D1519625

A Rumor of Justice

Tom Bernstein

Balustrade
Books©
Stairways to Imagination®

This book is a work of fiction. Names, characters, and incidents are the product of the author's imagination or are used fictitiously, except where noted in acknowledgements, and these are used by permission. Any other resemblance to actual persons, living or dead, is entirely coincidental.

Published in The United States by Balustrade Books

ISBN - 13: 978-1495423338
ISBN - 10: 1495423336

Cover photography by Melissa Bernstein
Cover design by Mishelle Johnson

To Lillian

Acknowledgements

The writing of any book is a time consuming process that in addition to the author involves numerous people whose contributions are invaluable. More than any other, I am indebted to Dave Kauffman, not only for the original idea for this story, nor for the benefit of his thirty-plus years of experience in local law enforcement, but more for his friendship and patience in answering my many thousands of questions, and for his suggestions in plot and character development, as well as his unflagging encouragement throughout the project. I truly could not have written this without him, and I look forward to his participation in the sequel.

I am likewise grateful to my soul mate, Lilly Dooris, for her immeasurable contributions, as well as for her patience and forbearance during the innumerable times that I pulled her away from whatever she was doing to listen to a passage I had just written, or to allow me to bounce an idea off her. This book is dedicated to Lilly.

My long-time friend and attorney, Randy Schwickert, was very instrumental in correcting my legal terminology and trial procedure, not to mention that he did it pro bono.

I would like to thank my daughter, Melissa Bernstein, for her suggestions and corrections, as well as her remarkable cover photography. It was much more than I had dared to hope for.

Furthermore, I would like to express my appreciation to Bob Brown for his technical assistance in formatting my novel for an eBook. It is both a rare and rewarding experience to witness such technical skills in a man of eighty-seven years.

For readings of the rough draft and ideas on how to improve it, my thanks go out to Jon Krack, Somer Treat, Cindi Blanc, Mickey Bernstein, and Diane Bernstein.

There are some very real people who graciously allowed me to use them as characters in this story: Jon Krack from Old Montana Building Company; Kim Abell who has waited tables at Cislo's Restaurant for twenty-seven years and was twice voted best waitress in the Flathead; Jennifer Young; Andre Floyd and Mood Iguana; and Scott Johnston of KXZI Montana Radio Café, front porch music served fresh daily.

1

Eli felt as much as heard the rhythmic thump of the helicopter minutes before he saw it approaching his position at the top of the ridge, soaring above the valley like some enormous flying insect. The sun just now climbing above the crest reflected blindingly off its Plexiglas bubble in brilliant contrast to the still darkened, snow-covered homes and farms below. As the shadow of the mountain raced back toward him, the entire expanse of the Flathead Valley was illuminated as when a curtain is drawn open inundating a room with radiance. The full moon was dissolving into the brightening sky, and in the gathering light across this snow-blanketed vastness he could now see clearly beyond the mouth of the Flathead River to the southwest where it snaked its way down the valley to empty into Flathead Lake, and all the way north to Big Mountain with its presently glistening ski-run corridors thirty miles distant. However, the uncommonly pure light of this particular morning spawned the impression that the mountain was no more than a mile or two away.

Most of the people below were just now beginning their commonplace morning routines - getting dressed, preparing for work, cooking breakfasts, shoveling driveways and sidewalks - completely unaware of the unfortunate, yet irreversible events of the previous night that had led him to be here, hunted and frightened. He had no doubt that those aboard the chopper were searching for him, and that others pursuing him would soon follow on all-terrain vehicles, and even more on foot with search dogs.

Plagued with uncertainty, he was nonetheless convinced that they were not likely to find him. During his ascent the night before he had taken much caution in leaving almost no trail, and last night's snow would undoubtedly cover what little there was. The wilderness that he was entering was perhaps the most immense in the lower forty-eight, and having spent a large portion of his youth hunting, fishing and exploring it's millions of acres with Uncle Dex, he felt that he knew it as well as any man alive; better than most. He possessed absolute confidence in his skills. His uncle had taught him well.

A sigh escaped with the frigid fog of his breath as he lowered his head to the ground in an attitude of prayer to avoid a reflection off his face, while the chopper flew noisily over the forest canopy making a sweeping turn along the crest of the ridge that slithered southward like some huge prehistoric reptilian backbone. As the reverberation of its rotors receded, he actually said a silent prayer for the man that he had injured.

Time to move. Adjusting his pack to ease the bruised tenderness in his shoulder and ribs, he continued walking carefully upstream taking cautious steps to avoid overturning rocks or stirring up silt in the glacial waters of the small creek, and by doing so he left no tracks in the new-fallen snow that coated the ground like a crystalline jeweled coverlet. Fortunately, in the aftermath of the previous night's madness, he had had the presence of mind to dress and outfit himself, not knowing how long he would have to remain in the high country. At the moment he found himself in an impossible situation, but he could stay well hidden for months if necessary, or at least until he had decided on the best course of action. He had debated with himself over whether or not to bring the rifle that was slung on his shoulder and the handgun that he carried in a holster on his belt, knowing that the weaponry would cause him to be considered "armed and dangerous" and making it more likely that he would be shot at if seen. Finally, he resolved that he would be better off in any case if he had them with him. He would have felt naked and unprotected without them.

Having heard what were probably unfounded rumors that a cell phone could be tracked electronically even if it was turned off, he had left the device behind, although it would have been advantageous to be able to communicate with those who would offer help. But he could ill afford to take any chances. Perhaps his smart phone was a little too smart. On the other hand, it probably wouldn't receive a signal where he was headed anyway.

This early in the season it was unlikely that he would encounter any campers or hikers in the back country, but regardless of the spring avalanche danger there were always imprudent snowmobilers who were willing to risk their lives for a transitory adrenalin rush. Before the morning had progressed another few hours, he hoped to be up in the basin where there would be limited risk of inadvertently being observed.

Turning things over in his mind again and again, he alternated between berating himself for what he had done and reassuring himself that he had had no choice but to defend himself. Yet, all along, he knew that it was his own fault for getting involved with Jolene in the first place. He had been warned that she had some kind of bipolar or schizophrenic thing going on, some said she was just fucking crazy, but the sex was great, and he chided himself for falling victim to the venerable, or perhaps venereal, curse of men since the dawning of the human race: thinking with the little head instead of the big one. But, even so, how had things gone so terribly, irrevocably wrong?

The helicopter made another pass overhead reminding him that he had to move a little faster. Nevertheless, as the lingering echo expired he paused to listen, but heard nothing more than the faint whoosh of a light breeze as it whispered uphill through the crown of the trees. On clear mornings such as this, the sunrise just now breaching the summit of the mountains could be relied upon to generate a rapid rise in temperature, producing an updraft ascending the slope that would help insure that his scent would be undetectable to the tracking dogs.

Those who pursued him on foot were without question already advancing below. He knew there was little likelihood that they would catch up before he passed over the saddle into a vast expanse of densely forested Douglas fir and spruce, an area with which he was well acquainted and within which he could easily vanish. Wincing at an abrupt spike of pain, he shook out three ibuprofen tablets and swallowed them with a sip from his water bottle. Although he had taken several hard blows he was sure his ribs were not broken if for no other reason than that he had been climbing steadily for hours and had experienced no respiratory difficulty. He had cleaned and dressed the knife wound in his left shoulder before leaving the house, and it had appeared to be only a little more than superficial.

As he moved on he reflected morosely on the recent twists of fate that had set him on this path. Although he had seen Jolene around town, mostly in the bars and always in the company of another guy, he'd never had an opportunity to speak to her until that Friday in late March, only a few weeks before, when he had stopped off at The Mountain Vista Tavern with Ray and Bennie for a couple of beers after work. She was seated at the bar, some sort of fruity drink in front of her in a tall glass with a straw poking out, wearing a short denim skirt, her dark hair in one of those French braids. A shaft of late sunlight streaking through a window highlighted her face in a way that he found attractive. She looked up and smiled at Bennie when they walked in, and for a moment Eli thought that she was smiling at him, so he grinned back and instantly felt idiotic for doing so. There was already a large, noisy happy-hour crowd in the bar, but they managed to find a table over by the stage and ordered a pitcher of Bud Light.

Ray leaned over and poked Eli with his elbow saying, “Hey, what are you drooling about?” and Eli gave him a look that said I don’t know what you’re talking about, as Ray said, “I saw you giving Jolene the eye.”

“Well, she is looking pretty hot!”

Bennie laughed sardonically. “It’s early. Just wait. She’ll be looking a whole lot hotter the closer it gets to closing time.”

Ray shook his head. “Old joke, Bennie. Not too original.”

Bennie shrugged as if to say ‘So what?’ “Well, anyway, she’s just another easy-lay bar chick.”

“How would you know?” Ray challenged.

“Oh, I know. Believe me, I know.”

“What’s that mean? Did you ever get any of that?”

“No, but I know plenty who have. Ya know her last name’s Sutten, but everybody calls her ‘Sucks ‘em’. I mean, she really gets around!”

Eli chuckled meaningfully. “Well I hope she comes around my way. I haven’t been laid in quite a while.”

“It wouldn’t be hard. Why don’t you go talk to her?”

“Yeah, Eli! Why don’t you go talk to her?”

Eli stood up, pushing his chair back with a scraping sound that was barely detectable in the din of the crowd. “I think I will.”

And it was just that easy. He walked up to her and told her his name was Eli, and she said, “I know”, and he bought a few rounds of drinks, and for a couple of hours they talked and joked about nothing of consequence, and then she accepted his invitation to go to his house where they could be alone. As they were leaving he waved across the crowded barroom to Ray and Bennie who waved back, know-it-all expressions on both of their faces. In the parking lot she simply said, “I’ll follow you,” and she walked to her car, a red Dodge Caravan. He got into his old pickup and she pulled up behind him as he crunched out of the gravel parking lot. It was not quite sunset and she had no difficulty staying behind him as he drove the winding sixteen miles out Foothill Road to his little cabin that sat on five wooded acres nestled up against nearly two million US Forest Service acres.

When they got there, they had a drink and talked about more trivialities, and then she kissed him and led him to his bedroom, and they undressed and got into his bed, and it was as if she was trying to demonstrate to him how skillful and uninhibited she was, a thing he found oddly exciting. He fell asleep completely drained of energy and everything else about two AM, and when he woke Saturday morning she was gone.

Monday morning at the job he was buckling on his tool belt, when Ray and Bennie walked up and asked him how it was with Jolene.

“It was crazy fuckin’ wild, is what it was!” Eli gloated triumphantly.

Bennie knew everybody else’s business and loved to gossip. “I’ve heard that about her, that she’s crazy.”

“I like ‘em a little crazy.”

“No, man. I mean like clinically, certifiably nuts. There’s something about her that’s just not right!”

“Well, no need to worry, man. Just havin’ some fun. I’m not going to marry her!”

⁂

For the next few weeks that was pretty much the way it was with them. Just having fun. She drove to his house a couple of times during the week, and left him used up and asleep, and drove herself home. On Fridays after work they met at The Mountain Vista Tavern, had a few drinks, visited with the crowd, and then went to his place where they had something to eat and shared some desultory and forgettable conversation before climbing into bed for another session.

So it was no small surprise when she reacted the way she had last night. One of his former girlfriends was in the bar, and, although their breakup had been mutual and amicable, it had been months since he had seen or even spoken to her, so he said hello, and how have you been, and was introduced to her new boyfriend, and introduced both of them to Jolene. That was it!

When they got back to his place, at first he thought Jolene was teasing him when she said, "So that's how it is, huh?"

"Uh, what do you mean, Jo?"

"What do you mean, what do I mean? You *know* what I mean! I saw the way you two were looking at each other! I saw the sparks flying! Whadda you think I'm stupid? Well, I'm not stupid! Not by a long shot. Let's see, how does this work? I get Friday, Monday, and Wednesday," ticking them off on her fingers, "and she gets Tuesday, Thursday, and Saturday, and on Sunday…" pointing the index finger at him, "on Sunday… why Sunday I do believe is the day of rest, is it not? And you must really *need* a day of rest after a week like that."

She wasn't teasing or joking. In fact, she was working herself into a pretty good rage, and Eli, with mounting apprehension, wasn't quite sure how to respond.

"Look, Jolene. There is nothing between her and me anymore except that we are still friends, and all I did was say hello. And besides, I think you're way off base!"

"Off base, huh? How so?"

"How so? *How so*?" Eli's face was molded in confusion, "Because you and I have never even talked about any sort of relationship. In fact, we've never talked about anything much at all. Mostly, we've just been having sex!"

"Just having sex? Is that all it is to you. Just sex? Oh, you men are all alike. I hate men!" And that was when she reached for the knife block on the counter grabbing the first one that her hand came in contact with and stabbed him in the shoulder. Luckily it was only a small paring knife and she hadn't struck with enough force to drive it in very deep, but it hurt like hell and bled like an open faucet.

"Holy shit!" He was backing away in alarm, "What did you do that for, you crazy bitch?"

"Don't call me crazy!" screaming now, "Don't you dare call me crazy!" She threw the paring knife on the floor and lunged wildly for the knife block again, searching for another, larger one. It suddenly occurred to him that she really was crazy, and, frightened, all he could think to do was to snatch the telephone off the wall and dial 911. Before he could speak into the phone she came at him with the butcher knife and he had to drop the phone to seize her wrists, trying to get it away from her. She had the inhuman strength of the truly insane and they struggled fervently for possession of the weapon. Several times Eli shouted at her to *stop it* and to *drop the knife*, but she persisted in her vicious efforts to stab him.

By some means she managed to hook a leg around his and they fell to the floor still grappling with each other for an indeterminate time, until finally she appeared to settle down a little, and Eli thought that perhaps she was tiring. But when he attempted to get the knife out of her hand, she seemed to have found her second wind and with renewed vigor she tried to stab him again. She was indefatigable, unrelenting, and he was truly terrified. Then he heard a car approaching the house and saw the shine of headlights through his front window, and hoped with all his being that his 911 call had been traced and that the cavalry had arrived.

Jolene suddenly doubled her efforts as if she was trying to finish this before anyone could help him. There was a banging on the door and he called out "*Come in*! *Come in*!" and heard the door open behind him and a man's angry voice saying, "OK, buddy, that's enough!" He felt his ankles being grabbed and he was pulled forcefully across the floor. Suddenly he felt something hard smash against his kidney doubling him over in severe pain as more blows rained down on him. He curled into a fetal position trying to protect himself with his arms and legs, but was roughly turned onto his back. Eli looked up and saw a uniform and then an enraged face as the officer raised his arm with a huge flashlight in his hand preparing to strike him again.

"Stop! *Stop*! Don't hit me," Eli cried, "It was me! I'm the one that called!"

There was a momentary pause in the beating, and for a fleeting instant Eli thought it had ended, but then in hard, curt words encrusted by taut lips the officer spoke, 'Oh, no! You're not getting' off that easy," and to Eli's complete horror he raised his arm to swing at him again.

In that suspended split-second the officer's deep-set eyes divulged a murderous loathing, a killing hatred, and Eli was consumed with a form of terror, a primal panic, far outstripping anything he had previously experienced while struggling with Jolene for the knife. Defensively, he grabbed at the flashlight and was able to get his hand on it. As the deputy tried to pull it from his grip Eli utilized that impetus to help him gain his feet, and in the same motion he managed to wrest the flashlight away from the officer's sweaty grasp.

There was a moment when it might have ended right there. There were just a few quick heartbeats that seemed to say *Stop! It's over!* But then, with a venomous snarl, the officer reached for his gun, unsnapping the retainer strap. Before he could clear the holster, Eli swung at him instinctively, the flashlight unexpectedly striking the deputy with considerable force on the neck just below his ear, and the officer's legs came out from under him and he landed on the floor awkwardly and lay still.

At this moment Jolene ran out the open door and when she reached her car she turned and gave him the finger, shouting triumphantly, "You're really fucked now, asshole!" and she jumped in the car and roared down the driveway and was gone.

She was right. He was really fucked now!

Checking on the fallen deputy he determined that he was breathing and that, other than being unconscious, he seemed not to be too badly hurt. There was no blood, and Eli prayed that he had only been knocked out.

Removing his shirt, Eli examined himself and concluded that nothing was broken, and then he bent over the sink and splashed warm water on the knife wound in his shoulder, which was still oozing blood and plasmatic fluid. Using a first aid kit that he kept in the bathroom, he hastily disinfected and bandaged the injury as best he could.

There was poor cell reception this far out Foothill Road, but it would only take fifteen or twenty minutes for Jolene to be able to make her own 911 call, which he was certain she would do, and perhaps another twenty minutes for the whole Sheriff's Department to arrive. He had little doubt about what she would tell them and how this would look. In that moment, primal survival instincts superseded rational thought, and he made the reflexive decision to go up into the mountains where he would be safe, and could think this through. But he had to move quickly.

Fortunately, all of the gear he would need was kept stored in his backpack so that he would not have to search for it when hunting season came around again. It didn't take long for him to change into his camouflage hunting clothes and waterproof boots, and fill his pockets and the empty spaces of the pack with all of the food he could find, and most of the ammunition he had on hand. Fresh snow was beginning to fall in the dark, shadowy forest when he left the house and headed up the creek. Up *shit* creek, he thought to himself, as he plodded through the icy waters to avoid leaving tracks.

Now he was standing motionless at the timberline scanning the clearing that he would have to traverse before entering the basin. It would take him only fifteen minutes or so to get across, but he waited patiently in the seclusion of the trees studying the terrain, plotting his route judiciously. When he had left the creek he had wrapped his boots in some scraps of tanned deer hide secured with duct tape to prevent leaving a discernable boot print. His feet would still leave an impression in the snow, but only a skilled tracker such as his Uncle Dexter would recognize it for what it was, and only because he was the one who had taught Eli how to do this. As soon as the helicopter had completed another flyover he moved out onto the barren slope but kept in the shadow of the cliff on the northeast side where he could not be seen as easily, using his camouflage clothing to its best advantage. The rocky ground and scant snow accumulation would leave his tracks yet more undetectable.

Hoping for the thousandth time that the cop he had hit was okay, it occurred to him that there were probably people in his cabin right now going through his things, maybe taking some things, and he felt intruded upon but helpless. He had lived in that cabin most of his life. His mother had bought it with the money she got from the divorce, and she had been able to pay cash for it; the only time in her life that she had ever had more than a few hundred dollars. This was back in the days before Flathead County, along with much of Montana, had been invaded by the super-rich who had driven up property values to where normal people couldn't afford to buy anything,

He'd never really known his father, Todd March, who had gone back to his family home in Ohio when Eli was still a toddler, and had only seen him a few times while he was growing up, and not once in the ten years since high school. His rich and snobbish paternal grandparents were racial bigots and had never approved of his mother and her tribal membership, judging her to be beneath their family; and had refused to claim him as a grandson with his own one-quarter Indian blood. In fact, they had considered the marriage itself to be nothing more than an impulsive, youthful episode that their son had, thankfully, outgrown. Regardless, Eli's mother had continued to be proud of her status as a member of the Kootenai tribe.

So it had just been Eli and his mother against the world in the little one bedroom cabin where his bed had sat in a corner of the main room with a curtain around two sides for privacy. His mother worked lunch and dinner shifts at a Mexican restaurant in town five or, sometimes, six days a week. She joked with him that she could pass for Hispanic and even at his young age he was perceptive enough to suspect that that might have been one of the reasons she had been hired in the first place.

As she had instructed, he always went directly home after school, and, because they lived so far out, he was usually the last one off the bus, so only rarely did he have after-school playmates. They had no television or computer, but there were lots of books. So when the weather was foul he read, but when it was tolerable he went into the woods. Facilitated by his uncle's tutelage, at a very early age he came to love the solitude of the forest, and he studied the ways and habits of the creatures of the forest, and his heart felt the rhythm of the forest. The woodlands and the mountains were both his playground and his school ground. And he became a part of it, never an intruder. He learned to snare birds and small animals and was extremely proud of the game he provided, and very fond of the way his mother cooked it. To the local deer population he became so familiar that they seldom ran from him.

His uncle had told him that Indian names are very important because they are unique and descriptive of the ones who bear them, not like the generic names of white people, and that often people give names to themselves that they feel represent something fundamental about them. Likewise, a person could have two names: the name by which others call him, and the name by which he thinks of himself.

There was a large black bear that had lived in the area for years that was so accustomed to seeing Eli in the woods that he treated Eli mostly with indifference. On a fall day, when he was ten years old, Eli was able to follow the bear from a safe distance and note the location of his den. Then one afternoon later that winter, when Eli got home after school, he put on his snowshoes and hiked up to the bear's cave. He crawled in quietly and carefully lay down close to the slumbering bruin, and closed his eyes hoping for a revelation. He longed to comprehend what it felt like to hibernate. In the stillness of the cavern he listened carefully to the hypnotically retarded rhythm of the bear's respiration, a slow and regular cadence that presently lulled him. And he dozed. It was nearly dark when he opened his eyes and made his way safely home. Not long after that episode, he secretly gave himself the name: Sleeping Bear.

He did have a father, in a sense. Dexter Ksunka, his mother's brother, had always been around, taking him up this very slope on wilderness excursions that often lasted days. The family name was also the ancient name of the tribe, translating as The People of the Standing Arrow, a symbol that stood for strength and unity. One summer when Eli was only eleven they hiked all the way into the Bob Marshall Wilderness and were gone for almost three weeks, and it was during this time that Dexter began calling him by the name, *Samose*, which he explained means "Walks Over Much".

On all of these backcountry expeditions Dexter had vigilantly and patiently instructed him in the ways of wilderness survival - skills that had been handed down from one generation to the next for thousands of years - and also educated him in the use of modern tools, weapons, and equipment. As he grew older and gained confidence, Eli went often to these places alone for long periods of time, spiritual occasions he equated with vision quests. By the time he was nineteen he was an expert and well-known wilderness guide, taking rich people, who lived their lives in big cities, down rivers and up creeks in pursuit of cutthroat trout and elk, and they tipped him well, not necessarily for the success of the hunt or for the numerous fish caught, but more for the experience he had given them, as well as for their gratitude that he had kept them alive in the wilderness.

When he was a senior at Flathead High School, his mother had left him on his own and moved back to Polson to care for her mother who was dying of cancer. Afterward, Eli's mother had remained in Polson because she had inherited her mother's house and had found a good job at the Kwa Taq Nuk Resort Casino on Flathead Lake. By that time Eli was well adapted to being on his own, and he had stayed, taking over the single bedroom that his mother had occupied. After a time, the little cabin had come to feel as his own.

Even though his mother had at this time begun using the Ksunka name again, Eli had kept the last name of his father, March, if for no other reason than that it coincidentally was close to the English equivalent of the name his uncle had given him.

After graduating from high school with Ray and Bennie, they had all gone to work for Bennie's dad's construction company, and Eli had learned carpentry and other house building skills. This was during the construction boom before the recession and there had been plenty of work, sometimes too much work.

Nonetheless, Eli had still found time to guide in the summer, as well as in the fall when everyone on the job would disappear during hunting season anyway. Those were good years with good pay, but Eli had learned the lessons of poverty well, continuing to live simply and save his money. Thanks to this frugality, when the recession hit and everything came to a grinding halt, he was not as adversely affected as many were. There was still some work, although the money was nowhere near what it had been, but everyone on the crew agreed to take a cut in pay and the construction outfit managed to limp along. Fortunately, there were yet rich clients who continued to pay well for the adventures that Eli could provide them with, so for him, anyway, life was still good.

He made it across the clearing unseen only moments before the chopper made another pass. Well hidden in the trees he watched it turn west and head back towards town, probably to refuel. He doubted that they would give up so soon. Taking careful steps, he moved through the landscape as if he were but another woodland creature. As he faded into the forest on the east side of the divide, Eli prayed with all his heart and spirit that he would find a solution to this situation and be allowed to resume his life in his little cabin out on Foothill Road east of Kalispell. A life begun in denial and adversity, and yet, a life he had come to love.

2

Every morning as soon as she got out of bed, Jennifer Lawson executed at least five sun salutations, but on Saturdays, when there was no urgency, she always went through her entire yoga routine. It was one of the many tools she had acquired to help her deal with the stresses of her profession. Her job however was one of the last things on her mind this morning. The new issue of Garden Design had arrived yesterday and she was anxious to begin planning a new border for her front walkway.

When she was done stretching, bending, and breathing, she turned on the television to get the weather report and went to retrieve the morning paper from her front porch. As she stepped outside she saw that a couple of inches of snow had fallen last night, and she was hoping that the forecast would be for another warm day so that the snow would melt and she would not have to shovel. Winter was over. She was sick of shoveling. Bob had always done all the snow clearing, and had offered to come by and do it this winter, but she had refused, wanting to prove a point.

The first shafts of sunlight were just fanning out over the Swan Range, sparkling lasers erupting so suddenly into the clear sky it was as if they were tangible, something you could just about reach out and touch. Mornings like this were the main reason she and Bob had bought the house in the first place. The one that they had built in Whitefish was a lot nicer, and larger, but it was never really home. They had always had the intention of selling it for a profit and moving on. Fortunately, that had come to fruition six years ago during the height of the economic boom, and they had done so well that they had been able to buy this place outright. A lot of people had not been so lucky. It was all about timing.

The house itself wasn't much. In fact, it was kind of funky. But the location was stunning! All of the residences on the west side of Woodland Drive shared the same spectacular view of the east valley, unrestricted because there were no houses along the narrow east side of the road where it plummeted abruptly from the top of a sixty foot bluff. Both she and Bob had told all their friends that they had bought a view that happened to have a house on it.

As she was bending to retrieve the paper the faint knocking sound of a helicopter caught her attention, and she stood shading her eyes with her hand against the glare that bounced off the new snow, and scanned the panorama before her until she detected the spin of its rotors against the backdrop of the spectral mountains that loomed twenty miles distant. *Oh God*, she thought, *it's The Alert Helicopter. Who's hurt or lost now*? It happened all too frequently that someone went up into the mountains unprepared, or had an unfortunate accident, and Flathead County Search and Rescue were called out in an attempt to find them. Sometimes they were successful. Sometimes not. Local television and newspaper reports had been warning people for weeks about the avalanche danger. She said a silent prayer for whoever might be in trouble as she turned to go back inside.

A young blond female reporter on the morning news program appeared to be talking about whatever was going on but Jennifer, preparing coffee in the kitchen, wasn't really paying attention and only caught snatches of what was being said. But then something caught her interest. A picture of a dark, attractive young boy that was obviously taken from a high school yearbook was projected onto the screen and the woman's voice-over was saying, "All police agencies in the area are on the lookout for Elias K. March, twenty-eight, who is said to be a suspect in the assault. March is described as being six foot two with medium length dark hair, no facial hair, and no visible tattoos. It is believed that he fled into the forest and an extensive search is in progress. Citizens are to be advised that March may be considered dangerous, and, if seen, should not be approached. Anyone with any information as to his whereabouts is urged to call Flathead Crimestoppers at the number now on our screen: 406-752-8477. Once again, that's 406-752-8477. The victim is listed in critical condition at Kalispell Regional Hospital. His name has not been released. Now we will have our weather report from meteorologist Aaron Fraser."

Jennifer opened the newspaper to the front page to see if she could learn more, but she could find nothing that seemed to refer to the partial story she had just seen. Probably happened too late to have been in this morning's issue, she guessed. That publication was always a day behind in the news anyway. She made a mental note to check it out on the Internet later on.

The good news, as she now saw on the chart that the weatherman was pointing to, was that the high temperature for today was expected to reach into the mid sixties. Several of her gardening magazines and seed catalogues were still spread out on the dining room table from the night before, and she sat with her coffee and started leafing through them, thinking that some autumn joy, a perennial that waited until early fall to bloom, might make a pleasant border for the front walk. Set among some well-placed rocks their medium height and green foliage would be charming against a sedum groundcover with a spattering of pansies. Maybe Angela would want to help. When she was little she had always enjoyed helping with the gardening. It had been a while since they had had a mother/daughter project.

The blond reporter was now onto another story about more local job layoffs, but Jennifer's mind was in the dirt and she ignored it. A person could only take so much bad news. She drained the rest of her coffee, got up and turned the television off and walked out into the sunroom. Among her many potted plants was a hanging basket with an enormous hoya in full bloom, giving off an almost sickly sweet smell and dripping its viscous honey onto the slate floor. But she didn't mind having to clean it up. This room was her salvation. It gave her a place where she could water and fuss over her plants all winter long.

Along with a couple of friends that he knew from working in the trades, Bob had built the sunroom for her when they bought the house. Removing a section of the south wall of the living room, they had temporarily supported the roof and inserted a glue-lam beam to carry the load, framing in an area ten by sixteen with operating windows all around, five skylights, and a sliding glass door that led to a patio in the rear of the house. Bob, who was a masonry and tile contractor, had laid an attractive offset diamond pattern slate floor that allowed her to spill all of the water she wanted to without worry of damaging anything.

She loved and depended on this room and often thought she would go crazy without it. She needed to have something to nurture, something to get a positive response from, because every day she had to deal with hopeless situations. With a sigh of relief she gave thanks that there would be no arraignments, or bail hearings, or motions filed, or requests of continuances today. The judicial processes for the most part were dormant on the weekends.

"Hi, Mom. Whatcha doin?" Angela was sitting amidst the clutter at the dining room table. Jennifer had been so self-absorbed that she had not even heard her enter the room.

"Hi, honey. Did you just get up? I tried not to wake you."

"No, you didn't wake me. I just woke up early."

"Here, let me get some of this stuff out of your way." Jennifer started restacking all of her magazines and catalogues. "Do you want some breakfast?"

"No thanks, I'm not hungry yet."

"How about some juice then?"

"Sure, I'll take some OJ."

Jennifer got a carton of orange juice from the refrigerator, poured some into a glass, and handed it to Angela as she sat down across from her. At twelve years old Angela was already starting to develop the contours of a woman. She was tall for her age, a trait she had inherited along with her eyes from Bob; but she has my mouth and fair complexion, thought her mother, and with a shudder she realized that they'd have to deal with the whole boy thing before long.

"Sweetie, I was just thinking that maybe you'd like to help me with a border for the front walk. I was thinking maybe some autumn joy like that nice lady at the Farmer's Market sells."

"Jeez, Mom, it snowed last night! The ground's still frozen!"

"Actually, the ground is just about thawed already, and, anyway, I was just hoping that you would help me design it for now, and maybe next weekend we'd dig the sod out and prep the beds."

"Sure, Mom, whatever. But I can't help today. I'm going to walk over to Dad's later."

"Are you going to stay there tonight?"

"I'd like to, if it's okay with you."

"Of course, it's okay. Why wouldn't it be?"

Angela looked up at her petulantly.

"I don't understand why you don't just get back together. Then I wouldn't have to go back and forth. I liked it better when we all lived together."

It always seemed to come back to this.

"I know, honey, and I'm sorry to put you through this," Jennifer was making an obvious effort to keep the tone of exasperation from her voice, "but it's…well, it's just complicated."

"That's what you always say," Angela grumbled, "*It's complicated.* I'm not a baby anymore, you know! You can talk to me!"

"I wish I could explain it better. I'm just as confused about it as you are."

"He still loves you, you know."

Jennifer smiled indulgently.

"Yes, I know, and I love him to. He's a very good man. But sometimes love isn't enough. You have to be able to get along, and I haven't been very good at that lately. Blame me if you want to."

Angela sighed and gazed out the window, refusing to meet her mother's eyes.

"I don't want to blame anybody. I just want us all together again."

"Me, too, sweetie. But you're just going to have to be patient with me for a while. Things will work out one way or another. They always do."

"Sure, Mom. Whatever."

Finishing her orange juice, Angela got up from the table and headed down the hallway.

"When are you going to your dad's house?"

"After breakfast, but I'm going to take a shower first."

"Be sure to hang up your towel."

"Right, Mom," she replied as she closed the bathroom door.

Angela had always been an exceptionally good kid, though there were some things about pre-teen girls that were universal. Mainly, they all needed to have a father in their lives, something Jennifer knew all too well, something she would always support. She acknowledged that she *had* been hard-headed about some things, like when Angela had been born and she had insisted that the baby's middle name be her father's last name: Angela Lawson Mayfield. Not a hyphenated last name. However, because of what had happened to her at that age, she would never do anything to interfere with Angela's relationship with her own father.

Bob had rented a house on 5th Avenue East just a few blocks away near Hedges School where Angela was in the sixth grade. Although his masonry business was not as lucrative as it had been in recent years, rent was affordable, especially since there was no mortgage on this house, and it was very convenient for everyone that he was so close. Jennifer was particularly pleased with the arrangement. She remembered how her own father had been taken away from her when she was twelve years old. She knew firsthand what it was like to grow up without a father. All the counseling had helped her to understand why relationships were so difficult for her, but it didn't change things. Only someone as kind and patient as Bob could have stayed with her for so long, even though she had consistently turned him down whenever he had suggested they get married.

Over thirty years had gone by since her father had been sentenced, and nearly twenty-five years had passed since he had died in prison. She and her mother had never stopped believing in his innocence, although her own innocence, in fact her very childhood, had been stolen from her long ago when she first realized that justice was for those who could afford it. A series of shrinks had all suggested that this was at the very core of her becoming a defense attorney; that she was attempting over and over to save her father. In a sense, they were right, but it was much deeper than that. She was no longer naïve or idealistic, in fact, part of the problem that she had in her relationship with Bob was that she was so jaded, but at the same time so driven.

Like plaids with stripes, cynicism and dedication were a bad combination, and it made her difficult to live with.

Always careful not to prejudge innocence or guilt, and vigilantly on guard for those who did, she truly believed that everyone was entitled to a vigorous defense; although, in truth the majority of her clients *were* accountable, and were willing to admit it in exchange for a plea bargain. Nonetheless, she was undeterred, in spite of the fact that the county did not pay a public defender enough to launch a full-scale defense. It was an imperfect system that made poor allowance for the fact that some people simply couldn't afford to put up much of a struggle even when their freedom was at stake. She never ceased to be haunted by the inopportune victims of this injustice.

However, she consoled herself with the knowledge that the system did work, sometimes. Occasionally she had a client who was indeed falsely accused and, more importantly, had the resources to pay for investigators and expert witnesses and dozens of other expenses, not to mention her retainer and fees. If and when they were victorious it made all the losses and plea bargains worth it, for a while, but it was a joy short-lived.

So many people these days were desperate and afraid, and burglaries and other crimes were becoming more and more common. Police departments were stretched to their limits, jails were overcrowded, and it was all she could do to keep up with her caseload at Lawson Law Firm. "Law Law" as it was called by certain insensitive people who thought they were being clever, but it was her father's name and she would never change it.

She was mercifully shaken out of her reverie by the ringing of the telephone, reminding her that it was the weekend and she didn't have to think about any of this until Monday.

"Hi, Jenny, it's me. I just got home and I wanted to call you before you heard it from anyone else."

Brenda Gunderson, an ER nurse who had been working the night shift, had been Jennifer's closest friend since grade school and had stuck by her during those terrible years when everyone else still believed that her father had committed that horrific crime; a time when Jennifer had felt that she herself was imprisoned, in a sense, by public opinion. Brenda had been her only visitor behind the walls of this socially imposed incarceration. It had forged a bond that was stronger than sisterhood, strong enough to allow her to ignore the fact that Brenda was a gossip who loved to pass on hearsay and scandalous rumors.

"What's up, Brenda? Is this about that alcoholic county commissioner, again?"

"No, it's something else, but remind me to tell you about that later. It's about what happened last night out on Foothill Road. Did you hear about it? About the deputy that was assaulted?"

"I think there was something on the news, but I wasn't paying attention. Something about a search for some fugitive and call Crimestoppers and so on. I only caught the tail end of it, and I don't think I heard anything about a deputy being assaulted. What's up with that?"

"Apparently, this officer was answering a call on a domestic dispute and when he got there this guy just went ape-shit on him. They brought him in last night and I overheard one of the other cops say that the guy beat him with his own flashlight. You know, those big metal mags they all carry?"

"How did he get the officer's flashlight?"

"I don't know! What is this? A cross-examination? Cut the lawyer crap and let me tell you. There's something you need to know."

"What's that?'

"Well, the cop was in a coma and was hurt pretty bad. I overheard Dr. Santay, the neurologist they brought in, say something about spinal injury, and that could mean paralysis, but I guess we won't know about that until he wakes up."

"Wait a minute, Brenda. Should you be telling me about all of this? Should you be releasing this sort of information even to me?"

"For cryin out loud, Jen! Stop being a lawyer for a minute, wouldja? This is important!"

"What's so important?"

"The cop that was assaulted?"

"Yeah, what about him?"

"Well, Jen. I don't really know how to tell you this…so here it is."

"What, Brenda? Here what is?"

"Jen…It's Scott Deaver!"

3

Sheriff Mike Montgomery was worried. When the call came in from The Lake County Sheriff's Department, he was sitting at his desk on the first floor of the Flathead County Justice Center thinking about how this business last night with Scott Deaver could easily get out of hand. The local media was hounding him for more information, and, if not already, it would not be long before the story was all over the state. It might even get picked up by the national media. The cyber universe was unlimited.

Deaver was still in a coma, a viable pretext for not releasing his name, and it was not likely that a statement would be forthcoming from him for quite some time. The media investigators were well in advance of his own people in digging up information on the March kid. It was discomforting, embarrassing even, that most of the department's background material on March was being accumulated from the special news bulletins that were airing almost every hour on the local television station, and on the Missoula channel as well.

But this was all to be expected, and was not his primary concern. As long as they stayed focused on the fugitive everyone had a common cause. But after seventeen years with the department, three years as sheriff, he had come to realize that the local journalists were just as devious, ruthless, and competitive with each other as those in LA had been, and if this incident caused them to start excavating inside the department they might unearth something he would rather they didn't know about. Something that could very likely create a setback in his re-election campaign.

He answered the phone.

"Sheriff Mike Montgomery."

"Monty, this is Charlie Nichols down in Lake County."

"*Sheriff* Nichols, what can I do for you?"

"Just wanted to see if you could use some extra manpower?"

"Thanks for the offer, Charlie, I might need to take you up on that, but I think we've got it under control for the moment." Montgomery tried to keep the worry and fatigue from his voice.

"Do you need a good tracker? There's this Indian fella that contracts with both us and the Tribal cops. He's really good at it. Do you remember last year when those people had wandered off from that small plane that crashed up in the Missions? Well he led us right to 'em!"

"You know, right now we've got our whole shift out there, we've got a guy with some dogs, three game wardens, the chopper's up. I think we've got it covered for now, Charlie."

Sheriff Nichols did not reply for a moment. Montgomery could hear him breathing on the other end.

"Well then, let me put this way, Monty. You've got a seriously injured deputy in the hospital…one of us, goddammit! …and the asshole that put him there is still on the loose. And it's hard for me to just sit here and do nothing."

"You know what, Charlie? There is something you can do. His mother lives down there in Polson. Her name is," shuffling through some papers on his desk, "Here it is. Dorothy K. March. We ran her through motor vehicles and the address on her driver's license is 287 Maple Street West. She works at the Kwa Taq Nuk. I can email all this over to you. Could you put some plain clothes on her? In case he tries to contact her?"

"You got it! No problem. But we'd still like to do more. If it's a budget thing, you know, we'll cover our own expenses."

"Well that's about always the thing, isn't it, Charlie? You've got county commissioners, too, don'tcha? But this is a special situation, you know. I don't think I'll have any problem justifying expenses. Nevertheless, I don't want too many people moving around up there. Somebody else might get hurt. I just want to see what happens over the next few hours. Maybe we'll spot him, or maybe he'll even turn himself in."

"Okay, we've got the mother, and let me know if you need anything else."

"I will, Charlie. And thanks. It really means a lot to me that you offered."

There was another thing troubling Sheriff Montgomery. The more he learned the more he realized that March would not be easily apprehended. This would not play well with the media. A deputy had been injured, and his fellow officers, in fact everyone who worked in law enforcement, along with most of the general populace, demanded justice, and it was Sheriff Montgomery's job to see that they got it. But March was only one person in an area larger than some states, an area that he was apparently well-acquainted with, and well-equipped for; an area so vast that an adequate search would be impossible regardless of how much help and manpower he received from other agencies. Usually when a fugitive hid in the forest, the policy was to simply wait, knowing that sooner or later his own survival would force him to come out seeking food, or maybe help from family or friends, and that's when they would catch him. But this would not be the case with March. The portrait that had emerged was of the kind of person who was exceptionally capable of staying up there indefinitely.

The sheriff leaned back in his chair with his arms above his head and stretched to help relieve the tension, and couldn't help yawning. He'd had so little sleep last night he was running on fumes.

The call telling him that he had an officer down had come in on his private cell phone at 2AM. He sat up in bed quickly and grabbed the phone hoping he could answer it before the ringing woke Annie. Promptly he remembered that she was in the guest room. She had not been sleeping well since she'd started this last round of treatments, and she'd decided to stay in the other room so she wouldn't wake him with her insomniac tossing.

He dressed hurriedly, put on his coat and hat, and was about to leave the house, but stopped and returned to the bedroom for his gun, a Glock .40 caliber that he wore in a pancake holster under his coat behind his back. It had been a long time since he'd worn a duty belt.

There was a light snow drifting dreamily across the road as he headed east on Hwy 35 at 65mph. There was no need for sirens; there was no traffic. In fact, there was no need to hurry. The dispatcher had told him that the shift sergeant was already on the scene with several deputies, and the paramedics were well ahead of him. This was all good news, because the road was starting to ice over.

When he reached the Flathead Electric Coop's substation where Lake Blaine Road becomes Foothill Road, he saw the pulsing lights of the ambulance approaching up ahead on its way back to town, and then suddenly it was passing him, kicking up snow, going at least 80mph, sirens blaring. He keyed his mic and got the shift sergeant on his portable.

"Who is it, Rube?"

"Deaver, Sheriff."

"How bad is it?"

"Don't know. He was unconscious when we got here, but he was breathing okay. When the paramedics arrived they tried to wake him, and then they loaded him up and took him in. Looks like the perp hit him with his own maglite."

"I wonder how that happened."

"Don't know. The detectives are here. They're working on it. What's your ETA?"

"About fifteen."

It wasn't hard to find the cabin. He could see the flashing lights through the swirling snow flurries when he was still a quarter mile away. He noted some of the Creston Volunteer Fire Department vehicles on the road as he pulled into the drive behind several patrol cars. Sergeant Ruben Broussard walked out to meet him as he got out of his car adjusting his hat.

"The forensics team won't let anyone in there for a while. It's a pretty small cabin." Broussard's breath fogged in the frigid air.

"What the hell happened here, Rube?"

"About ten-thirty we had a 911 call with no one responding, but the dispatcher could hear sounds of a struggle, so he put a trace on it. Deaver was already out this way, just finished up with another domestic, so he took the call, but he never checked back in. At eleven-ten there was another 911 from the girl," he tilted his head in the direction of one of the squad cars where Montgomery could see the silhouette of a woman in the back seat on the passenger side, "said this March guy was threatening to kill her so she called 911 but he knocked the phone out of her hand, then she grabbed one of his kitchen knives and when he came at her she stabbed him in the shoulder. He got the knife away from her and then tried to strangle her. She's still pretty hysterical, so her story gets a little confusing here. Somehow, they ended up on the floor wrestling for another knife, but when Deaver came in, March went after him. Deaver had his flashlight in his hand and somehow March managed to take it away from him and hit him with it. The girl escaped while all this was going on, and drove her car towards town until she got cell reception, and then called it in."

"Has anybody gotten a statement from her, yet?"

"We were letting her calm down a little first."

"That story you just told me has got more holes in it than Sonny Corleone. Maybe she's using the time to get her story straight."

"Look, Sheriff." Broussard held a hand up protectively, "I know a lot of it doesn't make sense, but, like I said, she's pretty freaked out. Go see for yourself."

"Don't have to get defensive, Rube."

"I just don't want you trying to make me look bad. Because of the election, you know." Sergeant Broussard was on the ballot challenging Montgomery in November for the Sheriff's job.

"You know that's not the way I work, Rube. Now, if you don't mind, I think I'll go have a talk with her," pointing toward the squad car, "Whose unit?"

"Morton's, but it's not locked, only the child-safety."

"What's her name?"

"It's Jolene. Jolene Sutten."

Montgomery walked through the falling snow to the squad car, opened the rear door on the driver's side, disengaged the child-safety mechanism, and slid in next to Jolene. He was a big man and the car settled some with his weight. The heater had been left on high and it was hot inside, so he removed his hat and unzipped his jacket.

"Ms. Sutten, I'm Sheriff Montgomery. Would you mind if I asked you a few questions?"

Jolene had a blanket around her shoulders and her disheveled hair hid her face as she nodded. Montgomery was hoping he could see her eyes. It was always the eyes that told him if someone was being truthful, or not.

"Why don't you just start at the beginning and tell me what happened?"

"Well," Jolene began in a weak voice, almost a whisper, "I was only teasing, but Eli got mad…"

"Excuse me, Ms. Sutten," Montgomery interrupted, "I meant at the very beginning. How do you know Mr. March, and how did you happen to be here tonight? And would you mind looking at me when you talk? I'm a little hard of hearing."

Jolene lifted her head and turned toward the sheriff. Even through the smeared and running eye makeup, he could see that she was an attractive young woman. Probably because he had told her he couldn't hear well, she spoke more loudly.

"Me and Eli have been sort of seeing each other for like a few weeks, but we weren't really going together, if you know what I mean. So anyway, earlier tonight we were at The Mountain Vista and he introduced me to his ex-girlfriend. When we left the bar we came here, except I drove my own car because I didn't want to leave it there. So, after we got here, we were talking and I kinda like teased him about his ex-girlfriend and that's when he got like really angry."

"What did you say about the ex-girlfriend?" Montgomery wanted the ex-girlfriend's name, but he would get that later.

"Nothin' much. I just said something about how I thought he still had the hots for her. I was only joking, but I guess he took it serious and it pissed him off, and he started yelling at me about minding my own business. I was getting kinda scared so I told him I was leaving and then he grabbed my arm and said 'You're not goin' anywhere!' and I asked him to let go of my arm and then he hit me. See? Right here!"

Jolene pulled her hair back and in the strobe of the flashing patrol car lights Montgomery could clearly see bruising at her left temple.

"Had he ever hit you before?"

"No! Never!"

She shook her head emphatically.

"Go on. Then what happened?"

"Well, when he hit me he also let go of me and I fell back against the kitchen counter, and this wooden block with all these knives were like right in front of me so I grabbed this little knife, you know, like to protect myself with. But he just reared back like he was going to hit me again, so I like swung at him with the little knife and it stuck in his shoulder. I wasn't really thinking about what I was doing, I just didn't want him to hit me again."

"Excuse me, Ms. Sutten. Are you right-handed or left-handed?"

"What?"

"Are you right or left-handed?"

"Uh, right-handed."

"So you stabbed him in the left shoulder?"

"Yeah, that's right."

"Okay. Go on, please."

"Well, anyway, after I stabbed him, he backed off, like he was kinda surprised that I would fight back; in fact he said, 'I can't believe you did that, you bitch!' For a second I thought it was over, but then he pulled the knife out and threw it on the floor and he got this real freaky look on his face and he said, 'I'm gonna kill you for that!' Well, I was like really scared, and I was still standing next to that knife block, so I pulled out this big butcher knife and I warned him not to come near me, and with my other hand, my left hand, I got the telephone off the wall and dialed 911. I text a lot, so I'm pretty good at dialing with my thumb. But then all of a sudden he came at me and grabbed my wrist so I couldn't use the knife, and he knocked the phone out of my hand. And he kept yelling, 'I'll kill you! I'll kill you!' He was tryin to get the knife out of my hand, but no way was I gonna let him have it, so I fought him! I fought him hard 'cause I knew I was fighting for my life! And then we like tripped over something and we were both on the floor rolling around and like struggling with each other and he was like cussing and calling me all these bad names, and we were still fighting for the knife when that policeman came in and pulled Eli off me. But Eli just jumped up and snatched that flashlight out of the officer's hand and hit him with it. The policeman had left the front door open, so I ran out and jumped in my car and locked the doors, just in time, too, because Eli was right behind me, and he was trying to get the doors open, and he was cussing a lot and banging on the glass, so I drove out of there as fast as I could. He even chased me down the driveway!"

"You had the car key with you?"

"What?"

"Did you have a purse or something with you? With your key in it?"

"Uh…no! I had left it in the ignition."

"Is that something you're in the habit of doing?"

"No, not usually, but it's pretty safe out here. Eli *always* left his key in his pickup. The first time I ever came here, he gave me a bad time about it because I locked my car."

"I see. Tell me what you did after you drove away."

"Well, I drove toward town, but as soon as I had two bars on my cell, I pulled over and called 911."

"So this would be your second call to 911?"

"Uh….yeah! Right! I like called 911 *again*!"

"Okay. Then what happened?"

"Well, I told the 911 guy what had happened. And he asked me was I in danger now, and I told him I wasn't. Then he asked me where I was and what I was driving and I told him, and then he told me to stay in my car and that a deputy would come to me. So I waited for fifteen or twenty minutes, and then I saw the cars coming with the flashing lights and all. And then one of the cars pulled over, and this officer came up and asked me what happened, and I told him the same thing I just told you. So, then he brought me here."

Jolene spread her hands palms up in a gesture that said 'that's all there is, folks'.

"Do you know where your car is now? I didn't see it when I drove out here."

"I think it's here somewhere. I gave the officer my key and he said someone would take care of it."

"Okay, Ms. Sutten, I think that'll do for now. I know it's late and you're tired, but would you mind if Deputy Morton drove you in to our office to tell this story one more time, while it's still fresh in your mind, so that we can get it on record. It would be very helpful. And I'll be sure to get someone to drive your car in."

"No, Sheriff. I don't mind. In fact, I'd feel safer with Eli still being on the loose and all."

"Thank you, Ms. Sutten. Whether you realize it or not, by getting that call in to us so quickly, you may have saved that deputy's life tonight."

It had stopped snowing. When Montgomery emerged from the squad car, Detective Mick Linnell was waiting for him. Linnell was a lean, tough Gulf War vet who had been with the department longer than the Sheriff himself.

"How'd that go?" he asked.

"Well," said Montgomery as he zipped his jacket and adjusted his hat, "It's a pretty good story."

"Are you being sarcastic, Sheriff?"

"No, not at all. It's a cohesive story, and she tells it pretty well."

"But?"

"But, there's a few things that'll need to be clarified. Go ahead and take her in and have her tell it again. Get a signed statement. Then we'll compare notes and maybe by then we'll have some forensics to work with. And, Mick, you might want to get a search warrant and have forensics check Ms. Sutten's car out."

"That's pretty much what I was thinking. I'm also going to listen to both 911 calls and see what I can learn from them. Are you headed home?"

"No, it's almost dawn. I think I'll come on in to the office, too."

Before leaving for town, Montgomery took another look around the clearing that encircled the little cabin. In the early morning glow, he spied a well-kept older model F-150, blue with chrome trim that he assumed belonged to the suspect, Eli March. He walked over to it and tried the passenger-side door. It was unlocked and he leaned in to take a look. There was no key in the ignition.

So much had happened since Sheriff Montgomery had arrived at the office, and he was so tired from having had less than three hours sleep, that the happenings of the previous night were taking on aspects of a dream. He stretched and yawned again, and his thoughts returned to the item that had been concerning him for months. The thing he was most worried about: the election.

Mike Montgomery had grown up here in Kalispell. His father had made a career in the U.S. Forest Service, and his mother had taught math at Flathead High School, the same school Montgomery had attended. He had excelled in academics, and was a star quarterback with The Flathead Braves the year the team won the state championship. He and Annie Richards had been a couple all through high school until he went off to college.

He attended UCLA on a football scholarship, where he earned a degree in criminal justice with a minor in economics, and was once more a valued member of the team, but not really good enough to be considered by the pros. This was only a minor disappointment for him. He had already been recruited for something else.

He joined the LAPD one month after he graduated from UCLA. His intelligence and aptitude were soon recognized, and, after only three years on patrol, he was transferred to the OCP. He was twenty-six years old, and he and Annie had been happily married for two years. Annie had a job as a medical secretary, with paid maternity leave, and their son, Chad, was about to be born. And he had just landed a job in the top office. Life was good!

But disillusionment soon followed. It was in The Office of the Chief of Police that he began to learn the politics of law enforcement, which had very little to do with law enforcement itself, but more to do with administration, finance, and public relations. It was not the job he had imagined himself doing when he had joined the department, but he learned it well, and stuck it out as long as he could. When their son was six and ready to start school, he talked it over with Annie – the poor quality of the public school system, the rising cost of living, the expanding crime rates, and his own disenchantment with the LAPD - and they decided to move back to Kalispell.

He applied to all of the law enforcement agencies in Flathead County, and was soon hired by the Sheriff's Department. After thirteen years on patrol, four of them as Undersheriff, he ran for Sheriff. With his background, and his family name, which had been known in Kalispell for several generations, he easily won. And now he wished had lost, or at least waited to run.

If he did not win the next election, he would not be able to return to patrol, and his career with the Sheriff's Department would be over. He would only have seventeen years on the job, and he needed twenty to receive retirement benefits. But what was even more important to him was the insurance. Annie was battling breast cancer, and the medical costs were astronomical. In addition, Chad was still in college and the income was needed.

His instincts told him that the Sutten girl wasn't telling the whole truth. He knew from experience that when March was apprehended his story would bear no relation to hers, and he was certain that when Deaver regained consciousness his story would be something else altogether. And he recognized from certain episodes in the past, that Deaver's story could not be trusted either. If the truth was what he suspected, and it became public knowledge, it could cost him the election.

Sheriff Mike Montgomery was worried.

4

"You know, Jen, this isn't going to just go away! It was on the front page of this morning's paper, for chrissakes! It's the feature story on every newscast, and it's the main topic of conversation everywhere you go. And you know what? I'd be willing to bet that sooner or later *you're* going to get involved!"

Jennifer and Brenda were sitting across from each other in a booth at The Buffalo Café in Whitefish having an early lunch after dropping their daughters off at The Big Mountain Ski Area at the north end of Flathead Valley. A few years ago the name had been changed to Whitefish Mountain Resort, but the locals never gave that any consideration. It had always been called Big Mountain. It was the second Sunday in April, the resort was closing for the season, and the girls didn't want to miss their last opportunity to go snowboarding together.

It seemed the natural course of their lives that Jennifer and Brenda's daughters would be like siblings themselves. Nikki, tall and imposing like her mother, was fourteen, two years older than Angela, and had always assumed the duty of protector. Both mothers accepted this, and were at ease with leaving them alone at the family ski area for their afternoon fun.

What a gorgeous day, thought Jennifer when they had dropped the girls off. There were only a few wispy clouds in the sky and from the base area she could see the entire expanse of the Flathead Valley, truly one of the most beautiful places on God's earth. Framed by the Swan Mountain Range on the east and the Cabinet Mountains to the west, the vista extended south to Flathead Lake, the largest freshwater lake in the western United States. Whitefish Lake and the town of Whitefish nestled at the base of the mountain.

Jennifer seldom came to Whitefish anymore. When she was growing up in Kalispell, Whitefish had been a friendly little railroad town, and she loved it. Bordered east and west by old, shady neighborhoods, Main Street defined the center of the sleepy business section. At the north end of Main was the old run-down Depot that dated back to the grand old days of Glacier Park, when the well-heeled of that time traveled on the trains in luxury to Montana to view the wondrous scenery and wildlife. Three blocks south, cater-corner to Haines Drug Store, stood the Orpheum Theatre, built half a century earlier, but yet still utilizing an ancient projector that typically broke down a minimum of three times per movie.

From almost any section of the small town, the virtually constant sounds of trains coupling, and moving in and out of the rail yard, could be heard above the usual noises of daytime commerce. The rail lines divided the town east to west, and access to the ski area, Whitefish Lake, and the homes on the north side was gained by way of a narrow, ancient two-lane viaduct. The south end of the lake offered a city park with a sandy beach, a boat launch and pier, a snack bar, and shaded picnic areas. As a young girl, back when they'd all still been together, her parents had brought her here on hot summer afternoons to play on the beach and frolic in the lake.

Whitefish in those days was like a hundred other small towns across the west; not much going on, but a good, safe place to live and raise a family. The location was a bonus, but the thing that made Whitefish special was the sense of community; ordinary people who were always there to help a neighbor in need.

But over the last fifteen years the super-rich had descended on the area around Whitefish, building vacation mansions, driving the real estate market to mind-boggling heights; and the town, aware of its new status, had changed. It had developed an attitude, you might say, of a bustling tourist town that catered to the affluent. Gone was the old viaduct – thank God - and a wider, safer one with a bike path had taken its place. The Depot got a face-lift. Gone were The Orpheum Theatre, Haines Drug Store, Gordy's Drive-in, the Coast to Coast store, Mr. P's Cafe and many more, and in their place came trendy tourist shops and upscale restaurants that seemed to go in and out of business at an astonishing rate. However, many of the old businesses, like The Buffalo Café had managed to remain; some even flourished. The town did not completely lose its look or its charm. Just its flavor; it's essence, you might say.

The community did not necessarily change with it; many of the longtime residents are still there, continuing to live in their considerate and cooperative ways. And many of them resisted the change, fearing that something precious, priceless even, would be forever misplaced. But the power of wealth is irresistible and so, for a while, until the recession at least, the population profited from it. Financially, that is.

But luckily some things never change: like huevos rancheros at The Buffalo Café. Brenda had ordered hers with chorizo, and she took a bite before she continued.

"They're going to catch that guy and, knowing you as I do, you'll probably step right up to the plate and defend him."

Jennifer took a sip of her green tea.

"What makes you think I'd want to do that?"

"Two things. First: you're a softhearted sucker for every underdog that gets pre-tried and convicted by the public before he's even had a chance to tell his side of things – and that's already happening here. Trial by headline. And second: the cop that got hurt was Scott Deaver."

"What's that got to do with it?"

"Oh, come on, Jen! For chrissakes! A few years ago he was about all you ever talked about. For months!"

"So?"

"So, this might be your chance to prove it."

"I thought I did prove it. But maybe there's nothing to prove this time. Maybe it happened just the way it's being reported."

Brenda's fork halted halfway to her mouth and she stared at Jennifer with incredulity.

"Do you really believe that?"

"I don't know what to believe. I don't know the facts yet."

"Yet! You don't know the facts…yet! See? You *are* thinking about it!"

"It's just a figure of speech, Brenda. I'm not thinking about anything except that it's a beautiful day and we both have it off. What I'm really thinking about is spending the afternoon shopping around Whitefish with you."

But Brenda was right: it had been weighing on her mind. Deaver was still in a coma, and in her own compassionate, forgiving way she hoped he recovered. At the same time, she hoped that somehow this would finally end his career in law enforcement. From past experience she knew all too well what kind of person he was.

Seven years ago she had been assigned the case of a homeless man by the name of Luke Foster who had been charged with trespassing, prowling, and resisting arrest. Foster was a Vietnam vet, originally from Pennsylvania, who had been living in the hobo camp located behind the old Wal-Mart building that had been abandoned when they built the new Superstore on the other side of town.

Seated in the detention center interview room at Flathead County Justice Center, she was reading the arresting officer's report of the incident when Foster was brought in. He was a thin man with long, lanky blond hair going gray, and he walked slightly stooped, and groaned faintly as he took a seat on the other side of the glass partition.

"Mr. Foster, my name is Jennifer Lawson and I've been appointed to defend you. I have just now been reviewing your case and I have a few questions. It says here that the arresting officer was investigating a report of a suspicious looking person on Fourth Avenue East, that he spotted you prowling around a house, and that when he approached you, you ran from him. He further states that when he tried to apprehend you that you became belligerent and had to be restrained. Is this correct?"

"I guess I'll have to agree with whatever they say," mumbled Foster.

"That's not what I asked, Mr. Foster. Is this statement by the arresting officer correct, or do you wish to contest this?"

"What difference does it make? It won't change nuthin'."

Jennifer tried to suppress a sigh. Why did it always have to be like this?

"Mr. Foster, you may be indigent, but you still have rights, and it is my job to defend those rights. It says here that you were caught prowling on private property and had to be subdued before the officer could arrest you. The officer further states that this arrest prevented you from committing a crime. What crime would he be referring to?"

"I wasn't committin' no crime. Unless it's a crime for someone like me to take a walk in a nice neighborhood."

"Okay, now we're getting somewhere. You say you were just taking a walk?"

"To see the fall colors. All the shades of red, orange, and yellow. I miss the way the trees turn back home. They got them elm and maple trees in that part of town. I was just admiring them." Foster was suddenly seized with a coughing fit and the exertion bent him over in evident pain.

"Mr. Foster, are you alright?"

"Bout as well as could be expected." He was only just able to choke out the words.

"What's that supposed to mean?"

"Don't mean nothing."

"I want you to tell me the truth. Are you injured and how did it happen?" There was a note of rising anger and insistence in her voice.

"It ain't all that bad. I'll be okay."

"Mr. Foster, it says here that the arresting officer had to use necessary force in order to arrest you. Now tell me the truth: did he beat you?"

"I done told ya, it ain't that bad! I don't wanna make no fuss."

"Have you been examined by a doctor since you were brought in?"

"No ma'am, I don't need no doctor. I'll be fine."

A look of frustration followed by righteous fury came across her face. She stood and walked quickly to the door.

"I'm going to get you a doctor right now! I want someone to take a look at you."

Stepping outside the interview room, she approached the window behind which sat a detention officer. Jennifer did not have to assume the expression of an indignant attorney. She was truly enraged.

"Why has Luke Foster not been examined by a doctor?"

"There didn't appear to be anything wrong with him when he was brought in," The deputy sounded genuinely surprised, "He didn't say anything."

"Well, I want a thorough examination! As quickly as it can be arranged! And I want a report emailed or faxed to me as soon as it is completed."

The diagnosis that she received that afternoon revealed that her client had bruised kidneys and traces of blood in his urine. He had been treated, given some prescription pain meds, and returned to lock-up. In the interview room the next morning, this was her first concern.

After reviewing the medical report with him she said, "Do you want to talk about this?"

"No, ma'am, I don't."

"Why not?"

"Like I tried to tell you yesterday, it'll just stir up trouble and no good will come of it."

"Mr. Foster, you need to tell me if that officer abused you, or in any way violated your civil rights, and you will need to testify to it in court. At the very least this will help us get the charges against you reduced, if not dismissed. Do you understand this?"

"I think I unnerstand this situation better'n you do."

"And how is that?"

"Because I've played this role before." He shook his head, "Lots of times. Me, you, the cop, and the judge; we all got a part to play. Let's just get on with it."

Jennifer shook her head in disparity.

"I can see what you're trying to say, but I don't agree with you. That's not the way it is."

"Sure it is!" He raised his head and for the first time actually looked at her. In his eyes she could clearly see all the hurt and humiliation that he had suffered for God knows how many years. "Same show, different town. 'Course all the actors change 'cept me. But it's always the same old show, ya know? There's always some cop gotta prove how tough he is, and then some lawyer gotta prove they're on your side, and then some judge gotta get re-elected. Never changes."

"If this is the way you feel, then why did you plead 'not guilty' at your arraignment? Why did you request a public defender, and why are we going through all of this?"

"If I had said I was guilty, then they would have turned me loose with time served. This way I get to spend a few days in jail with a warm place to sleep and three meals a day. The food's not exactly what you'd call gor-met, but it beats the hell out of what I've been eating, and besides, there's plenty of it."

The sigh that Jennifer had been restraining made its escape, revealing her aggravation, but she did not allow it to diminish her determination.

"Nonetheless, you pled 'not guilty', and I have your case now, and I assure you, Mr. Foster, this time you've got a very different kind of performer in the role of the lawyer. If you will tell me what really happened, I promise I will go to bat for you, and I won't quit until I see you vindicated."

It took some more persuasion, but Foster ultimately conceded and provided her with his account of what had taken place. Three days previous, he had been walking alone on the sidewalk along 4th Ave. East, when a Kalispell Police squad car pulled up alongside the curb. Because he had never been here before, Foster was unaware that this was a one-way street, and was a bit surprised at the car parking on the left side. He was doing nothing wrong, and, although he generally mistrusted cops, he felt he had no compelling reason to stop, so he simply continued his walk.

The officer got out of his car, and said, "Okay, buddy, hold it right there," and when he caught up to Foster he yelled, "When I say stop, I mean stop! Up against the wall, dirt bag," and began shoving him toward a narrow space between two houses. The cop then pushed him roughly up against the wall of one of them, and struck him viciously several times in the kidneys with a flashlight. The blows were severe enough to knock him to his knees. The officer then cuffed his hands behind his back, yanked him to his feet, and dragged him to the police car, locking him in the back seat. He was taken first to the Kalispell Police Headquarters, where he was booked, and then brought to The Flathead County Detention Center. The name of the arresting officer was Scott Deaver.

Jennifer was able to get a continuance of a couple of days to investigate this story. Bail had been set at $500 and she offered to cover it, but Foster declined, declaring that he didn't mind remaining in jail a few more days. In fact, he welcomed it.

She enlisted Brenda's help, and together they went door to door looking for witnesses. Most of the people they talked to had been at work that day, but they finally found a teenage girl who had stayed home sick from school and had seen most of what had happened.

In court, the girl testified that she had been sitting on the couch watching 'Regis' when she glanced out the front window of her home and saw the policeman take Foster to a side yard between the two houses across the street. She further testified that she witnessed Foster being struck by the officer several times in the lower back with a flashlight, cuffed, and then taken to the squad car.

On cross-examination, the prosecutor asked her why she didn't report this incident at the time it happened. Her reply was that she had assumed that the officer had a reason unknown to her for doing this, and that it was none of her business. She had, however, mentioned it to her parents that evening, and they had all speculated as to what it was all about.

When Scott Deaver took the stand he steadfastly upheld his original report: that he had found Foster peeking in windows, most likely looking for a way to break in, and when he had approached him, Foster had become belligerent and had to be restrained by necessary use of force. What Jennifer saw in Deaver's expression and heard in his tone when she questioned him, though, was sadistic arrogance. He was a big, anvil-jawed man, with large, square teeth that brought to mind crooked tombstones in an ancient graveyard. Throughout his testimony he glared at her malevolently out of cold, close-set, simian eyes from beneath a Neanderthal brow as if she were a deadly adversary, and, try as she might, she was unable to trip him up in his version of the events.

However, based on the teenage girl's testimony, and the medical report, Foster was found innocent of all charges and released from custody. Deaver was not officially reprimanded, but the judge did ask him to stay and have a word with him after court. Jennifer did not hear what transpired between them. She hoped that it would lead to an official investigation, but she doubted it. Most often this sort of thing was dealt with quietly.

She drove Luke Foster to Whitefish to catch an outbound train. Sitting in her car at the depot, she had to argue forcibly until she was able to get him to accept a gift of some cash from her. *That's some way to practice law! You're not going to get rich if you continue to pay the clients.* Then she wished him luck.

"Thank you, Ms. Lawson," he said earnestly, "Thank you for everything. You may not believe this, but you've given me new faith in the human race. I'm glad to know that there are people like you in the world."

Jennifer was deeply touched as she watched him heft his small backpack that contained all of his worldly belongings onto his back and walk up the tracks toward some freight cars. She assumed she would never see him again, but the experience had left a mark on her, and its outcome had given her renewed determination.

She had won the case, but it was a shallow victory. Justice would not be served until Scott Deaver was exposed. What Deaver had done was going to get swept under the rug, and Jennifer was furious! She wasn't going to allow a rotten cop to continue his predations. For months she placed phone calls and wrote letters to the Chief of Police, and confronted city councilmen, apparently to no avail. Searching through old cases she tried in vain to find documentation that he had done this sort of thing before. She came across several arrests Deaver had made using 'necessary force', but found no official complaints or investigations of brutality.

So it was quite a pleasant surprise when six months later she heard that Deaver had resigned from the Kalispell Police Department. She felt like celebrating. No longer would he be able to victimize those he arrested. Jennifer believed she had seen the very last of Scott Deaver. Until this weekend it had never occurred to her that he had merely transferred to the Sheriff's Department.

5

'Kalispel' was the name given by the Upper Pend d'Oreille Indians to the area where they had seasonal villages at the north end of Flathead Lake. The name means 'flat land at the top of the lake', and the Indians who lived there became known as the Kalispel tribe. The south shore was home to a band of Salish that had strayed upstream from the Columbia River basin; and a branch of the Kootenai tribe, the Ksanka, migrated down from Canada and resided along the west shore of the lake. Kootenai is a Blackfeet word meaning 'water people', a name given them because they always lived by water and fished from sturgeon-nosed canoes. Several other bands, such as the Shoshoni and Nez Perce, habitually visited the valley, and the Blackfeet routinely traversed the mountains to raid the other tribes for horses and children. Legend has it that, at times, Kootenai scouts were positioned on the cliffs above the narrow defile downstream of the confluence of the three forks of the Flathead River, and when Blackfeet war parties passed beneath, they rolled huge boulders down upon the would-be raiders to discourage further advancement. For this reason the gorge became known as Badrock Canyon. It wasn't until after The Stevens Treaty of 1855, commonly known as the Hellgate Treaty, established The Flathead Indian Reservation in the lower Flathead and Jocko Valleys that white settlers first began to drift into the region.

Northwest Montana was one of the last sections of the lower forty-eight states to be settled. In the 1870's, cattlemen like Nick Moon, Thomas Lynch, and an Irishman named John O'Leary established the first ranches in The Flathead Valley. A few years later John Dooley opened Fort Selish, a small trading post on the Flathead River, and before long the valley began to attract farmers, miners, and horse traders. Several small towns like Holt, Ashley, and Demersville were founded, and by the late 1880's there were numerous ferry's operating along the river. When the Great Northern Railway began to lay its route through Marias Pass along the Middle Fork of the Flathead River, Nick Moon left, telling his neighbors that the area was getting 'too damn civilized' for him.

In 1891, with apparent foreknowledge of the division point for the railroad between Cutbank and Troy seven miles north of Flathead Lake, Charles Edward Conrad, a banker from Fort Benton, used his own capital to form The Kalispell Townsite Company. The town was soon platted and lots were offered for sale. Along with his brother William, he established the Conrad Bank at the southwest corner of Main and Center Streets. He then began construction of a twenty-three-room Shingle-style residence, a monument to his own prosperity, on Woodland Drive, only a few blocks from where Jennifer Lawson now lives.

Conrad, a Confederate veteran, was something of a visionary. Having witnessed the near extinction of the American bison, he purchased fifty of the one hundred or so of the animals that remained in existence and started his own herd. He grazed them on Wild Horse Island in Flathead Lake for a while later moving them to

Smith Valley, after which they took up a more lasting residence in some fields north of Kalispell. To this day that area is still known as Buffalo Hills.

Charles Conrad died in 1902. His widow continued to manage the growing herd, selling a few as breeding stock, and in 1908 she gave 37 buffalo to start the herd at The National Bison Range in Moise.

The Conrad Mansion remained in the family for seven decades falling into ruin. In the 1970's it underwent a renovation and became a museum, offering guided tours daily. The Conrad Bank continued operations for more than eighty years. On May 18, 1980, at about 8:30 AM, Mount St. Helens in Washington State erupted, and by late that afternoon The Flathead Valley was engulfed in a cloud of volcanic ash. Within twenty-four hours all of the stores that offered surgical and dust masks were sold out, and residents had to use bandannas or whatever else they could find to protect their lungs from the fine dust that permeated the atmosphere. A few days later, the volcanic fallout still suspended in the air, the Conrad Bank was robbed. Police arrived only moments later, and were able to get very accurate descriptions of the perpetrator, and were also able to view him on the playback of the bank's surveillance cameras. The robber was wearing blue jeans, a white T-shirt, and a red bandanna was tied across his face. Within twenty minutes of the hold-up, police had rounded up over two dozen suspects fitting this description. The case was never solved.

In the early 1900's, the division point for the railroad was moved fifteen miles north to Whitefish, but the City of Kalispell was already well established and continued to flourish, nonetheless. In 1910, Mother Mary Agatha and the Sisters of Mercy purchased six lots at the corner of 5th Ave. East and 7th Street for $630.16, and began raising money for a new hospital. On May 8, 1912, The Kalispell General Hospital, a four-story red brick building, constructed at a cost of $46,000, opened its doors. A young doctor by the name of James Upton

Montgomery, a recent graduate of The University of Tennessee Medical School, was hired as one of the original fourteen resident physicians at the hospital.

Fulfilling a lifelong fantasy of living in the western mountains, Dr. Montgomery brought his young family to Kalispell, and moved them into a small house in the eastside neighborhood. In 1915, Michael James Montgomery, Sheriff Mike Montgomery's grandfather and namesake, was born in one of the operating theatres of the hospital with his own father attending. Altogether, there were nine children born to the family, eight of which survived, and, in 1925, mandated by his own reproductive prowess, the doctor had a large, five bedroom, frame house built on First Avenue West.

This was the same year that a woman, apparently seeking to murder her husband who was a patient at the hospital, convinced a young retarded boy to set a stick of dynamite on one of the windowsills and light the fuse. All of the windows on the west and south sides of the building were blown out, but, miraculously, no one was seriously injured. Glass was everywhere, even in the patient's beds. Hundreds of the townspeople turned up to help with the cleanup, and dozens of rough planks were donated to temporarily board up the shattered windows. This was the type of community to which the Montgomerys had migrated; a place where everyone pitched in to help those in need; a good place to put down roots and commence a dynasty.

Sherriff Montgomery's parents, Jonathan and Lydia, still lived in the old house on First Avenue West that his great-grandfather had built. Over the years it had undergone several renovations. Almost every Sunday afternoon, following attendance at the Episcopal Church, the family congregated there for an early dinner. This Sunday, Annie had felt well enough to accompany the Sheriff. Also present, along with his wife, Rachel, was his brother Stephen, who, in somewhat of a family tradition, was, like the original patriarch, a physician. It seemed there had always been a Doctor Montgomery in

Kalispell. In addition, they were joined by Stephen's grown daughter, Stephanie.

As the family sat down to a typical Sunday feast of roast chicken, mashed potatoes, and steamed broccoli, Stephen remarked to his brother, "Well, Mike, it sure looks like you've got your hands full!"

"I've always got my hands full," he quickly replied, helping himself to some chicken.

"No, seriously. I'm surprised you're here today with a deputy in the hospital and a fugitive on the loose. I would think you'd be right in the thick of things."

"Don't worry, we'll catch him."

Stephanie spoke up. "I know him! Eli March? I went to high school with him. I ran into him just a few months ago at Smith's grocery." Stephanie had inherited her mother's green eyes and auburn hair, which today she wore in pigtails making her look more like a teenager than a woman her late twenties. "I can't believe he would do that! He's really a nice guy! What's going to happen to him?"

"We still don't have all the facts," the Sheriff answered, "But, most likely, he'll end up in prison."

"As well he should!" Jonathan commented, emphasizing this statement with the drumstick he held in his hand.

Horror overwhelmed Stephanie's face.

"How can you say that, Grandpa?" She cut in springing to Eli's defense. "You don't even know him!"

"What about your deputy? How's he doing?" Jonathan asked, ignoring her.

"Don't really know. He was in surgery for several hours yesterday, but he still hasn't regained consciousness. A couple of vertebrae in his neck were fractured, and there may be some damage to his spinal cord. The doctor mentioned something about potential paralysis, but they won't be able to evaluate that until he wakes up."

"Of course, it's not my field," Stephen, who was in general practice, interjected, "but, in my limited experience, these kinds of injuries don't often result in permanent paralysis. Usually what you see are chronic problems with pain in the neck, shoulders, and hands."

"Well, let's all pray that it's none of that," suggested Lydia, "and that he'll have a full recovery."

"Amen, to that!" Mike's father agreed.

"Did you see the Sunday paper?" Stephanie asked, "It's all over the front page. I can't believe that picture they're using! Eli doesn't look anything like that anymore."

"It's from his driver's license, but it's eight years old. It was the most recent picture we could come up with." This was a major concern for the Sheriff. None of his men would be able to identify March if he walked right up to them. A police artist working with the Sutten girl had put together a composite, but it was, well, sketchy, at best.

"Did anyone by chance happen to read what the editor had to say about it in this morning's paper?" Jonathan inquired, "That guy is such an idiot! I can't for the life of me figure out how he got to be editor of a newspaper."

"What did he have to say?"

"It was so stupid; it's not even worth repeating. Somehow he had that Eli March confused with Muslim terrorists and Democrats."

This produced a chuckle around the table. Although Flathead was a very red county in a mostly red state, the members of the Montgomery family were characteristically liberal and habitually voted for Democratic candidates.

"Some of the rumors flying around are bizarre," Jonathan continued, "I was at the pharmacy yesterday picking up a prescription, and the lady behind the counter told me that she heard that March was one of those Neo-Nazi survivalists."

"I heard that one, too," said Stephen, "I also heard that he had a huge stockpile of weapons. Any truth to that, Mike?"

"None at all! We found a couple of rifles and a shotgun. Less than what you'd expect to find in most Montana homes, especially that of a licensed guide. We do assume, however, that he has at least one weapon on him. There were some empty ammunition boxes that didn't match up with the guns we found."

"The best one I heard," Stephen offered, "was that he had a bunch of bomb making equipment in his cabin and was related to the Unabomber!"

Everyone had a good laugh over that one. Everyone except the Sheriff, that is. Ted Kaczynski, a.k.a. The Unabomber, had been captured near the town of Lincoln at the southern tip of The Swan Range – the same mountains where they were now searching for Eli March – in a small cabin not much different than the one in which March lived. Montgomery was thinking about how, just as in the case of The Unabomber, gossip can spread across a small town like a whirlwind in a field of wheat, swelling and swirling, stretching the truth until there is no longer any resemblance of what it began as, or any memory of where it commenced. Once set in motion, it was unstoppable and inescapable. It doesn't take much of a wind to kick up an enormous mass of dust. Things were already getting out of hand, and he pondered how his opposition might make use of it.

"Michael, it's your turn to help me with the dishes!" Lydia had been a teacher for thirty-three years, and, although she was retired, she still ran her house like a classroom. Everyone was expected to pull their own weight, and so, without objection, the Sheriff followed his mother into the kitchen.

As he was rinsing dishes and placing them in the dishwasher, Lydia said, "I know both of those boys, you know. Had them in my classroom; not at the same time, of course, but I remember both of them." His mother had taught hundreds of students over the years, and, although most of them were grown with families of their own, she continued to refer to them as 'boys and girls'.

"Quite frankly, I agree with Stephanie," she continued, "I'm having a hard time believing any of what they're saying about Eli March. He was a good boy, very polite, and he always did his work. I had him for Algebra I, and then again for Algebra II. I can't really say I knew him well; I don't think anybody knew him well, because he was such a loner. Shy, you know. Always kept to himself. The girls all seemed to think he was 'cute', or whatever, but he never showed much interest in any of them. I think I remember that even Stephanie had a crush on him at one time."

"Didn't he have any friends at all?"

"I remember seeing him in the hall a few times with Bennie Greenwald, and Bennie's best friend, Ray Holt was with them sometimes. That was more than ten years ago. I don't know if they're still acquainted, but you might want to talk to them. Other than those two, he was always off by himself; never with a group like most kids. I think that's what made him stand out. Maybe that's why I remember him so well."

"So, who's the other boy you were referring to?"

"Oh. That would be Scottie Deaver. The reason I remember him so well is because I couldn't wait to get him out of my classroom. Fortunately, he turned in just enough work that I was able to pass him on to another unlucky teacher. I'm sorry he's injured and in the hospital, but, pardon my language, that boy was a pain in the ass."

"Really! In what way?" For his own reasons the Sheriff felt the same way about Deaver, but he asked the question anyway.

"He was very disruptive in class; speaking out of turn, always trying to get attention, that sort of thing. Most kids, by the time they reach the upper grades have learned how to behave, but I had to discipline him numerous times. And he was a bully with the other students; pulling pranks and using his size to intimidate them. More than once I saw him cause another kid to drop an armload of books. And I'm almost certain that he was the one that pulled the fire alarm that one time, but we could never prove it. Most of the Kalispell Fire Department showed up, and they……………."

Just then, the Sheriff's cell phone rang and he took it out of his pocket looking at the caller ID. "Excuse me, Mom, I better take this"

He stepped out the back door for a moment to have some privacy, and when he came back in his mother was just finishing up with the dishes.

"Well, speak of the devil!"

"What's that?" Lydia asked.

"Deaver. He's awake."

6

A pickup splashed past a clump of brush where Eli crouched in the rain along the east side of Highway 83, commonly known as The Swan Highway, near the intersection of Hollopeter Road, about a hundred yards from the Mission Mountain Mercantile. For four days he had traveled south, crossing and re-crossing the divide to take advantage of the trails that received the most sunlight, and therefore, would have the least snow, facilitating his progress and leaving less of a trail. This was further aided by the fact that the previous winter had been uncommonly mild, and the snowpack in the high country was significantly less than average. He was now about sixty miles south of his cabin, and his heightened, native instincts reassured him that he was no longer closely pursued.

After caching his pack and weapons, he had followed the stream down from Smith Creek Pass the night before, carrying only his small daypack, and crossed the Condon Loop Road, taking up this position where he could watch the store, nearly invisible in his camo raincoat. In the ditch nearby was the decayed and desiccated carcass of a roadkill whitetail deer. He had chosen this hiding place so that if he were recognized the stench might confuse the search dogs.

The store had opened a few minutes ago, but he was waiting for a few cars to park in front of it so that no one would notice that he had not driven in. Although he had knocked down a few grouse yesterday with his wrist rocket, and had been able to snare some other small game, his food supplies were running low, leaving only his packets of freeze-dried emergency rations. Moreover, in his haste, he had neglected to bring any fishing gear, which he generally kept separate from his hunting equipment. In addition, all of the bandages in his small first aid kit had been utilized redressing the wound in his shoulder, which, in truth, should have received stitches. The pain in his kidneys had receded to a dull ache.

The rain stopped, and there were now two passenger cars and several pickups parked in front. Creeping out from his place of concealment, he crossed the highway and walked toward the store. He was at least a few miles into Missoula County, and prayed that the search had not extended this far. It was a risk he had to take nonetheless. If all went well, by nightfall he would be back over the divide and well hidden in the wilderness, no one the wiser.

When Eli entered the building, he kept the hood of his camo rain gear over his head, in the hope that he would not be recognizable, and could not be identified by the store's security cameras. Most of the customers were lined up at the checkout station at the front of the store. Keeping his head down, he grabbed a yellow plastic basket off the stack, and quickly walked past them, turning down an aisle that looked as if it might contain miscellaneous items, such as fishing gear and first aid supplies. What they offered in the way of sporting equipment was very limited, but he did find some five-pound test line, along with some 5X tippet, and assortments of hooks and weights. With these he could easily devise a handline, enabling him to catch brook trout from the high-mountain lakes that would soon be thawing. On the opposite side of the same aisle, he found some bandages, tape, and antibiotic ointment, and dropped them into the basket, as well.

Two aisles over, he added a large supply of dried fruit and nuts, along with as many granola bars as he thought he could fit in his pack, hoping that this unusual quantity did not generate comment or arouse suspicion at the cash register. In a few weeks the first early shoots of edible plants would be available, fireweed stems and evening primrose, the roots of Canadian thistle and Jerusalem artichoke, and the entire foliage of glacier lily and wild chives, but these supplies would be needed to balance his diet until then. Obtaining meat would be no problem, and would be his major staple.

All of this had only taken about ten minutes, and he was relieved, wanting to be in and out as fast as possible. However, as he neared the checkout, something on the newsstand captured his attention. His own face gaped out at him from the front page of a newspaper, and adjacent to the photograph, looking somewhat like one of those Photoshop images, was a pencil sketch that had been rendered of his likeness. The snapshot was from his driver's license, and he was aware that his features had matured somewhat since the picture was taken, but the drawing, he believed, bore a reasonably fair resemblance to his current appearance. His initial impulse was one of alarm, urging him to get out of the store, and get away as hurriedly as he could, but his curiosity was more irresistibly dominant. One of his uncle's favorite sayings was that curiosity was the reason a cat needed nine lives. Heedlessly, he took the newspaper from the rack and put it in his basket.

Again keeping his head down, he stuffed his purchases into his daypack as they were scanned by the cashier, a teenage girl who never really looked at his face. He paid with cash, and left the store. The entire process, from the time he entered the store until he stepped back outside, had lasted less than twenty minutes, and no one had shown any sign of suspicion or recognition. The waterproof sportsman's watch on his wrist informed him that it was only eight-thirty in the morning. Unburdened by doubt, he walked back up the highway, and with no cars in sight, crossed in the same place as before, through the thicket of alder brush where the dead deer lay, and proceeded on the same track he had used for his descent the night before. The sky had cleared, and the expanding sun was just beginning to insinuate its beaming countenance through the cleft in the mountains toward which his path directed.

When he reached the snowline, he sensed he had covered sufficient distance to take a break and have some breakfast. Seated on a deadfall and munching a granola bar, he read the article in the paper that said that he had fled the cabin subsequent to assaulting and critically injuring a deputy sheriff. Discovering that the deputy's condition presented potential paralysis troubled him profoundly, and he wondered if he could have helped the man if he had remained with him. *Should* he have remained was the greater question. Perhaps if he had, it would have made him seem more innocent, or, at least, less guilty. However, possessing only a frail self-confidence in most social settings, he had never learned to deal well with conflict, and the mountain forests had always been his refuge, his sanctuary. Even on the rare occasions when he had quarreled with his mother, he sought the solace and solitude of the woodlands. It was only here that he found balance and harmony, only here that he could attain a sense of centeredness, and, consequently, he felt more socially adept in this, his own element. But now he fully understood how the momentary choices we make, like the flip of a coin or the drawing of straws, can alter the course of our lives forever. After the lot is cast, there is no way to retrieve it.

The rest of the article was, more or less, what he had guessed would be Jolene's story, containing just enough of the truth to make it believable. And people *would* believe it, if for no other reason than it was in print - in black and white. No poison could be more lethal than ink.

He understood now what it was that Bennie had tried to warn him about, that she was not right in the head, but still, he could not understand why she had suddenly become so bitter and hateful toward him. Perhaps he would never know. In any case, it seemed unlikely that she would recant her version and tell the truth. For lack of any clarity in the situation, he surmised that it was best to simply move on.

His intended route would lead him back through Smith Creek Pass, around the north side of Cooney Mountain, and he would follow Big Salmon creek down to where it flowed into Big Salmon Lake. The outlet of the lake emptied into the South Fork of The Flathead River. The river would be raging with the runoff this time of year, but there was a packer's bridge that would allow him to cross, gaining access to the depths of The Bob Marshall Wilderness beyond, where he could remain undetected indefinitely. The bridge was used by outfitters in 'The Bob' to move horses and gear across the river; in fact, he had utilized it many times himself, but no one would be there this early in the season with the river running so high. Later on, however, those very outfitters, some of which he knew well, would be an unwitting source of food and provisions. Most of them adhered to the well-defined trails and camped in established campsites, so it would be effortless to evade them. When preparing for daily forays, food supplies were hoisted into the trees to keep bears from raiding them, and while the camp was vacant it would be easy to pilfer small amounts without arousing suspicion.

Four hours later, as he was approaching the mouth of the pass, he heard the unmistakable whine of snowmobile engines. It was late afternoon; slanting sunbeams streaked through the forest spilling their iridescence upon the new shroud of snow that was troweled like a fresh coat of plaster over the forest floor.

Knowing that the unseasonably balmy weather would make the logging roads in this favored recreation area more accessible, Eli had followed a trail that wound up through the trees along the creek, insuring that he would be concealed; undetectable in his camo clothing. Therefore, he was only mildly alarmed.

Through an aperture flanked by tree trunks, he had an ample line of view into the exposed area along the slope to the south, and was able to see two snowmobiles as they entered the sun-lit clearing from a US Forest Service fire lane across from where he crouched, veering off on separate courses. There was a small ridge splitting the meadow, and one of them chose a route over the top of this, while his companion dropped down below, noisily carving a path through the unbroken sparkling snowfield.

As the first snowmobiler raced along the cornice, heavy wet chunks of snow fell from the edge, setting off a small slide that gained momentum as it hurled itself inescapably toward the other rider. In the past, Eli had witnessed avalanches much larger and louder than this one, but, nonetheless, it launched itself down the incline striking the unaware snowmobiler with ample force to overturn his vehicle and leave him buried face down with only one booted foot kicking above the surface as he tried to free himself. As the snowslide played out at the bottom of the clearing where the slope leveled off, Eli could see the other snowmobiler, oblivious of what had just occurred, plunge down the far side of the ridge, the clatter of his engine a diminishing echo as he dropped out of sight.

Having no way of knowing how long it would be before the other rider became aware that his friend was missing, Eli, although he was exceedingly aware of the great risk he was taking, did not hesitate hastening to attempt rescuing the trapped man. Thrashing through the soft snow as fast as he could travel, he reached the downed man quickly, dropped to his knees, and began digging down around the exposed leg with his gloved hands. Within minutes he had freed the other leg, along with the man's squirming hips, and only seconds later was able to get his head above the surface. Having lost his helmet in the crash, the man came up sputtering and gasping as someone might if he had been forced to hold his breath under water for too long. He had only been buried for six or seven minutes, and it was entirely possible that there had been a small pocket of air around his head, so that he may have not been deprived of oxygen for even that long, and Eli was relieved that he did not seem to be injured in any way.

At this moment, the other snowmobile came to a roaring halt beside them, and the driver jumped off removing his helmet.

"Is he okay? Should I call 911? Is he gonna be alright?"

Eli looked up formulating a reply, but received an unexpected jolt of adrenaline as he saw the light of recognition race rapidly across the man's countenance. It was all he needed to get him moving. Leaping to his feet, he darted swiftly back the way he had come, following his own trail back into the trees, and charged up the path along the creek toward the pass. From what the man had said he could only assume that he had a cell phone on him, and he did not know if having come to their aid would prevent them from reporting him. He had to move fast!

7

"I've been thinking a lot about religion lately. Not just Christianity, but all of them, you know; just religion in general."

It was a few minutes before Annie Montgomery's 3:00 PM appointment for chemotherapy, and they had just pulled into a parking space near the entrance to the infusion center at Kalispell Regional Hospital. Knowing how awful she would be feeling afterward, she had scheduled the session for later in the day so she could simply go home to bed when it was over.

"It's times like this," she continued, "that I wish I had something I could really believe in. I think it would help."

"You're doing just fine, Annie," the Sheriff shut the engine off and turned to face her, "In fact I'm amazed at how good your attitude has been. You're the bravest person I've ever known, and I'm very proud of you."

"Attitude is cerebral. It's just a matter of choice. But faith is something altogether different. I can't just pick a religion and choose to believe it. I need something more than that; some kind of revelation, I guess. I know it happens to other people, at least they say it does, but it's never happened to me. And right now…I wish it would."

A silent tear escaped from her eye, and Mike tenderly wiped it away.

"We're going to get through this, Annie. We'll beat this together. You'll see. It's going to be okay."

"Oh, Mike, you're so sweet! You're such a gentle person, you know, you just don't fit the profile of a western sheriff at all," She touched his cheek affectionately, "But that's not what I'm talking about. I'm not worried about getting *through* this, about *beating* this. And I'm not really afraid of dying. I got over that a long time ago. We all have to go sometime. I just wish I had some sort of belief in *where* we go, if we go anywhere at all."

"I wish I could answer that for you, but I think that's something we all have to decide for ourselves."

"But that's just it, Mike! How do you *decide* a thing like that?" she paused reflectively, "You know something? I've gone to church nearly every Sunday for my entire life, and *I don't know why*! I mean, I enjoy seeing everybody; it does give me a sense of community, I guess, but I don't really feel like I've ever been…*invested* in the religious part. It's just the way we were raised, you and me. We went to church on Sunday. It's the way we tried to raise Chad. It's the *right* thing to do! But, to be perfectly honest with you, when we all bow our heads to pray, I'm usually thinking about something else, like what all I'll need to do to help get Sunday dinner ready, or something like that. It's only in the last few Sundays that I've actually been thinking about God when we pray."

"Honey, I think you're being too hard on yourself. Not everyone in the service is praying. Everyone gets preoccupied at times."

"Oh, I know that! But I'm not talking about everyone else. I'm talking about me! And you know what I wonder about when I think about God? It has nothing to do with religion. As far as I'm concerned, all religions are pretty much the same; they all want to humanize their gods and deify their saints, and they all bless their soldiers and assure them that God is on *their* side. But when I think of God, if there really is such a thing, I can't help but wonder why God loves *me* so much! Why has God given me everything I ever wanted in life, and so many people never get anything? Why has my life been so blessed? What have I done to deserve such a wonderful life?"

He started to reply but she held up a hand cutting him off, and smiled in a way that was equally joy and sorrow, contentment and dissatisfaction.

"And you know, Mike," she continued, "more than anything, I wonder what I've done to deserve you."

"Okay, sweetie," he cut in, wiping at his eyes, "You're getting me teared up now. C'mon, let's go inside. We're running late, as it is."

The outpatient infusion center was located in an older part of the building in the rear of the hospital. When they entered, the nurses on duty fussed over her in a familiar and almost festive manner as if she had arrived for a hair appointment, or something equally benign. Annie took a seat in one of the elevated reclining chairs, and a CNA took her blood pressure and other vitals, and asked if she would like something to eat.

"No, thank you," she declined, "I really don't have much of an appetite these days. But I would like one of those hard lemon drops if you have any. I always seem to get a bad taste in my mouth. They really help."

As one of the nurses was drawing blood for the lab before starting her IV, Annie turned to the Sheriff who was standing next to her chair and said, "Mike, this will take about an hour or so and you'll just get bored. Why don't you go see how your deputy is doing? I'll be fine."

Spontaneously, she began to chuckle.

"What in the world are you finding so humorous, Annie?"

"Oh, nothing. It's silly!"

"What?"

"Well, I didn't mention it, but a few days ago the oncologist offered to recommend me for one of those medical marijuana cards. He said it would help with the nausea and appetite loss. And I was just thinking how funny that would look, the Sheriff's wife being a pothead. Not to mention what Sergeant Broussard would do with that in his campaign."

"Who cares, Annie? If you think it will help you, then do it! No one has to know anyway."

"Mike! Get serious!" she exclaimed in feigned indignation.

"I am serious!"

"Oh, go on! Get out of here!"

Leaving the infusion center, Sheriff Montgomery made his way through a labyrinth of corridors that led into what he still thought of as the new wing of the hospital. It seemed that there was perpetually a crane in the sky above Kalispell Regional Medical Center, aerial verification of incessantly unending expansion.

He had last visited Scott Deaver on Sunday night after receiving the call that he was conscious, but had found him too medicated to be coherent. Most of what he'd been able to say was either incomprehensible or illogical, and almost all of the reports he had received since then had informed him that Deaver's responses continued to be unintelligible. Hopefully, he would find him more lucid today.

Taking the elevator to the third floor, he walked down the hall to Deaver's private room, arriving just as Detective Mick Linnell was leaving.

"Hi, Mick. How's he doing?" The Sheriff inclined his head in the general direction of Deaver's room.

"Morphine's still making him groggy, but he seems to be a little more rational. Keeps complaining about numbness in his legs and feet, but I talked to Dr. Santay, the neurosurgeon, a little while ago, and she said that Deaver's pathological and involuntary reflexes seem to be okay, so she doesn't expect there to be any permanent paralysis."

"Thank God for that! What else did the doctor say?"

"Well, as you probably know, they had to fuse two vertebrae.........I think it was C4&5, or something like that. Dr. Santay said that she had operated right away because imaging had shown some small bone fragments near the spinal cord, but that she had been able to remove them with only very minor cord damage."

"What did Dr. Santay say about the numbness?"

"She seemed a little unsure about that. She said it could be from the minor cord damage, or related to the trauma, or possibly psychosomatic. To tell you the truth, the doctor seemed a little confused, and, personally, I'm wondering if maybe she didn't miss something."

"Well, let's hope not."

Linnell nodded his agreement.

"Anyway, they'll know more when they get him on his feet. They're going to start physical therapy as soon as possible."

"Santay? What kind of name is that?"

"I think it's Indian."

"Indian, huh? I wonder which tribe."

"No, not American Indian. *Indian* Indian."

"Oops! My mistake!" the Sheriff smiled inwardly, "Did you question Deaver again about what happened out at that cabin?"

"I tried, but he still can't remember anything much after receiving the call from dispatch. But you might ask Broussard. He's been spending a lot of time here and maybe Deaver said something to him about it."

"Mmm. Hey, Mick, could you wait out here for me. I won't be but a few minutes. There were some things in the forensic report that I wanted to ask you about."

"Sure, no problem. I'll be right down there in that little seating area."

When Sheriff Montgomery entered the room, he found Scott Deaver, his head, neck, and shoulders encased in a traction device, reaching awkwardly for a plastic mug of water on the bedside table. He stepped over to the table, lifted the mug with the KRMC logo on it, and held the flexible straw to Deaver's lips.

"How're you feeling, Scottie?" the Sheriff asked when he finished drinking.

Deaver mumbled something indecipherable.

"What was that? I couldn't hear you."

"Said………sleepy. So sleepy."

"That's probably the morphine. I just heard that they're gonna get you out of this contraption pretty soon, and into some therapy. Won't that be a welcome change?"

"At'ssss…nice."

"Scott, I'm not gonna stay long; I don't want to tire you. But I'd like to ask you if you can remember anything about what happened. Anything at all?"

"T'ssssalll………fuzzy. Don't…know."

There was a soft tap on the door and Linnell stuck his head in the room.

"Uh, Sheriff, sorry to interrupt, but could you step out here a moment? It's pretty important."

"I'll be right there, Mick. I was just about to leave anyway." Turning to say goodbye to his deputy, he discovered that Deaver had already drifted off to sleep again.

When he exited the room he found Linnell waiting in the hallway with a flushed, excited look on his face.

"We've had a confirmed sighting. Less than an hour ago."

"March? Where? How?"

"Two snowmobilers up in Smith Creek Pass above Condon. In the Swans. Apparently, one of them got planted upside down in a snow slide, and March pulled him out."

"Really! And they're sure it's him?"

"No doubt about it! One of them got a real good look at him!"

"This is good news, Mick," The Sheriff pulled his cell phone from his pocket, "Excuse me a minute. I better call the office."

Instead of calling the department's landline, Montgomery hit a speed dial number to Undersheriff Walter Holbrook's cell phone. He and Holbrook had been friends since playing football together in high school, and had remained close through all their years with the department. Holbrook's support had been instrumental in getting him elected last time, and he was assisting the current campaign.

"Hi, Mike. I guess they got hold of you."

"Yeah, I just heard. What have you done so far?"

"The sighting was called in on a cell phone about forty-five minutes ago. I'm surprised that they had reception, that's usually a dead zone, but maybe it was because of the altitude. It's pretty high up, right at the pass. But the roads are reasonably accessible. The snowmobilers were able to drive up there. Their position was just a few miles from both Missoula County and Powell County lines, so I notified all of their departments."

"Did you call Lake County?"

"No, that would be in the other direction, over the Missions. We don't think he's headed that way. Looks like he's moving into the Bob. If we don't catch him quickly, it'll be hard to find him in that much wilderness. But there's several good places to land a chopper in there, even at this time of year, so we already sent one out from here, and Missoula's got one on the way. They've got heat detectors, but there are so many big animals in those mountains, you know, they just confuse things," Holbrook paused for a moment, and then, expressing misgivings, said, "It's a bad spot, Mike. Right on all those county lines and so far from anything. The only law enforcement in the area is a highway patrolman, and he's totally unequipped to do anything. It'll be hours before any search teams can reach Hollopeter Road, and who knows how long before we get anyone up in the pass. And by then it'll be getting dark."

"You know, Walt, let's slow down a little bit. That rain last night almost certainly fell as snow in the mountains, so he has to have left fresh tracks. Instead of sending a bunch of men and dogs in to churn up the snow, let's see if we can get just two or three of our best trackers well-equipped and up there by tomorrow. It's not supposed to rain or snow for a few days, so his trail should stay visible. If they're all carrying sat-phones we'll be able to maintain communication."

"Good thinking, Mike. I totally agree with you. I'll get right on it."

"Okay. And I'm going to give Charlie Nichols down in Lake County a call and see what he can do to help."

Linnell was still waiting nearby when Montgomery ended the call and said, "Sorry, Mick. I'll be right with you. I just have to make one more call."

From his contact list he called the Lake County Sheriff.

"Charlie, this is Mike Montgomery. I think we could use that tracker if he's available."

"I'm way ahead of you, Monty. I heard the news about a half hour ago, and I figured you'd be needing him, so I put a call in to him and left a message on his voicemail. I'll get him up there as soon as he calls in, but I can't say when that'll be. He's one of those guys that live on Indian time, but he's real good. Worth waiting for. You've got my word on it!"

"No problem. Just do the best you can. We'll have a couple of other trackers on it as well. And even though he was spotted somewhere else, could you keep watching the mother?"

"You got it! Glad to help!"

After his conversation with Sheriff Nichols, Montgomery stood pensively in the corridor outside Deaver's room, running everything over in his mind to be sure he had not missed anything. Then he noticed Detective Linnell standing patiently nearby.

"Sorry, Mick. Everything seems to be happening at once. Thanks for waiting. I wanted to ask you about what forensics has come up with so far. I saw the fingerprint analysis, and a few things don't quite seem to jibe."

"Are you talking about the telephone?"

"What about the telephone?"

"The Sutten girl said that she called 911 from his landline and that he knocked the phone out of her hand. But her fingerprints weren't on the phone. His were, like you'd expect. It's his phone. But they didn't even find a partial on her."

"What do you make of that?"

"I'm not sure. You know, telephones and doorknobs are not very reliable for prints because so many people touch them. But we only found three sets of prints in the cabin: his and hers and Deaver's. She said she dialed with her thumb, and she has long fingernails, so maybe she didn't leave any prints."

"Yeah, I guess that's my take on it, too. Did you get anything useful off the 911 tapes?"

"Nothing useful. On the first call the phone had landed face down on the floor and the sounds were pretty garbled. And on the second tape the girl was hysterical which would account for some slight variations from her statement."

"So, what about the knife?'

"Which knife?"

"The little paring knife."

"Well, that checked out. It's got her fingerprints on it."

"I know. I saw that. But she told me that after she stabbed him, he pulled the knife out and threw it on the floor."

"That's not what she said when I took her statement. She said that she held on to it after she stabbed him, but that he knocked it out of her hand."

"My memory is pretty good, Mick. And it was only five days ago. I remember what she said because it didn't make any sense at the time. I remember thinking why would he pull the knife out and throw it on the floor if he wanted to hurt her? Why wouldn't he use it on her?"

"I don't know, Sheriff. Maybe she was confused, but that's not what's on her statement."

"I don't think she was confused, Mick. I think she changed her story. And what about her car? She said that March had tried to get in the car, but his prints were not anywhere on it."

"Yeah, you're right! I guess I missed that."

"Don't be too hard on yourself. On the surface this case looks like a slam-dunk. It's just when you start dissecting it that things don't quite come together."

"Yeah, maybe so. It's always the little things that tell the big story."

"Very true! But what I can't figure out is why would she lie? It doesn't make any sense. Unless she was the one who hit Deaver, but that doesn't add up either because March's prints were clearly on the flashlight." Sheriff Montgomery shook his head ponderously. "And another thing I was just wondering about. What kind of man would try to kill a woman, and then assault an officer, and five days later would save the life of a snowmobiler?"

8

The offices of Lawson Law Firm, conveniently located in the west-side neighborhood only a few blocks from the courthouse, were in the front rooms of the house that Jennifer's parents had bought when she was two years old. They had met and married while attending the business school at The University of Montana in Missoula, and after completing their degrees, had moved to Kalispell where Jennifer's mother found a job at a local bank, and her father went to work at an investment firm.

They rented for the first couple of years until they could qualify for a loan at the bank where her mother, Ruth, worked, enabling them to purchase the three bedroom house in 1972 for $18,000. Living so close to downtown allowed them both to walk to work except on the foulest of days, and, equally convenient was the daycare center run by Brenda's mom only two blocks from home.

Over the next few years, Ruth received rapid promotions from teller, to customer service representative, and then to loan officer. When Jennifer's father, Jeffrey, was taken away from them, Ruth was earning on her own enough to keep the house, and in 1997, the year that she retired from the bank, she made the final payment on the mortgage. This was also the same year that Jennifer graduated from the U of M Law School, and returned to Kalispell, moving in with her boyfriend, Bob Mayfield.

Ruth was only forty-nine years old, and felt much too young to stop working, and so she made an offer to her daughter. Jennifer could establish her new law firm in the front of the house, and Ruth would continue to live upstairs, and would work for the firm as receptionist and legal secretary. As a graduation present, Ruth offered to pay for all of the remodeling. It was a generous proposal, and it enabled Jennifer to start out on her own, something she had only dreamed of.

Her mother was sitting at the front desk when Jennifer walked in at 9:30 Thursday morning. In spite of the hardships she'd endured, the years had been kind to Ruth Lawson. At sixty-three she was trim and energetic, with only the first few web-like creases of advancing maturity beginning to show upon her face, mostly around the eyes, in a way that displayed sorrow and joy simultaneously. Her straight, shoulder-length hair, once dark brunette, had evolved to a glossy white. An attractive woman, she had assiduously, and successfully, avoided involvement in any sort of relationship, platonic or otherwise. Her entire life had been lived in devotion to her daughter.

"You had a call from that Deputy County Attorney, Jameson. He wants to talk to you about a plea bargain in the Watson case. And I'm supposed to remind you that you have to be in court this afternoon for Gunther's sentencing."

"Anything else?" Jennifer asked as she bent to kiss her mother's cheek.

"Yes. How's my granddaughter? I haven't seen her in over a week!"

"She's almost thirteen years old and I don't see her much either. If she's not at her father's house, then she's over at Nikki's, or out somewhere with her other friends."

"How long is it going to take for you and Bob to get back together again this time?" The ability to make quantum leaps from one topic to another was characteristic of Ruth Lawson, "It's been over four months and he still calls me almost every day wanting to know if you've said anything to me about it. I swear, that man loves you so much, but it drives him crazy when you're not together."

"I don't know, Mom. You know how I am. It just takes me a while." Jennifer really didn't have to explain it. Her mother knew her better than anyone, even Brenda. "Let me have the Watson file. I'll call Jameson first and see what his offer is." Jennifer took the file into her office to review before calling the County Attorney's Office.

Cody Watson, fifty-five years old, divorced, had been indicted for manufacture of dangerous drugs with intent to sell. His case, however, was further complicated by the fact that it dealt with what had recently become a very sensitive political issue in Montana, namely medical marijuana, and was receiving a fair amount of media attention. This could work to Watson's advantage. Jennifer knew the County Attorney would want to settle it quickly, but, regardless of how it turned out, Watson would lose everything he had.

Jennifer wasn't quite sure how she felt about the medical marijuana issue, a hotly contested debate in most sessions of the state legislature. An occasional recreational user in college, she had all but given up smoking pot during law school, however, she continued to think of it as a benign substance. Bob used it frequently, and it never seemed to impede or limit him in any way. Perhaps the real problem, as with so many laws, lay with the legislation itself, which was often vague and misinterpreted, leading to unfair prosecutions such as this one.

A native of the area, Cody Watson had graduated from Columbia Falls High School, and for the next twenty years had been employed at a variety of occupations ranging from various construction jobs, to driving a propane delivery truck, and working with logging outfits. In 2001, he landed a steady job at the Columbia Falls Aluminum Company, but seven years later he was laid off along with hundreds of others, when the CFAC was taken over by a Swedish corporation. Divorced years before, with one nearly grown son, Cody had only himself to fend for, and for over eighteen months he collected unemployment compensation and searched for a new job diligently, but in vain. He was a proud man, and it was difficult for him not to have work.

It was Cody's twenty-two year old son, Bridger, who came up with a possible solution: become a medical marijuana provider. Several years previous, voters in Montana had overwhelmingly passed an initiative allowing medical marijuana to be grown and sold to qualified patients, but Cody had never tried the stuff in his entire life, and, initially, was totally against the idea. Besides, what did he know about growing marijuana? Bridger, on the other hand, knew a little too much, and talked about it constantly for weeks, but it wasn't until he started calculating the potential profits that Cody began to get interested. Bridger had a friend who was already in the business and was more than willing to help them get started.

Cody applied for and received a caregiver's license. Using the last of his savings, they rewired and insulated the oversized garage, and purchased grow lights and hydroponic equipment. Bridger's friend gave them clones of nine different strains to get them started, and Cody got his name on caregiver lists at the offices of several physicians who were known to prescribe cannabis as medication. Six months later they were providing for numerous patients, and along with the income they earned from cutting firewood for sale, they were bringing in enough to pay the bills, at least. Better yet, Cody, filled with the satisfaction of self-sufficiency, was able to quit receiving unemployment benefits.

In the beginning, it was all about the money, but as time went by Cody began to find a more meaningful purpose in what he was doing, and to appreciate the fulfillment that comes from helping others. One of his patients was an eighty-three year old widow, a neighbor, who suffered from arthritis. She was overcome with gratitude that the cannabis he provided allowed her to function without any of the dangerous medications that were advertised on television showing lean, attractive older people enjoying active lives, voiced over with a long-winded but softly-spoken side-effects disclaimer that used up more commercial time than the sales pitch itself.

Another patient was a twenty-four year old woman who, for most of her life, had endured epileptic seizures that were so debilitating that she had dropped out of school and was unable to hold a job. Medical marijuana had all but ended her seizures, and now she was enrolled at the community college and hopeful of a career in computers.

A few months ago, sheriff's deputies had raided an underage drinking party, and two teenage boys had been caught with a small quantity of marijuana. When questioned about their source, frightened, they gave the name of Bridger Watson. Armed with a warrant, the police came to Cody's house, confiscated everything, and, since he was the license holder, charged him with the felony. Bridger, arguing that he was only working for his father, was able to get his charge reduced to a misdemeanor.

When she returned his call, the plea bargain that Jameson offered Jennifer was a two-year sentence with eighteen months suspended and time served. It was a good deal, a 'slap on the wrist' opponents of cannabis would say, but even a full acquittal would not change things for Cody. Once again, Jennifer felt that her client was a casualty of injustice. Cody had done no wrong, had followed the letter of the law, and had been victimized by his own son, but Jennifer was convinced that the court would not see it that way. In any case, it was too late. He had used the equity in his house to guarantee his bond, but with months of no income he had fallen hopelessly behind on his mortgage payments, and he was no longer eligible for unemployment compensation. Without a miracle, he would lose everything, and, quite possibly, become, like so many others these days, homeless.

Jennifer told Jameson that she would confer with her client and get back to him with an answer within twenty-four hours. After hanging up the phone, she leaned back in her chair brooding. When Jennifer was twelve years old, before her father had been arrested, she naively thought that courts were places where competitive games were played, like basketball and tennis. Recalling this, she was impressed with how unwittingly perceptive she had been. Gazing out the front window of her office she could see the sidewalk where she and Brenda had been playing on that summer evening in 1981 when her father had taken a stroll after supper around the neighborhood.

Jennifer's parents loved to take long family walks, but this particular occasion her mother was experiencing menstrual cramps and didn't feel up to it, and Jennifer, along with Brenda, had just completed drawing a hopscotch pattern in chalk on the sidewalk and was eager to play, and so, she declined to accompany her father. It was a beautiful, hot July evening, late afternoon really. Mid-summer this far north nightfall didn't occur until very late, and so both she and her mother were not surprised that he was gone for nearly three hours. They were stunned, however, when, early the next morning, two police detectives came to the house and arrested her father for the rape and murder of a nine-year-old girl.

Early in his walk, only a few blocks from their house, her father had encountered a little girl riding her bicycle toward him, and when she came upon a place where the sidewalk had buckled, she fell. He rushed to her and helped her up, and used his handkerchief to wipe a few droplets of blood from a scrape on her elbow. She thanked him, assuring him that she was okay, and rode on. Later on, acting on a call from the little girl's parents reporting her missing, police quickly organized a neighborhood search. At sundown, her body was found poorly hidden among the willows along Ashley Creek.

Numerous witnesses identified Jeffrey Lawson as the last person any of them had seen with her. His court appointed defense attorney could not produce one witness who would testify to having seen him later during his walk. Blood found on his handkerchief, which he freely admitted to be hers, matched the victim's blood type, but, even more condemning, semen found on the body matched his blood type, AB Negative, one of the rarest, possessed by only one in one hundred and seventy Americans. It was all circumstantial evidence, but compelling enough for him to be found guilty of the crime. It was only because there was no eyewitness that he was spared execution and was sentenced to life imprisonment at the state correctional facility at Deer Lodge.

The community was shocked and outraged by the crime, and most people agreed that the sentence was just, while only Jennifer and her mother, and a few close acquaintances, Brenda and her family among them, continued to believe in his innocence. For years afterward, many of the townspeople treated them with contempt and cruelty, and if it had not been for the kindness and compassion of their few remaining friends, they might have moved to another place.

Prison populations are notoriously contemptuous of men convicted of sex crimes, and Jeffrey, inexperienced in self-defense, was treated roughly, barely surviving five years until he was murdered by another inmate. Jennifer was only seventeen, still in high school, but it was at this time that she decided to devote her life to doing everything in her power to prevent anyone else from ever having to endure this sort of injustice.

When she graduated from law school and opened this office, her first client was her own departed father. For years she reviewed the transcripts of the trial, and questioned neighbors on what they could remember, trying to find some evidence that might clear her father's name. It wasn't until ten years ago, with the assistance of an organization that provides funds and expertise in cases such as this, that she was able to get the evidence tested for DNA, something that had not been available at the time of the trial. The blood on the handkerchief, of course, matched that of the victim, but the DNA provided by the semen sample matched that of a man who was already in prison for a similar crime.

She was liberated from the unpleasant memory by her mother entering the office, shutting the door behind her.

"There's a, um, 'gentleman' out front," Ruth turned toward the door as if she could see through it, "asking to see you."

"Oh, Mom, I don't have time. I haven't had lunch yet, and I have to be in court this afternoon. Tell him he'll have to make an appointment."

"I already told him that, but he's very insistent. He says he drove up from Polson this morning just to talk to you."

"Mom, just tell him I'm very sorry, but he should have called first."

"I did! But he said that whatever this is about happened over the weekend, and he couldn't call, and that it's urgent that he see you right now." Again Ruth glanced over her shoulder as if she were intimidated by this person and didn't want to face him again. "He said that he won't be available again until he needs your representation which will be very soon."

"Well that sounds suitably intriguing," Jennifer replied sarcastically, checking the time on her cell phone, "Okay, I'll just skip lunch, I guess. What's his name?"

"Something like 'Ka-sunka'. Dexter Ksunka."

9

"How in the hell could our men be following two sets of tracks when we're only after one man? Could you please explain that to me?"

Sheriff Mike Montgomery scowled irritably. He and Undersheriff Walter Holbrook were standing in front of a large US Forest Service map that was tacked to the wall in the office of the Search and Rescue Coordinator. Specific areas on the map were delineated by color: white for private land, orange for reservation land, and for US Forest Service land – what else? – Forest Service green. The green area to the east and south of the map was where the search was centered, where Eli had vanished: over two million acres encompassing the Hungry Horse and Spotted Bear Ranger Districts, The Bob Marshal Wilderness, The Great Bear Wilderness, and to the north, colored in a pinkish-purple, extended the additional vastness of Glacier National Park. This time of year most of the high country would still be deep in snow, but an experienced and well-equipped person would not have much trouble traveling through the lower elevations, and along the sunnier slopes. Searching for such a person in such limitlessness would be like probing for the proverbial needle in a haystack.

"No, Mike, I can't explain it. It just is what it is. Our men followed one set of tracks up the creek, and when they got to the east side of the pass, the tracks separated off in two different directions. So they split up, thinking that one set was false, and the other the true trail. That way they were covering all bases. The first set went north around Owl Peak, here," Holbrook placed his index finger on the map moving upward, "and then crossed the divide again at Lion Creek Pass, vanishing in some rocks. We were thinking maybe he came back down and crossed Highway 83, and then went up into The Missions."

"But that would have meant taking a chance on being spotted again. I don't think March would be that stupid. What about the other tracks?"

"That set went south to this pass above Holland Lake. But the tracker lost the trail in a thicket somewhere down along Smokey Creek, about here." Holbrook rested his finger on the map.

Montgomery made a face like he was suffering from severe indigestion.

"Didn't anybody look for tracks going east, downhill toward the South Fork? Wouldn't that be the rational direction?"

"It would seem that way, but there wasn't a trail leading in that direction. What were they supposed to do, Mike? Follow no trail at all?"

Montgomery shook his head.

"No, I suppose not. That would have involved intuitive thinking. The simple truth of the matter is that March is much better at this than we are, and he's making fools out of us."

"So what are we supposed to do? Neither of our trackers has been able to pick up the trail again."

"I guess just them call in. They're just wasting their time anyway."

"Alright, if you say so," Holbrook had his nose almost up against the map along the Swan Peaks trying to read the small print, "But I hate to give up so soon. What about that other tracker from Lake County? The Indian guy? Have you heard from Sheriff Nichols?"

"No, not yet. I'll give him a call."

"Hey, look!" Undersheriff Holbrook pointed at the map again. "There's a Holbrook Creek. Right there!"

"That's great, Walt," Montgomery said sarcastically, "Maybe we should look there."

Back at his desk, Montgomery placed a call to Sheriff Nichols in Lake County.

"Charlie? Did you ever locate your man?"

"Monty, I was just about to call you. Ksunka finally showed up, and we got a chopper to fly him over the Missions and the Swans, and drop him near that packer's bridge on the South Fork at the foot of Big Salmon Lake."

"Why did you take him there? The tracks didn't lead in that direction."

"I know. But Ksunka said that the logical trail was more important than the apparent one. And I trust his judgment. He's been right about this sort of stuff too many times. But there's something else you need to know. Something I just now found out."

"What's that, Charlie?"

"Well, I'm not sure what to make of it, but you remember you asked me to watch March's mother?"

"Yeah? So?"

"Well, I decided to do a little background on her to see what I could turn up. Maybe learn something useful. You never know."

"So, what did you find?"

"March is her married name," Nichols paused for a moment, "Her maiden name is Ksunka. Our tracker, Dexter Ksunka, is her brother."

"So, what you're telling me is that the guy you sent out to find March is his uncle?"

"I'm afraid so. I didn't find out until after the chopper had already dropped him off; otherwise I wouldn't have sent him."

"Great, Charlie! That's just great! I wonder what he's really up to. He's mistaken if he thinks March needs his help. March doesn't need any help. He's making jackasses out of all of us!"

10

The freshly slaughtered rabbit lay in the snow, its steaming viscera savagely torn from its abdomen, the hare's splattered life-blood adorning the snowy whiteness in a crimson mist. Strewn around the carcass in stippled profusion were the distinctive outsized footprints of a large mountain lion. The asymmetrical four digits with a prominent leading toe distinguishing left from right, followed by the characteristic triple-lobed palm pad, were clearly discernible, and Eli could see where the big cat had scratched with its hind feet in the snow with extended claws, and urinated to establish ownership of the killing ground, so recently that the cold mountain air was suffused with the acrid, pungent odor of ammonia. Diminishing to a vanishing point in the direction of a thimbleberry thicket was a set of over-step prints, hind feet landing ahead of the front, as the lion had taken flight from Eli's approach. The distance between these tracks was over thirty inches, and the front feet were nearly four inches across, the hind feet only slightly less. This was indeed an exceptionally large cougar, well over two hundred pounds, and it was undoubtedly at this moment scrutinizing him from a position of concealment.

Primarily a predator of ungulates, a mountain lion does not normally recognize humans as prey, but having seen few deer or elk tracks in the area, coupled with the killing of an animal as diminutive as the rabbit, led Eli to the conclusion that this was a hungry cat, and starving animals are unpredictable. Unshouldering his .30-30 lever action rifle, he thumbed off the safety with an audible click, and began moving gradually away from the carnage, his eyes constantly circling to prevent his back from being exposed to any direction for more than a few seconds, aware that a cougar attacks from the rear, sinking its sharp, pointed teeth into the neck of its victim, working them between the vertebrae and into the spinal cord. Hopefully, the lion would return to its kill as soon as Eli had vacated the area, but even now it could be stalking him. Cougars are known to be experts at camouflage that will wait patiently for their quarry to close within striking range, and he had to resist the urge to move too quickly, because a running animal presents itself as prey.

The reverberation of a gunshot would be heard for miles, and Eli would only use his rifle as a last resort. As evidenced by its hunting conduct, a cougar is fundamentally a coward, exhibiting a tendency to shy away from an equally aggressive animal, and if Eli could catch sight of it, he would spread his arms wide to make himself look as large as possible, and would shout at it in a tone of voice one might use to bluff a belligerently barking dog.

Half an hour later, well away from the lion's territory, he was moving into a dense stand of old-growth tamaracks, but his preoccupation with the predator persisted, causing him to neglect taking any evasive action with his own tracks. Instead, an instinctual awareness - a subconscious cognizance - imposed a quickening of his pulse, and a tingling sensation in the fine hairs upon the back of his neck and along his forearms, warning him that he was being shadowed, and to advance with immense caution. Cougars are exclusively carnivorous, and the absence of large game in the area apparently had given the lion abnormal determination. An icy breeze came up quickly, stinging his face, and caused him to shiver spontaneously.

Extensively cut for their timber decades before, the majestic trees through which he was cautiously proceeding were some of the last of their kind, only surviving in the sanctuary of designated wilderness. Several were over sixty feet in height, and in excess of three feet at the bole. Limbless to a height of twenty feet or more, these colossal conifers were grandfathers of the forest. About eight feet up one of them Eli saw where the bark had been scoured by a bull elk in an effort to remove this spring's velvet coating from its antlers. While staring at this Eli was suddenly overcome with a primitive perception that he was being watched, and he gripped his rifle and turned a slow circle, all senses on full alert, scanning the forest trying to discern some telltale movement that might reveal the lion, when his uncle, Dexter, stepped out from behind the tree with the elk rub.

"I don't know what you're so jumpy about, Samose. That panther is way back there feeding on the rabbit," Dexter pointed back up the trail. As always, Eli was first struck by his uncle's wide-set pale blue eyes – evidence of his white blood – acetylene eyes that seemed to glare boldly and confidently out at the world, penetrating. His hair had once been coal black, and he wore it long, Indian style, but, even though it was silvering now, with his lean, medium build, his age was indeterminate. He could have been anywhere from fifty to seventy-five.

"Could you point that thing in another direction?"

Eli reset the safety on his rifle and slung it back onto his shoulder.

"How did you find me?"

"Are you kidding? With the trail you've been leaving, Ray Charles could have found you! And he's dead!"

Laughing vigorously at his own joke, Dexter reached out and pulled Eli into a gentle hug, a fatherly embrace. When they separated, Dexter rewarded Eli with one of his infrequent compliments.

"That was a pretty good trick you pulled on those dummies up in the pass. Where did you learn that one?"

"I read about it in a book about the San people of South Africa. They eat practically anything, and they can go for real long periods of time without water. They're supposed to be the best trackers in the world. But the government and the settlers wanted to get rid of them. Thought they were a nuisance, in the way of expansion and greed. So they put a bounty on them. Tried to exterminate them. But when the bounty hunters came after them thinking that killing a few pygmies would be an easy payday, they were in for a rude surprise. The little Bushmen would lay down a very clear trail into the dry lands for them to follow far enough to get them lost, and then they would take off in another direction leaving no trail at all, and the hunters would perish.

"Only I decided to take it one step further, and I left two sets of false tracks to follow, so they'd have to split up and follow both of them, and then I went down the creek to the river and hid my trail the whole way. What normal person is going to give up on one of two obvious trails and follow no trail at all?"

"I did."

"Yeah, but you're not normal. No one can do what you can do," Eli smiled wryly, "So, seriously, how did you find me? I thought I'd hidden my trail completely. What mistakes did I make?"

"Not many. After you crossed the river, you leaned against a tree and ate a granola bar. I saw where some moss was rubbed off the bark, which, of course, could have been done by any animal moving through, but it made me look at the ground, and I found some oat crumbs."

"Well, okay, but that's not much to go on."

"It was enough to let me know I was headed in the right direction," Dexter laughed softly, "The success of a rain dance is really just a matter of timing. I have to admit, you had me fooled. If it had not been for you getting spooked by that panther, I don't know if I would have found you."

Eli's smile dropped and he faced Dexter.

"So that's *how* you found me. But *why* did you find me?"

Dexter chuckled good-naturedly.

"Well, they hired me to find you."

"Who did? The cops?"

"Yeah, man. I'm getting paid for this." Dexter chuckled again.

"So now that you found me, what are you going to do about it?"

"I'm going to try to talk some sense into your head."

"Good luck!" Eli snorted. "I suppose you think I should give myself up, don't you?"

"I do."

Eli looked into his uncle's eyes.

"I didn't do what they're saying about me," he stated emphatically.

Dexter comfortably held his gaze.

"I know that."

"Do you want to know what happened?"

"If you want to tell me. But let's sit over here and get out of this wind to have our little powwow. It *has* got a bit of a bite!"

Sheltered from the chilly wind that whispered through the trees, they sat on a dry natural shelf under an outcropping of rock and Eli told his uncle everything that had occurred since he and Jolene had first met. He didn't omit anything, and confessed to Dexter that he had been advised that she was volatile and unstable, but had failed to heed that warning. With her as the only witness - the only person beside himself who knew the facts - he felt that his situation was hopeless. And there was a very compelling reason for her to continue to lie: it would be self-incriminating if she were to tell the truth.

"It's all I've thought about since I took off. I just don't believe that she would admit that she started this whole thing when she stabbed me. And she certainly isn't going to admit that she tried to kill me with that butcher knife. Why would she own up to that?

"And what about that cop, man? I swear to you, that guy was going to shoot me! I saw it in his eyes! When he went for his gun I had to stop him. I'm really sorry I hurt him so bad, but he wouldn't listen when I tried to explain! He just kept hitting me with that damned Maglite! What was I supposed to do? Huh?"

"Calm down. I would have done the same thing," Dexter put a hand on his arm, "But I think we can get you out of this mess."

"I don't know how!"

"I do! Number one, I've already hired us a guide."

Eli glanced at Dexter with a puzzled look.

"A guide?"

"Yeah, someone who knows all the trails and passes in the backcountry of the legal system."

Looking even more confused, Eli asked, "What the hell are you talking about?"

"A lawyer, man! I hired us a lawyer. And a good one, too! And what's more, she has some history with that cop. He's done this before, and she thinks she can nail him to the wall."

"And what if she can't? What then? I'll tell you what then. I'll go to jail for the next twenty years. Maybe more. That cop's hurt bad! He's going to have a lot of sympathy on his side. I saw a newspaper. You know what they're calling him? 'The Fallen Hero'. No one's gonna want to believe that he's a bad cop and got what he had coming. And he's not gonna tell the truth either. It's just not gonna happen!"

Dexter smiled and spread his hands indulgently.

"So…what? You're just going to spend the next twenty or so years hiding out? Being a fugitive?"

An assortment of emotions pursued each other across Eli's face before he responded.

"I could go to Canada easily enough," he answered tentatively, "I could walk there from here."

"And then what? What are you going to do in Canada? Go on living like a wild animal? You don't think The Mounties will find you and send you back? They're a lot better at tracking than these guys," Dexter shook his head, "That's a foolish idea."

"What am I supposed to do? It's a lose-lose situation!"

"No, it's not. It's a lose-maybe-win situation. Your best bet is to turn yourself in and fight them in court. At least you'd have a *chance* of winning. You can never see where a path leads until you reach the end of the trail. Maybe our lawyer can get the girl to tell the truth. You said you were warned that she was nuts. Maybe she has done this before. If she has we'll find out about it. And the cop has definitely done this before – same MO, with a Maglite - and we can prove it. But the most important thing is that if you give yourself up, turn yourself in before they can catch you – and they will catch you sooner or later -- then you will look more innocent. Or, to put it another way, if you keep running until they catch you, then you will be pre-judged as guilty."

Dexter's words echoed his own thoughts, and Eli's head and shoulders slumped at their validity as if an enormous burden had finally collapsed him. Encumbered beneath this yoke of despair he replied fearfully, "At least out here I can breathe. I don't want to be locked up. I'll go crazy!"

"You won't be in jail for long. Whatever they set bail at; we'll come up with it, me and your mother. We own three houses between the two of us. No problem!" Dexter assured him. "We'll get you out real quick."

The mention of his mother made Eli suddenly homesick for his little cabin, and a fire in the woodstove, and a big piece of his mother's crispy sweet fry-bread.

"What about this lawyer? Do you trust her?"

Dexter turned the full power and authority of his gaze on his nephew.

"I do! She's got the fire in her eyes."

"Excuse me!"

Lorna Johansson looked up from her desk by the window in the front office of the Sheriff's Department, which was located in the entrance hall on the ground floor of the Flathead County Justice Center. Bending over slightly to talk through the small round chrome speaker set in thick bullet-proof glass was a pale, fair-skinned woman with frizzy reddish blond hair that she recognized as one of the attorneys often seen entering or leaving the building on their way to or from the courtrooms on the third floor. Standing beside her was an older man that, despite his striking blue eyes, had a Native American look about him. He had long, graying hair and was dressed in a western-cut shirt with a native pattern decorating the yoke, and he wore a bone necklace with some kind of claw hanging from it. A little behind them was a handsome young man clad entirely in camo that looked vaguely familiar.

"How can I help you?"

"We'd like to see Sheriff Montgomery, please."

"Do you have an appointment?"

"No, but I'm sure that he'll want to see us right away." The attorney woman seemed peculiarly confident, and somewhat sanctimonious. Lorna experienced an unusual defensiveness in her presence.

"The Sheriff is very busy at the moment. Could someone else help you?"

"Probably, but I'm pretty sure that Sheriff Montgomery will want to handle this personally." The woman's smugness was starting to annoy Lorna, and, regardless of her years of experience dealing with the public through this very window, she found herself becoming a little irritated, and less inclined to be of much service.

"Well, as I said, the Sheriff is very busy. I can probably get you an appointment for tomorrow or certainly by the first of the week."

The woman leaned in closer to the speaker.

"I am absolutely positive that the Sheriff is going to be very upset if you send us away."

"And why is that?"

"Because my client here," and she paused to indicate the young man standing behind her, "happens to be Eli March. Now would you please tell the Sheriff that we are standing out in front of your office waiting for him so that Mr. March can turn himself in?"

Lorna took another look at the young man in camo, and her mouth formed a perfect "O" as the surprise of recognition swept over her.

"Oh! Omygod! Don't move! Please! I'll let him know right away!"

Lorna picked up her telephone and punched in four digits. A few moments later she spoke into the receiver.

"Uh…Sheriff, there's some people here to see you."

A pause.

"Yes sir, I told them that, but I think you'll want to come on out here."

Another pause.

"Well, sir, it's…………it's the man you've been looking for. Eli March. And his attorney."

No pause.

Lorna looked up and said, “He’ll be right out.”

A few moments later, Sheriff Montgomery walked through the office followed closely by Sergeant Broussard. There was a distinct click as Lorna pressed the button on her desk unlocking the glass and steel entry door, and they stepped out into the lobby.

“Ms. Lawson,” the Sheriff first acknowledged Jennifer.

“Sheriff,” Jennifer nodded then turned and gestured with her hand, “This is Eli March.”

Eli stepped forward and stuck out his right hand, and Sheriff Montgomery, somewhat awkwardly, shook it, thinking that this was not how he had envisioned March’s arrest.

“Mr. March, you have given us quite a run for our money.”

“Yessir, I’m sorry, sir.”

Montgomery’s first impression was ‘he seems like such a pleasant, polite young man’, and he found himself taking an immediate liking to Eli, although he was about to book him for the attempted murder of a young woman, in addition to assault on a police officer.

“I’ve instructed my client not to answer any questions,” Jennifer informed him, but for now you can get him checked in, and as soon as it’s convenient we’ll all sit down together and see what we can hash out.”

She makes this sound like he’s ‘checking in’ to some kind of hotel or spa or something, thought Montgomery, and the irony of it was not lost on him. In some ways the procedure was very similar.

“I think the hashing out is going to be done in court, Ms. Lawson. The charges against your client are very clear at this time. But, along with the county attorney, we would welcome an opportunity to question him on a number of things. With you present, of course.”

“Of course,” then she turned to March, “Eli, you’ll have to go with them now.”

"Sergeant Broussard," said the Sheriff, "would you take Mr. March to the back and check… uh, book him?"

"Yes, sir," Broussard answered, "Should I cuff him and take him around to the back door?"

"He's turning himself in, Rube. Voluntarily. I don't think cuffs are necessary, and the front door is right there."

"Yes, sir. Uh, Mr. March, would you come with me, please?"

Lorna pushed the button on her desk again, unlocking the door, and Sergeant Broussard escorted Eli through the office.

Montgomery next turned to Dexter, and, meeting his gaze, experienced a disconcerting sensation. He had never seen eyes quite like Dexter's; a blue so pale that they almost appeared devoid of color, and tiny pupils that seemed no more than pinpricks of light. He was reminded of a National Geographic cover he had once seen of the eyes of some wild animal, a wolf perhaps, or maybe a bird of prey.

"You must be Mr. Ksunka."

"Yessir," With a wide, infectious smile Dexter also stuck out his hand to shake, and the Sheriff shrugged and smiled, as well, at the absurdity of the situation and shook his hand. His grip was strong, but not hard, and warm.

"I suppose you'll be wanting to get paid for this?"

"Well, Sheriff," Dexter chuckled, "I guess the door of opportunity swings both ways. I did do what I was hired to do. I found him, and I persuaded him to come in. So, yes, I do expect to be paid."

His voice, not unlike many Native Americans, possessed a singsong quality, each phrase ending in an upward inflection almost as if he were asking a question rather than making a statement.

"Yes, but there *are* extenuating circumstances, don't you agree? Nonetheless, I'll talk to Sheriff Nichols and see that you receive your agreed-upon fee. But would you answer a question for me?"

"Of course."

"Did you have prior knowledge of where your nephew would be?"

"No, I didn't"

"Then how were you able to find him?"

"Well, Sheriff," he replied enigmatically, "if I tell you what I know, then you'll know what I know *plus* what you know, and then you'll know more than me."

11

Jolene Sutten had never lived in a real house for any length of time, but the double-wide was by far the nicest trailer she'd ever occupied, even if she had to share it with a loser like Sharla. It was light-years better than that single-wide dump in Coram where she grew up living with her mom and Arnie. But the best thing about it was that for the first time in her life she had a room all to herself.

She was lying in bed in her room right now. Her alarm had gone off a few minutes ago, and she was enjoying being lazy for a little while until she had to start getting ready for work. Sharla seemed to be arguing or pleading with someone on the telephone in the front room, but Jolene couldn't really hear what she was saying and didn't really care. Sharla was always whining about something.

It felt good to have a little privacy, a place where she could shut the door and have her own things. Actually, she *had* had her own room when she was little, but when Arnie moved in he made her sleep on the couch so that he could have her room for his "shop". And then there were a few years that she lived in foster homes and had to share rooms with other girls; girls that were either so silly, or so fucked-up that they were impossible to get along with, although she always got blamed when there was trouble, and then got sent to live with another bunch of fucked-up people.

But this was her personal space. She never allowed anyone in here, never brought boys here, and even Sharla knew that she was not permitted to enter.

This was why Sharla was knocking on her door now instead of barging in.

"Jolene? I know you're awake. I heard your alarm go off. I need to talk to you. Jolene? Do you hear me?"

"*Go away!* I'll be out as soon as I get dressed."

Through the cheap hollow-core door she could hear Sharla exhale noisily in frustration and then stomp back to the living room. She was such a fat pig that the whole trailer shook whenever she lumbered through it.

Jolene took her time getting ready for work. She had a hunch what this was about and she wanted to appear unconcerned. After she had finished dressing, she reached into the top drawer of her dresser, took something out and slipped it into the front pocket of her jeans. When she finally walked into the front room she could tell by Sharla's face that she had been fuming, and Sharla wasted no time on pleasantries.

"I just got off the phone with Mrs. Windover. She claims that after we cleaned her house last Tuesday that something valuable went missing. Do you know anything about that?"

Jolene put on her best innocent and annoyed expression.

"I have no idea what you're talking about. What did she lose?"

"She didn't *lose* anything. It's a gold necklace with a diamond pendant and, she didn't come right out and say it, but she more-or-less implied that she thinks one of us took it! And she threatened me with the possibility of not cleaning her house anymore! Maybe that doesn't mean much to you, Jolene; you have a job, but this is my livelihood. This is all I have, and I can't afford to lose any clients, especially ones like Mrs. Windover. That's one of my best-paying jobs!"

Sharla cleaned houses for several lazy rich old bitches over in Whitefish, and occasionally when she got too swamped she asked Jolene to help out on her days off. They always paid Sharla well, and often tipped her on top of that, but Sharla only paid Jolene eight dollars an hour, and never in cash, but instead deducted it from her rent. *Cheap cow!*

"Like I said, Sharla, I don't know anything about it. She probably just misplaced it. But if you think I'm lying, you have my permission to go ahead and search my room."

Jolene knew that Sharla wouldn't bother looking in her room, not because it was off-limits, but because if she offered it up so easily then Sharla would know there was nothing to be found.

"Please, Jolene! If you know anything about it, please just make it right, okay? No questions asked, okay?"

The fat slut is whining again. Man, that pisses me off!

"First you called me a liar, and now you're calling me a thief. If you think I stole some stupid bracelet…"

"Necklace," Sharla corrected.

"Whatever! If you think I'm a thief then why don't you and miss rich bitch call the cops? Huh? Turn me in if you think I did it!"

"Calm down, Jolene. Don't get so damned angry. I'm just scared that's all."

"Well, I'm not scared! I didn't do anything to be scared about!"

"What's that supposed to mean?'

"Take it however you want; I don't care!" Jolene made a show of checking the time on her cell phone.

"Now you've made me late for work! I hope you're happy!"

And she left, slamming the front door behind her before Sharla could reply.

⁂

She was at her locker in the employee's area when Eddie Parelli came bursting through the doors at the back of the Treasure State Grocery. A highly orchestrated, banal version of "Raindrops Are Falling On My Head" was playing insipidly on the store's intercom system.

"You're twenty minutes late!"

Eddie was assistant manager, one of her bosses, but he hadn't worked here nearly as long as Jolene. She had started as a bagger when she was only sixteen and still in foster care. Social Services had helped arrange it. That was over ten years ago. By the time she was nineteen she was running the video rental department. Except now, with Netflix and On Demand Cable, nobody rented DVD's much anymore, so the department had been shut down and she was moved to the checkout. Which was okay with her; that's where she wanted to be anyway. It was the best job in the store. You didn't have to work too hard; didn't have to lift too much heavy stuff. Just ring up and bag purchases, and count money mostly. And the pay was more than her raggedy-ass mother had ever made in her entire life.

But she did have to deal with customers constantly, and some days it was all she could do to keep her cool. Some of them really got to her, but she recognized that if she didn't keep it under wraps she would lose her job. This was all she knew. It was the only job she'd ever had. She'd be lost without it.

A few times in the past she had close calls when she lost control with other employees, but by then she had some leverage, and only received a reprimand.

Which was also why she wasn't worried about being late, at least as far as Eddie was concerned.

"Shove it, Eddie. It's only eighteen minutes."

"No," Eddie pointed at the clock on the wall over in the lunch area, "It's actually twenty-two minutes."

Jolene gave him a hard look.

"Do you want to make a big deal out of this, Eddie?"

"No, Jolene. I just want you to show up on time and do your job. This is the third time this month."

"So what, Eddie? What are you going to do about it? You gonna fire me?"

"No, Jolene, I..."

"Cause if that's what you're thinking, maybe it's time I gave your wife a call..."

"Now, Jolene, there's no call to go and..."

"Yeah, Eddie! Maybe your *wife* and *kids* would like to know about me giving you a blow job in the store room when we were both working night shift!"

"Look, Jolene," Eddie lifted both hands palm outward, if not a gesture of surrender, at least one of defense. "No one said anything about firing anybody. Like I said, I just want you to do your job."

"Well, then," pushing past him, "get out of my way and let me go do it."

"Hold on a minute!" Eddie grabbed her upper arm and she stopped and looked down at his hand until he warily released her. "You're not up front today."

"What are you talking about? That's my job! That's where I work!"

"Not today."

"Why not?"

"Cause I already put Doreen on your register. You were late."

"Well, I'll just go and relieve her."

"No, it's her drawer now."

Jolene knew what this meant. Each checker was held accountable for a shortage at their till, and it was not allowed for two checkers to work out of the same drawer. The store's accounting system was very tight and it was almost impossible to steal cash. This was just as well; it's stupid to shit in your own nest.

"So, where do I go?'

"You're out at the pumps today."

"Oh shit, Eddie! I hate working out there!"

"I'm sorry, Jolene. That's where I need you. Casey's on it right now, but she's got a sick kid at home, and I promised her I'd send you out there as soon as you showed up."

Casey was one of the few people that Jolene honestly liked. She was totally a live-and-let-live kind of person, and was never a threat to anybody. Innocent and guileless, Casey was only twenty years old and already had two kids by two different dead-beat dads. *What a chump! Doesn't she know what abortions are for?*

"Oh, fuck it, Eddie! Okay, just this once!"

On her way out to the gas pumps, Jolene took the necklace from her pocket and casually tossed it into the dumpster amidst the trash and the stink of rotting vegetables. *Who is going to go looking for it in there?*

Casey's broad smile signaled her relief when she saw Jolene approaching the little building that housed the cash register where she sat behind a thick glass window flanked by wire racks that held cans of oil and transmission fluid. To one side of the tiny structure stood a line-up of coin-operated pop and candy machines. This was the only cash register in the store that was shared by more than one person. There was no toilet out here and the attendant, by necessity, had to be relieved – literally – every couple of hours.

The store's intercom system was piped out here also, and as she approached the pumps a song came on that Jolene recognized but could not identify in such an overly produced format. *What is that stupid song?*

"Thank you so much, Jolene? I'm so glad you're here!"

Casey got out of the chair as Jolene entered the tiny space.

"Yeah, no problem. I guess I've gotta work somewhere today."

"Well, don't think I don't appreciate it, 'cause I do! By the way, have you seen the paper this morning?" Casey held out her own folded copy, but Jolene didn't take it.

I got it! Listening to that song again. *It's "Brown Sugar" by the Rolling Stones! How can they do that to such a song?*

"I don't read that stupid rag! What about it?"

"You might want to read this one. It says that the guy that assaulted you? That Eli March guy? Well, he turned himself in!"

Jolene snatched the paper out of her hand and opened it scanning the front page until she found the article. Then she caught herself, not wanting to seem too interested, and tossed the paper onto the chair.

"So what? Maybe now he'll go to jail where he belongs!"

"But aren't you scared?"

"Scared of what?"

"Well, what if he gets out on bail or something? Don't you think you ought to get one of those restraining orders at least? I remember my mom got one against my step-dad once. It wasn't such a big deal."

"I'm not afraid of Eli March! That guy's a wimp!"

"Jolene! How can you call him a wimp? He tried to kill you, and he crippled that poor cop? You should be more concerned!"

Just then an elderly man who had been filling his gas tank walked up to the window.

"Oops! You've got a customer, and I gotta get going! Thanks again, Jolene. I'll probably see you tomorrow."

Late in the afternoon, just before her shift ended, a man and a woman at pump number four, next to the cubicle where Jolene sat, got into a heated argument. Or, really, a one-sided heated argument, because the woman mostly cowered while the man, thirtyish and thin, with wiry arms and long ropey muscles decorated with a vivid display of tattoos, called her a stupid bitch and a worthless cunt at the top of his vocal range, volume and pitch. They were both out of the car, standing next to the pump, and several customers were staring pointedly at them. A girl in her early teens who sat in the back seat of the car kept sinking lower and lower as if she did not want to be seen and associated with these poorly behaved people.

Jolene felt that she knew exactly what was going through the girl's mind because she had endured many moments such as this with her mother and Arnie. She never knew her real father; in fact, she didn't even know who her real father was. Her mother seemed to be a bit confused on that point. There had been several men around in her early years, but she could only vaguely remember any of them. Arnie was the only one who had ever stayed for any length of time.

Her mother worked nights as a bartender, and she was often left alone in the trailer with Arnie, who didn't work at all. He claimed to have suffered some sort of injury on a job, and was collecting worker's comp, but he also told everyone that he had been wounded in Vietnam and was living on veteran's disability. It was years later that Jolene figured out that Arnie would have only been ten or so when the Vietnam War ended.

She was seven years old, or thereabouts, when he moved in and kicked her out of her room. He put a padlock on the door, and wouldn't let anyone else in, but he spent a lot of time there himself. "Buddies" of his often stopped by, and Arnie would go to his "shop" and come back with a paper bag for them, and they would give him money. Sometimes they seemed to be arguing about the money, or whatever was in the bag; but there was always someone arguing in the house and Jolene got numb to it pretty quickly. All of this was just something adults did, and if she ever got curious enough to ask about it, she was told harshly to mind her own business. At any rate, it was impossible not to see what was going on. After all, she lived in the front room. The couch was her bed, and her clothes and other belongings were kept in wicker baskets stacked against the wall.

For the first few years Arnie treated her with either contempt or indifference, sitting in his recliner late at night watching loud TV shows with lots of shoot-outs and explosions, or hanging out in the living room with his buddies drinking beer and smoking dope, while she tried to sleep on the old sagging couch.

But when she was about eleven, Arnie started being a little nicer to her, often bringing home little gifts of cheap costume jewelry, or treats of ice cream or chewing gum. And sometimes when her mother was working late at the bar, while he was watching yet another cop show, he would lift her onto his lap and stroke her hair, and tell her how pretty she was getting to be. He had an unwashed odor only slightly masked by the smell of cigarettes and dope and rancid sweat that seemed to cling to him like a gauze shroud, and his breath stunk of stale beer and rotten teeth, but, nonetheless, at times, in the privacy the bathroom, she would pause to study herself in the mirror, and wonder if the things he said to her were true. Was she really pretty? She wasn't sure.

But she did notice that her body was changing. Rounding out. And she had definitely gotten taller. Her chest wasn't so skinny anymore, and she could plainly see that her nipples had gotten darker and were sort of expanding. Is this what he meant when told her she is getting pretty? Maybe so.

And there was something else she was puzzling about. It was almost as though he wanted something from her. What was it? She wasn't sure, but, even at her age, her instincts were sharp enough to tell her that, whatever it was, she was the one who could exercise control over it.

She found the answer one such night as she was sitting on his lap, the TV blaring, and he unceremoniously took her hand and placed it between his legs forcing her to rub up and down vigorously. As she felt him stiffen and grow beneath her hand, she likewise felt for the first time her own sense of command stiffen and grow. And as she continued, she experienced a momentary weakening of the power that Arnie had always seemed to hold over her; it seemed that she was now in charge and he was helpless to the point that she was actually able to cause him to shudder, like he was in the grip of a sickening fever.

It wasn't long before she was doing this to him without any encouragement, not so much to please him as to experience, if only for a little while, that sensation of being in control. Sometimes she would do it two, or even three times in an evening while her mother was at work and they were alone together. Until one night when it all changed; when Arnie told her he wanted to try something different, and he took her back into the bedroom that he shared with her mother and laid her on the bed, and pulled her pajama bottoms off.

After that, Jolene began to discover just how dominant she could be. Arnie wanted to do it again and again whenever they could, but he was recognizably afraid that she would tell someone, and because of that she was able to get him to do almost anything she asked. Soon he became resentful of her, almost as if it were he that was being forced to do something against his will. And this made him angry. So angry that he even threatened to do her serious harm if she ever spoke about this with anyone.

But Jolene was not afraid. She had uncovered a sort of sixth sense that told her that Arnie was weak; that he was all talk and was really no danger to her at all. He didn't have it in him, and she knew it. In fact, she became aware that it was Arnie who was afraid of her.

All along, her mother didn't have a clue as to what was going on. She would come home late, drunk, and would sleep well into the day. Jolene had to get herself ready for school and it was up to her to get to the bus on time. If she didn't feel like going, she stayed home and got Arnie to call in saying she was sick. When her mom woke up she was usually hung-over, and all she did was sit around drinking coffee and smoking cigarettes until it was time for her to go to work again. On her days off she would sometimes stay in bed all day.

By the time she was thirteen, Jolene had discovered that she could exert this influence over other men besides Arnie; his customers who came to their trailer, and even a couple of the male teachers at her school. Some of Arnie's friends would give her little gifts, and sometimes even money in return for her favors. After a while, she had quite a stash of cash hidden in the bottom of one of her wicker baskets.

And then one day she came home from school and discovered that her money was gone. She was crippled with fury, but when she confronted Arnie he vehemently denied any knowledge of it whatsoever. She was certain he was lying but was unable to prove it, and was equally unable to control her anger. She told him that she would get even, and he pleaded with her swearing an oath that he knew nothing about it.

At school the next day she approached the duty officer and sheepishly told him that she thought her mother's boyfriend might be dealing drugs. That was all it took. Things happened very fast. Sheriff's deputies came to the trailer with a warrant, the meth lab was found along with quantities of other substances, and Arnie was arrested. What Jolene had not anticipated, though, was that her mother would be charged as well, and that she herself would be placed in foster care.

Arnie had been in trouble with the law before for selling drugs, and, coupled with the sex offender charges, he was sent to prison for a long time. Her mother received a much lighter sentence, and was paroled after only a couple of years. Jolene knew she was living in Billings, but, other than a couple of brief letters, they had never gotten in touch with one another. Arnie, on the other hand, was up for parole now, or may even be out already, but Jolene was unconcerned. She knew he lacked the balls to do anything in retaliation, unless he'd acquired a set in prison, but she doubted it. Most likely it was the other way around; he'd probably been turned into some inmate's bum babe.

"Excuse me!"

Jolene was shaken suddenly out of her reverie by the woman who had been cowering at pump number four while her – boyfriend? – verbally abused her. She paid for their gas and bought two packages of Marlboros, which Jolene passed to her through the stainless steel sliding drawer under the window.

"Thank-you," Jolene said automatically, "Have a great rest of your day."

Later, after her shift ended, after she had clocked out, Jolene sat in her car and read the newspaper article about Eli. He had indeed turned himself in, but there was no mention about whether or not he would be granted bail. It also said that he had hired a lawyer, a woman named Jennifer Lawson. Jolene wondered briefly whether or not she should hire a lawyer, but then thought – why should she? If she hired a lawyer it might make her look like she was hiding something. Nonetheless, she knew she was in for a lot of grilling and cross-examination, and she hoped that Eli had not been able to afford a very good lawyer. One that might be able to trip her up in court.

12

"Your Honor, the defendant was the subject of an intense manhunt that covered several counties, he owns no property in Flathead County which poses a flight risk, and in view of the nature and severity of the crimes of which he stands accused, the prosecution requests that bail not be allowed."

Eli felt oddly detached as County Attorney Fred Wilkinson standing behind the prosecution table, an assistant seated beside him, droned on sonorously. He was sitting with Jennifer at the defense table in the oak paneled courtroom where his immediate fate, and soon his long-term fate would be decided. Judge Mildred Walker sat in a swivel chair behind the bench staring at her computer screen, and appeared to not be paying attention to the proceedings. Maybe reading her email, thought Eli. The bailiff, clad in a black uniform with various shoulder patches, and wearing a duty belt outfitted with a handgun and other equipment, was asleep in one of the red leather upholstered chairs in the jury box, snoring lightly. Eli's uncle and his mother were directly behind him on one of the long oak benches on the other side of the partition. There was a smattering of people from the news media, but the courtroom was otherwise empty.

The entire proceeding was nothing like Eli had expected; not at all like what he had seen in movies and on TV. There were no dramatics; it was all very businesslike. Boring; tiresome even.

"…and in addition, Your Honor, both assaults were perpetrated with the use of deadly weapons. In light of all this we believe that it is crucial that bail be denied."

The County attorney completed his argument and waited patiently for what seemed like more than a few minutes until the judge unenthusiastically pulled her interest away from whatever she was doing and re-focused on the matter at hand. Even though Jennifer had mentioned that they were lucky to be in her courtroom because she had a history of being very fair and impartial, Judge Walker was not at all what Eli had anticipated. Seated up high behind the bench in her black robe wearing half-lens bifocals she appeared small and frail, and somewhat grandmotherly, possessing none of the power and presence of judges he had seen in the movies. When she spoke into her microphone her voice, coming through the little black speaker on the wall above her, was tinny and distorted.

"Ms. Lawson, do you wish to rebut this?"

"Yes, Your Honor," Jennifer stood and Eli started to rise with her but she placed a hand on his shoulder and kept it there. "My client turned himself in voluntarily because, as stated in his not-guilty plea, he is innocent of these charges and is eager to prove this in court. In addition, he needs to be allowed to return to his job and continue earning a living so that he can better afford the costs of his defense. He has no history of violence, in fact, no arrest record whatsoever, and has been gainfully employed here in Flathead County for over ten years. In consideration of all of this, he is obviously not a flight risk."

The judge contemplated this for a moment and then turned her attention to the county attorney. "Mr. Wilkinson?"

"I strongly disagree, Your Honor! The defendant has no real roots in the community. Nothing to keep him here. The flight risk should be obvious!"

"Noted. Bond will be set in the amount of one hundred thousand dollars."

"Your Honor…" Wilkinson started to protest but Judge Walker cut him off.

"Bond has been set, Mr. Wilkinson. Anything else, Ms. Lawson?"

"No, Your Honor."

Jennifer had already explained to Eli that she would file a motion for a change of venue at a later time, and that it would most likely be denied, but that it would possibly come into play if it became necessary to appeal a verdict.

"Okay. Trial will begin on…" She paused and consulted with her clerk who was seated to the left of the bench, "July twenty-fourth."

"Your Honor, the defense requests a continuance so that we can have time to locate some key witnesses." Jennifer had likewise explained to Eli that this request would easily be granted, and would accomplish two additional objectives besides the one stated. The first would be to give public interest a chance to die down, perhaps aiding them in selecting a more impartial jury, and the other would allow time for Scott Deaver to, hopefully, recover sufficiently enough so that he would walk into court rather than be wheeled in.

Judge Walker leaned over and spoke to her clerk again.

"Very well. The trial will begin on October seventeenth. I expect both parties to be ready to proceed with no further delays."

⁂

The next day Eli's uncle, true to his word, posted a property bond. Dexter, shouldering an army-green backpack, was waiting for him in the back parking lot of the Sheriff's Department on the main floor of the Flathead County Justice Center - the same place where Eli had turned himself in only a few days before. He stepped through the metal door wearing the same camo gear he had worn when he came in, the same outfit he had worn in the mountains for most of two weeks. The clothing had been returned to him when he was released. Having been sealed in a plastic bag for days, they were dirty and sour smelling, but, nevertheless, Eli was more than glad to trade the orange jumpsuit and jailhouse slippers for them.

His jail stay had not been altogether unpleasant. The food was okay, and plentiful, and, although the mattress he slept on was thin and lumpy, and his pillow was flat, Eli had slept in worse places in the last few days. Despite any discomfort, he slept almost the whole time he was in jail. He had not realized how exhausted he was. Being a fugitive is hard work.

Dexter set his backpack, which contained a laptop computer, on the asphalt pavement and they grasped each other's forearms affectionately.

"Thanks for bailing me out," Eli cast his eyes around the parking lot; he could not look his uncle in the eye, "Are you disappointed in me?"

"Never! We all get into jams, and we all need each other's help at times. Right now you need me more than ever."

"Right now," Eli replied, "I need you to take me home. It's been two weeks, and I'm filthy, and I'm sure my cabin's a mess. I just want to clean up, have a quiet weekend, and then go back to work."

"Your lawyer wants to see you first."

"Can't we do that in a few days?" Eli felt so uncomfortably filthy that he was almost whining. "I really want to go home."

"She said it won't take but a few minutes. She just wants to ask you a few more questions and explain a few things. It's not far. We can walk there from here."

"Okay," Eli capitulated, "Let's get it over with."

It was early May, an unseasonably warm, perhaps even a record-breaking day. When Eli had stepped out into the blazing sunshine, he was astounded at how quickly the weather had changed, feeling somewhat baffled as if he had been in lock-up for weeks rather than only a few days. As they walked the three blocks to Jennifer's office, he was amazed and, to some extent, amused at all of the campaign signs that had sprung up in front of nearly every house they passed advertising the resident's favorite political candidates, several of which promoted Sheriff Montgomery for re-election. Why were these signs so early? It was still only May, and the elections were not until November. Could the June primary be this hotly contested?

Montgomery did not seem like a policeman to Eli. If he had met him under different circumstances, Eli would have taken him for a teacher or a coach, or maybe even a guidance counselor. There was a gentleness about him that Eli did not typically associate with law enforcement, especially since his recent encounter with the deputy, Deaver

It was the same sort of gentleness and compassion that always appeared to radiate from his uncle. Walking along beside him, Eli reflected on how much he depended on Dexter. More than a father, he was a mentor, protector, a guardian angel, even; and, perhaps the most unusual man Eli had ever known or heard of. Most men could be identified by, or associated with, what they did for a living; a doctor, or a plumber, and so on. But not so with Dexter. He did many things, all of them well. In addition to serving as a tracker for the Lake County Sheriff's Department and other agencies, he also was under contract with the county to keep their computers repaired and running smoothly, a service he likewise performed for the tribal government. *Just a G-*

man he lightheartedly referred to himself, which was not entirely a joke, as he had often served in the tribal government. As a hunting and fishing guide, he had repeat clients that had been following him into the wilderness for decades. Well respected in all capacities, he was likewise considered by many to be an exceptionally wise man.

Up ahead, Eli saw a sign in front of one of the houses that, instead of promoting a political candidate, was a sandblasted redwood sign with powder blue lettering advertising the Lawson Law Firm. There was a similar, smaller sign to the left of the front door that displayed the number: 131. The door itself bore a thick beveled glass supported in a wood frame coated with yellowing, fractured white paint; and a tarnished brass knob with a thumb latch and deadbolt that exhibited innumerable scratches from countless years of inserting keys into the slot. Above the door was a transom with leaded glass panes set in an elongated diamond pattern. It was an old house that looked like it had been refurbished at some time, and it was fronted by a covered porch with a slightly sloping tongue and groove floor painted blue-gray, and bordered by a white, lap-sided half wall in place of a railing. Not at all what Eli had expected a law office to look like, it felt more like somebody's house; like they ought to knock before entering. But Dexter reached out, grasped the knob and depressed the latch with his thumb; and they walked right in.

The front desk was unoccupied. Heavy crown moulding surrounded the tall ceiling, and wide painted casings with large, detailed headers framed the doors and windows. Eli noticed that the glass in the windows had that watery sagging look that glass gets when it's very old. The flooring was narrow oak strips that had been refinished, but there remained dark lines between the strips, and the plaster walls had been patched and painted so many times that they were the authentic version of the hand-textured distressed look currently trendy in most new homes.

Being a carpenter himself, Eli couldn't help but marvel at the workmanship performed at least eighty-five years earlier – maybe as much as a hundred years - all hand-cut, fitted and nailed in a time before there were compound miter saws and pneumatic nail guns.

"What a nice old house!' he remarked.

"Thank you. I grew up in this house." Eli had not noticed Jennifer standing just inside the door to her office. Standing behind her was a remarkably fit looking older woman with very straight, shockingly white hair. "My mother still lives here. This is my mother, Ruth."

Eli stepped forward and shook hands with Ruth. Dexter had often counseled him to always shake hands with white people. It makes them more comfortable, he explained; less threatened.

"Let's go into the conference room," Jennifer gestured to the door across from her office.

The conference room had obviously once served as a formal dining room. Encircled by the same crown moulding as the front room, in the center of the ceiling hung a crystal chandelier, and the table, an oak antique, looked as if it had always been there. As they were getting seated, it felt more like they were sitting down to a meal. On the back wall was a floor to ceiling bookshelf stuffed with volumes of law books. Eli had never been in a law office before, but the collection looked impressive.

"Eli, I know you've been through quite an ordeal," Jennifer began, "and you must be very tired, so I promise to keep this meeting brief."

She paused momentarily to shuffle through some papers in front of her.

"I think," she went on, "that the real key to winning this case is Ms. Sutten. We will have to either get her to change her story and admit the truth, or, failing that, find a way to totally discredit her. Do you have any information about her that might be helpful?"

Eli answered hesitantly; a little embarrassed to admit that he knew practically nothing about someone with whom he had been sexually involved.

"Not really. I guess I never really got to know her that well. I mean, I was warned that she was kinda nuts, but never anything specific."

"Who warned you?"

"A friend of mine. Bennie. Bennie Greenwald. I work for his dad. Greenwald Construction."

Jennifer made some notes on a legal pad, then put her pen down and sat back in her chair lost in thought for a moment.

"I can see we're going to need to hire an investigator. I'm afraid that it could get expensive, and I promise I'll try to keep it within limits, but there are other reasons that it seems necessary. One of them is that I need to find a man named Luke Foster, a homeless Vietnam vet that I defended in a case seven years ago. In the course of being arrested he was beaten in exactly the same manner; about the kidneys with a large flashlight, by the same officer who beat you…Scott Deaver. If we can find him, and convince him to testify, it will go a long way in establishing a pattern of behavior for Mr. Deaver. The only problem is that he hit the rails right after his trial and I haven't heard of him since. He could be anywhere, living on the streets or in a hobo camp. Or he may not even be alive anymore. I guess what I'm trying to say is that the search could be hopeless."

"Don't worry about the cost," Dexter spoke up, "There will be none. I will do the investigating myself."

"I didn't realize that you were an investigator. Are you licensed?"

"No license needed. I'm not charging for my services."

"But what are your qualifications? Do you have any experience?"

"I have experience enough to know that you have to turn over a lot of stones to find the hiding place of a snake. I've been a professional tracker for nearly fifty years. I can follow *this* trail."

Jennifer was beginning to get the impression that Dexter did not only appear to be eccentric, but that he might be playing with a just a few cards short of a full deck. She tactfully changed the subject.

"Well, we don't have to decide this right now. Just a couple more questions, Eli, and we can end this meeting."

"Do you have a wireless router?" Dexter asked, apropos of nothing.

"Excuse me?" His sudden question had caught Jennifer off-guard, confusing her.

"Do you have wireless Internet?" Dexter repeated his question.

"Well," Jennifer hesitated, attempting to regain her composure, "as a matter of fact, we do."

"Would you mind giving me your password?"

"There is no password. You don't need one. We often have clients in the office that need to get online with their own devices."

"Thanks."

Pulling his laptop out of his backpack, Dexter put it on the table in front of him, opened it up, and began pecking intensely, almost frantically, on the keyboard. Jennifer watched him for a moment, his fingers festooned with several turquoise and silver rings flashing on the keys, and his long, graying hair hanging in his face; his concentration obsessive.

More than just a few cards, she revised her opinion.

"Eli," she continued, ignoring the intrusion, "I haven't checked Deaver's arrest record in seven years, but I will be doing so very soon. Maybe I can find something that will help us to establish a pattern that will support your testimony. We have to tread very lightly in this area, because there is no denying that he is seriously injured. Sentiment will be strongly on his side. But that's a stone we can't afford to leave unturned, snake or no snake."

She paused again examining her own thoughts.

"Okay, I guess that's about it, unless there's anything else that you can think of that might help. Anything about Ms. Sutten?"

"Only that she's got a really bad temper!" Eli certified emphatically, "That's what Bennie tried to warn me about; he said that she wasn't right in the head, but I guess I wasn't really listening, if you know what I mean."

"That might be helpful. If we can't get her to change her story, I may be able to elicit a reaction from her while she's on the stand that will put her in an unfavorable light with the jury, and help me to convince them that she's lying."

"Do you really think you can win this?" Eli asked both hopefully and skeptically.

"No, Eli," Jennifer shook her head, "I think *we* can win this. All of us. Together. As a team."

"Here he is!" Dexter interrupted.

"What are you talking about?" Jennifer was having trouble not showing her annoyance at his outburst. "Here who is?"

"Luke Foster. I found him."

"What do you mean you found him? How?"

"Easy! I just followed his trail."

"What trail? Mr. Ksunka, you're not making any sense!"

"You said he was a Vietnam vet. I cross-referenced his arrest record here in Flathead County with the VA's records – all those homeless vets go in to the VA from time to time – and I found him. He's not homeless anymore. He's in Spokane and he has a job as a janitor at the VA Hospital, and he also has an address. I have a phone number…"

"Wait a minute! Are you telling me that you just hacked into the county's court records, not to mention the United States Veteran's Association?"

Dexter shrugged and started to speak, but Jennifer put up a hand silencing him.

"Never mind! Don't answer that! I seriously don't want to know!"

Dexter merely smiled, tilted his head slightly, and replied cryptically, "They don't call me the hacker-tracker for nothing." He pulled out his cell phone. "Should we give him a call?"

"You really found him? That easily?"

"Nothing to it!"

Jennifer smiled mischievously. "You know," she mused, "You might just be useful after all!"

Dexter held up his phone. "So, what do you think? You wanna try to call him?"

"No. I don't think so. He might get spooked for some reason. I should probably go to Spokane and speak to him in person. Face to face."

"Would you like me to go with you?"

"No, thanks." Jennifer smiled inwardly, "I've already got someone who will go with me."

"I guess I can give these back now."

Dexter was reaching into the back seat of his king cab and handing Eli's guns and knife to him. He had held on to them for safekeeping, and also so that the authorities would not know that Eli had had them with him up in the mountains, and, therefore, would not be able to allege that he had been an armed fugitive.

They had just pulled into Eli's driveway and were parked behind his old blue pickup. Nothing seemed out of place, but Eli could only imagine the mess that must be inside.

As if he were a mind reader Dexter asked, "Do you want some help cleaning up?"

"No thanks," Eli replied, climbing out of the truck, "I think I better do this myself."

"Well, if you need anything...well, just let me know."

"I will. And Dex..." Eli searched for something to say, something that would let his uncle know what he was feeling, how grateful he was, but, for some reason, he had difficulty forming the words, and merely stood and watched as the fluid surface of the moment skittered past like a leaf in a stream; and all he could manage to say was, "Thanks."

But it was enough. All that really needed to be said passed between them on an indefinable current, and Dexter's usually intense gaze softened - and he put the truck in gear and backed out of the driveway.

Eli walked around his pickup carrying his guns, but was startled, brought up short by the snarl of an animal. Standing on the porch guarding the front door like he owned the place was a huge dog with the black and tan markings of a German shepherd, but his head was rounder and completely black, suggesting maybe some Labrador retriever. Eli had never seen him before. The dog was thin, his ribs easily defined along his flanks, and his coat was dull. Probably a young dog, thought Eli, but also underfed. At any rate, the animal seemed intent on preventing Eli from entering his own house.

"GO HOME!" He shouted and the dog flinched but continued to stand his ground. "GO ON! GET! GET OUT OF HERE! GO HOME." Eli waved his rifle in the air and false charged and the dog finally cowered and slunk off the porch and toward the edge of the forest.

I hope he goes back to wherever he came from. I hope that's the last I see of him.

The front door was locked and across it was a yellow crime scene tape. Eli seldom locked his house, but he kept a key under a flat rock at the end of the porch for just that eventuality. After removing the 'Do Not Enter" tape, he retrieved the key and opened the door.

He thought he had been prepared for what he was going to find. *Not*! It appeared as though everything he owned had been strewn randomly about the cabin. Most of the furniture had been overturned and his mattress was leaning on its side against the wall next to the bed, sheets and blanket draped haphazardly over it. Once muddy boot prints were now dried and crumbling on the rough plank floor.

His block of knives was gone – there was a receipt from the Sheriff's Department on the kitchen counter – but he was surprised to find his guns and fishing gear untouched in the closet in his bedroom; and his cell phone still plugged into the charger, along with the key to his pickup, was on his dresser. It looked as if someone might have been on his computer; the keyboard drawer was pulled out and the mouse was displaced, but, other than that, it appeared to be undisturbed.

Feeling overwhelmed, he picked up his cell phone and went back outside and sat down in one of the bent-willow chairs on his front porch. In spite of having no reception out here, he could, nevertheless, check the time, and he was surprised to see that it was only two o'clock in the afternoon. After all that had already happened today, it seemed as if it should be much later. He sat there quietly for a half hour watching through the trees as the occasional automobile passed by flickering in the fragmented sunlight out on Foothill Road. In the cloudless sky a red-tailed hawk flew lazy circles like a figure skater. Finally heaving a sigh he pushed himself up off the bench, went back inside, and got to work. It was nearly midnight by the time he got the cabin back in order, and he was so exhausted that he fell onto his bed still dressed in his camo gear and was instantly asleep.

13

Eli woke to a surreal world as if he were yet dreaming. It had been so long since he had slept in his own bed that he initially felt apprehensive and displaced in what should have been familiar surroundings. But nothing seemed the same. His reality had been shattered, and for a few minutes, he simply lay there, re-acclimating, before climbing out of bed, and, finally, taking the time to wash the accumulated stink off of himself. In the shower he soaped and rinsed numerous times and then stood under the needle spray until the hot water began to fade. After drying off he dressed in clean blue jeans, a polo shirt, and tennis shoes, and then started to make breakfast.

Breakfast was quickly aborted when he remembered that the refrigerator door had been left open during the search of his cabin and all of the food was spoiled. Luckily, the freezer door had remained closed and what little venison and elk meat he had left from last season was okay. It was nearly twenty miles to Kalispell, so to save gas Eli tried to limit his trips, but this morning he decided to go out to breakfast and then go to the grocery. He grabbed the key to his pickup and his cell phone, and as he approached the front door he heard a scraping sound. When he stepped out onto the porch, he saw the tail and hind legs of the dog, disappearing around the corner of the house. *Damn! I wish he'd go home.*

It was Friday morning, another bright sunny, warm spring day in May. In Montana these days are rare and must not go unappreciated, but as he drove to town he morosely reflected on all the misfortune that had attached itself to him like a leech, and in a mere two weeks had sucked his life away. How could he have gotten himself into such a quagmire? And was there truly any way out of it, or was he doomed to spend years in prison? He swore to himself that if he did get out of this mess he would never again let his dick do his thinking for him. In fact, he didn't care if he ever got laid again. He knew guys like that - guys that had one bad thing happen with a woman and decided right then that they were through. That was it. No more for them. Many of them were big, macho guys who acted tough on the outside, but inside they were so devastated by the pain, that the fear of that ever happening again drove them to remain single and alone for the rest of their lives. Totally gave up on 'The Montana Dream'. Maybe that would be him.

Cislo's Restaurant on LaSalle was Eli's favorite breakfast spot - good café food in an inviting, unpretentious atmosphere; a place where the staff treated him with familiarity and made him feel at ease. But today was different.

On his way in he picked up a free copy of The Flathead Beacon from the newsstand, his favorite local newspaper – the only truly local newspaper – walked past the cash register desk at the front of the cafe, and seated himself in a booth by the front window. Laminated to the tabletop were advertisements for local businesses: a body shop, an insurance agency, a hair salon, and so on.

Eli pulled his cell phone out of his pocket and saw that he had several texts and voicemails that had come through now that he was in a place with good reception. The first one he listened to was from Bennie:

"Dude! I heard that you like beat up a cop and took off up into the mountains! What's up with that? Call me."

He scrolled through several others without listening, knowing that they would be just as inane and irrelevant, until he saw that there was one from his mother:

"Eli, if you get this message call me right away. I talked to Dexter. We can help. I can't say any more in case someone else is listening to this. Call me. I love you."

On impulse he deleted all of the voicemails and all of the texts except for the one from his uncle:

Stay where you are if you can. Either way I'll find you.

A cute young girl about eighteen years old brought iced water and a pot of coffee and asked if he would like some.

"Sure." Eli slid his cup over and she poured steaming coffee into it, and left a menu. Taking a small sip of the hot coffee, Eli began to read his newspaper.

When he opened the paper to page five, he got a sudden shock. There, once again, was his own picture looking out at him from what could only have been his booking photo; an image that made him look sullen and angry, accurately reflecting his mood at the time it was taken. The accompanying article related the details of his recent court appearance, along with a recap of what had happened at his cabin two weeks ago – the official press release version, far from the truth – and the subsequent manhunt. Eli scanned the story quickly; it was mostly a rehashing of what he had read last week. The only thing he learned from the article that he didn't already know was that Deputy Scott Deaver had been released from the hospital and was at home recuperating, still in a wheelchair. He felt terrible that he had crippled the man, but he held tight to his conviction that he had had no choice. Deaver had been beating him savagely and might have permanently injured *him*, or even killed him.

Then, with an uneasy feeling, he glanced up from his paper and took a look around the restaurant. It seemed as if at least half of the other customers having breakfast at Cislo's this morning were reading the Beacon, and although he might have been mistaken, he could swear that many of them were stealing glances at *him*, and whispering at their tables. *Don't look now, but I think that's the guy who beat up that cop!*

"You ready to order, Hon?" Kim, his favorite waitress, was standing over him with the coffee pot in her hand. She had been working here for as long as he could remember, and had known him since he was a child coming in for meals with his mother. He liked her a lot, but he was suddenly feeling a wave of paranoia and wanted nothing more than to get out of there.

"No thanks, Kim. I think I'll just pay for my coffee and go."

Kim looked around the café and then with an audible sigh looked back at Eli.

"Ya know, Hon, you shouldn't let it bother you. This is a small town and people need something to gossip about. But I'll tell you something for what it's worth: that deputy? Deaver? He comes in here a lot and *nobody* wants to wait on him. Always throwin' his weight around and actin' like such a big man, if you know what I mean. I'm sorry he's hurt so bad, but that's just the plain truth. And that girl? Jolene? I used to know her mother before she went to prison, and, take it from me, they were nothin' but trash."

Even though Eli had said he was leaving, she, nonetheless, poured him a fresh cup of coffee before continuing. "But I've known you since you were just a little guy. And I don't even know what your side of the story is, but I can tell you one thing: I'd believe your story before I'd be taken in by either of theirs. And I'm sure there's plenty of people who feel the way I do, or, at least, are willing to listen to what you have to say."

"Thanks, Kim. I really appreciate you saying so."

"Now, what are you gonna have?"

She was right, of course, that he should ignore their stares and gossip, but it was more than that. If he was going to get through this, he was going to have to grow a thicker skin, and he might as well start right now.

"Okay, I guess I'll have the ham and two eggs. Over-easy."

"What kind of toast? White? Wheat? Rye? Sourdough?"

⁂

After breakfast Eli drove to Smith's grocery on Idaho Street. He usually did his shopping at Smith's, but he was also careful to steer clear of the Treasure State Grocery where Jolene worked. This was not only because he wanted to avoid her, but also because his attorney had informed him that Jolene had sworn out a restraining order against him and he was not allowed within fifteen hundred feet of her - not that he would want to be anywhere near her. As he pushed his cart around the store, he detected that look of recognition on the faces of several other shoppers, but this time he just tried to ignore them. As he was paying for his groceries he noticed Stephanie Montgomery at one of the other registers. She looked up, waved, and launched a small smile from across the checkout stands. He waved back tentatively, picked up his change and left the store.

"Hey, Eli! Wait up!" Stephanie caught up with him in the parking lot pushing her cart up alongside his.

"Oh, hi, Steph."

"So," she asked with a sympathetic look on her face, "How're you holding up?"

"Okay, I guess. I seem to be pretty famous all of a sudden, at least locally. I'm not sure I like it all that much, but I guess there's not much I can do about it."

"Just so you know, Eli: I don't believe a word of what they're saying about you." She brushed a strand of auburn hair from her lightly freckled face, and her green eyes assessed him earnestly. "I've known you all my life. We went all the way through school together. And I know you wouldn't do anything like that. You're just not that kind of person."

This was the second time in less than two hours that he had been offered essentially the same words of encouragement.

"Well, thanks, Steph, for saying so," They had reached his pickup and he started loading his groceries into the passenger seat, "but I'm afraid you're in the minority. It seems like most people have already convicted me in their minds."

"Don't be so fatalistic." Stephanie touched his arm reassuringly, "I think there are more people around here with open minds than you give them credit for."

"Maybe so," he shook his head, "but it doesn't stop them from staring at me everywhere I go. One woman in the grocery just now pulled her kids in close and headed in the other direction when she saw me. It was as if she thought I was going to attack them or something – right there in the cereal aisle!"

"Oh, Eli, they're just people. You have to cut them a little slack. I'm sure all that will change once the truth comes out."

"You don't even know what the truth is, Stephanie."

"I'd like to know. If you want to tell me, that is."

"Not that much to tell."

"Well, I'd like to hear it anyway, if you've got time." Stephanie beamed an encouraging smile, "Today's my day off, so I'm in no hurry to get anywhere. You want to get a cup of coffee?"

"You sure you want to be seen with me?"

"C'mon, Eli," she punched him playfully in the shoulder, "You look like you could use a friend."

Eli locked his truck and waited while Stephanie loaded her groceries into her car, a blue Subaru, and then they walked the two blocks to Julie's Center Street Café. Eli had only seen her occasionally in the ten years since high school, so on the way there Stephanie filled him in on what had been going on in her life. He learned that while she was pursuing a degree in forestry at The University of Montana she had gotten married, but that it had been a big mistake and only lasted a year. She seemed embarrassed and reluctant to talk about it and did not elaborate. After finishing college, she had gotten a job with the US Forest Service – thanks in no small part to a recommendation from her grandfather who had spent his entire career there – but her job had evolved to where she spent most of her time at her desk and not enough time in the field to suit her. She had been there for six years but was not certain that she would stay. She had even considered going back to school for something else, but she wasn't sure what.

"Just listen to me going on about job dissatisfaction when there're so many people out of work and losing their homes and everything! I should be ashamed of myself! I'm lucky to have a job at all."

"Anyone who has a steady job nowadays is lucky," Eli agreed.

The owner of the café, a soft-spoken Chinese woman, greeted them warmly and seated them at a table next to a window. Stephanie ordered a latte and Eli asked for a black coffee. After their drinks were served, Stephanie gently began to pry the story loose from Eli, who was reluctant only because he didn't know how to begin. He liked and respected Stephanie, and he found it very difficult, and somewhat shaming, to tell her about his sordid involvement with Jolene. But there was no other way to tell it. Stephanie listened patiently with a neutral expression, and once he had gotten past that part he found the rest of it easier to share.

There is a frequently repeated saying in Montana that if you don't like the weather just wait a few minutes and it will change. As Eli was finishing his narration he glanced out the window and noticed that what had started out as a sunny day was now clouding over, dark and heavy, and threatening to rain.

Stephanie reached across the table and touched his wrist lightly to bring his attention back to their conversation.

"You know, Eli, I probably shouldn't be telling you this, and I don't know what you can do with the information, but, for what it's worth, I overheard my uncle talking to my grandmother, and he was telling her that he had had trouble with that Deaver guy in the past for getting too rough with people. He said that he had reprimanded him several times."

Eli turned to look at her, his confusion apparent.

"Your uncle?"

"Yes. He said that a judge had even warned him to rein Deaver in, and that he had considered firing him."

Eli looked even more perplexed.

"I guess I don't understand what your uncle has to do with it," he said apologetically.

"Are you trying to tell me that you didn't know that the Sheriff is my uncle?"

"Sheriff Montgomery is your uncle?" Eli was truly surprised. "I guess I never made that connection. I mean, I know your grandmother - she was my math teacher – but I didn't know you were related to the Sheriff."

"I'm sorry. I guess I should have said something, but I assumed you knew. There's a lot of Montgomery's around here, and most of us are related. We're what you might call a Kalispell dynasty, dating back over a hundred years to when my great-great grandfather came here to work at the old hospital, only it was new then. It's not even a hospital anymore – I think it's an apartment building, or something."

"So, the Sheriff is really your uncle?" Somehow the information just wouldn't sink in.

"Well, yeah," Stephanie looked at him closely, "That's not a problem is it? I mean, for us to be friends. Cause I really like you, and I was kind of hoping to see you again."

"No, it's no problem at all," Eli was surprised to find that he was smiling, maybe for the first time in weeks, "As a matter of fact, I kinda like the Sheriff, as weird as that might sound – after spending a couple of weeks in his jail. He seems like a pretty nice guy."

Just then the parking lot outside was lit up with a flash of lightning, followed closely by a loud clap of thunder. The lights in the restaurant dimmed but came right back on.

"Uh oh! You know what, Steph? Why don't you wait here and I'll run back to Smith's and get my truck and drive you to your car. No sense in both of us getting wet."

Eli stood up.

"It hasn't started raining yet." Stephanie protested, "Maybe we can make it."

"It's okay," Eli smiled at her, "Finish your latte. I'll be right back."

He started to leave some money on the table but she would not allow it, insisting that she had invited him. He left in a hurry, but had only gone a block when the sky opened up – a real gully washer. By the time he got to his pickup he was thoroughly drenched.

Stephanie was waiting by the front door of the café when he pulled up and she ran to his truck and jumped in. When they got to her car in the grocery parking lot she turned to him and touched his shoulder gently.

"You know, Eli, I believe this is all going to work out okay. I don't know how, but I just know it will." She handed him a piece of paper. "That's my cell number. Please call me. And thanks for being so gallant."

She kissed him quickly on the cheek, and then ran through the downpour to her car.

When Eli pulled up in his driveway he could see the dog through the curtain of rain, slinking off the porch. Still soaked from earlier, he didn't care how wet he got as he carried his groceries into the cabin. As soon as he was inside he changed into dry clothes, but he still felt chilled; so, even though it was May, he kindled a fire in the woodstove. As he was putting things away he thought about how both Kim, the waitress, and Stephanie had counseled him to ignore other people's reactions and get on with his life, and he resolved to do just that.

He began by calling his friend, Bennie, to see how the job was progressing and let him know that he would be back to work on Monday. Eli had been with the outfit for ten years and, like everyone else, had periodically missed work for various reasons – illness, hunting season, vacations, and so on – and he had little doubt that he could resume his place on the crew.

Bennie answered his cell phone on the third ring. There was a lot of loud conversation in the background smothered in pounding music.

"Dude! What up? When'd ya get out?" Bennie shouted into the phone to elevate his voice above the racket.

"Dex bailed me out yesterday."

"So what the hell happened, man? The papers say you beat a cop with his own flashlight and, like, crippled him for life. What's up with that? That doesn't sound like the Eli I know! I've known you most of my life and I don't remember you ever being in a fight at all! What the fuck happened?"

"Well, actually, Bennie, my lawyer told me not to discuss the case with anyone, especially over the phone, so I guess that means you, too."

"That's okay. I bet I can guess. That Jolene went wacko on you, didn't she? I told you so! Me and Ray, we both warned you that she was nuts!"

Eli could hear Ray's affirmation above the clamor.

"Like I said, Bennie, I can't talk about it."

"Yeah, whatever!"

There was a sudden clash that sounded like someone had dropped a tray or something, and Bennie asked him to hold on a minute.

When he came back on Eli asked, "So, what's going on with work?"

"Oh, we tried to work today, but the rain blew us out, so me and Ray are at the bar having a few brews. Wanna join us?"

"Not really! No, what I meant was what's going on with work in general? I haven't been there in a few weeks, but I was planning to show up on Monday."

There was a detectable hesitation in Bennie's voice and his volume dropped a few decibels.

"Oh! Well I guess you should talk to my dad first, ya know?"

"What do you mean 'I should talk to your dad'? I haven't been fired have I?"

"Well, no, I don't think so. But you should check in with my dad before you show up for work. See what he says. Ya know what I mean?"

Bennie was being purposefully evasive, and Eli began to get a sinking feeling in the pit of his stomach.

"No, I don't know what you mean, Bennie, but I can guess."

"Now don't go jumping to conclusions. Just call my dad."

Eli felt himself getting angry and he fought to control it, taking a deep breath and letting it out slowly.

"No, Bennie. I'm not going to call your dad. I'll be at work Monday, and if he has something to say to me he can say it to my face."

Eli hung up without waiting for a reply. *Damn! This can't be happening!*

The rain continued unabated for the remainder of the day, and Eli paced the cabin restlessly. For a while he tried to lose himself in one of his favorite adventure epic novels by Wilbur Smith, but he was unable to focus and found himself reading the same sentence over several times before he could comprehend it. Finally he gave up and decided to prepare an early supper.

After putting some water on to boil for pasta, he opened a jar of spaghetti sauce, poured it in a pan, and set it on top of the woodstove to heat. When his meal was ready, he sat at the table and discovered that he had no appetite, and so, annoyed with himself, he took the plate of food and set it outside the front door, knowing that this would do little to discourage the dog from continuing to hang around.

In compensation for his poor judgment, he sat at his computer and posted an ad in "Lost+Found" on Craigslist. Ms. Lawson, his attorney, had cautioned him against using Internet media at all – warned him that you never know what might be used against you in court – but Eli didn't see any harm in putting it on Craigslist.

He did not sleep well that night, and when he slept at all he was besieged by vague and troubling dreams that he woke from in a clammy, apprehensive sweat, and then lay restless in the small hours listening to the roar of the rain assaulting his metal roof. At last exhaustion won over and he fell into a deep slumber, not opening his eyes again until almost ten o'clock in the morning, once again feeling confused and disoriented. The cabin felt cold and damp, gloomy, and Eli kindled another fire in the woodstove in hopeful anticipation that its warmth might help diminish his despondency.

The rain had moderated to a mild drizzle that dripped lightly from the corrugated eaves, and when Eli stepped out the front door, he saw that his dinner plate had been scooted a few feet across the wooden decking and had been licked clean, and the dog was lying down but eyeing him warily from the far end of the porch.

"*Go home*!" Eli yelled, but the dog just ignored him and laid his head down on his front paws. Exasperated, Eli picked up the plate and went back into the house to check his email and see if, by chance, anyone had responded to his lost & found notice, but there was nothing.

As the morning wore on, he was feeling more and more anxious, and with the constant rain and accompanying inactivity he was beginning to develop a severe case of cabin fever. Eli had always been comfortable with being alone, but on this particular morning he was feeling a need for human interaction, and on impulse he dug the scrap of paper out of the pocket of the shirt he had been wearing the previous day and called the number written on it in a neat, precise hand.

She answered on the second ring.

"Hello, this is Stephanie!" Her voice sounded bright and cheerful.

"Uh, hi, Steph, it's Eli."

"Eli! I was hoping you would call! What's up?"

"Oh, just going kind of stir crazy. I was wondering if maybe you wanted to hang out or something."

"Sure! I'd love to!" she beamed, "My family usually has a big Sunday afternoon get-together, but I skipped church this morning, so I don't think anyone would notice if I wasn't there. I could drive out to your place if you'd like. I'd love to see where you live."

"Yeah, that sounds great! Do you play cribbage?"

"I love to play cribbage, but I have to warn you, I'm not very good at it."

"Yeah, I bet! That's what all card hustlers say."

He gave her directions to his house and she promised to be there in about an hour. Almost instantly, Eli felt cheered up, and, although he had spent most of the previous day cleaning, he, nonetheless, went about straightening things up, and preparing a lunch for them to share.

Given that it was such a cold, wet day he thought a stew might make a good meal, but since the police had confiscated his knives, he had to use his folding hunting knife to cut up the ingredients. As he worked over the stove he thought about Stephanie. In school she had always been one of those people who laughed loudly at things that other people only found mildly amusing - or not funny at all. But it was something Eli had always liked about her. It seemed to him that she had always possessed a more acute sense of humor than most people, and that made her fun to be with.

The consistent rain on the roof was sufficiently loud that Eli did not hear Stephanie's car pull up an hour and fifteen minutes later, and was unaware that she had arrived until he heard the sound of her voice outside his front door.

"Oh, what a gooooood boooooy! Aren't you a friendly baby? Yeah! Doesn't *that* feel *good*?"

He opened the door and looked out. Stephanie, clothed in a bright scarlet poncho, was on her knees scratching the dog's back and shoulders, and the dog was squirming and wagging its tail and enthusiastically trying to lick her face. While tussling with the eager canine some of her ginger-colored hair had come loose and was hanging in her face, and glowing through the tangled tresses her emerald eyes smiled up at him.

"What a great dog! What's his name?"

"Uh...I don't know."

She shot him a quizzical look that almost made him duck as if she had thrown a rock at him.

"He just showed up a couple of days ago," Eli continued, "and he's been hanging around and won't go home. Wherever that is."

"He looks starved! Have you fed him?"

"Uh, sorta. I gave him some spaghetti."

“Spaghetti! What kind of food is that for a dog? Don’t you have anything better than spaghetti?”

The dog seemed to be giving him a look of agreement.

“Well…there’s some venison stew on the stove.”

The dog licked his chops. *Really*!

“Perfect!”

“But that’s our lunch,” Eli protested weakly.

“Oh, I bet there’s more than enough to go around. Just look at him! His ribs are sticking out, and he’s all wet and shivering. C’mon, let’s get him inside and dry him off and least.” She turned and talked to the dog again, “C’mon, baby! C’mon sweetie! Let’s go warm you up and find you something to eat. You *good boy*!”

“Fifteen for two, fifteen for four, fifteen for six, fifteen for eight, and a double-run makes sixteen,” as Stephanie moved her peg she declared, “and that’s a game!”

Eli threw his cards down on the table in mock exasperation.

“What was all this talk about not being very good at cribbage?” He protested. Stephanie laughed and Eli laughed with her. Six games, and she had won four of them! “I just knew you were a hustler!”

“You should try playing with my grandfather or my uncle. They both make me look terrible.”

“I doubt it!”

The fire crackling softly in the woodstove cast a warm glow about the cabin, and the dog was curled up on the floor nearby sleeping off more than half of the pot of stew.

“I love your house,” Stephanie declared looking around, “It’s so cozy! How long have you lived here?”

"All my life. I grew up in this house. It belongs to my mom, but she lives in Polson now." Eli was suddenly reminded that he had not spoken to his mother since he got out of jail, and made a mental note to call her tonight. "I've never lived anywhere else."

"What about your father?"

Eli looked away.

"I don't know much about him." Raindrops trickling down the windowpane were superimposed on his face like a cinematic projection, "He left when I was just a baby."

"Oh, I'm sorry, Eli," She reached out and laid her hand on his wrist, "I shouldn't have asked."

"No, it's okay. That was a long time ago. I hardly ever think about it anymore. And it's not like I didn't have a father. My uncle, Dex, was always there. And he was more than a dad to me. He was everything: father, teacher, friend…and still is…and much more."

The statement itself caused him to pause for a long moment.

"But you know what really seems strange to me? Somewhere out there…" He waved his hand to encompass perhaps the whole world, "…I probably have all sorts of blood relatives. Half-brothers? Half-sisters? Aunts, uncles, maybe even grandparents? And I know absolutely nothing about any of them. Doesn't that seem weird to you?"

Stephanie didn't really know how to answer that question, or if it even required a response. From her perspective it did seem odd. Almost all of her relatives lived right here in Flathead County, or, at any rate, in Montana - and there were *a lot* of them – and she knew every one of them, along with almost everything about them: their ages, where they went to school, what kind of work they did, the names and ages of all of their children…everything.

She gave his forearm a gentle squeeze. "I'm sorry, Eli. I didn't mean to touch on a painful subject. It was my intention to try to cheer you up."

"And you have! Almost anything is a painful subject nowadays." Eli began stacking and shuffling the deck of cards absentmindedly, "I guess I have to admit I started the day out feeling kinda down, but I just now realized that for the last few hours I've hardly thought about any of it. So…I guess what I'm trying to say is…thank-you."

Stephanie smiled wryly, "Don't mention it."

"No, seriously! It's been the best afternoon I've had in quite a while."

"It *has* been a nice way to spend a rainy Sunday afternoon," she agreed as she stood up glancing at her watch, "but it's going on five o'clock already, and I need to go home and get ready for the work-week."

Work-week! Eli suddenly stopped shuffling and wondered what would happen when he showed up for work tomorrow. Stephanie detected an expression of trepidation skittering across his face.

"Is something wrong?" she asked.

"No, not really! Something you said made me think about something else. Totally random." Eli waved his hand dismissing the subject.

The dog got up from his nap by the fire, and walked over to Stephanie. She ruffled the fur on the back of his neck.

"You really ought to give him a name. Any ideas?"

"No. I haven't thought about it at all. I'm still hoping someone will claim him."

"Well, if not, you should keep him. He's a nice dog!"

Eli set the deck of cards on the table, stood up, and walked to where she stood next to the front door.

"That might not be possible, Steph." Looking down at her, "I might not be here."

"Oh, Eli, don't even talk like that! Think positive!" Searching his eyes.

"I'm tying real hard, Steph. I fully realize that I've got to keep a good attitude; otherwise, I'll go nuts!"

"Eli, listen to me. You're innocent! I *know* you're innocent. And I believe the truth will come out. And I believe this nightmare will end. And I believe…in you."

As if to offer emphasis to her statement, she cupped his face in her hands, and kissed him. And through the conduit of her kind words and affection, she endeavored to replenish the dry well in his spirit where hope and faith reside. To be the answer to a question that he had not asked.

Monday morning the rain had finally let up. Eli, determined to show up ready to work, packed a lunch and threw some tools and his nail bags into the back of his truck, and hoped for the best. As he was opening the cab door, the dog jumped past him up onto the truck seat and assumed the shotgun position, looking back at him as if to say 'Let's get going'. At first he was surprised and a little annoyed, but then he just shrugged and climbed in. A lot of guys brought their dogs to work with them. No big deal!

The house that Greenwald Construction was building was located just outside of Lakeside, about twenty miles south of Kalispell on the west side of Flathead Lake. It was a medium-large custom – about four thousand square feet – for a rich couple from California, predominantly to be used as a vacation home. The jobsite was partway up Blacktail Mountain and offered spectacular views to the east across the expanse of the lake to the Mission Mountain range which rose up from the opposite shore, a book-match reflection of the snow-capped peaks upon the placid water. On days like this, when the sky was nearly clear and the lake was still, it looked more like an artist's rendering than reality, so strikingly colorful as to be the envy of even the greatest of painters' palettes.

It was a few minutes before eight and the sun was already high as Eli pulled in next to Bennie's pickup. A lot of progress had been made since he was last here. All of the walls had been framed and the roof was dried in. There were several large piles of siding materials under tarps, and a stack of windows and exterior doors was in the garage waiting to be installed. It suddenly struck him just how long he'd been gone.

"Hey, dude! Where'd you get the dog?" Bennie was stepping down from his truck with a coffee mug in his hand.

"He just showed up. I'm trying to find out who he belongs to," Eli responded as he and the dog hopped out.

"The way he's acting kinda looks like he belongs to you!"

The dog sat on the ground next to Eli and gazed up at him as if in agreement.

Eli looked at Bennie and in a somber tone said, "I can't be taking on a dog right now."

Before Bennie could reply, his father, Gary Greenwald, stepped out of his job trailer. Gary, a hands-on builder, already had his nail bags on, and his hammer slapped his thigh as he approached them.

"Bennie, I want you to run down to the feed store and get as many bales of straw as you can carry in your truck. All that rain this weekend has turned this place into one big mud puddle. If we spread the straw around the house it might help some."

Ray was just pulling up in his white van.

"And take Ray with you," Gary added.

Ray got out of his van and walked over to them.

"Hey, Eli. Nice dog! What's his name?"

"I don't know. He's a stray."

"C'mon, Ray," Bennie interjected, "We gotta go get some straw."

"Straw?"

"Yeah." Bennie tilted his head toward his truck, "For the mud."

“Oh…right! For the mud!”

Ray nodded his understanding, and they got into Bennie’s pickup and crunched gravel as they drove out and turned right down the county road.

Gary watched them leave and then seemed hesitant to speak, so Eli asked him. “Where do you want me to get started?”

“Well, Eli…fact of the matter is…I can’t keep you on.”

Eli didn’t say anything. He only stared at Gary in a way that said ‘I was expecting this’.

“It’s like this, Eli. I’ve known you most of your life, and I know that whatever happened, it wasn’t the way the papers are reporting it. To tell you the truth, if it was up to me, I’d let Ray, or even my own son, Bennie, go before you. You’re by far the best worker I’ve got. But, unfortunately, it’s not up to me. I have to do what my customers tell me to do. They’re not locals, they don’t really know you, and they only know what they read in the papers. I tried to explain it to them, but they wouldn’t budge. They kept insisting that there must be some truth to it or you wouldn’t be charged with it, and that unless you’re proved innocent – which I believe you will be – they don’t want you on the job.”

Eli remained silent. He looked down at the dog who appeared to be staring back at him sympathetically.

“Times are bad, Eli. We’ve been in a recession for four years, and I’m lucky to have this job. These are not bad people to work for. They just don’t understand. But if this was four or five years ago, when things were still booming, I’d just tell them to fuck off and we’d go start something else. But there isn’t anything else, and if we walk off this job then we’re all out of work.”

Gary walked over to his pickup and got an envelope off his dashboard and handed it to Eli.

“That’s two weeks wages. I wish it was more, but it’s all I could manage. I’ve been asking around to try to find you another job, but, so far, I haven’t come up with anything. But I'll keep looking, and you know I'll give you a great reference."

Eli stared at the envelope in his hand for a moment, and then looked at Gary. He wanted to say that he understood, but he couldn't find the words. Instead he turned and opened the door to his truck, told the dog to load up, and climbed in behind him.

Gary walked up to his open window.

"I'm really sorry, Eli."

"Yeah. Me, too."

⁂

Eli's face was flushed and his scalp was burning as he drove down the mountain road. That same poetic view of Flathead Lake was laid out in front of him, but he was in no mood to appreciate it. The reality had been worse than the expectation, not to mention that his fragility was barely subcutaneous. Although he thought of himself as a strong person, he realized that he was afraid, phobic even, and he consciously made an effort to reclaim himself.

He needed to work. Although he had considerable savings, it wasn't just about the money. He had to stay busy, keep his mind occupied, if he was going to have any hope of getting through this with his sanity.

There was one more thing he could try. When he got to the town of Lakeside, he pulled into a convenience store parking lot, turned off his engine, and called the number for Flathead Fly Shop and Guide Service from his cell phone's contact list. It had been the principle shop that he had guided out of for more than ten years; in fact, it was where he had started his guiding career. He had been there longer than anybody, and there was a time when that seniority had meant something. But a couple of years ago the shop had been bought by a Texan named Charley Gant, and his wife Maureen, and they had not continued to place any value on employment longevity. Nonetheless, it *was* still early in the season, and Charley *had* always treated him fairly. So, think positive!

"Flathead Fly Shop. How may I direct your call?"

"Hi, Maureen, it's Eli."

"Eli! Are you okay? I've been so worried about you!" They were the right words but something was missing, sincerity maybe. It didn't really matter, though. Maureen was responsible for the retail operation, but it was Charley who ran the guide service.

Trying not to allow this presumption to be detectable in his voice, Eli answered, "Yeah, I'm okay. Just fine. Is….uh…. Charley around?"

"Sure, I'll get him for you," sounding a bit relieved. Apparently, her interest in his troubles was only fleeting.

"Hello, Eli." As soon as he heard Charley's voice, Eli's hopes sank like a lead balloon. There was no 'How are you? Are you okay? We've been so worried about you!' however insincere. There was no 'What can I do for you?' or anything like that. There was only 'Hello, Eli' with no inflection whatsoever.

Suspecting that his chances were slim he, nonetheless, plowed ahead.

"Hi, Charley, just wondering if there was any guide trips for me?"

"Sorry, Eli. They're all booked."

Just as he suspected, but he continued through the motions regardless.

"How about day trips? Anything?"

"Nope, sorry, nothing."

"Well, if anything comes in will you let me know?"

"Sure. You bet."

On the way home Eli stopped at Murdoch's Ranch Supply and bought an eighty-pound bag of dog chow and a large food and water dish. He loaded his purchases into the back and, when he climbed in the cab, he looked at the dog and said, "I must be crazy! Don't go getting any ideas. This is still only temporary. It's just that you showed up at the wrong time, and I have no idea what's going to happen to me."

The dog cocked his head a little, looking slightly confused. Other than shouting while trying to chase him off, Eli had never spoken to him.

"Maybe my whole life has turned to shit, but I can't let you starve, can I? But you have to understand that I can't keep you. If I can't find your owner, then I'm going to have to find someone to take care of you. But I will promise you one thing. No matter what, I won't just drop you off at the shelter. Okay?"

The amber eyes seemed compassionate, and for a moment Eli thought, my God, he actually understands me.

"Okay, that's that. But I guess I've got to call you something, so how about if I just call you...Random?"

14

Bob Mayfield was losing his hair. He stood at the bathroom sink and stared at his reflection in the mirror trying to figure out how he should comb what little was left on top. Maybe he should just give up on hair all together and shave his whole head. That was kind of trendy nowadays anyway.

Thinking back to his college days when he and Jennifer had first started going together, he remembered having a full head of wavy dark brown hair that hung nearly to his shoulders. What was left now was mostly gray and only thick on the sides and in back. Hell, he was barely forty-three years old. It didn't seem fair. Back then long hair had been the style among the teens and young adults, now it was tattoos and piercings. The apparent difference was that there was no permanence in hair. It went away on its own. What were some of those tattoos going to look like when those kids got older and *their* bodies started to sag? The mental image made him shudder.

Finally he gave up, put a ball cap on his head, and glanced at his watch. It was an old-fashioned analog wristwatch with a braided leather band that Jennifer had given him for Christmas years ago at a time when they were first living together. It was almost eight o'clock. He needed to get moving if he was going to pick her up on time.

She had called him last week and asked him to drive her to Spokane and help her locate a witness for an upcoming trial, and, of course, he eagerly agreed to be of service. It had always been that way. He would happily do anything she asked.

He loved Jennifer completely and unconditionally, and understood her better than anyone, with the possible exception of her mother. Some of his close friends, and most of his family, thought he was crazy to put up with her. And maybe they were right; at least the part about him being crazy. Crazy for her, that is. From the first moment he had ever seen her – stepping out of the main entrance to her dorm at the U of M – there could never have been anyone else for him. It was a love-at-first-sight sort of thing. And in all the time since, she had never shown any interest in anyone else. Or maybe she scared them all away. She was, and still is, pretty intense.

They say you can't really love anyone until you love yourself. And maybe that was part of the problem, because, at times, Jen was so damned hard on herself. But equally problematic was that during those times she was also hard on those around her, and Bob was the easiest target, because, not only was he the closest, but years of following this pattern had given her confidence that Bob would never leave completely.

And she was right. Undaunted, Bob hung in there, year after year. His patience with her emotional issues was infinite, and even during the numerous times that it seemed better if they lived separately, Bob, nonetheless, thought of her as *the* major element of his life. Nothing meant more to him. Just a fool for the girl.

Angela had spent last night with her friend Nikki, and was going to stay there again tonight in case Bob and Jennifer were late getting back, or decided to stay over in Spokane. It was only about a four-and-a-half-hour drive each way, and could easily be done in a day, but Bob secretly hoped that their business would take longer than expected. A night in a motel with Jennifer might be just what was needed to get them back together, especially if her interview was successful and she was in a good mood, something he had not seen for months.

He left the house full of anxious, but, at the same time, pleasurable anticipation.

"So, even if we do find Luke Foster, and he agrees to testify, I'm still going to need someone to corroborate his testimony. With what little I've learned already I'm pretty sure that I'll be able to discredit the Sutten girl, but if I'm unable to get her to tell the truth, then I'll have no other choice than to go after Sheriff Montgomery. He may be the key to this whole thing, anyway. He's got to know what kind of deputy Deaver is! I just have to find a way to make him admit it..." Jennifer threw her head back in exasperation, "God! This is just like déjà vu all over again!"

There was road construction on I-90 heading up Lookout Pass into the narrow Idaho panhandle, and Bob was forced to keep his speed down to 50mph as he maneuvered Jennifer's SUV between interminable rows of orange-striped barrels that divided one side of the Interstate into two opposing lanes. From the moment they left Kalispell she had spoken of nothing other than the case she was working on. It was starting to seem more than a little protracted, bordering on monotony.

But it also reminded him of seven years ago when she had last confronted Scott Deaver, one of those times when living with her had become too challenging and he had been forced to stay somewhere else for a while; to back off and give her a lot of space. It was a difficult thing to do, but he had learned the hard way that it was the only way their relationship could survive.

"Do you really think that Sheriff Montgomery would do that? Testify against one of his own people? Especially one who's been seriously injured? In an election year?"

Devil's advocate had always been Bob's role.

"I don't know," Jennifer turned, scrutinizing him in profile, "But I'll tell you what I do know. Mike Montgomery is a real decent man, and he knows right from wrong. And I've got a hunch that if I put it to him directly, he'll at least *try* to do the right thing."

They had gotten past the road construction and were driving through the alpine forest at the top of the pass now. Noticing that she had a strong signal on her cell phone, Jennifer took a second to send a text to Angela containing a list of motherly instructions, wondering if her daughter would read it or simply delete it.

Bob took advantage of the pause in their conversation to try to change the subject surreptitiously, to get her to talk about something else for a while, and he knew all too well that Jennifer was as passionate about politics as she was about most things. "Speaking of elections, do you think Romney will get the Republican nomination?"

"Probably. He's the best that they've got. But I don't think he can win."

Jennifer had unmatched multi-tasking skills. It always amazed him that she could do two or more things at once, like carrying on a conversation while texting with her thumbs. How do you divide your concentration like that?

"He'll for sure win in Montana."

"Yeah, but Montana only has one electoral vote," she replied all the while drumming away at the screen of her phone, "so our votes for president don't count for much. Obama will win all the densely populated areas, and it'll most likely be decided by one or two states, but, in spite of his marginal performance, I think he'll be re-elected. He's still very popular. And Michelle is the best First Lady ever!"

"I kinda like her, too."

"I *love* her! And it pleases me that she is recognized as the primary representative of American womanhood. And she has an absolutely lovely family! Those adorable girls! And it also makes me happy to think that they are an example of the ideal of the American family – as perceived by the rest of the world."

Bob frowned.

"You'd better be careful about how you express those opinions around the Flathead. There're a lot of very loud, very rabid Republicans there."

"Do you know what the difference is between a Democrat and a Republican?"

Bob shook his head, not to say that he didn't know the answer, but only to say that he knew something cynical was forthcoming.

"A Democrat thinks the glass is half full," Jennifer paused for effect, "And a Republican thinks the glass belongs to him!"

Bob smiled obligatorily.

"Besides," she went on, "I think there are a lot more liberals in The Flathead than you are aware of. They are just, by their very nature…quieter."

Bob was a lot more moderate, and a lot less vocal politically than Jennifer, but even though they weren't exactly on the same page, they were usually in the same book. The difference was that Bob considered all politicians to be parasites, indiscriminately sucking the life out of the American taxpayer; living like royalty, traveling to exotic places to deposit illicit funds into offshore accounts all the while partying it up at taxpayer expense. Maybe Michelle Obama was a good representative of American womanhood, but most members of Congress were atrocious, embarrassing representatives of American leadership.

"Well, but, who wouldn't love Michelle?" Jennifer continued, "She's so real! Remember when Sarah Palin was running for Vice-President and she went out and spent some four-hundred-thousand dollars on clothes out of campaign funds, and about the same time Michelle revealed that she bought all of her stylish outfits off the rack at J.Crew? And how about her organic garden on The White House lawn? I mean doesn't that prove that she's one of us? And she's beautiful, and smart, and accomplished! What's not to love?"

Jennifer ceased speaking abruptly and looked at Bob accusingly. "Wait a minute! How did we get on this subject, anyway? You got me sidetracked on purpose, didn't you?"

"Did not!"

"Did, too!"

"Did not!!!!!"

"Did, too," and they both started laughing at the old, dumb litany – something they used to do way back when.

"Anyway," Jennifer refocused, "it all seems too easy. Finding Luke Foster like this. I sure hope this isn't a wild goose chase."

"Why would it be? The information is valid isn't it?"

"Oh, it's valid enough! It's just the way it was obtained that's got me wondering. And that Dexter Ksunka! What a…different…sort of person! I'm not sure what to think of him. He's somewhere between a clairvoyant criminal and a cosmic charlatan!" This started them both laughing again, although Bob had yet to meet Dexter. "I guess this trip will prove which."

"Well, we'll soon find out."

They drove through the forested mountains in silence for a while past Wallace then Kellogg, Idaho, each left to their own private thoughts. Bob remembered when he was in high school there was a brothel in Wallace that several of his classmates had bragged that they'd been to, but all of their descriptions varied so widely that nobody believed any of their stories. Continuing on over Fourth of July pass, they were soon driving along the cobalt waters of Lake Coeur d'Alene to the south of the highway.

"I really don't know what to expect." Jennifer broke the silence, "The last time I saw Luke Foster he was about to hop a train to who knows where? He was thin and ragged, and other than the times he'd spent in lockup, I don't think he'd been sober in many, many years. Now, according to the information we have, he has a job and a house…he even has a telephone."

She stared out at the lake dotted with several precipitously jagged islands. A mysterious looking body of dark indigo water, one that could easily be the dwelling place of sea monsters, she mused.

"I wonder what happened. What changed him?"

As they were pulling into Spokane on the Interstate, Jennifer entered the address into the GPS on her smart phone and the computerized feminine voice directed them through the city streets to a small house in an older, tree-shaded neighborhood not far from the Spokane River. She was especially grateful for the technology. Finding the address without it would have been a daunting task. With nearly a half-million inhabitants, Spokane was the largest city between Minneapolis and Seattle, and both she and Bob, having spent most of their lives in a much more rural setting, were intimidated by large cities and metropolitan traffic.

Bob pulled to the curb and shut off the engine. Emerging from the SUV into the warm sunshine, they each took a moment to stretch the kinks out from their journey. It was a bungalow style house, with a metal roof, and there was an older model Volvo parked in the driveway. The yard was neat and tidy and Jennifer admired the abundant flower gardens that framed the building and lined the walkways. With a hint of jealousy she noted that the peonies were in full bloom, whereas just this morning as she was leaving, she had glanced at her own peonies, and all of the buds were still tight little balls that looked like red and white tootsie pops, and had ants dancing all over them. And these hostas were totally unfurled while hers at home were only little points just now breaking ground!

A trio of hummingbirds was dive-bombing a red feeder that hung from a bracket attached to one of the posts supporting a covered porch, and nearby some wind chimes pinged softly. The overall effect of the place was enchanting.

“Are we in the right place?” she wondered aloud, not really expecting a response, but Bob answered anyway.

“This is the address you gave me.”

“Well, then...here goes,” Jennifer said as she mounted the two steps onto the porch and marched up to the front door, determinedly. Bob remained in the sunlight below on the concrete walkway.

A formidable-looking black woman with graying hair and coffee-colored skin answered her knock. She wore a lavender housedress and was glaring at them through the screen door.

“I hope you two people haven’t come knockin’ on my door tryin’ to sell me on your angle of religion ‘cause I can tell you right now that I already got my own angle...and it’s a good one...and I don’t need any help with it at all. Now, you look like two nice young people, so please tell me that’s not why you’re here.”

“That’s *not* why we’re here!” Jennifer quickly replied.

“Good! That’s what I wanted to hear.” She pushed the screen door open and Jennifer was forced back a few paces as the woman stepped out onto the porch, right hand extended. “Hi, honey, my name’s Mayvelle Jefferson and the answer before you ask the question, believe it or not, is yes, I am a direct descendant of Thomas Jefferson, third president of the United States of America. Now that we got that out of the way, what can I do for you?"

As she shook hands, Jennifer found herself instinctively liking this good-naturedly over-bearing woman very much, even though she was now totally convinced that she had come to the wrong place.

"Ms. Jefferson, I'm sorry if we've bothered you, but I think we have the wrong address."

"Well, who're you lookin' for honey?"

"Well, I was looking for a man named Luke Foster."

Mayvelle nodded her affirmation.

"Well then you got the right house, only Luke isn't here right now. He went for a run about an hour ago, but he'll be back any minute. Usually, he only runs a few miles every day."

We might have the right address, but we most certainly have the wrong Luke Foster!

"Ms. Jefferson, I don't think we're talking about the same man. The Luke Foster I'm looking for is a white man about sixty-four years old."

"Yeah, that's my Luke and here he comes now."

She pointed up the block and Jennifer turned to see a lean, athletic-looking man with short gray hair dressed in blue sweats; a man who was not at all identifiable to her, running energetically up the sidewalk towards them. When he reached the driveway, he stopped suddenly and shading his eyes looked past Bob up onto the porch, an astonished expression shaping his face.

"Ms. Lawson? Can that really be you?" He called out in a strong voice as he bounded up the stairs and impulsively wrapped her in a sweaty bear hug.

Jennifer looked up at this man - this man who when last seen had seemed shorter than her – a man cowered by the circumstances of his life; and now he appeared so vibrant and virile! And, for one of the few times in her life, she was struck speechless.

Mayvelle, sensing that this was going to take some explaining, took control of the situation, "C'mon' now everybody. Let's go in the house and sit down. I'll fix us a pitcher of tea and some lunch and we can talk this thing out."

They sat sipping iced-tea at one end of a large trestle table that would seat at least twelve, positioned comfortably in the kitchen/dining area, which must have been the largest room in the house. Several framed photos of smiling black children were displayed on one wall. Jennifer, assuming them to be grandchildren, asked, "Is this your family?"

"Those are my babies, my daughters' children. The youngest one there, Shania, can't make a 'V' sound so she calls me May-Belle. But that's okay. She'll get it right soon enough. They all call Luke 'Grampa' or sometimes 'Grampa Luke'."

Mayvelle kept up a verbal patter, dominating most of the talk until she could finish putting a variety of food on the table: platters of cold-cuts with an assortment of cheeses along with some flavorsome dark bread and spicy hot mustard to make sandwiches with. Alongside these she placed bowls of potato salad, Cole slaw, and cold baked beans along with jars of pickles and green olives with pimentos. All this was accomplished in a matter of minutes, and Mayvelle took a seat at the head of the table.

"Let's all say grace," Mayvelle suggested.

And so they all held hands across the table and bowed their heads.

"Dear, Lord," Mayvelle intoned, "Thank you for this food we are about to eat, and bless these people you have led to our door. In Jesus Christ's name. Amen! Now let's eat!"

Everyone dug in and started putting food on their plates. Finally with an opportunity to ask questions, Jennifer was nevertheless feeling too overwhelmed to know where to start.

"So, Luke," she began tentatively, "I must admit, I'm completely…flabbergasted. Would you mind summarizing for me how you got from where I last saw you to here?"

Luke stopped spreading mustard purposely onto his bread and smiled across the table at her.

"Well, Ms. Lawson…"

"Jennifer…please."

"Okay. Jennifer. I guess I'd have to say it was mostly because of you."

"Because of me?" Jennifer was incredulous.

Luke put his knife on his plate.

"Ms. Law…Jennifer. I was drunk and homeless for most of thirty years. In all that time, you were one of only a few people who ever treated me as if I had any worth. Apparently, you have no idea what that meant to me."

No one was eating. They were all listening to Luke. Watching him.

"I never hopped that train in Whitefish. I stood in that rail yard and I thought about my life. I had hit bottom and stayed there for far too long. And I decided right then and there that you were right: my life *was* worth something. Or, at least it was going to be worth something. And that was the turning point. So I hitched a ride to Kalispell, and I used some of that money you gave me to buy a bus ticket to Spokane. Then I went to the VA hospital, because I had been there a time or two before and they had treated me decent. And right there at the front desk I broke down and started to cry, and I told them that I needed some help, otherwise I was going to die."

Luke used his napkin to wipe a tear from his eye, and Mayvelle reached for his hand.

"That was seven years ago," Luke continued once he had regained his composure, "and I've been sober every day since. One day at a time, as we say in AA. And then I met Mayvelle! Right there at the hospital. That's where she works. She's in charge of the sanitation crew."

"That still means I'm just a maid." Mayvelle interjected.

"Oh, she's a lot more than a maid. She's in charge of keeping that hospital clean, and she's the supervisor for over forty employees. That's no small job," he gazed at her with respect and admiration for a moment before continuing.

"They call it post-traumatic stress syndrome. I'm sure you've heard of it, and I've had it bad! I'm not going to describe the horrors of Vietnam to you, because I choose not to go there anymore. Besides, I'm sure you've heard enough about it already. While I was still there, I got a letter telling me that my young wife had left me for someone else. And she didn't even have the guts to write the letter herself. It was from her mother.

"I got home just in time to tell my own mother goodbye. She died of cancer a month later. My dad had died years before, and I was twenty-two years old and all alone in the world. I tried to find a job, but it seemed like while I was gone the world had passed me by, and all the decent jobs had been filled. I had no training for anything other than fighting, and everywhere I went there were always people who treated me as a pariah, something to be loathed and feared merely because of where I had been. And it made me feel so much like an outcast that that's what I became.

"I started having these overpowering anxiety attacks that would go on for days, sometimes even weeks, and then I would sink into depressions so low that I didn't think I would ever find a way out. So I turned to alcohol for self-medication.

"At first it helped. Just a little drink or two now and then to take the edge off, and I was able to function a little – get a job on a construction crew for a few weeks – or work as a bouncer at a bar. But alcohol is very seductive - an evil temptress that will lure you with her charms and not show you her true colors until you're already too far gone. By the time I was in my late twenties I was on the skids – homeless, and completely out of touch with society. And that's pretty much where I was thirty years later when you found me in that jail in Kalispell. And if it hadn't been for you, I would probably still be in some jail or hobo camp somewhere."

Jennifer actually blushed. She was suddenly aware of an enormous value of her job that she had never conceived of before.

"I think you give me too much credit," she said modestly.

"Not at all," he protested, "In all that time you were the only person who ever showed me any respect, or even real concern. The only person who ever treated me like a human being. It was all I really needed. It made me want to be worthy…worthy of myself. And it made me want to see that look of respect again, in the faces of other people."

Jennifer, humbled and somewhat uncomfortable, waved her hand dismissively.

"Oh my! That was quite an eloquent dissertation!" She stole a look at Bob who appeared vaguely amused.

"It should be!" Mayvelle interjected, "He's given that speech about fifty times at AA meetings!"

"So how did you two meet? How did this relationship come about?"

Luke and Mayvelle smiled at each other fondly.

"Do you want to tell it?" he asked.

"No, you go ahead. You're doin' pretty good. I'll jump in if you need any help."

"Well," he gave her hand a gentle squeeze, "after I had been at the hospital for a few weeks, a psychologist that was helping me – an Asian lady named Dr. Chen – suggested that some part-time employment might help me feel more useful. So she talked to Mayvelle and arranged for me to work a few days a week for her. The first time I met her, I felt something I had never felt before. Something I can't really describe, except to say that she gave me a feeling that I had not felt since I was a child. A sense of belonging - of home. I guess it was the way that from the very start she made me feel like I was a part of things. Not just someone she was trying to help out as a favor to someone else.

"It was menial work, but Mayvelle has a convincing way of impressing on you how important it is. And she always does it in a cheerful way, with kindness, consideration, and humor. She's a born leader."

Mayvelle was positively preening at his praise.

"Oh, hush now, and get on with it. You're embarrassing me."

"Mayvelle, you deserve all the praise I could possibly give you, and then some."

"Now, stop that, you hear! Go on with your story."

"Okay. Anyway, over the next few months of counseling, AA, physical therapy, and working a regular schedule for Mayvelle, I had progressed enough to rent a small place of my own. My confidence was improving, and I knew in my soul I was going to make it. And it was about that time that I started thinking of Mayvelle in a different way. I wanted to get to know her better, to be more than just an employee, to be…friends. And so I started asking her if she would like to do something together. Go to a movie or a concert or something.

"At first she just laughed me off. Joked her way out of it. But I was persistent. Finally, she put her foot down and told me that she would not go out with me until I had been sober for a full year."

"I'd done run off two drunks in my life already," Mayvelle interjected, "I sure as hell didn't need another one."

"So, you made it a year," Jennifer prompted.

"Yes, I did. But then she came up with something else. She said she could not go out with me because I did not share her beliefs. I had not been baptized. I was not a Christian.

"I argued that I was not talking about marriage or anything like it. I just wanted to be friends. To do stuff together. But she was insistent. She said if I really wanted to do something together, then we could go to church together. And so I figured sure, why not?"

He paused, musing about something. "Isn't that funny? I was thinking to myself – what harm could it do? Without even considering how much good it could do. But from almost the very first time I set foot in that church, I felt something I had never really known in my life. Everyone was so welcoming and friendly, I felt like I was part of a community.

"A few months later, I did it! And it wasn't just a little sprinkling of water. The whole congregation went down to the river, and I was completely submersed. And, to my complete surprise, on that day something changed in my life. I really did feel all of my transgressions washing away. I was a new person, and from here on out, I could be whoever I wanted to be. Just like that old cliché – today is the first day of the rest of your life. And I was able to forgive myself and all others. I now understood what it meant to be reborn."

"Praise the Lord!" Mayvelle cried out softly.

There followed a brief silence, each of them considering what this confession meant to them.

"So that was it?" Jennifer finally asked, "That was what brought you two closer."

Luke smiled contentedly.

"Mayvelle asked me to come to her house for dinner that night, and I've pretty much been here ever since," he replied simply.

"Can't get rid of him," Mayvelle agreed.

"Are you still working at the hospital?"

"Yes, but I'm no longer a janitor. I attended the community college for two years and got trained as a CMT. So Mayvelle doesn't get to boss me around anymore," he quipped fondly.

"Oh, don't you worry. I keep him in line." Mayvelle retorted.

Everyone else had finished eating, but Luke had yet to taste his food, and he bit into his sandwich hungrily as if the telling of his story had given him an appetite. Mayvelle stood and started clearing the others' empty plates away.

"So what brings you here?" she asked Jennifer pointedly.

"Well, Luke," setting her napkin on the table, Jennifer pushed her chair back and folded her hands in her lap, "first let me express how pleased I am to find out that you're life has turned out so well. It is truly a miracle! I never in my wildest dreams…"

Her thought went unsaid, and as Mayvelle once again praised God, she took a deep breath and continued.

"I've come to ask a favor."

Luke swallowed quickly and said, "Anything! I'd do anything for you!"

"Not so quick, Luke. Let me tell you what it is first, and then you can decide. I have a trial coming up in October. I'm representing a young man who has been accused of assaulting a police officer and crippling him. The truth of the matter is that my client was defending himself against a brutal officer who intended to do him bodily harm."

"Yes, ma'am, that's something I know about – police brutality. I've experienced it more than once. So, how can I help you?"

"The officer in question is Scott Deaver, the same one who attacked you. I need you to help us establish in front of a jury just what kind of policeman he is. What he's done in the past. At the risk of bringing back bad memories, things I understand you would rather forget, I'm asking you to testify at this trial as to what this man did to you."

Luke stopped eating and, bowing his head slightly, merely sat still for a while. At first Jennifer assumed he was giving consideration to her proposal but soon comprehension came to her that he was praying. After a duration of several minutes, he looked up.

"The good Lord tells us to forgive our enemies. This is the only road to salvation. To hate is like drinking poison and then expecting the other guy to die. I do not wish to bear testimony against this man, but I would welcome an opportunity to face him publicly and forgive him."

"But, in order to forgive him, you would first have to make him aware of what it is you are forgiving him for, wouldn't you?"

"Yes, I suppose so."

Jennifer clapped her hands together, once, but with enthusiasm.

"Works for me!"

For a half hour they discussed arrangements for Luke and Mayvelle to come to Kalispell in October. Jennifer assured them that all of their expenses would be covered although both of them insisted that that was not necessary. Jennifer was ecstatic! Luke would make a very compelling witness.

Standing out in the front yard before they left, Jennifer asked Mayvelle about one of the blooming plants in her garden.

"Is that a poppy of some sort?"

"It sure is! That's a blue Himalayan. Isn't it beautiful?"

"It sure is! I think I've seen them in my catalogues, but I've always been a little afraid to try them. They seem so fragile, and our climate is little behind yours."

"Nonsense! These are hardier than they look. Let me dig up some seedlings for you to take with you."

Cradling a black plastic pot containing a few small plants, Jennifer smiled out of the car window at Luke and Mayvelle as they pulled away from the curb.

"Well, that certainly seemed to go well!" Bob had only spoken a few sentences all afternoon. It was now nearly five o'clock. "What do you think? We could be home by ten or so, and it doesn't get dark until about eleven."

"I'm feeling too wired to sit in the car for long. Besides, I feel like celebrating. Let's drive over to Coeur d'Alene and have nice dinner and stay in a motel."

Bob's eyebrows shot up.

"In the same room?"

"Yeah, Bob, in the same room. I *would* like to be with you tonight. If that's okay with you, that is."

"Of course it's okay with me. I'd like nothing better!"

"Don't go getting any ideas just yet. It's just for tonight."

Bob assured her that he understood. It would not be wise, he realized, to try to re-establish their relationship until this trial was over with.

15

Juvenile records, along with those of foster care, are purported to be sealed, but with only minimal effort Dexter had quickly added that information to what he'd already been able to assemble about Jolene Sutten. Along with a copy of her driver's license, he also had her income tax records for the last five years. He knew her address and her cell phone number, and had a copy of her current work schedule, along with the names and schedules of her supervisors and fellow employees. She had no arrest record, but from inferences he was able to make from other sources, Dexter felt sure that this was only because she had never been caught.

He had also done extensive research on her mother, and her roommate, Sharla Bowen, as well as Arnold Simpson, the man who her juvenile records indicated had sexually abused her when she was a young girl. Simpson had been paroled last month, but there had been no official reports of him having been seen in the Kalispell area, and he doubted that Jolene was aware of it.

In Dexter's mind, an electronic footprint was every bit as intriguing as one found in the forest; it took the same level of skill and cunning to follow it and determine its implication and significance. An inclination was beginning to come into focus, with several paths leading in different directions. One of the surest ways to learn about a particular predator – and that was how he thought of Jolene – was to inspect her den, and, so that was the track he chose first.

It led him to a newer double-wide located in one of Flathead Valley's nicer mobile home parks, about two miles north of Kalispell. Titled to Sharla Bowen, it had an outstanding mortgage of $21,248, and some change. A paved driveway led to an adjacent carport where a white '05 Chevy Cavalier was parked - Montana license plate 7C37584, registered likewise to Sharla Bowen, with Glacier Bank as lien holder. There was nothing distinguishing about the exterior, no flower or rock gardens, but what little lawn there was had apparently been recently mowed.

Sharla Bowen's background was very transparent, and Dexter had been able to learn almost all there was to know about her. Born and raised in Kalispell, she had attended Flathead High School and graduated in 1998 with average grades. Her driver's license photo showed an overweight and not very attractive woman of thirty-one. She had never married. As her tax records showed she operated her own one-person cleaning business as a sole proprietorship, netting about $22,000 a year, and she followed all the rules meticulously; her business was registered with the Secretary of State, she paid regularly into worker's comp and unemployment, and made all of her quarterly tax estimates on time. As a matter of fact, she paid all of her bills on time. Even though her earnings were not much, her credit score was well over eight hundred with all three reporting sources he had checked. Every year she renewed her city business license allowing her to work in Whitefish, even though it was a requirement that was never enforced. She made very few credit card purchases and never shopped online. Her medical records indicated that she had visited a psychiatrist several times in the past few years, and had prescriptions for various sedatives; apparently she was a nervous sort of person. It didn't seem to Dexter that it would take much effort to gain her cooperation, but, even so, he was surprised at how easy it was.

When she answered the door he didn't give his name, but only said, "Ms. Bowen, I'm working on an investigation of your roommate, Jolene Sutten, and I was wondering if I could ask you a few questions."

Her face suddenly colored with apprehension. Dexter could see that his question had achieved its intended purpose of making her assume he was with law enforcement, and she answered fearfully, "Oh, God! Is this about that necklace?"

Her response presented an unexpected detour, and he quickly changed direction from what he had charted.

"As a matter of fact, that is what this is about," he replied authoritatively, "Perhaps I should come inside. It would be in your best interest to tell me all you know about it."

The front room was a combination kitchen and living room crowned with a shallowly vaulted popcorn ceiling, and the doors and trim were photo-finish fake oak. It was un-tastefully decorated in a style that Dexter thought of as 'foo-foo' feminine – lots of peach and aqua fuzzies with open jars of sweet herbal potpourris and scented candles interspersed about the room. She offered him a chair with lace doilies on the arms and over the headrest, but she remained standing, pacing and fretting as she spoke, scarcely pausing to breathe.

"I just knew this was going to happen. I told Mrs. Windover that she must have misplaced it and that it would surely turn up, but I knew she didn't believe it. And I just know that Jolene took it. I just *know* it! She vacuumed the master bedroom and walk-in closet where the jewelry was kept. She was the only one in there that day. It *had* to have been her! But I can't prove it and she's probably gotten rid of it by now...pawned it or something."

Sharla was still walking back and forth speaking excitedly, gesturing frenetically, and Dexter sat on the edge of the doily-infested chair permitting her to continue her rant uninterrupted. It was purely a stroke of luck that his search had proven so fruitful so soon, and he did not want to get in the way of his own good fortune.

"And that necklace was worth a lot of money! It had *diamonds* in it! *Real diamonds*! I'm lucky Mrs. Windover hasn't fired me yet, but I know she's suspicious because she never leaves the house anymore when I'm there working, and every time I move a piece of furniture to clean under it, she's right there, looking to see if that damned thing is underneath. It's nerve-wracking! I wish I'd never let Jolene move in with me in the first place. I didn't even know her, and I had no idea what I was getting myself into. Last year I ran an ad on Craigslist looking for a roommate. It seemed like a good idea at the time. I had that extra bedroom that I wasn't even using, and the rent I'm getting from Jolene is actually a little more than my monthly payment, and she's always paid her rent on time. She seemed okay at first, and I thought maybe...maybe we could even become friends, 'cause I don't hardly have any friends and I thought that might be nice. But, NOOOOO! As it turned out, she's one of the coldest people I've ever known. Like she's made of solid ice! It's *weird*! The only time she ever shows any emotion at all is when she gets angry, and, believe-you-me, it doesn't take much to set her off! I mean, like, I'm not very confrontational, but she's got this hair-trigger temper that goes off sometimes for *no reason at all*! I try real hard not to provoke her, but sometimes she leaves me wondering what did I do? What did I say? I wish she'd just move out, but I'm afraid to even suggest it...afraid of what she might do... Well, there you go! I've admitted it! I'm afraid of her! I really am! And I'm afraid of what's going to happen with this necklace thing. I asked her about it but she only got angry and denied it, but what would you expect her to do – hand it over? No way, Jose'! She'd never do that. So I haven't mentioned it again, but she knows I've been thinking about it. Not that I've even seen that much of her lately. I've been staying over at my mother's house a lot, you know, trying to avoid her. Isn't that crazy? I've practically moved out of my own house just so I don't have to see Jolene. My *own house*! I'm only home right now because she's at work. Is that insane, or what? So, what am I supposed to do? Huh?"

She stopped raving abruptly and was staring somewhat psychotically at Dexter as if he might be able to suggest some simple but life-saving solution, so he tried to offer some hope, albeit false.

"It might not be as bad as you think," he implied in his most soothing voice, "especially if we can recover the necklace. And if it turns out that Ms. Sutten is indeed responsible then there would certainly be…consequences…for her that might possibly work in your favor. So, if you wouldn't mind, I'd like to ask you a few questions."

His confident tone left her slightly encouraged, and she briskly nodded her ascent.

"Does she have any friends or acquaintances that she hangs out with; someone she might have confided in?"

Sharla bit her lower lip.

"Not that I know of?"

"Boyfriends, maybe?"

"No. Or if she does, I don't know about it. She's never brought anyone home."

"How about fellow employees? Has she ever mentioned being friendly with anyone she works with?"

"No, not really," She scrunched up her rather porcine eyes as something seemed to jog her memory, "There was this one guy she talked about – Eddie, or something like that. But, come to think of it, it didn't sound like they were all that good of friends. Maybe he was her boss or something."

Dexter stood up and said, "I want to thank you for your cooperation, Ms. Bowen. You've been very helpful."

"So, what happens now?" Sharla asked in a panicky voice, "Do you think you can find the necklace?"

"I don't know, but I'm going to try."

"And then what? What if you find it? Then what happens?"

"I'll make a deal with you, Ms. Bowen," he answered reassuringly, "If I do manage to find it, and when I don't need it anymore, I'll give it to you," pointing a finger at her, "so that you can put it back in Mrs. Windover's house in a place where she can conveniently discover it. And all I ask from you in return, is that you don't mention this visit to anyone."

Frantic hope gradually lit her eyes, but it was encumbered with perplexity.

"You can do that? I mean, wouldn't you get in trouble?"

"Not if I'm careful."

"But, aren't policemen supposed to turn in evidence like that?"

"I suppose they are, but I'm not a policeman."

"You're not?"

"No."

"Then…what are you?"

Dexter's smile was inscrutable, as always.

"You might say that this is a…private investigation."

At eleven PM there were only a few customers still shopping at Treasure State Grocery and Doreen Morningstar, manning the only register still open, was starting to get bored. She had just finished spraying and wiping down the counter in front of her for the third time in fifteen minutes, when she saw a familiar face enter through the automatic doors.

"Dexter Ksunka! What are you doing off the rez?"

"I could ask you the same thing, Dorrie."

"I work here! I live in Kalispell."

"Oh, yeah? How long you lived here?"

"Only about…ten years, Dex," she replied with a touch of sarcasm.

"That long, huh?"

Doreen's obsidian eyes flashed a knowing look in his general direction.

"C'mon, Dex, what's up? You didn't come in here at eleven o'clock just to go grocery shopping."

"Well, maybe I came in to see you Dorrie."

"Oh, really? What for?"

Dexter shrugged nonchalantly.

"Maybe I wanted to see if maybe you wanted to get together. Talk about things."

"Oh, for chrissakes, Dexter! That was like a hundred years ago, and it never was all that serious, anyway. We were just kids. It was all over even before you left for the Army."

"Yeah, you're right. But I wasn't asking you out on a date or anything."

"So, then, what *are* you doing?"

"I'd just like to talk some. Ask you a few questions about something I'm working on."

Comprehension suddenly colored her face and pursing her lips she nodded her head.

"Does this have to do with that nephew of yours? The one that's in all the papers?"

"Well…yes. Indirectly."

Doreen smiled sympathetically.

"Ya know, your sister was once one of my best friends. Still is, I guess, although I don't see much of her anymore. I don't know how I can help you, but I'll be glad to do whatever I can," She stole a look at the large clock high up on the wall at the front of the store, "Tell ya what. I get off in about an hour. Meet me at Scotty's Bar."

"I don't drink, Dorrie."

"I know, but I do. And you can buy."

Montana is the third largest state in the lower forty-eight and only has a population of about nine-hundred-thousand people, but every summer millions of visitors descend upon its expanses, clogging roadways such as Going-To-The-Sun Road in Glacier Park, and jamming into the hotels, restaurants and bars. Tourist season had arrived, evidenced by the fact that it was past midnight on a weeknight, but Scotty's Bar was, nonetheless, still jam-packed. Dexter and Doreen made their way through the loud, boisterous throng to a booth that would afford at least a modicum of privacy. A waitress stopped at their table and Doreen ordered a bourbon ditch - in Montana that means bourbon and water – and Dexter asked for a cup of coffee.

"That's going to keep you up all night," Doreen warned.

"That's okay. I have to drive back to Polson tonight. And I never sleep that much anyway."

"For someone who doesn't sleep, I sure remember you snoring really loud."

She flashed her eyes at him again, and for a moment Dexter could see the young girl she once had been, saucy and flirtatious. She's still a good-looking woman, he thought.

"That was a long time ago, Dorrie. People change."

"Some things never change. Like you, Dex," She lowered her brow and appraised him shrewdly, "I bet I know what you wanted to talk about. Or 'who', I should say. You want to know about Jolene."

Dexter feigned abashment.

"I never could fool you, Dorrie."

"Oh, you fooled me plenty." She chuckled derisively, not at him, but at herself.

"But, yeah, you're right. That is who I wanted to talk about."

"So…what?" She spread both hands. "You think because I work with her that I know what's going on inside that twisted mind of hers?"

"Well, you at least seem to know that her mind is twisted. That's a start. What else do you know?"

"Not much, other than that she's a mean-spirited manipulative little bitch with a barely controllable temper."

"Nice girl, huh?"

"Oh, you bet! The nicest!" She took a sip of her drink and grimaced, whether at the bite of the bourbon or at the thought of Jolene he wasn't sure. "But, seriously, that girl has got a sharp tongue on her! I've never seen her turn it on any customers, but all of us who have to work with her have been lanced by it at least a time or two."

"Doesn't she get along with anybody?"

Doreen considered the question for a moment.

"Well there's one girl, Casey, who seems to like her, but Casey's just a sweet little hippie chick who's nice to everybody. A while back it seemed like maybe Jolene had something going on with Eddie, but lately he seems to be avoiding her like the plague."

"Who's Eddie?" Dexter knew the answer but asked the question anyway.

"Eddie Parelli. He's an assistant manager. Like I said, a few months back it was looking like maybe something was going on – you know how people gossip at a place like that. But Eddie's married. Got a couple of kids. So I didn't pay much attention to what people were saying. None of my business, anyway."

She took another drink, dismissing the subject, but Dexter prodded her a little more.

"So, you say he's been avoiding her?"

"Yeah, that's what it seems like anyway. The rumor now is that she's got something on him, or something like that, but I try not to pay too much attention to that stuff. It's just a bunch of workplace bullshit and I really don't want to buy into it."

"Yeah, I suppose that's wise."

Doreen finished her drink as Dexter mulled this over for a few moments before continuing.

"Has she ever talked about what happened that night out at my nephew's house?"

"Not to me."

"Has she spoken about it to anybody else that you know of?"

"Right after it happened it was, as you might expect, about the only thing anybody at work talked about. And everyone told her how happy they were that she had survived such an ordeal, and all, and how they all had her in their prayers, and so on, but, as far as I know, she never said anything to anybody that was any different than what was in the papers. Mostly, she just acted like it was no big deal, not even worth talking about. But, then, that's just the way she is, you know. Kinda anti-social. A real icy bitch if you know what I mean?"

Dexter nodded.

"Yep, I'm picking up what you're laying down! So, that's it, huh? Nobody else that you can think of that she might have confided in?"

"Well, you might try asking Eddie. They *were* kind of friendly for a while, and being assistant manager and all, you know, she might have said something to him."

Dexter was quiet for a while, thinking.

"I'm sorry, Dex. I guess I'm not much help, am I?"

"Actually, Dorrie, you've given me quite a few things to think about."

The bar had quieted down and the crowd had thinned out. The waitress stopped by their table to see if they wanted anything else before last call.

"You want another one?" Dexter asked.

"No, thanks. One's enough for me."

When the waitress walked away, Dexter turned to her and asked pointedly, "What do you know about a necklace?"

"A necklace," She looked confused, "Nothing. I don't know anything about a necklace. Why do you ask?"

"Oh, nothing. Forget it. Just something I came across – probably doesn't mean anything."

He pulled his cell phone out of his pocket and checked the time.

"It's getting pretty late. I guess I ought to get going."

Doreen reached across the table and laid a hand on his.

"You know, Dex, you really shouldn't drive all the way to Polson this late."

"But that's where I live."

"You could stay at my place tonight." She pouted her lips in an evocative way.

"Oh, really?" He pretended to be shocked and raised his eyebrows suggestively, "Like old times, huh?"

"Well…yeah. Kinda like old times." She raised a cautious finger, "But just for tonight."

"Sure, Dorrie. That sounds real nice. Just for tonight."

This far north in late June when the northern hemisphere is nearing the time of the summer solstice, darkness descends very late in the day and sundown seems to extend for hours. At eight o'clock the next evening when Eddie Parelli was due to get off work, Dexter was waiting at the far end of the Treasure State Grocery parking lot where the employees were supposed to park so that the closer spaces would be available for customers. It was full-on summer now, and the heat rose in waves off the asphalt. Eddie was shaking a death stick out of his pack and lighting it with a Bic, as he sauntered up the parking lot squinting at the slanting shafts of sunlight.

Dexter had learned many interesting things about Eddie. About five years ago, Eddie, and his wife, Stacie, along with their two kids, had moved from Philadelphia to Kalispell, ostensibly to make a change from a crime-ridden environment to one that was safer. At least that's what they had told all of their new acquaintances in Montana. But the truth of the matter was that it was done in an effort to save their marriage after Eddie was arrested for trying to solicit sex from a woman he thought was a prostitute but in reality was an undercover police officer.

In marriage counseling after the incident, Eddie had somehow convinced Stacie that he had suffered some sort of breakdown due to a mid-life crisis – he was only thirty-two at the time – and that it would never happen again, and she had finally agreed to try to forgive him and start over. Since all of their family, and most of their friends knew about what had happened - and they felt that would be a hindrance to their progress - they decided to do their starting over in another place far away.

In Philly, Eddie had worked as an assistant manager at a Target store, and Stacie had worked in the appliance department at Home Depot - a job that she had held for over ten years - and she was fortunately able to transfer to a new location, which was the primary reason for moving to Kalispell. When Eddie applied for the position at Treasure State Grocery, he had tautly stretched the truth on his resume', although he had brought with him a 'decent' recommendation from his former employer. After taxes he netted about $34,000 per year, and Stacie, because of her longevity with Home Depot brought home nearly an equal amount. Both jobs came with excellent benefit packages, and for all intents and purposes they should have been doing very well, but somehow, during and since the move five years ago, they had accumulated credit-card and other time-pay consumer debt that nearly equaled their combined yearly incomes. The interest alone was more than the rent they paid each month on a three-bedroom house in the east-north section of town, and had prevented them from being able to buy a home of their own.

That kind of debt can be stressful on a relationship, and they were in marriage counseling again, not only on account of the financial pressure, but also because a few months ago Eddie had been caught - literally - in bed with one of Stacie's fellow employees, a twenty-three-year-old woman named Pamela Albrecht. Their therapist's records showed that this time Eddie was trying to convince her that Pamela had come on to him repeatedly and that he had had a 'moment of weakness'. So far, Stacie wasn't buying it, but she recognized that a divorce would mean financial ruin for both of them, not to mention the difficulties and outright trauma that would be visited upon their children.

In a well-hidden file in his home computer Eddie maintained an extensive array of pornography, something, Dexter was certain, Stacie knew nothing about. It all added up to a portrait of a very deceitful person; the kind of person that, in Dexter's experience, is often the easiest to deceive.

Eddie's car was a silver BMW convertible; albeit an older one, it was, nonetheless, well beyond what a person at his income level could afford, as evidenced by the hefty monthly payment it generated. Stacie had pleaded with him to get rid of it, but Eddie insisted that he would actually lose money if he did, since he owed more than he could currently expect to receive for it.

Eddie was using the remote device on his key ring to unlock the vehicle when Dexter turned his ball cap around and walked up on his blind side.

"Eddie, my man," Dexter called out deliberately employing a poorly-done ghetto accent, "Whuddup?"

Dexter had purposely chosen a position where the sun would be just over his left shoulder and shining directly into Eddie's eyes.

"Uh…hey, man! How'ya doin'?" Eddie responded, obviously unsighted. He was rocking his head from side to side to try to see who was approaching him, but the face could only be seen backlighted, silhouetted, and its features were indistinguishable. "Uh…who is that? D'I know you?"

"Sure, man. Don't you remember? I'm the guy who is always comin' up to you in the store? Complainin' that I can't find anything? And then, you're always tellin' what isle's it on?"

Using his hand as a sunshade, Eddie showed no obvious sign of recognition, but answered in a friendly manner, "Oh, yeah! Sure dude! Whasshappnin'?"

"Nothin' much…Hey, Eddie, I wanted to ask you somethin'."

"Sure, man."

"So, like, what's the deal with that Jolene chick?"

"Jolene?"

"Yeah, you know, always works one of the registers up front? Wears her hair in one of those French braids?"

"Yeah…what about her?"

"Well, don't you think she's hot, man?"

"Yeah…sure, I guess."

"So, what's her story, man?"

Eddie dropped his cigarette on the asphalt and stepped on it as he moved to the side to get a better look. He seemed a little shocked, and perhaps even a little intimidated, when he saw Dexter more clearly.

"Aren't you a little old to be asking about her?" he asked with a touch of false bravado.

"Hey, man! A guy can look, can't he? Maybe dream a little? Know what I'm sayin?" Dexter leered suggestively.

"Sure, man," Eddie agreed readily, "We all like to look."

"Oh, I bet you do more than look, Eddie! Good-lookin' guy like you! I bet you've already had a slice of that, haven't ya, Eddie?"

"Well..."

"You did! You dog! I knew it! I knew it! You lucky son-of-a-bitch!"

Dexter made a snap-assumption that Eddie was the type that liked to brag to other men about his extramarital dalliances, and his arrow solidly hit the mark.

"Well, the bitch was begging for it! What was I supposed to do?" Eddie spread his hands making this pronouncement as if it happened all the time.

"So, let me ask you, Eddie. Was she as hot as she looks?"

"Well, her mouth was hot!"

"Are you shittin' me? She gave you head? Oh, man, you are one lucky mothafucka!"

They beamed shit-eating grins at one another, and then Dexter dropped the phony accent and asked abruptly, "But what about that necklace, man?"

Eddie's smirk quickly faded and was replaced by an expression of alarm, and Dexter instantly knew that he was on the right path.

"What necklace? I don't know what you're talking about."

"Oh, sure you do, Eddie! I can see it in your eyes! The *stolen* necklace!"

"*Stolen*? I didn't know it was stolen!"

"So you do know about it." It was a statement, not a question.

"Well...yeah. But I didn't know it was stolen! A few weeks back I happened to see her toss something in the dumpster, and I took a look to see what it was. If it hadn't landed on a cardboard flat it would have sunk to the bottom, but there it was. I'm no expert, but it looked like real diamonds, but I didn't know what it meant. I mean, I couldn't figure out why she would throw something like that away. At first I thought about maybe making nice with the old lady and giving it to her, but then I decided that wasn't such a good idea."

"Why not?"

"Well, to tell you the truth, that Jolene's a cunt! She's been threatening to tell my wife about the blowjob, and it's not like things aren't already bad enough with my marriage. So, I couldn't take the chance that Jolene might see her come into the store, or something, wearing it. Don't you see?"

"Yes. I do!"

"I swear I'd like to kill the bitch! I'd like get my gun and blow her away!"

Dexter chose to ignore this declaration.

"So, what did you do with it?"

"What? The necklace? I kept it. It's in my locker. But I swear to God I didn't know it was stolen! I swear to God!"

"I believe you, Eddie. But I'll tell you what! You better get rid of it, and quick! If the cops catch you with that thing, telling them that you fished it out of a dumpster is going to sound a whole lot like 'my dog ate my homework' if you get my meaning."

"Yeah, but what should I do with it? Throw it away?" He was acting agitated; his unease was apparent.

"Hell, no, don't throw it away! If it ever turns up it'll have your DNA all over it."

Dexter was betting that Eddie had no idea what kinds of cases warranted that sort of forensic testing.

"So what *should* I do with it?" Eddie asked anxiously.

"You should probably go get it right now and bring it back here and give it to me."

"Give it to you?" Eddie sounded suspicious, "Why should I do that?"

"Simple!" Dexter spoke reassuringly, as if offering him an easy way out of this. "You should turn it over to me because I know who it was stolen from, and I can arrange to have it put back in a way that no one will ever know it was stolen."

"You can do that? You're not just bullshitting me?"

"No lie!' Dexter held up his right hand in a classic red man pose, "That's the honest truth."

Eddie's despair began to morph into hope, and along with that hope came slyness.

'You know what, man? I'm going to trust you. At least if I give it to you, it won't be in my possession anymore; it'll be your problem."

"That's right, Eddie. The problem will be all mine."

"Wait here. I'll be right back."

Dexter was leaning casually on the BMW ten minutes later when Eddie came walking back up the grocery store parking lot, his right hand balled in a fist. The sun was nearly horizontal now and once again shone directly into Eddie's eyes as he unceremoniously dropped the necklace into Dexter's hand.

"So, who are you, anyway?' he asked shading his eyes against the glare, "What's this all about?"

"Let's just say that this is part of a…private investigation, and leave it at that."

16

Every summer for the past twenty-one years Kalispell's Department of Parks and Recreation has organized and hosted a free public outdoor concert series titled PICNIC IN THE PARK, featuring many of the area's talented local musicians. Held in Kalispell's Depot Park for nine consecutive weeks, a different two-hour act is featured every Tuesday evening at seven o'clock and every Wednesday morning at eleven. Staged in a large octagonal gazebo sheltered by a weathered moss-covered shake roof, the singers and instrumentalist perform before an audience that is spread out across an area the size of a city block shaded by venerable maple trees. At the park's north end garnished in orangish-brown stucco façade - the result of its' most recent renovation - stands the old Depot Building, an historic landmark, which houses the offices of The Kalispell Chamber of Commerce. The railroad tracks still traverse like parallel steel ribbons to the north of the building, merely an ornamental reminder of the town's origins; for trains are seldom seen in Kalispell anymore. There is a First Interstate Bank branch office cater-corner across Main and Center, on the same site where once stood The Conrad Bank, Kalispell's first banking establishment.

A large PA system is provided to insure that even those at the far end of the park near the war memorial can hear the concert. On the lawn in front of the Gazebo small children can always be found cavorting amongst a smattering of dancers, while a few hundred patrons of all ages relax in folding chairs or on park benches, many of them enjoying various food and drink they may have brought with them, or purchased from one of several vendors set up in the east parking lot.

Eli was feeling more than a little self-conscious as he stood in the ice-cream vendor's line with Stephanie. Uncomfortable with being recognized everywhere he went, he had for the past couple of weeks allowed himself to be seen in public only when necessary, and had even tried to alter his appearance by buzzing off his long black hair and growing the beginnings of a goatee. But on this Tuesday night, Stephanie's favorite local band, Andre Floyd and Mood Iguana, was performing, and she had somehow talked him into meeting her there; he wasn't sure how. She had employed all of her feminine skills: gentle persuasion, cajoling, and even a little coercion, and despite his resistance he had, nonetheless, eventually agreed; and now here he was hoping fervently that his disguise was effective. It was put to the test sooner than he expected when he saw his attorney, Jennifer Lawson, coming right toward him with a tall, balding man, and a teenage girl, each of them carrying a collapsible chair in a green canvas sheath with a shoulder strap.

And it almost worked. Although they had conferred regularly on the phone, there had been no reason over the past few weeks for them to meet, so Jennifer had had no opportunity to see him with a beard and no hair. She was about to walk right past him when suddenly she looked him in the face and exclaimed, "Oh, Eli! I almost didn't recognize you. How are you?"

"Uh… Okay, I guess." Eli stammered. He liked Jennifer a lot, but he was nevertheless somewhat disappointed that she had identified him so readily. If it was that easy for her, how difficult would it be for those who had known him for a much longer time? Then again, did it really matter all that much? Most of the people that he had seen around town who knew him well had undeniably voiced their support for him. Mostly he was concerned about the ones who might recognize him from the photos that had appeared in the newspapers, and he continued to hope that this new look might yet fool them.

"Eli, I'd like for you to meet Bob Mayfield, and this is our daughter, Angela."

Eli shook hands with Bob and said hi to Angela, and then said, "This is my friend, Stephanie."

He wasn't quite sure why, but for some reason he was reluctant to give them Stephanie's full name. Perhaps it was because of her relationship to the Sheriff. But he should have realized that Jennifer would cross-examine her. Ever since he had become her client, she had become as protective as a grizzly with a cub. She would undoubtedly want to find out what she could about whomever he was hanging out with.

"Hi, Stephanie," Jennifer stuck out her hand, "I'm Jennifer Lawson. I didn't catch your last name?"

"Oh, sorry. It's Montgomery."

"Oh! Are you one of the local Montgomerys?"

"Yes. My father is Stephen Montgomery. He's a doctor."

"Yes. I know him very well. I've actually consulted with him before," Jennifer smiled, "A small town, isn't it?"

"It sure is!" They all agreed nearly in unison.

Eli wasn't sure whether 'consulted with him before' referred to medically or legally, but even though she showed no change in facial expression, he was all but certain that Jennifer had made the family connection. However he totally forgot these concerns when, utterly out of the blue, something opportune but totally unexpected happened.

"Eli," Bob said, "I think we've met before. Weren't you working for Gary Greenwald?"

"Well…yeah, I *was*. That is, up until a couple of weeks ago."

"I thought so! I was the stonemason on the Grosweiler project."

Eli nodded his head in acknowledgment.

"Oh, yeah! I remember you!"

Even though they had just shaken hands, they shook again in mutual agreement that they had worked together and had liked each other.

"So, you're not working for Gary anymore?"

"No, he had to lay me off."

A multitude had been laid off during this recession, so Eli felt that he was under no obligation to provide further explanation.

"Are you doing anything now?" Bob inquired.

"Not really. I was thinking about filing for unemployment. I've never done that before. Never had to. And I don't really want to. But I can't seem to find any work."

"I might have something for you."

"Really! What's that?" Eli was suddenly very alert.

"Well, I've got a pretty good-size tile job coming up, starting in about a week, on a big house in Whitefish. These last couple of years I've been mostly working by myself, but this job is big enough that I could use some help. Are you interested?"

"Well, hell yeah, I'm interested! But I don't have much tile experience."

"Oh, that's okay. If you've been working for Gary, I know you've got good basic skills. All I need is a helper. Someone who knows how to work. I can show you in the first couple of days almost everything you need to know. I probably can't pay you quite as much as you're used to, but I'll come close. And the job is probably only going to last a couple of months. I can't say what'll happen after that. So…what do you think?"

Eli couldn't say what's going to happen in a couple of months either.

"What do I think?" Eli looked like a mild breeze would bowl him over. "I think I don't know how to thank you."

He put out his hand and they shook yet again.

"I should be thanking you. I didn't know where I was going to find the right guy." Bob took his wallet out of his back pocket and dug out a business card. Handing it to Eli he said, "Call me on Monday and I'll let you know when we're starting and where to come to, and all that stuff."

"Okay. Thanks. I'll call you Monday."

"You bet! Enjoy the concert."

As they were walking away Eli overheard Jennifer say, "That was a nice thing to do!" and Bob reply, "Yeah, it *was* nice of him to agree to help me." And then he saw her punch him in the shoulder playfully.

"Eli, that's so wonderful!" Stephanie exclaimed. "I'm so glad you got a job!"

"Yeah, me too."

"You see? It's just like I've been telling you. Everything will work out, if you just allow it to."

After they got their ice cream, they returned to the place on the lawn where they had set up their folding chairs amongst the crowd gathered in front of the gazebo. There was a charge of electric anticipation in the air of the upcoming music as they took their seats, and Eli was feeling better than he had felt in months. Just the prospect of steady work had boosted his spirits immeasurably.

Jennifer Young, director of Kalispell Parks and Recreation, and the organizer of this event since its conception, was on the stage dressed in a bright yellow summer dress. She was making some announcements over the microphone, and the band behind her was going through their final preparations, as Eli took a moment to surreptitiously observe the crowd nearby to see if anyone was looking at him. Nobody seemed to have noticed him, and he was starting to settle down when suddenly his heart leapt up into his throat. Jolene was sitting about twenty yards to his right, but was looking in the other direction, and had apparently not seen him.

"Oh, crap!" He quickly turned his head to the left and down, and pulled his ball cap low to cover his face.

"What's the matter?" Stephanie asked.

"Jolene!" Eli pointed with his thumb over his shoulder.

"Which one is she?"

"Sitting on a park bench with a guy in a Hawaiian shirt. Kinda dark brown hair in a French braid."

"Oh, so that's her!" Stephanie was checking out Jolene with conspicuous curiosity.

"C'mon, let's get out of here."

"What? The band's just about to start!" Stephanie protested, "Besides, what can she do? You should just ignore her."

"I know, but I can't stay. You can stay if you want to, but there's a restraining order. I'm not supposed to be within fifteen hundred feet of her, and I don't want to be."

"Well, then, let's move over next to the Depot building." Stephanie pointed across the park, "That's about fifteen hundred feet, I guess. Close enough! And we'll be able to hear the band just fine. There must be over six hundred people here. She'll never see you!"

Actually it was only about two hundred feet, but Eli didn't want to waste time arguing, he just wanted to move quickly.

"Well, okay. Let's go."

Scott Johnston, from KXZI, Montana Radio Café, was introducing the band, and Eli was careful to keep his head turned away from Jolene as they gathered up their belongings and moved to the other side of the park. They set up their chairs against the wall of the Depot just as Andre Floyd, one of the area's most appreciated performers, played a handful of notes on his guitar, asked Lenny, the sound man, to make some adjustment to his monitor, and then after welcoming everyone to Picnic in the Park launched into his first song.

Stephanie was right. They could hear just fine, and they were well obscured by the crowd, so Eli was finally able to relax and eat his ice cream and soon found himself enjoying the high-energy first set. Fifty minutes later when the band took a break, they had been having so much fun that he had all but forgotten that he had seen Jolene. Taking advantage of the intermission, he told Stephanie he'd be right back, and went to the men's room on the other side of the Depot.

Jolene was standing on the sidewalk when he exited the bathroom. Waiting for him.

"Hi, Eli."

"Leave me alone, Jolene. I don't want to talk to you."

He started to walk away, but she stepped in front of him.

"I bet you're sorry you fucked with me!"

He tried to step around her, but she moved with him continuing to block his way.

"Get out of my way, Jolene. I'm not supposed to be within fifteen hundred feet of you."

"You're going to prison, you son-of-a-bitch!" She snarled venomously, "That's what happens to people who fuck with me! And you know what? You're gonna have to take it up the ass every night for years!"

Eli turned and went the other way.

"Say hi to Bubba for me," she shouted at his retreating back.

Her maniacal laughter echoed in his ears as he turned the corner of the building.

When he got back to where Stephanie was seated, he folded up his chair and said, "I'm sorry, Steph, but I'm leaving."

"Why? What happened?"

"Jolene." He answered simply.

"What? You saw her?"

"Yeah. She was waiting for me when I came out of the bathroom."

"What did she say?"

"You don't want to know."

"Yes, I do."

"No, you don't." There was finality in his tone, so she did not press it.

Instead, she tried to placate the circumstances. "So she's had her little say. She probably won't bother you anymore."

"Look! I'm feeling pretty freaked-out about this right now. Okay? You can stay if you want to. It's okay. But I'm leaving."

"Well I don't want to stay if you're not staying. At least we got to see the first set."

A week later, Eli started his new job. He had given himself extra time to find the job site following the directions Bob had given him over the phone, and it had proven easier than he had anticipated, so he arrived about a half-hour early. Bob was not there yet, but there was a pickup equipped with side-mount toolboxes parked in front of but facing away from the house. Both of the truck's cab doors were wide open, and as Eli got out of his rig, he could hear a talk-show program projected from the truck's speakers at full volume. Before Eli could even make out what was being said, he felt assaulted by the radio show host's angry tone of voice.

A slightly overweight middle-aged man carrying a yellow Dewalt drill stepped out of the house and saw him standing there.

"Well. Did you buy your flat screen TV yet?" He shouted above the radio program.

The question was so apropos of nothing that Eli didn't know what to say, so he merely stammered out, "Come again?"

"Didn't you hear what they were just talking about?"

"Who?"

"Rush! On the radio. Weren't you listening?"

"Uh…no. Not really."

"Well you should! You should pay attention. This shit affects you! You should keep yourself informed about what's happening to this country."

Eli's confusion was evident in his expression.

"I'm sorry. What does this have to do with flat screen TV's?"

"It's Obama, man! He's passing a new law that's going to make it illegal to import TV's from China. You know what that's going to do? It's going to make them cost ten times as much! So, if you want one, or even think you might ever want one, you better buy it now before that new law goes into effect."

"How can that be true?"

"Oh, it's true, man! Didn't you hear Rush?"

"But, the President doesn't pass laws," Eli disputed. "That's what the Senate and the House are for. At least that's what I learned in High School Civics class."

"Yeah, that's the way it's supposed to be! The way our founding fathers set it up." he bellowed on top of Rush Limbaugh's angry tirade, "But Obama doesn't care about the Constitution. Nooooo! He just goes ahead and does whatever the hell he wants to. He's nothing more than a dictator!" As if to reinforce his conviction, he pointed at the rear window of his pickup where Eli saw an enlarged photo of Barack Obama with a Hitler mustache drawn over the upper lip.

This was starting to feel very weird, but Eli was thankfully saved by the arrival of his new employer. Bob came up the driveway, quickly parked and got out about thirty yards away near the garage, and waved Eli over. "Come over here and help me with this stuff."

When Eli approached him, Bob turned away and motioned him closer, saying in a lowered voice, "Sorry. I didn't know that guy was going to be here, or I would have warned you."

Speaking in hushed tones was totally unnecessary with Rush Limbaugh still braying at full volume, but Eli asked in the same mode, "Who is that guy?"

"Oh, that's Delroy. He's the plumber. Don't pay any attention to him. He's a nut case. He does this on every job. I'm surprised anyone will hire him, but you know how it is! He's actually a really good plumber, and he's not as expensive as most of them. So that's why he's here, Rush or no Rush. But I think it's only for today, so just ignore him."

"Okay, I'll try." Eli agreed tentatively.

Another pickup arrived pulling up next to them. As its occupant emerged, Bob said, "Mornin', Tom."

"Hi, Bob."

"Eli, this is Tom. He's the finish carpenter."

"Hi there, Eli. How ya doin'?" They shook hands.

"Are you working by yourself today?" Bob asked.

"No, Adam will be here any minute. In fact, I'm surprised he's not here already. And Greg will be stumbling in around ten or so."

Bob and Tom had a little laugh about that, and Eli realized that Greg was probably not known for starting early.

Tom nodded his head over to where Delroy's radio continued to spew forth Rush Limbaugh.

“I see we have to put up with Delroy today.”

“Hopefully it’s just for today.” Bob answered.

Tom reached back into his pickup extracting a pair of headphones, which he fitted over his ears plugging the jack into an IPod that he took out of his pocket.

“No problem!” He said merrily as he headed into the house.

“C’mon, Eli, let me show you around and get you started,” Bob offered as he followed Tom through the front door.

The project, which was being built by Old Montana Building Company, was located on one of those rare lots on Whitefish Lake where, rather than being on a steep grade, there was a nearly level spot down next to the lake that was large enough to put a house of this size on - and still have room for a driveway and some landscaping. In the great room, there was a huge bank of windows looking out on the lake where a pair of sailboats was tacking lazily, the summer morning sunshine reflecting luminously off their dazzling white mainsails. The house had so many rooms that Eli felt a little disoriented. This must be at least a five million dollar house, he thought to himself. The lot alone had to have been over a million!

Other workers started showing up and soon the house was full of the clamor of construction noises. Bob put Eli to work installing some tile underlayment for the laundry room floor, something that only took about fifteen minutes of instruction, and Eli was totally at home with, so Bob left him alone telling him that he would be working in the master shower if Eli needed anything. While he was prepping the floor, Delroy, the plumber, came in to the room ostensibly to check something on the washer connection.

“I just heard that Obama has come up with some kind of governor that they’re going to put on all the cars that will only allow you to use a certain amount of gasoline each day, and then your car just shuts down wherever you happen to be!"

"How could he possibly do that?" Eli said without looking up.

"Exactly! How does he get away with all this shit?"

Eli didn't respond; he just kept working and tried to do what Bob had told him to do: pay no attention to it. But Delroy proceeded undeterred.

"You know what's going to happen if he gets re-elected don't you? Socialism! That's what! No free enterprise! No one will get a paycheck anymore! Instead the government will dole out an allowance. And you won't get to choose what kind of work to do, either. The government will choose it for you. And no more home-ownership! You'll have a little cubicle that's assigned to you, like they do in Japan. *BIG GOVERNMENT*!!! That's what I'm talking about! That's what'll happen if you vote for Obama. That's what he's trying to do to our country! The good old US-of-fucking-A!"

"Okay, Delroy, that's enough. Leave Eli alone and let him work. I'm not paying him to listen to you." Bob must have overheard and come to Eli's rescue.

"Sorry, Bob," Eli apologized after Delroy left the room grumbling, "I was trying to ignore him."

"That's okay. No worries! He does that to everybody. I don't like having to be the heavy, but sometimes you just have to tell him to shut up." Bob took a moment to inspect what Eli was doing. "How's it going?"

"No problem. This is easy."

"See! I told you there was nothing to it."

Delroy didn't bother Eli again until the end of the day. He had finally turned off the rant on his truck radio, and the jobsite was mercifully silent. As Eli was about to leave, Delroy came up to him, and standing a little too close asked, "I know you from somewhere, don't I?"

Alarms were going off in Eli's head as he tried to shrug indifferently and answered, "No, I don't think so."

"Oh yeah! I've seen you somewhere." He scrunched his brow, "Just give me a minute. I'll remember where it was."

Eli walked away headed for his pickup, but before he reached it Delroy came up behind him and exclaimed, "Wait a minute! You're that guy that crippled that cop! Aren't you?"

Eli didn't say anything. He just opened the door to his truck and started to climb in.

"It *is* you. Isn't it? I knew it!"

"Delroy, you don't know what you're talking about!" Bob said as he walked over to them. "Eli's not even from here."

"Yeah!" Delroy actually snapped his fingers, "Eli! That was the name in the paper! It's him!" He jerked a thumb towards Eli.

"No, it's not! Different Eli. It's just a coincidence. He just moved here last week."

"Are you sure?" Delroy asked skeptically.

"Would I lie to you?" Bob spread his hands palms up.

"Well, he sure looks a lot like the guy in the paper! Sorry, kid, but I'll tell you what! If it's not you, you should probably change your name, or use your middle name or something. Take my advice. There's a lot of people – myself included – that would like to teach that little asshole a lesson!"

After Delroy left them, Eli thanked Bob for running interference for him.

"No problem," Bob reassured him, "It's unfortunate that some people think they have to be like that. And the ones who are the most opinionated always seem to be the loudest! Luckily, most of the guys on this job are pretty cool. Delroy won't be around again until we're done and he comes back to install his fixtures. So we won't be seeing much more of him."

Eli nodded, but he looked so forlorn that Bob asked, "Are you okay?"

"Yeah, I'll be okay. It's just hard…the way people treat me everywhere I go."

"Well, for what it's worth, Eli, I don't know you all that well yet, but from what I do know, and from what little Jennifer's been able to tell me, I believe you're innocent. That you were only defending yourself. So you can count on me to be in your corner."

"Thanks Bob. That really means a lot to me."

Bob smiled reflexively.

"But I do have a favor to ask."

"Sure. What's that?"

""'Well, Jennifer told me that you've worked as a fishing guide, and I've always wanted to learn more about fly-fishing. I've got a fly rod and everything, but I've never had anyone show me how to cast, or what flies to use, or where to go. So it's always been kind of a mystery to me. So I guess what I'm asking is…"

Bob's hesitancy prompted Eli to finish for him.

"You want me to take you fishing?"

"Well….yeah!"

"I'd love to, Bob. How about this weekend? Sunday?"

"Cool! Sunday would be great!" Bob appeared indisputably delighted.

"That little stretch of the South Fork below Hungry Horse Dam has been fishing pretty good lately, "Eli informed him, "I've got a couple of those little one-man pontoon boats, so we'll take both pickups and set up a shuttle from below the Hungry Horse Bridge. You know where that is?"

"I do."

"We'll meet there about seven-thirty. Is that too early?"

"Not at all! Seven-thirty will be great! I can't wait!"

Bob was smiling like a schoolboy and Eli found himself grinning back.

"So…I've got a little favor to ask you, Bob?"

"Shoot!"

"Well, I was wondering if it would be okay if I brought my dog to work with me."

"I don't see why not. The guy that owns Old Montana Building Company, Jon Krack, is a pretty good guy, and I don't think he'll mind. And this is a vacation home for a Canadian couple, and I doubt we'll ever see them…so, sure!"

"Awesome. Thanks."

"No problem. And Eli?"

"Yeah?"

"You did real good today. I'm glad you're here. Thanks."

"No, thank *you*."

"See you tomorrow."

"You bet!"

As Eli was driving home he came to the realization that today he had gained one of the most valuable things a person can have. He had found a friend.

17

Sometimes on a summer afternoon when Jennifer Lawson was in her early teens, she and Brenda would walk across town to a matinee at The Liberty or Strand Theaters. Both movie houses were of the old style with the ticket window on the street next to glass encased posters of upcoming films, and inside the crowded red-carpeted foyer stood the concession stand; the permeating smell of buttered popcorn followed you into the hushed theater with high draperied walls rising to a small balcony in the rear protected by a brass rail. Both theaters are gone now and the buildings that once housed them are currently occupied by The Fresh Life Church.

More than a decade ago, The Hutton Ranch Plaza, a huge retail development, was built at the corner of Highway 93 and Reserve between Kalispell and Whitefish, at the site of a former gravel pit and concrete batch-plant north of Flathead Valley Community College. Anchored by a Wal-Mart Super Store, and a Home Depot, the shopping center is likewise home to numerous other box stores. Directly across the highway stand Lowes and Costco, fronted by a variety of outlets and fast food restaurants. Almost every community in America has a generic development just like it, and most metropolitan areas have several. The only variation is the surrounding scenery.

It was this scenery that briefly caught Jennifer's attention as she was driving Angela, Nikki, and their friend, Cricket to catch an afternoon showing of The Avengers at The Signature Theater Complex in Hutton Ranch Plaza. Descending the hill in front of the community college, she could see all the way to the 'V' between Tea Kettle and Columbia Mountains that mark the entrance to Badrock Canyon, the main route to Glacier Park, and she thought fleetingly that summer was already half over and she had yet to visit the park, something she had done every year for as long as she could remember. Bob was going fishing this weekend, but perhaps Angela would go for a hike with her.

Jennifer had a soft spot in her heart for Angela's friend, Cricket Linnell. She had lost her mother in a car accident when she was still a toddler. In fact, she had been in the accident with her mother, strapped into her car seat, which was properly installed in the rear seat of the vehicle, and had been unharmed. Her father, Mick Linnell, a detective with the Sheriff's Department, had done an admirable job raising her, but Jennifer could see that as Cricket was reaching puberty she would be very much in need of a mother.

For the past few weeks, ever since Eli had gotten him started, it seemed like all Bob wanted to do was go fishing every weekend, not that they had spent much time together since the trip to Spokane. But for the first time in all the years of their on-again-off-again relationship, Jennifer was feeling a twinge of jealousy; and it seemed especially strange to her that it was not over another woman. God knows, she had given Bob every reason in the book for seeking companionship elsewhere, but he had never once gone down that road. Instead, he was finding a different kind of solace and fulfillment and all she could do was accept and support it. It's just that she was so accustomed to being the center of his life and attention. He had not fallen in love with someone else, but he *had* fallen in love with some*thing* else; and Jennifer was having trouble getting used to it. Conflicting emotions, however, were a common aspect of her life.

The vast Signature Theater Complex had over a dozen movies showing at the same time, and was so imposing and sterile that it made Jennifer nostalgic for the old Strand and Liberty Theaters. She wondered if thirty years from now her daughter would miss this with a sentimental wistfulness. How could she? There was nothing alluring about it. What was there to miss?

After dropping the girls off, and reminding them that Brenda would pick them up, she was driving across the theater parking lot when her cell phone rang and she pulled into an empty parking space before answering it.

"Hi, Jennifer. It's Fred Wilkinson. Your office gave me this number."

Before being elected County Attorney, Fred Wilkinson had been a deputy county attorney for many years, and for as many years had been a bitter foe in more cases than Jennifer could remember. Not to mention that she just plain didn't like him. He was arrogant and condescending and in her mind he was little more than a ladder climber. It was no secret that he was planning to run for Judge Walker's job when she retired – which wouldn't be long. Eli's case might not be the most important trial of the year, but there was no denying that it was getting a lot of publicity, and if it went to court she was certain that Wilkinson would see it as an opportunity to put another feather in his war bonnet. He would no doubt milk it for all it was worth, and Jennifer was determined to make sure that this would be one plume that would not get added to his collection.

"What can I do for you, Fred?" she asked curtly.

"I wanted to see if you could stop by my office. I want to discuss the March case with you."

"I'll be happy to discuss the case with you, but since you're the one who called, we can meet at my office."

His patronizing laughter was so condescending that it made her cringe.

"Take it easy, Jennifer. It's just an informal discussion. We don't have to play tactics here." There was a very insincere tone of conciliation in his voice. "Suppose we meet somewhere neutral. Get a cup of coffee or something."

Jennifer glanced at the clock on her dashboard. "It's one-thirty. I'll meet you at Coffee Traders in thirty minutes."

She was hoping the short notice would throw him off guard, but he replied after only a moment's hesitation, and with just a very slightly supercilious tone, "Thirty minutes would be fine."

It only took her ten minutes to drive to the bistro on Center Street across from the mall. The lunch rush was over and there was only a smattering of customers left. Some light saxophone jazz seeped out of the café's sound system. She got a cup of Kenyan Dark Roast and sat at a table in the back reading a copy of the Great Falls Tribune that someone had left behind. The editorial page was overflowing with widely varying opinions of the candidates and issues for the upcoming election, only a few of which she found herself in any sort of agreement with. She was, nevertheless, so absorbed in one of the letters that she was unaware that Wilkinson had arrived until he plopped a steaming mug on the table and took the chair across from her. He did possess a certain rugged handsomeness, but his tie was knotted too perfectly, and his hair was way too important.

"Interesting article?"

"Nope! Just a bunch of dumb, self-righteous opinions."

"Mmmm."

Wilkinson took a sip of coffee and Jennifer, finding herself already growing impatient, decided to skip the small talk and get right to it.

"Let's try to make this brief, Fred. I have to get back to the office. What did you want to talk about?"

"Well…I thought it might be a good time to start a plea bargain discussion."

"Plea bargain? Are you kidding? We don't go to trial for almost three months! I'm still preparing my case. I don't even know what all I have yet!"

"You don't have zip, Jennifer! This case is a slam-dunk. We've got two corroborating testimonies *and* an officer in a wheel chair – and you know how that's going to play to a jury. Not to mention that, to the best of my knowledge, there has never been a single case in the State of Montana where a defendant charged with assault on a police officer has won by reason of self-defense! You've got nothing!"

"I've got witnesses, too." Jennifer replied calmly.

"What? A recently reformed indigent alcoholic who claims that Deaver beat him, too? It won't take much to destroy his testimony. If that's all you have, I think it would be in your client's best interest to at least consider an offer."

It wasn't all she had. Among other things like Deaver's arrest record, she knew the Sutten girl was lying, and she believed she could get her to tell the truth when she cross-examined her, or at least trip her up enough to convince the jury that she was lying. But she played along with him and went through the motions, nonetheless, because she didn't want to reveal this tactic, even though she suspected that Wilkinson already anticipated it.

"What kind of offer?"

"Well…of course, nothing official at this time, but I think I could get the judge to agree to two ten-year sentences to run concurrently, with time served.

Allowing for good behavior your boy could be out in two-and-a-half to three years."

To stop herself from drumming her fingers on the table, Jennifer took a sip of her coffee but found it had gotten cold.

"I'll talk it over with my client, but don't expect any kind of answer - yes or no - until you're ready to make it official."

She stood up abruptly and left without any further discussion.

⁂

Late the next day, seated around the table in her conference/dining-room, Jennifer summarized this conversation for Eli and Dexter. All during this dialogue she observed Eli staring at her wall of law books as if in awe; perhaps he was trying to determine if she had read them all or merely used them for reference. As she had come to know him better these past months, she had come to understand that Eli was a daydreamer, maybe a little ADD even. The kind of person that the winds of fate might blow in any direction, and it made her feel very protective of him. This case was becoming more personal than most. She knew in the depths of her heart that he was an innocent victim of circumstances, and this gave her even greater conviction to fight for him. At the same time, it was her duty to keep both Eli and Dexter informed. Give them the lay of the land, so to speak.

Dexter had proven to be an anomaly, albeit a valuable one, and Jennifer found herself relying on him more and more. He had managed to provide her with a lot of useful information about all of the principals in the case, but she sensed that he was holding something back. She hoped it was only his methods and sources that he was keeping secret, because that was something that she really *did not want* to know about.

"...Of course it's only an informal offer," she was saying, "which leaves the door open for a lot of negotiation, so all in all, it's not a bad starting place if it comes to that."

"No!" Eli's full attention had returned to the room, "I'm not going to plead guilty to something I didn't do! At least not the way they're telling it! If I had not hit that man, I believe he would have shot me. Everything he had done since he came in my door made me believe that. If I had not hit him, I'd be dead now."

"I know, Eli! I know," Jennifer assured him appeasingly, "I believe in you one-hundred percent! But I also need to help you to understand that if we go to trial, and we lose, then you may be facing a much harsher sentence than this."

"Well, I guess that's the chance I have to take. No matter what happens, I still have to live with myself. And I won't be able to do that if I cave in. Simple as that."

Eli's jaw was set and he glared at both of them obstinately.

"Before you start doing that rock-paper-scissors thing," Dexter broke in, "Maybe you should just take a step back and try to be patient for a while longer."

"Patient for what?" Eli asked impudently, "Seems like what I need is a miracle. You got one of those in your hat?"

"Matter of fact...I might," Dexter smiled that enigmatic smile again, ignoring Eli's impertinence.

"So are you going to tell me what it is?"

"Nope. Not till I'm sure. It's a foolish idea to show the pieces of a puzzle until they're fitted together and you can see what the picture actually is."

18

Two days later, on Friday evening, Dexter was already seated with a tonic and lime in front of him at the bar in The Mountain Vista Tavern amidst the noise and bustle of happy hour, when Jolene came in the front door. He had tailed her for the last couple of weeks and was familiar with all of her routines, such as coming to this bar after work on Fridays. For the past two Fridays she had sat by herself at the same stool nursing a tall tequila sunrise, until some guy approached her and offered to buy her a drink. She had left the bar with the first Friday's admirer, but last week she had accepted a few drinks and then blown the guy off – figuratively. Tonight Dexter figured on making his play; it was time to face the predator head-on.

Dexter finished his drink and casually moved down a few stools to the one beside her.

"Hi there, young lady! Would you allow an old man to buy you a drink?"

Jolene glanced his way, and then sat more erect, leaning her head back to get a better look at him, as if she was a bit baffled, and perhaps even more so amused, by what she saw.

"You are a little old for me, don't you think? What are you? Some kind of cradle robber?"

"Nope. Nothing like that. Just a lonely old man looking for someone to talk to."

He seems harmless enough.

"Sure. Why not? As long as you're buying."

"What'll you have?"

She rattled the ice in her glass.

"Oh, I guess another one of these."

"Excuse me, miss!" Dexter called to the bartender making a twirling gesture with a downturned index finger, "Could we please have another round?"

As they were waiting for their drinks, Jolene initiated some small talk; something at which she was very proficient.

"I saw you sitting in here last week, didn't I? You were right over there," she pointed down the bar, "all by yourself."

"Yep. That was me. Trying to hide in plain sight."

Jolene took this as a joke and chuckled a little.

"What have you got to hide from?' she asked a bit coquettishly, "I'll bet you've got, like, six kids and maybe a couple of wives, and that's what you're hiding from."

"Maybe so. Or maybe I was just trying to hide from you!"

Jolene chortled again. She enjoyed this kind of flirting, even with older men. Ever since her teenage experiences she had often more-or-less preferred older men.

Their drinks arrived and Dexter gave the bartender a hundred-dollar bill. She placed his change on the bar in front of him and he left it lying there.

This guy's got some bucks! And he seems pretty easy with it!

Jolene held up her glass and said, "Here's to…what should we drink to?"

"Here's to," Dexter lifted his glass and held it next to hers, "Truth, Justice, and The American Way!"

They clinked and drank.

"I know that one!" Jolene laughed, "That's from Superman!"

Dexter merely smiled at her and sipped his drink.

"So, really! Don't you have a family? A wife? Kids?"

"No, I never married. All I have anymore is a sister. And a nephew. But he is like a son to me!"

"Sounds like he's really special."

"Oh, yeah. He is. I would do anything for him."

"Well, take it from me; he's lucky to have an uncle like you!"

"And I'm lucky to have him." Dexter nodded in agreement.

Giving him an appraising look, Jolene dismissed the subject.

"Say, are you, like, some kind of Indian the way you're dressed and with your braids and all? Or are you just some kind of refugee from Woodstock?"

"I'm about one-half redskin. But you need to see me in better light to be able to tell which half."

This comment caught her in mid-sip and she snortled, "That's a good one! You're funny!"

Dexter pretended to be pleased with her assessment. "I'm glad you think so."

"So, have you lived here all your life?"

"I don't know. My life's not over yet."

Jolene smiled to show that she found his response amusing.

"No, I mean are you, like, a *native* native? Were you born here?"

"I grew up in Polson. Still live there."

"What brings you up this way?"

"Oh, I've just had some business to take care of in the area."

"Well I hope it's the kind of business that makes you richer."

"Yeah! Me too!"

They went on like this for another hour or so through a few more rounds of drinks, until Jolene started feeling the effects of the alcohol.

"I better stop," she protested when Dexter offered to buy yet another round, "I've had too much already, and I better stop and sober up a little before I head home."

"Oh, you don't have to go so soon, do you? It's still early."

"It's been a long day. Hell, it's been a long week! I really ought to go home and get some rest." She stood and picked up her small handbag from the bar.

"Aw, don't go yet! I was really enjoying talking to you!"

"Sorry, big guy, but this is late for me! I really should be going."

Dexter stood also.

"Well, I should walk you to your car, at least," he offered.

"That's not at all necessary. I'm sure I can make it by myself."

"I'm sure you can, too. But I'm old-fashioned; and I just wouldn't feel right about letting a lady leave a bar by herself and walk to her car unescorted. It wouldn't be good manners."

"Well, alright then. But that's all this is," she warned him, "You're just walking me to my car."

In a classic Indian pose he held up his right hand palm out as if to say, "I promise. Honest Injun!"

As they exited the front door the noise of the happy hour died behind them. It was almost nine o'clock but the sun was sill high in the sky, and their feet crunched gravel as she led the way across the parking lot to her red minivan.

She turned toward him saying, ‘Well, thanks for the drinks….” and then stopped abruptly staring incredulously at what was in his right hand. It was already too late to mask her expression, and she knew it was all too obvious that she had recognized the necklace that he held dangling in front of him. But at least she had the presence of mind not to acknowledge it.

“What is this?” She demanded. “And who the hell are you?”

“Oh, I think you know what this is. I know who you stole it from, and I have a witness who saw you throw this in the dumpster at the grocery.”

“Eddie!” She made the logical assumption out loud. “I’ll get even with that asshole.”

“You’ll do no such thing, or the deal is off.” He cautioned her.

“What deal? What are you talking about?”

“We’re going to make a deal, you and me.”

She glared at him warily.

“Oh we are, are we? What makes you think so?”

“Because you have no other choice.”

“You’re full of shit. You are one fucked-up Indian hippie if you think you’re going to get me to make a deal with you!”

“You have to make a deal with me. Unless you want to go to jail.”

“Bullshit! You can’t prove anything.” She continued to bluster but her resolve was already beginning to wane.

“Try me,” he dared.

He seemed very confident and she was beginning to feel trapped, but she continued to question him, looking for some chink in his armor, for some avenue of escape.

“Who the hell are you? You’re not a cop! What’s all this to you?”

“I’m just a guy who is looking for ‘Truth, Justice, and The American Way’. It’s like I said. I’d do anything for my nephew.”

"Your nephew? What the hell has he got to do with this?"

"Eli is my nephew." Dexter answered simply, taking note of the comprehension appearing swiftly in her eyes.

"Oh, I get it!" Jolene was not dumb. She could easily see where this was leading, and she understood that she would have to at least pretend to cut her losses, and see what kind of arrangement he was proposing. "So, what's the deal?"

"Simple! As soon as you take the stand and tell the truth about what happened that night at Eli's house, I'll see that this," again he held up the necklace, "gets returned in such a way that it will appear to have been misplaced all along."

"And if I refuse?"

"Well then, like I said: I'll turn you in and you'll probably do some jail time."

"So, what is it you want me to say?"

"Just the truth. Even you can tell the truth if you want to, can't you?"

"But then I'll go to jail anyway, won't I? For lying."

"You haven't perjured yourself yet. If you're asked why you changed your story, you can just say you were scared at the time, or something. About all they can do to you is charge you with simple assault for stabbing Eli, and I doubt they would bother. And you have my promise that Eli will not file any civil charges. He just wants to be done with it."

"How do I know I can trust you?"

"You don't! But you don't have any choice do you?"

Jolene scowled at him defiantly, but she knew she was beat; and Dexter knew it, too.

"Yeah...alright...whatever!"

⁂

On his drive back to Polson, Dexter passed through the little reservation town of Elmo along the west shore of Flathead Lake. The sun sinking low in the western sky fashioned a shimmering stripe upon the lake that darted to a vanishing point in the mirror image of the Mission Mountains that was replicated upon the placid waters. On his right was the pavilion where next weekend The Standing Arrow Powwow, the annual gathering of the Kootenai Tribe, would be held, featuring dancing, drumming, singing, and stickball competitions attracting contestants from all over the country and Canada. This was to be the event's thirty-third year, and Dexter had not missed a single one.

Checking his cell phone he saw that he had four bars and decided to call Jennifer at home to give her the good news.

"I had a talk with the Sutten girl. She's agreed to come over to our team."

"What do you mean: she agreed?" Jennifer sounded dubious and Dexter laughed at her skepticism.

"Just like the Godfather. I made her an offer she couldn't refuse. It was actually pretty easy to get her to flip."

"Dexter, what the hell are you talking about?"

"She's going to tell the truth in court."

"Dexter, what have you done?" Her disbelieving tone had now turned to one of alarm. "I'm afraid you've done something illegal, something that might get me fined for contempt, or even disbarred. Why in the world would she change her mind?"

"Don't worry. I haven't done anything that can come back to bite us in the ass. All I can tell you is that I had a talk with her, and convinced her to tell the truth in court."

"If that's true, then this is indeed wonderful news, but this sounds suspiciously like witness tampering. Don't you realize that there are such things as ethics?"

"Yes, I do. But ethics only work when both sides are following the same code of honor. And what's more important, to me anyway, is to keep Eli out of jail. Or, to put it another way, Eli is my nephew, but he is also the only son I'll ever have. Are you telling me that if your daughter was in some kind of trouble that you would not be willing to bend some rules to help her, especially if you knew she was falsely accused? You have to understand that I am the only one that this could possibly come back on, and I'm more than willing to take that risk. So, it's better if you don't know any more than what I've told you, and I promise that I would not do anything that would put him or you in any kind of jeopardy, legal or otherwise. So just trust me on this and don't worry."

Jennifer was silent considering this for such a long moment that Dexter wondered if he had lost the connection.

"Are you still there?" he asked.

"Yes, I'm still here. I was just thinking about what you said. I do trust you, Dexter. More than you know. But you play by a different set of rules than I do. I can't just make it up as I go like you do."

"That's a good thing, too! You need to keep up a solid, respectable front, and let me do the dirty work. I can't tell you any more than that. But, like I said, you're just going to have to trust me. I know what I'm doing."

Dexter could hear her sighing over the phone, whether in relief or displeasure he could not tell.

"I guess I don't have any choice at this point. Whatever you've done, it's done. We'll just have to make the best of it."

"Good. I'll call Eli and tell him the good news."

"Okay, but please caution him to keep it to himself. The fewer people who know about this, the better."

"Not to worry! Eli knows how to keep his mouth shut."

19

One week later, on Sunday morning, Eli and Bob launched the pontoon boats at Big Creek Campground on The North Fork of the Flathead River, planning to float down to Blankenship Bridge at the confluence of The Middle Fork where they had left Bob's truck earlier to set up a shuttle. It was about a sixteen-mile float with some Class III sections that Eli felt Bob was ready for. Over the past few weeks they had taken the boats on several easier excursions, and Bob had performed very well. Eli owned two of these Water Skeeter one-man pontoon boats. In reality they were very stable, but, because you sit on an exposed swivel-seat mounted to the frame above the pontoons, there was more danger of falling off of the boat than of capsizing. Safety required a modest level of skill and experience. Montana law required that there be an equal number of life jackets to the number of passengers in any watercraft. Eli thought this was a silly law because it did not require the passengers to actually wear the life jackets, rendering them as ineffectual as an unloaded gun. Regardless, Eli always made sure that he and his clients – Bob in this case – wore them at all times.

The North Fork, which forms the western boundary of Glacier National Park, pours volubly through a narrow basin hemmed by timbered slopes that rise precipitously on both sides of the stream; and it possesses a reputation as one of America's Wild and Scenic rivers. Fiercely protected by every environmentalist group in the country, it is an area that has constantly been fought over by developers and oil interests. In recent years there had been a mountain of controversy over a development on some private land only a few miles north of where Eli and Bob were now preparing to begin their float. It was a large, high-end gated community that was built around a golf course. Boasting extreme exclusivity, lots sold for four-hundred thousand dollars and up, and HOA dues, that included a golf course membership, were twenty-five thousand dollars a year. The average cost of a home in The Glacier Club was five million dollars and a few of the homes had topped twenty million.

Environmental groups had argued that chemicals used on the golf course would leach into the river. The developers had defended themselves with laws that were designed to reinforce the rights of property owners. In the end, big money had won out, and the development was built.

The Glacier Club was also shrouded in mystery. A few years ago, one of the partners in the development had crashed his private plane in the deep waters of Lake MacDonald in Glacier Park. Because the wreckage of the plane had never been recovered, the cause of the crash, and the subsequent death of the pilot, had never been determined.

It was another glorious sunny day; only a few white clouds were strung like bed sheets on a clothesline in the translucent sky above the peaks across the river, and there was a gentle breeze bearing downstream fluttering the cottonwood leaves and promising a slight supplementary source of propulsion at their backs as they drifted with the current.

At the boat-launch they readied their gear and made their final arrangements as the incessantly surging waters kept up a continuous chatter. Clouds of steam rose off the turquoise river in the morning sun and the air was suffused with the ripe smells of humus mixed with the acrid aromas of pine and juniper. Shattered shards of sunlight bounced on the riffles like fragmented gemstones, and fish were hungrily snapping morning mayflies off the robin's-egg blue surface of the water. About thirty yards downstream, a fairly large group of day-tripping tourists stood around waiting as some river guides were putting in order two large rafts, Glacier Raft Company displayed in large lettering on either side of each vessel. Two women - who looked remarkably like sisters - and a teenage boy, all three of them dressed in Hawaiian shirts, Cargo shorts, and designer sandals, were staring pointedly at Eli, and were actually whispering behind their hands to each other.

"Now what do you suppose they're staring at?" Bob had also taken note of their apparent interest.

"They're staring at *me*," Eli commented without pausing in his preparations. "I guess I'm getting used to it. It doesn't seem to bother me so much anymore."

"Maybe they're gawking at you because you're so good-looking," Bob quipped.

"No," Eli responded decisively, "You know as well as I do why they're looking at me. My picture is in the paper at least once a week. I've given up even trying to hide. It's no use. Happens everywhere I go. You've seen it enough yourself, Bob."

"Well, then it's a good thing you've developed a thick skin," Bob assured him.

"Yeah, I suppose. But the good thing is that in a few months everyone will know the truth about what really happened, and this will all be over."

"That's the spirit!" Bob congratulated him.

Eli was thankful that Bob had seen it that way, not in gratitude for his opinion, but for his misinterpretation of what Eli had just said. He had been warned to keep his mouth shut, and he had very nearly blown it.

Just as they were about to set out, the two sisters and the boy walked across the launch-site and approached Eli.

"Excuse me!" One of the women implored solicitously, "We're so terribly sorry to bother you, but we just couldn't help ourselves. We had heard that there were a lot of famous people who live around here, but we never *dreamed* we'd actually get a chance to *meet* one!"

Eli shot them a wary look, but at the same time his confusion must have been apparent. "I'm sorry but I don't know what you're talking about. I'm not famous!"

"Oh!" the other sister exclaimed, "I find that kind of modesty so attractive! Don't you, Louise?"

"Oh, yes!" Her sister agreed, "This is so exciting!"

"Now, wait a minute! Where do you think you know me from? Is it because you've seen my picture in the paper?"

"Well…yessss! In the paper? At the movies? In the tabloids? Magazines! Everywhere!"

"Now, hold on! Who do you think I am?"

"You mean you're not him?" Embarrassment was gradually creeping onto all of their faces.

"Not who?" Eli almost shouted.

"You mean…you're not Keanu Reeves?"

"Keanu Reeves?" Eli repeated in astonishment.

"Well…yeah! Keanu Reeves! The movie star! Aren't you him? Oh, God, this is so embarrassing! Please tell me you're him!"

"No ma'am. I'm not Keanu Reeves. I think he's a lot older than me, and I don't think we look anything alike. I'm sorry to disappoint you." Eli turned his back dismissing them. "C'mon, Bob. Let's get on the river."

They shoved their boats into the water and jumped backwards onto the seats, bobbing away in the flowing current. Bob had a goofy smirk on his face, and

Eli pointed his oar at him and said, “Not a word, Bob. Not one damn word. We’re here to fish!”

Before the current swept them away, Eli glanced once more at the tourist trio on the beach who all three continued to stare at him in dumbfounded disbelief. He then rowed hard for the far side of the river, wanting not only to put some distance between them, but also to separate himself from Bob for a while and provide himself with a moment or two to regain his composure. The vacationers had stirred his emotions, but he was also irritated with himself. He had almost let the secret slip out of his mouth. As instructed by both Dexter and Jennifer, he had not said a word about it to anyone – not Bob, not Stephanie, not even his mother. It had not been easy either, especially yesterday when he had taken Stephanie to meet his mother at the powwow in Elmo. On the drive down along the lakeshore, it had taken all of his reserves to keep from sharing the good news.

Stephanie had confessed that although she had lived her whole life here, she had never before attended a powwow, despite the fact that it was held every year only thirty-something miles from home.

“I’m almost ashamed to admit it,” she acknowledged.

“No reason to be,” Eli assured her, “I would guess that most of the people in Kalispell have never been.”

“Well, anyway, I’m glad we’re going. I’m really excited about it!”

“Me, too!” Eli agreed, “I enjoy it every year.”

They found a parking place alongside a barbwire fence in a pasture next to the powwow grounds. Cars and foot traffic had already trampled most of the tall grass. Permeating the air were the heady aromas of fry bread and Indian tacos. As they approached the pavilion the pounding of drums and the wailing of singers increased in volume to a nearly deafening crescendo, and Stephanie felt her heart begin to race with the forceful, persuasive rhythm. Everywhere she looked there was color. Men and women of all ages moved about dressed in elaborate, vividly feathered and bejeweled costumes, the bells on their feet raising a continuous jingling that was in counterpoint to the pulsating drums, like cymbals and tom-toms. Dancers in the dusty arena, their competition numbers draped on their backs, gyrated in a circle moving counter-clockwise, each with his or her own unique styles, shards of light reflecting off myriad mirrors and shiny beads attached to their outfits, while unintelligible announcements boomed over an echoing PA system. It was chaotic, spirited, and stimulating.

Looking around her, Stephanie saw that there were actually a large number of white people who had come to enjoy the event, and it made her feel a little more at ease, or at least, less out of place. They found Eli's mother and his uncle sitting up in the wooden bleachers along with a pretty middle-aged woman who looked vaguely familiar. Stephanie was sure she had seen her somewhere else, perhaps in a different circumstance.

Before Eli had a chance to say anything, his mother stood up and offered her hand.

"Hello, Stephanie. I'm Dorothy, this is my brother, Dexter, and this is my dear old friend, Doreen Morningstar." She had to shout to be heard above the tumult. "We're so glad you've come. We've heard so much about you, and from what I can see so far every word of it was true."

Dorothy invited Stephanie to sit next to her, and throughout the afternoon she kept up a dialogue patiently answering Stephanie's questions and volunteering explanations of what was going on in front of them and all around.

"These are the Fancy Dancers. It's one of my favorite events. One year when Eli was still in grade school, he took a second place in this event."

Stephanie glanced at Eli and despite his dark complexion she could detect that he was blushing at his mother's praise.

"Is that true, Eli? You had the costume and everything?" she asked, trying to picture Eli dressed in buckskins and feathers.

Before he could reply, his mother answered for him.

"Of course he did! I made it for him myself! In fact I still have it. I'll have to show it to you sometime."

At one point Stephanie asked her, "Could you explain to me why all the dancers move in a circle counter-clockwise?"

Dorothy gave her an impish look – a look that bespoke some basic dissimilarity in their cultures - and proceeded to enlighten her.

"Don't you realize that centuries before white people discovered that the world was not flat, our people were dancing in a circle, counter-clockwise, because," she paused making a point, "that's the way the earth turns?"

Eli sat between Stephanie and Dexter. Although he and Dexter only talked about inconsequential topics, he could tell by the way that his uncle kept placing his hand warmly on his shoulder that he was thinking about their recent fortuitous change of outlook. Nothing needed to be said, and the secret was kept.

Almost immediately after Eli had learned that Dexter had somehow convinced Jolene to tell the truth, he had experienced an almost profound sense of relief. He had found himself smiling more, even laughing, playing with his dog, and actually enjoying himself; and he no longer had dark dreams that clung to him like spider webs throughout the daylight hours.

⁂

Yesterday had been a lot of fun and Stephanie had remarked repeatedly about how much she had enjoyed it, and how much she liked his family, and now Eli's thoughts returned to the present as his boat was tugged into the main current, and he and Bob were borne swiftly downstream. At the bottom of this first set of exhilarating rapids, they beached their boats and caught several nice-size rainbows on small nymphs, gently releasing them into the glacial silt-colored water. After a short while the two guided rafts drifted by, their occupants laughing and screaming with glee and fright, and both Eli and Bob were glad that they would be far downstream for the rest of the day. There was a lot of river traffic this Sunday, and they were strategically trying to avoid most of it.

There were several sets of rapids ahead of them, and a couple of places where the river funneled between two large boulders in a raging torrent. Eli cautioned Bob to let him go first and watch how he gets his boat lined up before proceeding through the chute.

At the first of these, Eli was at the mouth of the trough back-stroking powerfully to keep the nose of his boat pointed with the current, when a red canoe with two occupants, a man and a woman, appeared on his right in his peripheral vision. Eli fought hard to maintain control as the canoe came in sideways in front of him, and was lodged against the two boulders that formed the mouth of the chute. Only with extreme effort was he able to keep his boat from crashing into them, as they pushed vainly with their paddles against the rocks. Getting no results from this method, the man stood up and pushed with his hands against the boulder, capsizing the canoe and tossing them both into the torrent, which swept them away, along with their canoe.

Eli released his boat and shot through right behind them, landing effortlessly in the calmer waters on the other side. The couple appeared to be unhurt, their life jackets keeping them afloat, and other boaters were already coming to their assistance. Eli spun his boat around just in time to see Bob coming through the chute – backwards. It was a testament to the craft's stability that it righted itself and floated easily. Bob heard Eli's laughter and scowled at him in humiliation.

They stopped for lunch at the downstream end of a gravel island in the middle of the river, and although it was a little early in the season they had some success with small hoppers. The fish they caught were generally smaller than those hooked previously on nymphs, but it was exciting to watch them rise for the take.

Bob was standing knee-deep in the water, which was cutting a 'V' around his legs, a bottle of Black Star beer poking out of one of the many pockets of his fly vest. After a few false casts, he lightly laid his dry fly into an eddy, mending his line neatly.

"I sure appreciate you bringing me out here, Eli. I've been needing this for a long time."

Eli was about twenty yards to Bob's left, drifting a #16 Joe's hopper on a foam line.

"No problem. This is exactly what I've been needing, too."

"I hope your girlfriend – Stephanie? Isn't that her name? The girl I met at the park? – I hope she doesn't mind you spending so much time on the river without her."

"Stephanie? She's not really my girlfriend. She's more like…well, I don't know what to call it. We've known each other since we were kids. She's a real nice person, and I like her a lot. We spent the whole day together yesterday, but she's not the kind of person who would say anything if she did mind."

"Neither is my girlfriend! But I've known her for a long time, too, and I can sense her moods. And lately she's been acting like my going fishing is interfering with something, but she won't come right out and say what's on her mind."

Bob looked up and across the river for a moment, and then with an odd look on his face turned to Eli and said, "Women!"

At that moment a large rainbow snapped up Bob's fly, and an instant later Eli had one on, also. Both landed their fish easily and held up their catches to show each other.

"Hey, Keanu!!! That's a nice one!"

"That's a nice one you've got, too! And my name is Eli!"

Bob put on an amused expression as he gently removed the hook from the fish's mouth with the hemostat that he kept clipped to the flap of one of his vest pockets. For the next thirty minutes they busied themselves with catching and releasing fish almost non-stop.

They saw the couple in the red canoe go by, waving to them, apparently no worse for wear, and they both waved back companionably. The rest of the day continued to be productive, and by the time they reached the take-out at Blankenship Bridge in the late afternoon they had both lost count.

There was only a fragment of the orange sunset left reflecting off a few wispy clouds in the darkening sky when Eli pulled up to his cabin. Random was barking excitedly and running in circles in a most peculiar way, and Eli, not yet attuned to his efforts at communication, interpreted this as merely enthusiasm at his arrival. When he entered the cabin, however, he felt an instinctual perception that someone else had been inside recently. Nothing seemed out of place; it was nothing that he could put his finger on, and he thought that maybe his suspicion was only due to Random's strange behavior.

As he was falling asleep that night, pleasantly exhausted from his weekend, he could still feel the drift of the river and the undulating waves beneath him as if his bed was floating merrily, merrily down the stream; he could still hear the coyote wailing of the powwow singers and the steady heartbeat of the drums providing him with an almost euphoric liberation from his torments, an answer to his innermost prayers; and he slept in peaceful dreamless slumber, unaware that the worst was yet to come, the hammer was yet to fall.

20

As she mixed another bourbon ditch, Jolene fully acknowledged that she had been drinking too much lately, but it was the only thing that seemed to dull the anger and frustration she felt. How in the world had she let that old Indian creep maneuver her into a corner like that? Not only that, but somehow that fat-ass Sharla had found the balls to tell her that she had to move out, and the resentment was consuming her! At least Sharla was staying at her mother's until Jolene found a place of her own. A good thing, too! Otherwise Jolene would – well, she wasn't sure what she would do. She was so wrought with hostility that she could not trust herself.

And then there was Eddie! He now had as much on her as she had on him. There was no longer anything she could threaten him with, and at work he treated her just like any other employee, otherwise smugly ignoring her. It all made her feel very powerless and aggravated, and she had no one to vent her anger on.

Bourbon wasn't really her drink, but Cody had left a half-empty bottle here a few nights ago, and it seemed to do the trick. Usually she stopped at The

Mountain Vista on Friday's after work, sat at the bar and bought herself a tequila sunrise or a margarita, and waited to see if some guy would buy her another. But tonight no one had even spoken to her, and she had begun to feel as if she had recently acquired a cloak of invisibility; so she had come home early and poured herself some of Cody's whiskey. It was Labor Day weekend, pretty much the end of summer, and she was spending it alone, unless Cody had not passed out yet and decided to come over and drink with her. Staring at the bottle she wondered if it was half-empty or half-full. *I guess that depends on how much it takes*!

Cody was at least twenty-five years older than she, and had shown no interest in her other than someone to drink with. A few weeks ago he had moved into the trailer next door with his divorced sister, and Jolene, contrary to her principles, had allowed him to visit with her in her home. Whenever he stopped by they had very little to say to each other; he would sit on the couch, and Jolene usually sat in the doily-chair, while they sipped their drinks and watched inane sitcoms – and even more inane commercials - on Sharla's flat screen, each alone with their own private seething.

He was a sad looking man who seemed to be aging rapidly. All she knew about him was that he had gotten involved in some sort of medical marijuana growing operation, and that it had somehow gone to shit, and he had lost everything he had. On top of that, he had been sent to jail for six months, except they had let him out early. But at least he didn't whine about it, and so Jolene didn't mind it when he knocked on her door. She hated whiners! And he always brought a bottle with him, which was both a blessing and a curse. Alcohol added to Jolene's dread of being out of control, but lately she had found it difficult to disallow the numbness that it provided.

So when someone started rapping on the door, Jolene naturally assumed it was Cody, and opened it without looking through the peephole, and then gasped.

Standing in the dim glow of her porch light, wearing blue jeans and a wife-beater, his ropy arms covered in jailhouse tattoos, and a filthy smirk on his mouthful of rotten teeth, was Arnie Simpson.

"Hello, Jolene." he crooned insouciantly. Even through the taste of bourbon in her mouth, she could smell his fetid breath, and she saw something putrid and decaying lurking behind his shifty eyes.

"What the fuck do you want?" She spat at him vehemently.

"Oh, come on, Jolene. It's been a long time. Aren't you even a little bit glad to see me?" His weak mouth draped itself over his almost nonexistent chin.

"No! I'm not! And I want you to leave right now! I don't want to see you!"

"Well…I can't just leave! At least not until we talk some things over."

"I have nothing to discuss with you, Arnie!"

"Don't you even want to hear about your mother?"

"My mother? What about her?"

"Well, I'm not gonna stand out here on the porch and tell you about this, Jolene. You're gonna have to let me come in."

"I don't have to let you do anything!"

"Yes you do, Jolene! That is, if you want to learn what I have to learn ya!"

Jolene hesitated. Maybe it was on account of the angst and frustration she had been having lately, or maybe the effects of the booze - whatever - but, against her better judgment she opened the door wider and stepped back allowing him to enter the house.

"So, what about my mother?" she asked as soon as he was inside.

Arnie spied her drink sitting on the kitchen bar, and crossing the room he picked it up and drained it, grimacing as the alcohol scalded its way down his throat and brought tears to the edges of his eyes.

Jolene had not seen nor heard from her mother in many years, but whatever else, there would always be a fundamental maternal association, regardless of however indifferent she may portray herself to be.

"What about my mother?" Jolene repeated in a voice that demanded an answer.

Arnie burped loudly and a rancid stench slid across the room.

"Sorry, sweetheart, but she's gone."

"Gone? What you mean?"

"I mean dead, honey. Your mama died a few months back."

"How do you know that?"

"I was there. When I was in Deer Lodge we wrote and talked on the phone once in a while, and after they let me out, I went to see her in Billings. She was nearly gone when I got there."

"What killed her?"

"It was the cancer. It was in her lungs and throat and who knows where else. That's what smokin'll do to ya. I'll probably go the same way." He shrugged and then grinned at her mindlessly.

Jolene was surprised at how much the news saddened her. She and her mom had not been close for a long time, but they were once. She remembered being a little girl in the days before Arnie had come to live with them; she remembered her mother taking her to a small park and letting her play on the swing set and the jungle-gym; she remembered feeding bread crumbs to the birds and the buoyant sound of her mother's laughter.

Jolene had an odd feeling - a sense that everything was falling apart and there was nothing she could do to stop it - a buried alive sensation that she was unfamiliar with, and suddenly all she wanted was to be alone.

"Arnie, thanks for letting me know, I guess. But now I think it's time for you to leave."

"Okay. But before I go, I was hoping maybe you could do a little something for me." Arnie offered an odd smile and raised his eyebrows expectantly.

"Like what?" she asked guardedly.

"Oh, you know. I was thinkin' maybe you could…help me out a little bit."

Jolene's brow creased in misperception.

"Help you out? How?"

"You, know! Maybe you could give me a little somethin' to tide me over?" His tone was equally pleading and demanding.

"Arnie, are you really asking me for money?" Jolene questioned with incredulity.

"Well, I don't need much! A couple hunnerd oughtta do it!"

"Ya know, Arnie, you've got a lot of nerve, comin' in here and asking *me* for money. This whole thing started because you stole money from me!"

"I didn't steal your money, Jolene! It was your mother took that money!"

"My mother! What makes you say that?"

"Oh, c'mon, Jolene. Don't you remember that just before we got arrested your mama went and put a down payment on that '97 Capri? Where do you think she got the money?"

"You're a fuckin' liar! She saved that money and kept it hidden from you! I wish I'd of hid my money better! How dare you try to blame my dead mother for what you did, you *mother-fucker*! Get the fuck out of my house!"

Arnie pointed a bony finger at her.

"You're a heartless cunt, Jolene, you know that!"

"I don't give a flyin' fuck what you think, Arnie! So just get the fuck outta here before I call the cops. I'll bet you're violating parole right now just by being here in the first place!" She could tell by the shift of his eyes that she had hit a mark, and she pressed the advantage. "Don't think for a second that I don't mean it! I'm calling 911 if you're not gone in one minute!"

Arnie puffed up his chest and got in her face, his rank breath convincing her to take a step back.

"You know what happens to people like you where I've been, Jolene? Where I've been you can't disrespect people like that without getting' a shank shoved in your gut!"

"Oh, you really scare me, Arnie." Actually, Jolene was beginning to feel apprehensive, but was determined not to show it. "You always were a fuckin' limp-dick coward, except when you were molesting little kids, and I doubt that being behind bars has changed you all that much."

"Yeah, well, I'll be more than happy to show you how much I've changed!" He was shouting at her, spittle flying from his lips, "I survived a dozen years in the slammer! Do you know what that means? Do you know what that does to a guy? Don't fuck with me, you bitch!"

"Alright! That's it! I'm dialing the phone."

Arnie backed off still pointing his finger at her.

"Okay! I'm leaving. But I'll be back before you know it! And you know what I'm gonna do? I'll tell ya what I'm gonna do! I'm gonna smoke your sassy little ass!"

He slammed the door behind him as Jolene continued to yell "*Mother-Fucker*!" at his back. After he left she stomped around the room agitatedly, and then furiously dumped a knick-knack shelf onto the floor shattering a number of Sharla's insipid gewgaws. Crossing to the kitchen she poured herself another drink – in a fresh glass. Even in her unsettled state she had the presence of mind not to drink out of the same glass as Arnie.

When she heard the rapping at her door again her fury boiled over. In a rage she threw the door open screaming, "I warned you, motherfucker. I'm calling the cops on you right now!"

What registered foremost in her mind at that moment was how large the muzzle of the pistol pointed at her seemed to be, and then something punched her hard in the chest, and in the next instant she was lying on her back on the floor, her life leaking out beneath her into the orange and yellow shag carpet.

Gaping in bewilderment at the face of her killer just as her eyes clouded over, her last conscious thought was: I can't believe *he* shot me!

21

When Eli got home from fishing a little before sunset Saturday evening, the Sheriff's Detective showed up so soon that it seemed he must have been waiting somewhere nearby. He arrived in a billowing cloud of dust driving a mid-size white sedan that looked recently washed but already gathering a film of grime. Mid-size himself, and compactly built, the detective got out of the car and walked up to where Eli was standing on the front porch. There was something about the way he carried himself that made him seem much larger and more imposing than he actually was.

"Mr. March, I'm Detective Mick Linnell with the Flathead County Sheriff's Department. I'd like to ask you a few questions if you don't mind."

"What kind of questions?"

Before Linnell could reply, Random came bounding up from the direction of the forest to greet Eli, but when he saw Linnell he came up short, and began backing away slowly, growling softly.

"Is that dog a biter?" Linnell asked, his hand moving toward a canister of pepper spray on his belt.

"I don't know," Eli replied, "I've only had him a couple of months. *I've* never seen him bite anyone, but that doesn't mean he never has."

"Uhm..." Linnell pointed toward the front door, "Do you mind if we talk inside?"

"Uh...okay." Eli opened the door allowing Linnell to enter, but as he was following the detective into the cabin Random pushed past him and then stood beside him protectively.

"Sorry," Eli said, and he had to grab the dog by his collar and practically drag him outside, shutting the door quickly behind him.

"Mr. March," Linnell began, "Could you tell me where you were last night at about 11:30 PM?"

"Uh...here. I was here all night."

"And was anyone here with you? Is there any way you can confirm that?"

Eli hesitated for a moment. "No. I was here alone, except for my dog."

"Unfortunately, your dog can't talk." Detective Linnell pulled a small notebook out of his pocket and consulted it. "Mr. March, you have a Ruger .357 Magnum pistol registered in your name. Do you still have that weapon?"

Eli had no idea what this was about, but at the mention of his gun, his heart began to race.

"Uh...yeah. Why do you want to know? What's this all about?"

"Hopefully, nothing at all. Where is this pistol?"

"It's in my closet. Why do you want to know?"

"Would you show me where it is, please?" Linnell asked, ignoring his question.

"Okay, I guess."

Eli led him into the bedroom and pointed up onto the shelf where he kept his gun.

"It's right up there. On the shelf."

Linnell felt around on top of the shelf amid some clothes and sporting paraphernalia, but other than some boxes of ammunition he came up empty-handed.

"It's not there."

"What! Let me see!"

Eli, who was much taller than Linnell was able to stand on tiptoes and see the top of the shelf. After pulling every item down and looking again, he turned to the detective and said, "I just cleaned it a few days ago! I know it was there!"

Linnell's gut feeling was that Eli was telling the truth, but he thought it best to follow procedure.

"Mr. March, perhaps you'd better come down to my office with me and we'll see if we can clear this up."

Eli, having no idea what was going on, was suddenly very afraid that he was going to end up in jail again.

"I want to call my lawyer!" he demanded, a note of panic in his voice.

"You can make that call as soon as we get there."

"Okay. I'll go with you," he agreed, feeling trapped, "but I'm not answering any more questions without my lawyer."

"Fair enough."

⁂

By the time Sheriff Mike Montgomery managed to get off the phone with Jennifer Lawson he was totally exhausted. It was late Monday afternoon, and she had been haranguing him for two days, but this last call was the worst. He could just refuse to take her calls, but the truth was that he felt just as bad as she did about having to hold the March kid. His instincts told him that March was innocent, but the evidence so far, circumstantial though it may be, was just too compelling. Legally he wasn't allowed to hold March for more than forty-eight hours without charging him, but because of the Labor Day weekend he would not hear from forensics until tomorrow. When the judge had returned his call, he had explained that there was motive – March was already under indictment for allegedly trying to kill Jolene Sutten. There was opportunity – March had no alibi. And there was the fact that Jolene Sutten had been shot with a .357 caliber bullet – a slug had been found in the rear wall of the trailer house - and March could not account for the whereabouts of his own .357 handgun. Judge Walker had put her rubber stamp on holding him in investigative custody for an additional twenty-four hours – long enough to see what turns up initially with the forensic evidence – and Jennifer Lawson was livid.

"Excuse me, Sheriff. You got a minute?" Sergeant Broussard was standing in his office doorway. Apparently, Montgomery had not heard his knock. "I didn't mean to eavesdrop, Sheriff, but your door was open and I…"

"No, that's okay, Rube. C'mon in. What's on your mind?"

"Like I said, sir, I wasn't trying to listen in. Sounds like you were just talking to March's attorney?"

"Yes. I was."

"Well, I just wanted to say that I'm glad you're being tough on this one. March deserves to be in jail. That kid's way out of control. And so is his lawyer. I don't envy you, Sheriff. I wouldn't wish that woman on anybody. She's a pit-bull with lipstick, if you don't mind me sayin' so."

"Well, thanks for your opinion on that. Anything else, Rube?"

"Well, yeah. Sorta. Just thought you might want to know that I spent yesterday afternoon with Scott Deaver. Thought you might want a report on how he's doing."

This was a recognizably feeble attempt at reminding the sheriff that he had not visited Deaver in months, but he refused to take the bait.

"And how is he doing?"

"Better, actually. In fact, he's getting around a little now with the aid of a walker, and he seems grateful that he's finally able fend for himself without any help."

"Well, that's good to hear."

"And, Sheriff, I, uh…well I told him about the murder and the March kid's arrest. Seemed like the right thing to do, I mean, technically, he's still with the department. Not to mentioned how this is connected to him personally. And, you know, it really seemed to upset him. He feels like he failed in his duty; that if he had not allowed March to get the better of him that the Sutten girl would still be alive. He blames himself."

"That's absurd. He's not to blame for what someone else does."

"I know. I told him that very thing. But Deaver refuses to see it that way. He thinks it's because he didn't do his job."

Montgomery's desk phone rang and he picked it up.

"Sheriff, your niece is out here asking to see you. She says it's an emergency."

Sensing a sudden quickening of his pulse, Montgomery sent up a quick, silent prayer that this was not what he feared.

"Okay, Lorna. Send her back. We're about done here."

He put the phone down and looked at Broussard.

"Sorry, Rube, but it seems I have some sort of family crisis. We'll have to finish this later."

"That's okay, Sheriff," Broussard responded backing out of the office, "I'm done, anyway. Thanks for your time."

"Don't mention it." Montgomery said as his favorite niece came walking briskly up to him.

"I have to talk to you," she said indicating his office, "In private."

Montgomery led her inside and shut the door.

"What is it, Stephanie?" he asked fearing the worst. Annie had not been doing well at all this past month, and his heart was in his throat.

"You have to let Eli go!" she pleaded, "He didn't do it. I *know* he didn't!"

Montgomery was both surprised at this outburst, and relieved that this had nothing to do with Annie or any other family member.

"I'm sorry, Stephanie. I know you went to school together and that he's a friend of yours, but there's too much evidence against him."

"What evidence?" She threw up her hands. "How can there be any evidence?"

"Stephanie, please calm down," He gently grasped her shoulders; almost an embrace, "I can't just let him go. A murder has been committed and, like it or not, he's the main suspect."

"Why is *he* the main suspect?" Small drops of moisture appeared at the corners of her eyes.

"There are a lot of reasons that I am not at liberty to discuss. And, besides, he has no alibi. He says he was home alone at the time of the murder."

"That's not true."

"What do you mean, that's not true? Why would he lie about that?"

"Because I was there with him. At his house." Her eyes flared boldly.

Montgomery released her and took a step back.

"What are you saying, Stephanie? Are you trying to tell me that you were with March Friday night at the time of the murder?"

"No, Uncle Mike." She shook her head. "What I'm telling you is that I was there at Eli's house with him all night long."

He stabbed both eyes unwaveringly into hers.

"Stephanie, do you know what perjury is?"

"Of course I do! But I'm not lying." Montgomery recognized that defiant look that his niece wore. He had seen it before. "Eli and I have been seeing each other all summer."

The Sheriff was visibly surprised.

"Oh! I see! Is it serious?"

"It's too soon to know for sure, but I think I've fallen in love with him."

"Well, I would call that serious. Do your parents know about this?"

"Of course not! They wouldn't understand. And I hope you'll be gentleman enough to keep it to yourself."

"So that's why March wouldn't tell us you were with him," the Sheriff suggested.

"Yes. It is. Eli didn't want to embarrass me in front of my family. He would go to jail before he would hurt me in any way. That's just one of the reasons I feel this way about him."

"Well! This certainly changes things. I guess I'll have to order him released right away."

"Oh, thank you, Uncle Mike! Thank you so much!"

"Stephanie, I'll do my best to keep this…relationship…private. But I do have to put it in my report. Hopefully it won't get out, but I can't guarantee that. But, I promise I'll do what I can."

"I understand. Thank you."

⁂

"I suppose this is all over the newspapers, isn't it?" Eli asked as Stephanie was driving him home after being released, "I can only imagine what all the self-righteous vigilante-minded citizens are saying about me now."

"Don't even go there, Eli. It's not worth it!"

"I can't help it. There're some things I haven't told you about. I guess I didn't want to worry you. But I've been getting threatening phone calls with the Caller ID blocked, and sometimes when I don't answer they leave vulgar messages on my voice mail. And a few weeks ago I found a rag doll with a noose around its neck in my mailbox. I know I should just ignore it, but it still kinda freaks me out."

"Have you told anyone about this?"

"Sure! I told my lawyer, and she reported it to the Sheriff's Department, but there's really nothing they can do about it.

"Can't they trace the calls somehow? Or maybe fingerprint your mailbox?"

"I don't know. I suppose they could, but they don't seem to care enough to even try. My lawyer had me file a report on my stolen handgun, and it seemed to me that they were just treating that as something routine and unimportant, or maybe they just plain didn't believe me. But it is important; at least to me it is. It means someone was in my house snooping around. This is rural Montana, for chrissakes! I've never locked my house in my life, and now I have to lock it every day! Not that it would do much good. Living way out where I do, with no neighbors in sight, if someone wanted to get in my house they'd just break a window."

They were on the Hwy 35 Bridge over the Flathead River, and Eli's gaze shifted downstream for a few moments, the mentality of a fisherman, his focus involuntarily drifting just below the shimmering surface of the water. And then an appalling notion transported his attention back to the matter at hand.

"What if…just what if, whoever stole my gun used it to kill Jolene? The detective, Linnell, said that the murder weapon was a .357 and so is my gun!"

"That's pure coincidence, Eli! Whoever stole your gun was probably one of the same creeps who've been calling you and putting weird stuff in your mailbox. You're right to be concerned, but there are lots of .357 handguns around. Even my dad has one! I'd try not to worry about it too much, if I were you. It doesn't do you or anybody else any good for you to fret about it."

"But don't you realize what this really means, Stephanie? Jolene was going to clear my name! And now she's dead! And there's no way she can testify."

"*She* was going to clear your name? What are you talking about?"

"I'm sorry, I couldn't tell you before because my lawyer made me promise to keep it a secret from everyone, even you. But my uncle got something on her, I don't know what, but, whatever it was, he convinced her to tell the truth in court. But what's worse is that she was murdered! And now everyone thinks I did it!"

"Not everyone."

"Maybe not, but enough that I'll never get a fair trial. Don't you see that?"

"No, I don't! I still believe that this will turn out okay. I'm not giving up, and I'm not going to let you give up either. We've got a good thing going on, and I believe it's worth fighting for. So no matter what happens, you know I'll be in your corner."

To Eli, what this meant was that if he went down, they would go down together – fighting. That was at least something to be grateful for. Stephanie was right: it *was* a good thing they had going on, and it gave him courage, and strength. But above all else, it gave him hope. And if he had learned anything at all from this colossal upheaval in his life, any sustaining revelation or deeper philosophical epiphany, it was uncovered in the eye-opening discovery of the immense power of that thing they call love.

When they pulled up to the cabin Random recognized Stephanie's car, and he started barking joyously, leaping involuntarily in excited circles.

"I'll bet he's really hungry. He hasn't been fed for days." Eli felt remorse at having been so self-absorbed that he had forgotten all about the dog.

"Of course he's been fed! I've been staying out here every night." Stephanie informed him.

He turned in the seat and looked at her, his face softening tenderly.

"You're really good to me, Steph."

"Yes, I am. Now come on inside and let me fix you both something good to eat."

22

Sheriff Mike Montgomery had only just entered his office Tuesday morning, when Detective Mick Linnell walked in right behind him.

"Sheriff, we got the first forensics report in this morning, and there's a very interesting, and possibly fortunate coincidence."

"What's that, Mick?" Montgomery inquired.

"Well, Friday night, same night as the murder, patrol picked up a guy hitchhiking out on Highway 93 near the trailer park where the murder happened. He turned out to be an ex-con named Arnold Simpson who was in violation of parole. He'd left Yellowstone County without notifying his parole officer. So, guess whose fingerprints are on a drinking glass found at the murder scene?"

"Why do I have the impression that you're going to tell me it's this Arnold Simpson?"

Linnell dipped his head.

"The one and only! I checked with the his PO; Simpson did fourteen years on a twenty-year beef for child molestation which included sexual intercourse without consent, and also for manufacture of methamphetamines with priors. He was paroled about six weeks ago."

"So how does this play in to the murder?"

"Simpson's common-law wife passed away in Billings two months ago. She was Jolene Sutten's mother."

"The victim in the SIWOC charges was Jolene Sutten." the Sheriff finished for him, nodding his head in comprehension.

"She was fifteen at the time of arrest, but the speculation was that it had been going on since she was about eleven years old." Linnell had an angry, revolted look on his face. "The guy's a regular pedophile."

The Sheriff sat on the corner of his desk and folded his arms.

"Where is Simpson now?"

"He's waiting in the interview room."

"I remember when it was called the 'interrogation' room." Montgomery reflected.

"We don't interrogate suspects anymore." Linnell reminded him. "We 'question' them."

Montgomery stood up.

"Well, then maybe we should go *question* him."

When they entered the room, Simpson was seated at the table, his ropey tattooed forearms stretched out in front of him, his face displaying the wary expression of a cornered animal.

"What's this shit all about? I didn't do nothin' wrong! Why am I getting double-teamed?" His pathetic attempt to appear confidently defiant only added to the obviousness of his apprehension.

Sheriff Montgomery stood against the wall, allowing Linnell, who was seating himself across the table from Simpson, to initiate the interview.

"Mr. Simpson, would you mind telling us where you were last Friday night at about eleven-thirty?" Linnell began.

Arnie's eyes grew wide and he looked down and started picking at his dirty fingernails.

"I don't know nothin' about it!"

"About what, Mr. Simpson?"

"About whatever it is you're askin' about!"

This guy's not the hottest skillet on the stove, thought Montgomery.

"Mr. Simpson" Linnell continued in an even tone, "Your fingerprints were found on a glass at a murder scene at the North Star Trailer Park. What can you tell me about that?"

"Yeah, I was there, but I didn't do it!" His eyes were fearful.

"Didn't do what, Mr. Simpson?"

"I didn't shoot Jolene!"

The Sheriff looked down and covered his mouth with his hand to mask his expression.

"What makes you think she was shot?" asked Linnell.

Arnie stopped and looked back and forth at the two cops, his Adam's apple bobbing up and down. He couldn't conceal the fact that he recognized he'd been trapped. He should have known better than to say another word. At this point he should have asked for a lawyer, but in his weak, dim-witted mind an idiotic impulse overpowered his judgment - a reckless, foolhardy compulsion - and he launched an imprudent effort to talk his way out of this.

"I saw it, but I didn't do it."

"What did you see?"

Arnie hesitated.

"What did you see, Mr. Simpson?" Linnell asked again.

"I just stopped by to tell Jolene that her mama died. That's all! I swear! She offered me something to drink. That's how come my fingerprints were on that glass."

"Let's start at the beginning, if you don't mind. How did you get to the North Star Trailer Park? Did you drive yourself there?"

"No, I didn't have no car. I came in on the bus from Billings, and I hitched a ride out to the trailer park. Jolene's mama gave me the address. Asked me to break it to her gentle."

"Break what to her?"

"When her mama died."

"Do you remember who you hitched a ride with? What he looked like? What kind of car?"

Arnie pretended to concentrate.

"Well, let me see. He was about thirty-five or so. I think he wore glasses, but maybe not. Just a guy! I think it was a black car, but maybe it was blue. It was dark. I don't know."

"Did you have any kind of conversation? What did he say? Anything about himself?"

"Naw! He just talked about the election, ya know. Who oughtta win, and so on. But I didn't know nuthin about any of it. So I didn't say anything much at all."

Linnell could not help but sigh in frustration.

"Okay, Mr. Simpson. What happened when you got to Ms. Sutten's trailer?"

"Well, when she answered the door, you know, she seemed kinda surprised to see me, but then she invited me in and fixed me somethin' to drink, so, like I said, that's how come you found my fingerprints. Anyway, I tole her about her mama, and she cried for a while, and so on, and then I tole her how sorry I was, and then I said ga'bye and left."

Simpson spread his hands to indicate that that was all there was to it.

"You said you saw something, Mr. Simpson. What did you see?"

"Uh…no, I didn't say that. I didn't see anything. That's all there was."

Sheriff Montgomery was beginning to feel that they were about to lose Simpson's cooperation, and he broke in. "Mr. Simpson? Do you mind if I call you Arnold?"

"No, that's okay. Most people call me Arnie."

"Okay, Arnie. Look…we're just trying to find out what happened," Montgomery said in the most appeasing voice he could muster, recognizing that however involuntary it might be, he was spontaneously falling into the role of 'good cop'. "You haven't been charged with anything. If you saw something that's relevant to this case, it would be in your best interest to speak up. I wouldn't want to have to charge you with withholding evidence in a murder investigation."

Arnie seemed to be weighing this and before he had time to think it through Montgomery spoke again, prompting him. "Tell us what you saw, Arnie."

"Well…it was dark, and I had just walked away from Jolene's place when this car came driving in. I was standing beside a tree a little ways away, and he didn't see me."

"Who didn't see you, Arnie?"

"The guy. The one driving the car. He stopped in front of Jolene's trailer and got out and left the engine running with the headlights on. It looked like he wasn't planning on staying long, so I kinda hung around hoping I could bum a ride when he left."

"Go on."

"Well…he walked up to the door and knocked on it, and when she opened the door he shot her. Just like that!"

"One shot?"

"Yeah, just once. Real quick like, he turned and walked back to his car."

"What did he do with the gun?"

"I don't know. I guess he took it with him."

"And what were you doing while this was happening?"

"Well, I really didn't want him to see me 'cause he might shoot me too, so I hid behind the tree until he drove away."

"What did this man look like, Arnie?" Linnell asked him.

Simpson looked down, studying his tattoos.

"I couldn't see him real good. It was dark. Maybe he was a kinda big guy, I think. I don't know, I was scared, man!"

"What did the car look like? Did you think to get a license plate number?" Montgomery continued.

"No! Like I said, I was scared shitless. I don't know what kind of car it was! Just a car! I've been in the can so long they all look the same to me, anyway."

"Was it a big car, or a small car?"

"Well…it wasn't a car, really…it was a pickup truck."

"A pickup truck? I thought you said it was a car!"

"Well, a pickup truck's a car, ain't it? You *drive* it!"

Montgomery took a deep breath and let it out slowly.

"So why did you call it a car? Why didn't you call it a pickup?"

"I don't know…maybe it was because it had one of those toppers, ya know! It made it look kinda like a big car."

"Did you happen to notice what make it was? Ford? Chevy?"

"No, man. I couldn't tell."

"Okay, then, what color was this pickup truck?"

"I don't know. Like I keep tellin ya, it was dark. I couldn't see too good. But it musta been a dark color. Black, maybe, or dark brown. Somethin like that."

"Was it an old pickup, or was it a newer model?"

“Uh…I guess it was kinda newish.”

“Was there anything else that you noticed about this pickup? Anything unusual?”

Arnie shut his eyes and twisted his lips around in a pantomime of profound examination.

“Oh yeah! I remember somethin’! It had like four headlights instead of two, like most cars.”

“Four headlights?”

“Yeah! There was these normal size ones, and below them there were these smaller ones.”

“Do you mean fog lights?”

“Yeah! Yeah! That’s what they’re called: fog lights!” Arnie pointed an index finger in the air as if recalling another oddity, “There was sumthin’ else, too. It made a loud clacky noise.”

“Do you mean like a diesel engine?”

“Yeah, that’s it!”

Linnell exchanged a dubious look with Montgomery, as if to say ‘well that pretty much describes half of the pickups in the state’, and then broke in with a question of his own.

“Okay, Mr. Simpson. Let me see if I’ve got this straight. You saw this dark colored, late model diesel pickup pull up to Jolene Sutten’s house, and a big man got out, left the engine running, and walked up to Ms. Sutten’s door. He knocked on the door and when she answered it he shot her once, then he walked back to his pickup, got in, and drove off. Is that correct?”

“Yeah, that’s pretty much what happened.”

“And all this time you were hiding behind a tree?”

“Yeah, that’s right.”

“So then what did you do?”

“I did what anyone would do! I got the hell out of there! People had heard the shot, and lights were comin’ on everywhere, so I ran out to the highway and tried to hitch a ride back to town. Just my luck that one of your patrol cars turned out to be my ride.”

Montgomery looked at Linnell and they silently agreed that this was going nowhere.

"Okay, Arnie. That's all for now. I'll have the deputy take you back to your cell."

"So…are we cool on this? I told you everything I know!" Simpson's voice contained a note of hope.

"We appreciate your cooperation, Mr. Simpson." Montgomery said noncommittally.

After the detention officer led Simpson away, Linnell remarked, "What a crock of shit! I've heard some far-fetched stories in my time, but, quite frankly, this one's a champ. He was just making this shit up as he went along! The only grain of truth in the whole thing is the part about hitchhiking back to town."

"I'm not so sure." Montgomery said shaking his head.

"Oh, c'mon, Sheriff! You're not going to tell me you believe that song and dance, are you?"

"I don't know. Who would make up a story that lame?"

"The guy's a moron, Mike. That's about all the explanation you need. It seems pretty likely that he did it."

"Where did he get the gun? And where is it now?"

"Guns aren't hard to come by in this state. You know that. He probably got rid of it. Threw it in the river or something. On the other hand, it might turn up; and if it does we'll probably be able to connect it to him. It's still early. We'll have to wait and see what transpires when we get the rest of the forensics report. But my money's on Simpson. I think he's our man."

"What about the gun that was stolen from March? Do you think there's a connection?"

"I really don't." Linnell shook his head, "I think the fact that they're of the same caliber is just a coincidence. With March himself in the clear, there's absolutely nothing else to tie them together; no evidence that Simpson even knew March."

"Well, I guess about all we can do at this point is just wait and see what else pops up."

The Sheriff started to walk back to his office, but then turned around and came back to where Linnell was standing.

"What about when you questioned the neighbors? Was there anything that might corroborate Simpson's story?"

"Not really. The guy that lives next door heard the shot, but he says he didn't see anything. He's a paroled con himself, so anything he says would have to be qualified anyway. None of the other neighbors admit to hearing or seeing anything unusual at all." Linnell answered dismissing any hope of an eyewitness, "But, I mean it, Mike, my gut tells me Simpson killed her. He had motive, and he even admits to being there. I think he was just trying to bullshit his way out of this. Just give me a little time, Mike. I'll find something else to connect him to this."

"Well, Mick, even if he lawyers-up, with the parole violation we won't have any problem getting his PO to allow us to hold on to him while we investigate this. Let me know if there are any new developments."

"You got it!"

23

Eli quickly discovered that there was at least one positive outcome from this recent turn of events. Public interest had shifted. His case was suddenly old news, and all of the rumors flying about were centered on Arnold Simpson and the murder of Jolene Sutten. For the first time in months, Eli was no longer the main subject of gossip in Flathead County.

Of primary concern was that it was now mid-September. The trial was barely a month away, and from where he stood his chances didn't look so hot. Without Jolene's testimony, it seemed his goose was cooked. Over-cooked, for that matter!

For the past few months Eli had been on an emotional rollercoaster, and it had been so tiring, so arduous, that he felt like he was a hundred years old. Only a few weeks ago he was under the delusion that his troubles were nearly over, but that was then and this was now, and now he could see no way out. It would be just his word against Deaver's. Who would the jury believe: Him or a crippled cop? Him or a public servant stricken down in the course of performing his sworn duty, his oath, his obligation to the community? What chance did he have?

His lawyer kept reassuring him that they still had excellent prospects for an acquittal. In addition to the witness she had coming from Spokane, there were others who had agreed to step up and tell about the abuse they had suffered at the hands of the deputy, Scott Deaver. But, in truth, every one of them had gone to jail for one thing or another, and no complaints of brutality against Deaver had ever been filed. Eli couldn't help but wonder what good their testimonies might do. He knew that if he were on the jury he would merely see these witnesses as a handful of malcontents, and not give their statements much credence.

Jennifer had also informed him that Deaver's records showed more arrests employing 'necessary force' than any other officer in the department. Eli could see where this might be of assistance in pleading his case, but, to him, it was likewise inconclusive. Even so, Eli steadfastly refused to accept a plea agreement. He could not under any circumstances allow himself to plead guilty to something he did not do.

It was late Thursday afternoon. Eli was out on his front porch just winding down after a day of work, scorching a venison steak over a red-hot fire on the charcoal grill, when, through the haze of dust suspended in the slanting sunbeams streaking between the tree trunks, he was pleased to see his uncle's pickup turning off Foothill Road into his driveway. Before the vehicle came to a stop, Eli had pulled another steak from the freezer and was putting it on the grill. Random stood by watching expectantly, but when he saw Dexter emerge from the pickup, he wagged his tail blissfully in greeting and sauntered over to be petted.

Dexter settled into one of the bent-willow chairs that they had built together, and Eli handed him a cold bottle of Black Star beer from the cooler. He took a sip of the offered beer and then rested the bottle on his knee saying nothing for a long time; just staring through lidded eyes out at the fading light, possibly dozing.

Dexter was a gifted man in many ways, not the least of which was an almost Shakespearean quality of always being able to view the world around him, and the lives of the people in it, as one colossal comic tragedy. He seemed to perpetually wear a secretive smile – no more than a slight upturn at the corners of his mouth – an implication that perhaps he had discerned some universal truths that remained concealed from the rest of us, or obscured at best.

Finally, he took another lazy sip and remarked matter-of-factly, "Well, it looks like they indicted that Arnold Simpson."

"Yeah, I know. It was in the paper."

"I don't know what they think they've got on him, but my guess is that it's all circumstantial. I doubt they have any indisputable evidence."

Eli shot him a look.

"Why do you say that?"

"Cause it's too neat and tidy." Dexter eyes were still fixed intently upon the now darkening forest. "Something tells me that it's more complicated than that."

"Like what?"

"I don't know. It's just a feeling. There's something missing. Just because you find a spider web, it doesn't prove which spider spun it. I keep casting about for sign, and now and then I feel like I'm looking right at it, but can't quite see what it is."

"That makes no sense at all, Dex."

"It's not supposed to make sense. Sense is for sensible people. You'll never find anything new if you always follow the sensible path."

Eli could think of no reply to this, so they sat quietly for a while, companionably, savoring their beers while the steaks sizzled, and watched the darkness descend, each exploring his own private thoughts.

If he had any hope at all, any expectation that this could still work out, Eli recognized the answer lay with his uncle. It was Dexter who had somehow gotten Jolene to change sides, and if he could manage that, he could most likely come up with something equally redeeming. If anyone could save him now, it was Dex. In all of their wanderings in the wilderness, his uncle had never gotten them lost. Dexter would find a way. It may take them over some rocky ground, or through some thorny brush, they may have to wade across some deep, fast flowing streams, but he would eventually lead them safely to the other side. Knowing this helped to set Eli's mind at ease and his thoughts turned to other things.

"Dex, how come you never married?" Eli had never asked this question before, had always accepted that that was just the way it was. Dexter had always been a bachelor. But now, especially in light of what his personal future might, or might not hold, he wondered why a man would choose to spend his life alone.

He could just barely make out Dexter's diminutive smile in the fading light.

"I don't really know. When my father died, it felt like it was up to me to take care of my mother and my sister. Then you came along. I guess that was about all the responsibility I could handle. Besides, I've always liked the ladies a little too much. Seems like all I ever really wanted was to bed them, not wed them."

"What about Doreen? She's really nice, and even at her age she's one of the prettiest women I've ever seen. I may not have your well-defined instincts, but even I can see there's some history there."

"Oh yeah, there sure is! Doreen and I go way back to when we were just kids." His smile acquired a wistful aspect. "Perhaps she should have been the one."

"So, why not now? It's not too late!"

"No, I guess not. But maybe there's a little too much history. Too much water over the dam, under the bridge, whatever. It would never work, and we'd just end up making each other unhappy. It's better this way."

"Don't you think you're being a little close-minded?"

"Maybe so. I used to try to be more open-minded, but my brains kept spilling out."

Eli pulled the steaks from the grill and they went inside. He added a couple of spoonfuls of beans to their plates from a pot simmering on the stove. Random was being somewhat annoying begging for meat scraps, so Eli filled a bowl with dog food and put him back outside to eat. Opening a couple of fresh beers, they sat at the table and tucked in.

"Sorry, I don't have a salad. I wasn't expecting company."

"That's okay. This is just perfect." Dexter replied between bites. "So, what about you and Stephanie? Is this serious?"

The question was so abrupt, so out of left field, and yet so precisely mirrored his thoughts, that Eli had difficulty formulating a reply.

"Yes and no…or, whatever. I don't know. We haven't really called it a relationship. Just the beginnings of a good thing. I think we're both a little afraid to make a commitment at this time. You know…until we see how it turns out."

"Commitment has a way of sneaking up on you when you least expect it. The question is whether you accept it or run from it."

Strangely, this was what kept echoing in Eli's mind as he was trying to fall asleep that night after Dexter had gone. Somehow his uncle had left him with the faith that his legal problems would get worked out, maybe not at the trial, but certainly on appeal. Eli had known his uncle all of his life, well enough to know that if Dexter said something was missing, then something *was* missing. It was going to be next to impossible to find an impartial jury, but he knew that Dexter would never give up until he found the elusive answer.

Consequently what kept pinging around his cranium had nothing to do with his upcoming trial. Instead he was wondering what *would* be next with Stephanie. She had most certainly stepped up to the plate where he was concerned, and in doing so she had risked compromising her close relationship with her uncle, the sheriff. There was no doubt now how he felt about her, especially considering what she had done for him, and, for the same reason, no doubt in his mind that she felt the same about him. With the exception of his mother, he had never felt this close to any woman. It was a new feeling, and he was unsure how to proceed. Just as he had explained to Dexter, there had been no declarations or promises made, only a mutual acknowledgement that what they had so far felt good, and a mutual, yet unspoken, agreement that it would advance no further until the outcome of the trial was known.

All things considered, it was a good problem to have; just thinking about it left him with a sensation of warmth, and despite any lingering self-doubt his mind soon quieted, and he found himself yawning, and drifted off to sleep. And he dreamed.

It was the track of an animal he had never seen before. It looked like that of a great cloven-hoofed mammal, but a hoof with long, extended claws, and it frightened him. He followed its hideous imprints cautiously through one of those quiet woodland glades full of ferns that often materialize in low lying areas shrouded in the sinister and ill-omened shadows of a mountain, and he saw where the animal had stopped and gouged great clods of rotting humus from the forest floor, like an earth-moving machine in its unyielding obliteration - its obstinate annihilation - of paradise. Quite unexpectedly, alarmingly, all of the diverse creatures of the forest were suddenly racing past him screeching, bawling, and howling in fear, like a Walt Disney movie gone psycho. Nevertheless he stood his ground, his heart beating fiercely, paralyzed, overwhelmed by terror but preparing to face whatever came, no matter how menacing; convinced that his skillfulness and his weaponry would shield and protect him from the horrifying beast, certain of his power to vanquish the monster before it devoured him.

But it was no living, breathing being that the forest animals fled from, although it did consume everything in its path. Eli smelled it first, and then began choking on the harsh smoke that had suddenly engulfed him, pursued by the flames that were now leaping all around him. And then Random was there, barking wildly, sinking his teeth into Eli's wrist, and pulling him out of bed and across the floor...

The cabin was an inferno, the conflagration had already destroyed the front wall and the place where the door used to be, now gaped openly, the only route to safety. Coughing out his lungs, the intense heat scorching his skin, Eli crawled across the floor, Random urging him on. Crossing what was left of the front porch, Eli momentarily detected the piquant odor of lighter fluid. They made it outside only a few moments before the entire structure gave way. The old cabin had burned to the ground in mere minutes, and along with it everything that Eli owned; every possession, every scrap of memorabilia that had defined and described his life. Gone! He sat in the dirt, his back against a tree, still coughing painfully against the smoke inhalation, and watched in horror and agony as his home - the only home he'd ever known - vanished for all eternity.

By the time the Creston Volunteer Fire Department showed up with their pump trucks there was not much left to extinguish. The only personal items that had survived the fire were his pickup and the few tools and other things he had left in it. Everything else was lost forever.

"Eli? Are you okay?"

Nate Newman, one of Eli's closest neighbors, an aging, but kindly man, approached him, a concerned look furrowing his brow. Eli still sat propped up against the tree, Random nearby whining fretfully. Someone, perhaps one of the firefighters, had draped a blanket over his shoulders, but he had no recollection of it. He tried to answer, but his throat hurt so badly that he could only croak a reply.

"I…think so."

Nate seemed to accept this without further reassurance, and simply stood next to Eli in his checkered robe and slippers staring in shock at the smoking ruins that the firefighters were now picking over.

"I'm an old man…thought I'd seen about everything, but I never seen anything go up so fast," he said shaking his head of tousled gray hair, "Good thing I have to get up a lot at night. I stepped out to take a leak and saw the flames and called it in. Wish I'd of seen it sooner. Might have been able to save *something*."

Eli merely sat there, dazed, saying nothing.

"I'm so sorry, Eli. I truly am. Is there anything I can do for you? Anyone I can call?"

His initial notion was to ask Nate to call Stephanie, but he quickly decided against it. He knew she would come right away, but for other considerations he didn't want her to know about this just yet. He would call her tomorrow. Dexter had driven all the way back to Polson, and although Eli was certain he'd come running as fast as he could, he was reluctant to ask. And his mother had suffered through this with him more than enough.

Finally, he managed to croak out Bob's name and number, and Nate patted him gently on the shoulder and left to go make the call, just as paramedics arrived and started working on the worst of his burns. One of them gave him a cold bottle of water, which he drank gratefully. It was soon determined that, thankfully, none of his injuries was severe enough to warrant a trip to the hospital.

Bob showed up in less than thirty minutes; he must have driven very fast. Jennifer had come with him. After their primary concerns of his physical condition were satisfied, they offered every reassurance that all of his immediate needs would be provided for.

The initial conclusion was that the fire had started in the front of the house, most probably by the barbeque grill containing smoldering coals being overturned, perhaps by the dog sniffing for scraps of meat. This sounded logical, but Eli distinctly remembered smelling the reek of charcoal lighter on the porch as he was crawling out of the burning building. When he told the firemen this they responded that they had found a can of lighter fluid, but that it was empty. *Well of course it was empty, you idiots! Someone poured it out all over my porch. And how dare you try to blame my dog! I wouldn't even be here if that dog had not saved my life!* Eli's conclusion was that the same devious, and perhaps drunken, would-be vigilantes who had been harassing him for weeks had intentionally started the fire.

Jennifer gently counseled him against this train of thought. There was no evidence indicating arson; it was most likely exactly what it appeared to be: a very unfortunate accident. But Eli's conjecture would not be reversed, and it infuriated him to the point that he became determined to fight back, determined to prove his innocence and show these assholes how wrong they had been.

He rode back to Kalispell in the back seat of Jennifer's SUV, the scent of soot and smoke still redolent in his nostrils. Random sat on the seat beside him, two of his paws bandaged from burns he had received while he was trying to drag Eli out of the cabin. Bob turned around in the passenger seat and promised Eli that he and Random could stay in the rental house with him as long as he wanted; and Bob likewise pledged to advance him whatever funds might be required to purchase clothes and other necessities. There were plenty of tools for him to use, so work would continue uninterrupted. Life would go on. We would all get through this together.

Eli was still in a state of shock, in sensory overload. The sight of his cabin burning, the overpowering smoke, the pain and anguish all hovered around him in a haze. He put his arms around his dog and hugged him tightly, burying his face in the dog's fur and gaining a small amount of comfort from the animal's warmth. And he swore a silent oath that if he could somehow found a way out of this mess that his life had become, that from now on whenever he ate steak he would cook one to perfection for Random.

24

"Let us pray."

Except for the slight shuffling noise of packed humanity, the large chapel was silent, adding to the illusion of the expansiveness of the pastor's voice - enhanced by the church's PA system in a nearly acoustically ideal venue. Not unlike, he surmised, what many in the congregation would imagine that the voice of God himself might sound, if he ever chose to make himself audible to mere mortals.

The pastor raised his arms in benediction.

"God is our refuge and strength…a very present help in trouble. Therefore we *will not fear*!" here he paused strategically, not quite but almost theatrically, "Even though the earth be removed, and though the *mountains* be carried into the midst of the sea…Though its *waters* roar and be troubled…Though the *mountains*…shake…with its swelling. Amen."

He paused again, much longer this time, as if to emphasize the poignancy of this passage delivered, as it was, to an assemblage of worshippers that lived their lives surrounded by unimaginably glorious peaks. The response from the congregation was an echoed murmur of 'Amen's'. One and all raised their heads, and the pastor looked over his flock and held them with his benevolent gaze. His tone softened but the amplified volume decreased only slightly.

"We are gathered here this morning to remember the dear and precious life of one of our most beloved sisters. I know that for many of you this is met with very mixed emotions. On the one hand, your hearts are filled with sadness at the loss of such a dearly beloved wife, mother, sister, daughter, neighbor, and life-long friend to our community. A woman the loss of whom can never be measured. A sadness that we can never overcome.

"On the other hand…there is joy! Great joy! It is the joy of knowing that because of the very personal relationship that Anne had with the Lord that she is already in his presence! Everyone here this morning knows that it was always Anne's desire to go home and be with the Lord. Any of you who ever talked to her for even a short while, recognized by her very nature that she understood what Jesus meant when He said, 'Don't let your hearts be troubled'. I think trouble was the last thing on Anne Montgomery's mind…"

Mike Montgomery sitting in the front row, the comforting presence of his mother on his right, and his son, Chad, on his left, began to tune out the pastor's voice, his focus shifting inward toward his own spiraling thoughts. *That preacher never really knew Annie at all!* What was it, just a few months back when Annie had acknowledged her lack of faith? She had said she couldn't just *choose* a belief, that she would need some kind of revelation to make her a believer, and as far as Mike knew, she had never experienced such a spiritual epiphany.

Annie had further confessed that she only came to church because it was "the right thing to do". But then, that was Annie all the way, wasn't it? She always did the right thing, and always encouraged him to do so as well. He only hoped that now that she was gone, he would be able to live up to her expectation.

About the only thing he could think of at the moment that brought him any solace at all, was that her suffering was over; but although he had suffered along with her, through all the doctor visits, hospital stays, chemotherapy, and so on, his own torment was, truthfully, only just beginning. The preacher droned on, and as Mike sat there pretending to be comforted by the words he did not hear, he had a sudden, unbidden visual recollection of a moment nearly thirty-five years ago. It was during his senior year of high school and The Flathead Braves were playing The Whitefish Bulldogs, their local rivals. At half-time the Braves led 7-0, and as Mike came running off the field he caught a glimpse of Annie Richards in her cheerleading outfit just floating back to earth after leaping in the air like a gazelle. At that moment she happened to turn toward him and caught his eye. They were already a couple then, in fact had been for years, and the look she shot his way sent an arrow through his heart, and a hot spear to his loins. Other men talked openly about their multiple experiences with the opposite sex, but Annie Richards was all Mike had ever wanted; the only woman he had ever loved. How could he go on without her?

But somehow he had to! Annie would accept no less. Chad would need him even more now. And his job presented him with an enormous responsibility to his community; he must continue to perform his duties to the best of his abilities. He would have to set his anguish aside for now until he had the time to grieve properly. This is what Annie would want him to do.

But how? Where do you find that kind of strength? Where do you find the will, or even the desire, to carry on? It wasn't supposed to be like this! We were supposed to grow old together, to share our golden years in comfort and joy. Why was this taken from us?

Mike was only fifty-one years old; still a young man by most standards. But what was left for him? Chad would be grown soon, hopefully with a young family of his own; hopefully with the kind of joy he and Annie had had when they were young, just starting out. Even if he won the election next month, his job would only last for four more years. What then? What would he do? Would there be anyone for him to share his time with? At this point, sitting in the church at the funeral of his wife of thirty years, he couldn't even begin to imagine himself with anyone else. How absurd!

Nonetheless, regardless of the yoke of sorrow we carry, life does go on. You never get over it; you merely get through it. And hopefully, eventually some of the weight of that heartache evaporates, and what's left turns out to be somewhat less of a burden.

It's just going to take some time. But how long? How long do I have to go on with this unbearable hurting, this constriction in my throat that makes it excruciating for me to swallow, let alone speak? This sensation that my heart is being savagely torn from my body? How long?

It was with a great effort that Mike drew himself away from this line of thought. This sort of self-pity was exactly what she would be likely to chide him over. It wasn't right. And the most important thing of all was to always try to do the right thing.

⁂

At the graveside service Mike's concentration continued to wander in and out, and he only heard snatches of what was said, freeze-frames of "dust to dust" and "He maketh me to lie down in green pastures". It was a sunny Indian summer day with just a tinge of autumn in the air. He was distracted by a V formation of geese flying high overhead, their honking faint with the distance, additional evidence that a change of season was imminent. The dizzying strain of just trying to keep himself upright was verging on overpowering him. Taking a deep breath he looked north across the valley; not yet October, but Big Mountain had already received a fair powdering of snow on the ski runs.

As the mourners were dispersing at the end of the service, stopping to shake his hand and pat his shoulder, offering what they hoped would be words of comfort and condolence, Mike felt an uneasy presence approaching and turned to see Scott Deaver being pushed in his wheelchair by Ruben Broussard across the close cropped yellowing lawn of the cemetery.

"Sheriff." They both acknowledged.

"Scott. Rube."

"Real sorry about your loss, Sheriff. A great loss to us all."

Deaver spoke for both of them, Broussard nodding his likewise sentiment.

"Thank you. Thank you, both." Mike, still finding speech difficult, more or less garbled his reply.

"Haven't seen much of you lately, Sheriff." It sounded as much an accusation as regret.

"Sorry, Scott. I meant to get by, but there was always something urgent to deal with." *Why did he feel a need to explain?* Deaver had caught him at one of his weakest moments, and seemingly was aware of it.

"Sure, I understand. No problem. You've had your hands fuller than usual, what with the Sutten girl's murder and all, not to mention your wife's illness."

He said there was no problem, but his eyes didn't. True, it had been months since the Sheriff had visited him, but he seemed to be doing reasonably well. Considering the fact that he had been seriously injured and was confined to a wheelchair, he actually looked pretty good. Granted, his legs through the thin material of his cotton slacks appeared to be a little emaciated, somewhat atrophied even, but his upper body looked strong in the way that many crippled people's torsos and arms developed in compensation. In a strange sort of way it made him appear even more menacing than was his characteristic manner before the injury.

It was no secret that the Sheriff had never cared for Scott Deaver. If he had not inherited him with the job, he would never have hired him. He was not

Montgomery's idea of the model patrolman, and on several occasions he had found it necessary to reprimand him.

It was all too glaringly obvious that Broussard had no real liking for Deaver either, but was trying to portray himself as a friend to the 'fallen hero' for purely political reasons. It was likewise evident that Deaver was using Broussard as his minion, someone to fetch things for him, as well as to keep him informed as to what was going on within the department. A match made in heaven!

"At least you caught the guy right away." Deaver went on, "I heard Morton picked him up hitchhiking not twenty minutes after he killed her. Imagine that! What luck, huh?"

Not wanting to extend this unpleasant encounter any longer, Montgomery started to walk away.

"Thanks, Scott, for your understanding. I have to be going now. See you around."

"Wait a minute, Sheriff."

Montgomery paused, attempting patience and restraint, but in reality longing to be on his way.

"What is it, Scott?"

"I just wanted to say…I guess I'll be seeing you real soon. At the trial, I mean." It may have been simply a product of Montgomery's mental state, but for some reason this resonated as a challenge.

"Yes. I suppose so." He replied noncommittally.

"And I wanted to let you know that afterward, when it's all over, I'll be moving on. There's not much left for me here anymore, and my disability pay will barely cover my expenses, so I think I'll go somewhere that's more affordable. Maybe Mexico, even."

"That sounds like a good plan, Scott." The concept of Scott Deaver leaving the country did not distress Montgomery in the least.

He had ridden to the cemetery with his mother and father, and Chad, but as he was about to climb back into the limousine, Stephanie approached him offering a ride.

"I would really like to have some time alone with you, Uncle Mike, if you're up for it that is."

"Sure, Stephanie, I would like that. Let me find Chad and give him my keys so he can drive my car home from the church. I'll be right back."

He was back in five minutes lowering his considerable bulk into the passenger seat of her little blue Subaru.

"So I guess that guy in the wheelchair that you were talking to was the deputy that tried to kill Eli. Am I right?" she inquired as they were pulling through the gates of the cemetery.

"That was Scott Deaver. As to the truth of what happened, that will be decided in court."

"Truth? Does anybody really want the truth? Eli has already been tried and found guilty in the papers, and on the local news, and in all the ridiculous rumors and idiotic gossip that gets kicked around this town like a hacky-sack. They even burned his house down, for Christ sakes! Unless there is some kind of miracle, Eli will never get a fair trial. Anyone on that jury that swears that they have no prior knowledge of this case is a liar. There's no way you could live here and not have seen and heard it all."

Stephanie stopped for a red light at the intersection of Main and Center Street, and turned toward her uncle who sat motionless staring straight ahead, his face a mask. All day he had worn this neutral expression that seemed to say: *I'm not going to let it show! I'm going to hold it inside, keep it hidden away for my eyes only.* They had always been very close, and she was one of the few who knew how to see through his forbearance.

"I'm sorry, Uncle Mike. This must be the worst day of your entire life, and I should not have bothered you with my problems. Please forgive me."

"Nothing to forgive, Stephanie. This trial is important to all of us, in many different ways. Like everything else, it just makes me wonder what Annie would have to say; what she would expect."

The light changed and Stephanie made a left on Center and then a right on 3rd Avenue, and drove into the shady eastside neighborhood, dappled sunlight sorting itself languidly through the changing leaves of the elm and maple trees, flickering sympathetically on Montgomery's face, un-sighting him dreamily.

He opened his eyes as they turned into his driveway. Unbelievably, he must have dozed off. Cars were parked end to end on both sides of the street, and scores of nicely dressed and well-meaning friends and neighbors were arriving bearing flowers and platters of food. Before he got out of the car he reached across the seat and grasped Stephanie's hand, and seized her with his sad eyes.

"It'll be okay, honey. I promise."

She was not sure what he meant exactly. Was he telling her that having all of these people in his house all afternoon would not be too bothersome? Or was he saying that in time he would get past his grief? Or was it something else altogether? She wanted to ask him, but before she could form the words he had risen out of the car and was greeting his guests.

The house was packed with people. Because Mike was Sheriff of Flathead County, he was acquainted with almost everyone involved in city and county governments, along with many of the area's merchants and business people, which resulted in a large number of the well-wishers crowded into his home being just that: mere acquaintances rather than close friends and family; strangers, more or less. And, although his job often required it, Mike had never been comfortable with playing politics, especially at a time like this. He tried to smile, shake hands and remember names, but he failed miserably, and soon found himself seeking refuge and solitude in the cool evening air on the back deck.

He was resting his elbows on the handrail, leaning forward slightly and staring out at the gathering darkness, as his mother approached softly and stood wordlessly next to him in protracted stillness. For longer, if not even more so, than Annie, Lydia Montgomery had always been the most stabilizing influence in Mike's life, his bridge over troubled waters. Volumes of thoughts were exchanged in those moments of quiet; nothing needed to be spoken, for the need for words between them had long ago been refined to irrelevance.

The cool night air turned suddenly chilly and the wind picked up, swirling fallen leaves, and breaking the spell of silence.

"Perhaps we'd better go back inside, Mike," Lydia suggested, "I think your guests are beginning to leave. They'll be wanting to say goodbye."

"Sure, Mom."

She slipped her arm into his and gently led him back into the house.

Several people, women mostly, were in the kitchen cleaning up. With somewhat of a shock Mike noticed that those were Annie's dishes and silverware that they were handling, and not just her everyday tableware, but the good stuff, too. If anything gets damaged, or put away in the wrong place, she's going to be upset, he thought unexpectedly; and then, just as swiftly, he was saddened once again. Nevertheless, he stood by the front door and shook hands and thanked one and all for coming, and was truly grateful for their departure.

25

"Your honor, at this time we'd like to call Deputy Scott Deaver to the stand!"

Eli was sitting next to Jennifer in the same chair at the same table where he had sat during his bail hearing, but he noticed that this time the courtroom was full, the judge was alert, and the bailiff was awake. Dexter, Stephanie, and his mother were all seated on an oak bench on the other side of the rail directly behind him. Bob had come in a little late and was leaning against the wall in the back, not far from the double doors where Sheriff Mike Montgomery stood with folded arms, a somewhat disinterested cast to his eye. But the eyes of the jurors and spectators alike were all on Deputy Deaver in full uniform as another officer wheeled him into the courtroom as if his arms were as useless as his legs.

Kalispell is a pretty small town and does not usually attract the attention of outside media, but this particular trial evidently was still big news. When Eli had arrived at the Justice Center this morning, as on all previous mornings during his trial, in addition to the local media there had been TV vans and reporters from

Missoula and Great Falls, and even as far away as Spokane. Eli flinched every time someone shoved a microphone at his face, as if he were being forced to run a gauntlet like his Indian ancestors had once done to torment prisoners. He had hoped that by now public interest would have waned, but it had been renewed by the unfortunate murder of Jolene, purportedly an act of revenge by her parolee stepfather – unfortunate because Jolene had agreed to tell the truth in court, and, as the saying goes, the truth shall set you free. But beyond that calamitous tragedy, what Eli lamented most was his loss of anonymity. It had cost him the comfort that accompanies being nobody special.

It was the morning of the third day of the trial. The day before there had been a very damaging reading of Jolene's deposition, which Jennifer had disputed fervently, pointing out discrepancies in the forensics reports. Jolene had claimed to be the one who had placed the first 911 call, but her fingerprints were not found on the telephone. Likewise, Eli's prints were not found on her car, although she had alleged that he had tried to enter her car after she had locked it during her escape.

Most of the other witnesses called by the prosecution on the previous days had been experts on one thing or another, and nearly all of their testimonies had been enlightening, but individually not very harmful to the defense. This was about to change.

County Attorney Fred Wilkinson stood by while Deaver was sworn in before asking his first question.

"Officer Deaver," Wilkinson began, "How long have you served with the Flathead County Sheriff's Department?"

"Going on six years," Deaver responded in a prideful manner.

"And before that how long were you with the Kalispell Police Department?"

"Actually, I worked as a private security guard for a year or so before I joined the Sheriff's department."

Deaver replied in the same tone, "Before that I was with The Kalispell Police Department for ten years."

"And where were you employed as a security guard?"

"At The Glacier Club. It's a high-end real estate development up the North Fork."

"Yes, I think we all know what The Glacier Club is." Wilkinson stiffly waved his arm to encompass the entire room, "And before you joined the Kalispell Police Department, what did you do?"

"I was in The United States Army. I served in The Gulf War as a demolition expert."

"So altogether you have served our country and this community – often risking your life - for over twenty years. Is that correct?"

"Just doing my job!" Deaver declared in an uncommon stab at humility.

"Are you married, Officer Deaver?"

"No, I'm not. Marriage didn't work out for me because the job always came first."

Jennifer had learned that the reason Scott Deaver's marriage had not worked out was because he had repeatedly physically abused his wife, who had never reported this abuse because apparently she couldn't see how she would be able to file charges with the same people that he worked and drank with? After the divorce she had continued to be so afraid of him that she had moved away and had her name legally changed, but Jennifer had managed to find her – or rather Dexter had found her. When Jennifer had contacted her she was still so frightened of Deaver in spite of him being handicapped that she had adamantly refused to come back and testify. Without the ex-wife, it would be a pointless pursuit to try to contest this remark.

That was when Wilkinson threw his first low blow.

"In all the time that you have been in law enforcement has a suspect ever attacked you before like the defendant did?"

"Objection!" The question made a vague presumption of guilt and normally Jennifer would not have bothered objecting, but she wanted to score a small point with the jury, a little prod, before Wilkinson went any further with trying to establish Deaver as a model law enforcement officer.

"Sustained. Please rephrase the question."

"Of course, Your Honor. Deputy Deaver, in all the years that you have been in law enforcement, have you ever been attacked by a suspect?"

"Sure! Plenty of times."

"And how did you handle these situations?"

"The same way any other patrolman would! I used whatever force was necessary to subdue the suspect, cuff him, and get him in the back of my car."

"Could you be more specific as to what you mean by 'necessary force'?"

"Sure! Most of us carry a Taser, pepper spray, and a gun - which is only used as a last resort. It's not a pretty world out there, what with the kind of people we have to deal with to keep the rest of the community safe. Sometimes we have no choice but to use these things, especially when someone's welfare is at stake, not to mention our own. It's what we're trained to do."

At this point Jennifer was powerless to disrupt Wilkinson's strategy, and had to sit quietly while he anticipated and attempted to pre-empt her forthcoming cross-examination. *Good luck!* She thought, *I still have a few tricks up my sleeve, and maybe even a rabbit or two to pull out of my hat.*

Wilkinson picked up an evidence bag from a table and carried it over to where Deaver sat.

"Do you recognize this, Deputy?"

"It looks like my flashlight."

"It *is* your flashlight!" Wilkinson made this pronouncement as if it were a startling revelation. "Have you ever been forced to use this flashlight as a defensive weapon before?"

"Sometimes. Maybe it's dark and I already have it in my hand when someone tries to jump me. At a time like that, I wouldn't have time to reach for anything else."

"I see. So, sometimes the choice of defensive weapon is made by the urgency of the situation. Is this correct?"

"Yes. It is. Whatever is most expedient."

"So do you have any particular weapon of choice?"

"No, sir. It all depends on what seems most appropriate at the time."

Jennifer could see that Deaver had been well coached. His answers were too perfect, and she doubted that he was in the habit of using words like 'appropriate' and 'expedient'.

"Officer Deaver, we have already heard testimony from your neurosurgeon, Dr. Santay, that as a result of injuries you received at the home of the defendant on the night of April 7 that you are now unable to walk. Is this truly your current state?"

"As you can see for yourself, I'm pretty much stuck in a wheelchair for the rest of my life." Deaver spread his hands displaying his hopeless situation.

"Dr. Santay also said that you underwent extensive physical therapy. Is this true?"

"It sure is! And it really kicked my…it was pretty rough!"

"And did this therapy help at all?"

"A little! I can get around a little at home now with one of those aluminum walkers like old people use. But I'm not too steady on it."

"Do you have any hope that this condition will improve?"

"Well…there's always hope, I guess. But we've been at it for seven months and that's about as good as I've been able to do. You'd think if I was going to get better then I would have by now!"

"Yes, I would think so." Wilkinson turned meaningfully toward the jury. "Officer Deaver, would you please tell us in your own words exactly what happened on the night of April seventh, at about eleven PM?"

There was complete silence in the courtroom, the clichéd pin-dropping type of silence. Deaver shifted awkwardly in his wheelchair, and it was necessary for him to use his hands to adjust his useless legs. Watching him, Eli, in spite of himself, felt remorse over what had happened, but all regret soon vanished as he listened in mounting incredulity to Deaver's version of the story.

"A little before eleven PM on Friday, April seventh, I was driving north on Foothill Road returning from answering another call in the area, when dispatch reported a non-responsive nine-one-one. This happens all the time, but it has to be investigated, because you can never tell when someone in real need was able to dial the phone, but was unable to speak. As it turned out, the address was only about a quarter mile from my current position, so I took the call.

"It was dark when I arrived at the location, so I grabbed my flashlight. As I was approaching the cabin I could hear the sounds of a struggle from inside, so I knocked on the door, announced my presence and entered the cabin."

"And what did you find upon entering the house?"

"The defendant was on the floor struggling with a young woman, who I later learned was Jolene Sutten, for possession of a large butcher knife. I could see the fear in her eyes, and it was obvious from the way he was after her that he was intent on doing her bodily harm."

"So how did you respond to this emergency?"

"I said something like 'that's enough, buddy' and I grabbed his legs and dragged him away from her. In doing so, I dropped my flashlight, and he somehow was able to get a hold of it. When I saw him do this, I let go of him and reached for my Taser, but before I could bring it to bear, he jumped to his feet and swung the flashlight at me. I saw it coming and tried to duck, but he hit me real hard across the neck and I blacked out. The next thing I remember: I was waking up in the hospital."

Deaver raised both hands in a way that said "that's about it".

"Looking back on it, is there anything you would have done differently?"

"No, sir. I followed procedure. There was no apparent need for backup. It's just one of the many dangers that we face on the job, that we might be hurt, but it's part of what I signed on for. I felt a calling a long time ago to protect and serve, it's just unfortunate the way it turned out."

"Yes, unfortunate in the least! That'll be all Officer Deaver. Thank you for your testimony." Wilkinson nodded toward Jennifer, "Your witness."

Jennifer kept her seat for a while taking notes on a yellow legal pad, purposely ignoring Deaver, intentionally forcing him to wait in livid expectation until Judge Walker finally asked her, "Ms. Lawson, are you ready to question the witness?"

"Yes, Your Honor. More than ready."

Jennifer rose but remained standing behind the defense table. Scott Deaver's rawboned face was set in a perpetual scowl.

"Mr. Deaver," She intentionally refrained from addressing him as 'Officer' or 'Deputy', "In checking your arrest records with the Flathead County Sheriff's Department, it seems that you hold the record! You have used – and I quote – 'necessary force' in more arrests than any other person in the department. How do you explain this?"

"Luck of the draw, I guess!" Deaver was endeavoring to appear insouciant, "That distinction has to go to someone. Just happens to be me."

"Hardly distinguishing, I would say. I wonder if you would care to tell us why you have received that...*distinction*, as you call it, for each of the six years you have been with the department. And while you're at it, maybe you would also like to tell us why you likewise held that record for five straight years with the Kalispell Police Department?"

Deaver lifted his shoulders to demonstrate his indifference to the question.

"Maybe it's because I'm a little more willing to put myself on the front lines than most cops; maybe I'm just more dedicated to protecting the good people of this community." Deaver's smugness demonstrated that he was pleased with his response. He was not a brutal cop; he was a hero. A fallen hero, at that! "I've certainly had to deal with more than my fair share of the bad ones. Maybe that's why I ended up like this."

"Yes, Mr. Deaver, maybe so! Perhaps it is as you so modestly suggest."

Jennifer abruptly redirected her line of questioning.

"You said that on the night of April seventh, when you entered the cabin you found the defendant, Eli March, *attacking* Jolene Sutten with a large butcher knife. Is this correct?"

"That's right. It was obvious that he was trying to do her bodily harm," Deaver repeated himself with a note of defiance in his voice.

"I see. And you also testified that Mr. March picked up your flashlight after you dropped it. Is that what happened?"

"Yeah. I had to get both hands on him to drag him off her before he could stab her." Deaver turned his head and glared accusingly at Eli.

Jennifer studied her notes for a moment wrinkling her forehead confusedly.

"I don't understand something, Mr. Deaver," she said in a way that conveyed her perplexity, "Did Mr. March release the knife and then pick up the flashlight that you had so opportunely dropped, or did he still have the knife in his other hand?"

Apprehension arose abruptly, quickening his pulse as he looked around the courtroom with the stricken face of an animal that suddenly realizes it has been cornered by a clever predator.

"Please answer the question, Mr. Deaver," Jennifer demanded.

"Uh…I, uh…I don't know…uh, he was on top of her with his back to me…so he must have dropped it where I couldn't see, or something…" Deaver's voice trailed off.

If it had been quiet in the courtroom when his testimony began, the silence was now deafening; the kind of frozen stillness that must exist only in the outer reaches of the universe, a gripping, motionless muteness. It was broken by the insignificant click of her heels as Jennifer paced purposefully across the courtroom and positioned herself in front of the jury box. Throughout the trial juror number three, a short balding man who always wore an American flag pin on the lapel of his warm-up jacket, had refused to allow her any eye contact, but she now stood directly in front of him and locked eyes with him as she proceeded in a louder voice, her back to Deaver.

"Which brings us to another question, perhaps the bigger question, Mr. Deaver. If Mr. March truly had a knife in his hand as you have avowed, why would he drop it - a much more lethal weapon - in order to pick up a flashlight?"

She now turned away from juror number three and strode deliberately across the room to stand explicitly facing Deaver from only a few feet away.

"Can you explain this… *anomaly* for me, Mr. Deaver?"

"How do I know?" Deaver's face was reddening and he was beginning to show signs of losing control, "Why does anybody do anything? That's just what happened. He stood up and swung that flashlight at me before I had a chance to protect myself. The last thing I remember is trying to duck and feeling a sharp pain in my neck. I don't know what else happened."

"Oh, come on, Mr. Deaver!" Jennifer exclaimed angrily, "You are a veteran police officer! A trained observer! You must have been keeping your eye on the weapon that my client supposedly had in his hand! So *tell* me, Mr. Deaver, what did Eli March do with this big butcher knife?"

"I told you, I don't know! It all happened too fast!"

"Or perhaps that's not what happened at all! Perhaps my client did not have a knife in his hand for the simple reason that the knife was in the hand of Jolene Sutten. In fact, this was exactly what Ms. Sutten's deposition revealed – that she had grabbed the knife, supposedly as protection. She further testified in this same deposition that Mr. March had wrested the flashlight away from you. Isn't it true, Mr. Deaver, that the reason Eli March had your flashlight in his hand is because he took it away from you to stop you from beating him with it mercilessly?"

"OBJECTION! Your Honor," Wilkinson was practically pleading, "Counsel is being argumentative!"

"Objection overruled!" Judge Walker laconically waved a hand in dismissal, and stared pointedly over the tops of her half-glasses at the side of Deaver's head and observed him glaring menacingly at Jennifer. "I want to hear this. The witness will please answer the question."

Deaver's eyes blazed hotly as his anger boiled over.

"Look at me, lady!' He practically spat the words at Jennifer and pointed both hands down at his legs with a jabbing motion, "Just look at me! You think this is some kind of lie? Well, then let me ask you a question? Which one of us ended up in a goddam wheelchair? Which one of us has to live the rest of his life as a helpless cripple? Do you have any idea what that feels like? Do you? And he's the one who did it to me!"

Deaver stabbed an index finger in Eli's direction.

"That punk over there is the one who put me here; he's the one who's responsible for this, and I won't rest until he's put in prison where he belongs for a very long time! He deserves harsh punishment, and if I could get out of this wheelchair it would be my personal pleasure to show him exactly what I mean by *harsh*!"

Deaver shouted these last few words, as Judge Walker rapped her gavel and called for order. "Mr. Wilkinson, please restrain your witness or I will find him in contempt and have him removed from the courtroom!"

Deaver had finally ended his rant, but he continued to glower at Jennifer with a lowered brow. A Cro-Magnon on wheels.

"Please continue, Ms. Lawson." Judge Walker said after a moment of silence.

But Jennifer simply turned and walked away, her mission accomplished. The jury had just been given a small, but insightful, suggestion as to Deaver's true nature.

"No further questions at this time, Your Honor."

Judge Walker turned to the County Attorney and spoke in a way that implied that she had had just about enough, "Mr. Wilkinson, do you wish to re-examine the witness?"

"Yes, Your Honor, just a couple of questions if you don't mind," Wilkinson replied diffidently as he rose from his chair and went to stand next to Deaver, unceremoniously resting his hand on one of the grips at the back of Deaver's wheelchair.

"Officer Deaver," he began, "Have you ever been dismissed from a position with any police department for reasons of brutality."

"No, sir, I have not!" Deaver responded adamantly, regaining some of his pride and composure.

"Have you ever had any charges of brutality brought against you?"

"No, sir, I have not!"

"And have you ever even been reprimanded by a superior officer for being unnecessarily forceful?"

Deaver's eyes shifted quickly, but uncomfortably, across the faces in the courtroom. "No, sir, I have not!"

"Thank you. No further questions, deputy. I wish I could say that you may now step down. You have my utmost sympathy that that is not possible in this case." Wilkinson turned meaningfully toward Eli. "Thank you for this trying testimony, Officer Deaver. You are…excused."

Sergeant Broussard stepped forward to wheel Deaver from the courtroom, and as they passed the defense table Deaver glanced briefly at Jennifer, shooting her a surreptitious look of unmodified hatred; a swift assurance of retribution, a fleeting promise of payback.

"You may call your next witness, Mr. Wilkinson."

"Your Honor, the prosecution rests."

"Very well! We will break for lunch and meet back here at one-thirty to hear the first witness for the defense."

"That was amazing the way you turned his testimony around! I've never seen anything like that!" Stephanie exclaimed to Jennifer as they all reached for slices of pizza.

"Perhaps," Jennifer replied modestly, "but you never know how a jury is going to react to those kinds of theatrics. There is still the fact that Deaver looks pretty helpless and ruined. That'll earn him a lot of sympathy. Could be that they'll decide that he had every right to be angry."

They were seated in a large booth at Mackenzie River Pizza, a short distance from the courthouse – Jennifer, Bob, Stephanie, Eli, Dexter, and Eli's mother, Dorothy. On the table between them were two large thin-crust pizzas. Everyone seemed to have worked up a ravenous appetite during the morning session - everyone except Eli who sat picking at his meal with a fork, but scarcely transferring any of it to his mouth. As the courtroom was clearing for lunch, Jennifer had informed him that she would be calling him to testify later in the afternoon. Although he truly wanted an opportunity to tell the factual details about what had happened that night, he likewise dreaded having to do so. In preparation for this day, Jennifer had coached him extensively on what specific questions she would ask, and on what likely questions the prosecution would ask, and there was little doubt that the County Attorney would go for his jugular. If Eli did, indeed, want the truth to be known, there was simply no other way to tell it; and for that reason alone he would almost – just almost – rather go to prison than to have to tell a jury of his peers, along with a courtroom full of spectators, not to mention the news media, about his sordid lust for a skank like Jolene.

Over the span of these past months Jennifer had gradually grown to be conscious of how much she had come to value and rely on Dexter's quiet intelligence. In the course of preparing for this trial, he had set up a temporary office in her library, and she had often consulted with him. And so, it seemed only natural to ask for his inferences. "What's your opinion, Dexter? How do you think the jury will see this?"

Dexter sprinkled copious amounts of crushed red pepper on his pizza, then took a bite, chewing thoughtfully.

"I don't know. I know how I would feel if I were on the jury – but I'm not on the jury, and I don't know how to read the tracks of other people thoughts. It's a skill I've never acquired to any great degree."

"Dexter, you're being too cryptic again." *My God that man can be exasperating*, thought Jennifer. "Can't you just answer the question? Was there anything that you heard – or saw, for that matter – that you think is worth commenting on?"

"Not really. Nothing that all the rest of you haven't seen or heard. No, all I got from it was just a nagging feeling!"

"What kind of feeling?"

"It's the same feeling I've had all along. It's like there's something I've missed, like a depression in the leaves on the ground where something has bedded down, or where the grass has been compressed by a passing animal, something hidden in the brush where I can't see it too clearly. But I know it's there. I can feel it! And when I finally track it down, I think it will explain everything."

Something that the others at the table seemed to already accept effortlessly, Jennifer had only lately arrived at: knowing beyond doubt that Dexter's premonitions were legitimate; and so her response merely reflected her own self-doubt.

"Well, for all our sakes, I sure hope you find whatever it is real soon!"

26

After lunch, Eli rode back to the Justice Center with Jennifer so that they could have a few minutes to discuss his case privately.

"This afternoon's testimony will be the most difficult part of the trial," she confided in him, "Somehow, I have to try to impeach a dead witness, and that won't be an easy thing to do, especially considering that she is a murder victim whose killer is in jail awaiting trial. There is already a lot of sympathy for her, and my unfortunate task is to not only destroy her, but also destroy any memory of her."

"But you're only trying to get people to tell the truth, Jennifer!" Eli reassured her.

"I know," she agreed readily, "That's what really sucks about it!"

Once they had all reassembled in the courtroom, Jennifer called her first witness. Steve Watts was a tall thirty-something with a prominent scar over his left eye, and the overdeveloped torso, neck, and arms of a serious weightlifter.

“Mr. Watts,” Jennifer began, “Did you know Jolene Sutten?”

“Yes. I did.”

“And what was the nature of your acquaintance with Ms. Sutten.”

Watts darted his eyes across the courtroom before answering.

“It was sexual.”

“I see. And how did you meet?”

“I met her in a bar. The Mountain Vista.”

“When was this, Mr. Watts?”

“About two years ago.”

“And did you leave the bar together?”

“Yeah. We went to my place. She followed me in her car. I asked if we could go to her place, ‘cause mine was kinda messy, but she said something about a nosy roommate and pretty much insisted that we go to my place.”

“I see. So when you got to your residence did you engage in sex?”

“Well, duh! Why do you think we went there?”

A mild chuckle skittered across the courtroom, and Watts looked up appreciatively, warming to his audience.

“So, when you had finished having sex, did Ms. Sutten stay the night?”

“Nope. She just got in her car and left.”

“And was that the last time you saw her?”

“Oh, no. She came back for more!” Watts flexed his steroid induced muscles, his self-image likewise inflating.

“So how many times altogether did you see Ms. Sutten?”

“I don’t know. It went on for a couple of weeks, at least. Maybe ten times.”

“And how did this…liaison end, Mr. Watts.”

“This what?”

"What brought this sexual relationship with Ms. Sutten to an end? Did you part on pleasant terms?"

"No, I wouldn't call it pleasant!" He pointed to the scar woven above his eyebrow. "She busted my head open!"

A fusion of amusement and astonishment swirled amongst the spectators.

"Mr. Watts, Jolene Sutten weighed a hundred and twenty-five pounds, and none of us can help but notice that you are a large, very well built man! Are you expecting us to believe that a woman of her diminutive stature could overpower a man of your dimensions?"

"Well, I wouldn't exactly call it overpowering. I'm just not the kind of guy that would fight back against a woman. It's not the way I was raised."

"So then, what was the cause of Ms. Sutten 'busting' your head open, as you have so stated?"

"I still don't really know! I was just teasing her about something and she went berserk on me! I told her that if she couldn't calm down then she was gonna have to leave, and she picked up this trophy I won in a bodybuilding contest and threw it at me. I wasn't expecting it, and it hit me right in the head." Watts pointed at his scar turning his head so that everyone in the room could get a good look at it.

"And did you retaliate in any way?"

"No. I was bleeding like a stuck pig and I hung my head over the kitchen sink and pressed a wad of paper towels to the cut. I thought she was going to say she was sorry or something, but she just called me a muth…a bad name, and left. I couldn't get the bleeding stopped, so after a while I covered it up as best I could with some gauze and tape, and drove myself to the emergency room. It took seventeen stitches to close it up!"

"After this encounter did you ever see Jolene Sutten again?

"No, thank God! I didn't want anything else to do with her!"

"Understandably!" Jennifer waited a long moment, allowing the impact of this testimony to have time to be absorbed before she continued her questioning.

"Mr. Watts, was your testimony today solicited?"

"Was it what?"

"Did anyone ask you to come here today and testify?"

"No, I volunteered."

"Why was that, Mr. Watts?"

"Well, needless to say, I've been following this whole thing in the papers and on Facebook and stuff, and I thought maybe I should come here and tell everybody what Jolene was really like. You know, like, maybe Jolene did the same kind of thing to him." Watts dipped his head in Eli's direction.

"Maybe so indeed! Thank you Mr. Watts. No more questions. Your witness."

Wilkinson shot right out of his chair and approached Watts.

"Mr. Watts, are you married?"

"No."

"Have you ever been married?"

"No, I haven't."

"Do you currently have a girlfriend?"

"No."

"But you've had girlfriends?"

"Yeah, sure."

"Would you categorize any of these as serious relationships?"

"Well, sorta. A couple, anyway."

"But none to which you've been committed enough to consider matrimony?"

"No, not really."

"Why not?"

"Just haven't found the right one yet, I guess."

"So, until that right one comes along, you prefer to make do with…casual acquaintances. Is that how you see yourself?"

"Yeah, more or less."

"So, would you describe yourself as the kind of man who is in the habit of picking up women in bars purely for the purpose of sex?"

"Well, why else would you pick up a woman in a bar?"

This observation brought on an eruption of laughter, and even Judge Walker tried to conceal a smile.

"Why, indeed, Mr. Watts!" Wilkinson also was struggling to mask his mirth. "You stated that you and Ms. Sutten had sex ten times over a two week period. That's impressive. Is that accurate?"

"No! What I meant was on ten different nights. We probably had sex more like twenty or thirty times."

The courtroom exploded in uproarious laughter, and Judge Walker was obliged to rap her gavel to quiet them. Watts seemed to be enjoying the commotion precipitated by his comment.

"I *am* impressed!" Wilkinson admitted, "But let's move on to something a little more serious, Mr. Watts. Earlier you testified that Ms. Sutten reacted violently to something you were teasing her about. What exactly was that?"

"It was something personal."

"Something personal? In what way?"

"Objection, Your Honor!" Jennifer rose from her chair, "This is irrelevant."

"You opened this line of questioning Ms. Lawson, so I'm going to allow it," Judge Walker responded, "The witness will please answer the question."

"Well," Watts was visibly trying to find a way to frame his words, "I just made a little joke about something she liked to do in bed. Something that turned her on. I didn't mean nothin' by it. In fact, I thought she would laugh about it. But, instead, she came unglued! Man, she went like totally off the air!"

"Did you file any charges against Ms. Sutten for assaulting you?"

Watts had been leaning forward in his chair, but now he sat back and looked down at his immense hands.

"No, I didn't."

"Why not?"

"I don't know. Didn't even think about it."

"So, when you got to the emergency room, what did you tell them was the cause of your injury?"

"I said I slipped and fell and hit my head on the edge of a table."

"And they believed you?"

"Yeah. Seemed to, anyway!"

"But why did you lie? Why didn't you tell them the truth?"

"Well, I was embarrassed that I let a little bitty thing like her do that to me. I didn't want anyone laughing at me."

"Yes, I can see how some people might find that amusing."

Wilkinson seemed to accept that he had made whatever point it was that he was trying to impress on the jury, and he moved in for the decisive stroke of his cross-examination.

"Mr. Watts. You stated that you would never fight back against a woman; that it would be contrary to your upbringing. But isn't it true that you were once arrested for domestic violence?"

Watts looked at him confusedly.

"What are you talking about?"

Wilkinson walked to the prosecution table and picked up a piece of paper.

"I have here Exhibit twenty-six, a copy of a Kalispell Police report from January first, in O-eight. It says that Steven Watts, that's you, I presume, was arrested on charges of domestic violence. Is this, or is this not you, Mr. Watts?"

Watts fired a very skeptical look at Wilkinson.

"Oh, I get it. I've seen this on TV. You're like holding up a racing form or something. You can't fool me!"

Wilkinson was nonplussed. "Mr. Watts, I assure you this is not a prank."

"Let me see that!"

Wilkinson handed the report to Watts, who read it thoroughly before responding, "This is bullshit!"

"Mr. Watts, I repeat, is that or is that not you?"

"Well, yeah, but…"

"Just answer the question, yes or no. Are you, or are you not, this Steven Watts?"

"Well…yeah."

"Thank you, Mr. Watts. No more questions."

Wilkinson walked back to his table and sat down next to his assistant. He was obviously trying to keep his expression neutral, but was unable to avoid an insinuation of smugness.

"Do you have any more questions for this witness, Ms. Lawson?" Judge Walker inquired.

"Yes, Your Honor, if it pleases the court."

Jennifer rose from her chair giving Wilkinson a look that said 'What a cheap shot!' and strode to the stand and stood in front of Watts facing the jury.

"Mr. Watts, what were the circumstances of this arrest?"

"It was a New Year's Eve party that got out of hand and the cops showed up. I'd had a little too much to drink, and I sorta mouthed off to one of the cops. Told him to get lost. So he cuffed me and took me to jail."

"Were you ever aware that you had been charged with domestic violence?"

"No, I don't remember what the charge was! Or, for that matter, if there was any charges filed."

"And what was the outcome of all of this?"

"They let me go."

"So there never was any violence on your part."

"None whatsoever!"

"Thank you, Mr. Watts."

This time when she passed the County Attorney her look said 'Nice try!'

Judge Walker called for a fifteen-minute break and left the courtroom hastily. When court reconvened Jennifer called Eddie Parelli to the stand. Eddie seemed to have aged ten years since Dexter had questioned him in the parking lot just a few months ago.

"Mr. Parelli, you are an assistant manager at the Treasure State Grocery; is this correct?" Jennifer began.

"Yes it is."

"And in this capacity were you one of Jolene Sutten's supervisors?"

"Yes, I was."

"Was there anything personal about your acquaintance with Ms. Sutten?"

Eddie shifted uneasily in his seat.

"Yes, there was one…incident."

"What kind of incident, Mr. Parelli?"

"A…sexual incident."

"And was there any consequence of this incident."

"Yes, there was. She was sort of blackmailing me."

"She demanded money from you?"

"No, no money."

"Well, what then?"

"She used it to override my authority. To get me to let her do whatever she wanted. And if she didn't get her way, she threatened to tell my wife."

"And did your wife ever find out?"

"Yeah, she did." Eddie affirmed.

"Did Ms. Sutten tell her?"

Eddie shook his head introspectively.

"No, I told her. It didn't matter anymore; our marriage was already over. A couple of months ago she took the kids and moved back to Philadelphia."

"So would you describe Ms. Sutten as being manipulative?"

"Well, I'm certainly no expert, but I would describe her as being a lot worse than that! If you ask me, she was completely off her rocker! I only saw it a few times, but she had this unreasonable temper, I mean like anything could set her off! Anything! It was scary! It's like something wasn't right in her head!"

Jennifer nodded her head as if in agreement, hoping that by now the jury was getting the same idea.

"Mr. Parelli, were you subpoenaed to testify in this trial?"

"No, I was not."

"So why did you willingly agree to be here today?"

Eddie response was preceded by a remorseful sigh.

"I've done so much wrong in my life. I guess I thought that this was a chance for me to do something right for a change. I worked with Jolene for several years. I knew very well what she was like, what she was capable of. And I just felt like it was about time everyone else knew. She was not a good person, and I don't believe that what happened was Mr. March's fault at all. Whatever happened, I believe she either started it or drove him to it."

"Your honor," Wilkinson piped in, "The prosecution moves to strike this last comment from the record. It is entirely speculative."

"Sustained."

This was okay with Jennifer. The jury had heard what she wanted them to hear.

"Thank you, Mr. Parelli. No more questions at this time."

Jennifer sat back down and Judge Walker turned the witness over to the County Attorney. Wilkinson rose slowly to his feet and addressed Eddie from where he stood.

"Mr. Parelli, what exactly was this incident you referred to?" Wilkinson asked intriguingly, walking out from behind the table and approaching the witness as if to show that he was captivated by the mystery.

"Like I said, it was a sexual incident."

"I see! And where did this 'sexual' incident take place?"

"In the store room."

"This is in the back of the Treasure State Grocery?"

"Yeah, that's right."

"So you claim to have been having sex with Ms. Sutten during store hours?"

"Well, we weren't exactly having sex."

"Well then what was it, Mr. Parelli? Was it sex or was it not sex?"

"Well let me put it this way,' Parelli replied in an annoyed manner, "There's a former President of the United States who says it isn't sex, but to me it was definitely sexual."

There was a soft murmur and some light laughter as every person in the courtroom seemed to comprehend this remark, and County Attorney Wilkinson looked completely chagrined and made the obvious decision that there would be nothing to gain by questioning the witness further.

"No more questions, Your Honor."

Gary Greenwald was called next as a character witness, giving Eli a glowing recommendation as an honest, hardworking employee. Gary told how he had had to let Eli go at the request of his clients on account of the bad publicity Eli had received, but that he would be pleased to re-hire him as soon as this was cleared up and Eli's good name was restored. Wilkinson declined to cross-examine.

After Gary, Jennifer called two more witnesses who each briefly told of having seen Jolene on several occasions come to the Mountain Vista Tavern alone and later leave with one man or another. Wilkinson refrained from interrogating either of them, as well.

Over the years Jennifer had come to think of trials as well-rehearsed plays, a stage show that was enacted for the benefit of an audience – the jury – who then decided which of the players had given the more convincing performance. But, as in any live show, often things don't go exactly as planned, and the best performers must demonstrate their level of experience by being adept at adlibbing.

Luke Foster was her next witness. Dressed casually and looking fit and alert, Foster entered the courtroom through the double doors and walked down the wide aisle, passing Scott Deaver who sat in his wheelchair behind the oak partition that separated the spectators from the players in this drama. With a kind expression, Luke compassionately laid a hand on the deputy's shoulder, but Deaver immediately shrugged him off and frowned up at him malignantly. Undaunted, Luke continued on through the double-swinging half doors to the witness stand. As he was being sworn in he looked across the room to where Mayvelle was beaming at him proudly, and he smiled reassuringly back at her. Bob, sitting next to her, gave him a 'thumbs up'.

"Mr. Foster," Jennifer inquired, "You currently live in Spokane, is that correct?"

"Yes, it is."

"But you've been to Kalispell before?"

"Yes, I have."

"When was that?"

"Almost exactly seven years ago."

"Mr. Foster," Jennifer's voice took on a sympathetic nature, "Would you mind telling us what your circumstances were at the time, and how you happened to have come here?"

"No, I don't mind at all," Luke answered matter-of-factly, "I was homeless. I had hopped a train to Whitefish, and then managed to hitch a ride up to

Kalispell. I had heard that there was a camp behind the old Wal-Mart building where people like me were tolerated."

"How long did you stay in that camp?"

"Not very long. A few days."

"Why did you leave?"

"I was arrested."

"What were the charges against you?"

"Trespassing and resisting arrest."

"And were you found guilty of these charges?"

"No, I was not. There was a trial and they let me go."

"So, why were you arrested in the first place?"

"I don't know. I was just walking down the street, minding my own business, enjoying the fall colors, when this police car pulled up beside me. I wasn't doing anything wrong, so I just kept walking. So this officer got out and yelled at me to stop, and when he came up to me he yelled at me again and called me a 'dirt bag'. Then he shoved me off the sidewalk and made me walk over between these two houses, and he told me to put my hands up against the wall of one of them. I did what he told me to do, but then he hit me with his flashlight in my lower back. When I cried out, he hit me again."

"How many times did he hit you, Mr. Foster?"

"I don't know. I wasn't counting. I'm guessing maybe five or six times."

Jennifer's gaze swept the jury box.

"After beating you, what did the officer do?"

"He put handcuffs on me…real tight, and then he made me get in the back of his car and he took me to jail."

"Is that arresting officer in this courtroom today?"

"Yes, he is. He's sitting in that wheelchair right over there by the gates."

Luke didn't point; he didn't have to. All eyes followed his and came to rest on Scott Deaver.

"Thank you, Mr. Foster. Your witness." Jennifer offered.

It seemed that the objective of Wilkinson's cross-examination was not only to discredit Luke Foster as a witness, but also to reduce him as a human being.

"Mr. Foster, are you an alcoholic?" Wilkinson asked bluntly.

"Yes, I am."

"Are you drunk right now?"

"No, I haven't had a drink in well over seven years."

"But you were drunk at the time of your arrest by Officer Deaver, were you not?"

"Yes, I was."

"And at that time how long had you been drinking?"

"For more than thirty years." Luke's response was straightforward, candid and sincere.

"Thirty years!" Wilkinson feigned astonishment, "Did I hear you right? Did you just say that you were drunk for thirty years?"

"Yes, I did."

"And were you also homeless for those thirty years?"

"Yes, I was. I was on the skids most of my life."

"So what changed? What happened that you suddenly became a sober, upstanding citizen again?"

Wilkinson was on a roll; he was so certain that this was all a ruse, that Jennifer had gotten Foster cleaned up for court, that he unexpectedly found himself unprepared for Luke's earnest answer.

"Jesus saved me," he replied simply.

"Jesus?" Wilkinson sputtered.

It was not evident if this was a question or an exclamation, but Luke chose to answer it nonetheless.

"Yes, Jesus came into my heart and made me whole again."

Wilkinson suddenly found himself wading through murky water. Somehow the script had been discarded and he was forced to improvise.

"Did this happen gradually over a long period of time, or was it a sudden transformation?"

"Actually, it was quite sudden. It happened all at once at the moment of my baptism."

"Your baptism?"

"Yes. When I was lifted out of the water, I felt it all wash away." Luke stated simply. "The bitterness, the frustration, the sorrow…all of it! All the years of sleeping in flophouses, or worse, in alleyways and makeshift shelters. All of the filth and self-loathing. All gone! Jesus had given me a new life, and a promise that I could be whoever I wanted to be from that day on."

"I see."

At this point Wilkinson apparently decided that there was nothing to be gained, and perhaps all to be lost, by pursuing this line of questioning any further. The jury had not been vetted on their religious views and he had no idea how they were receiving this, so he returned to the subject of Luke's arrest and alleged beating.

"Mr. Foster, you accused Officer Deaver of having beaten you during your arrest. Did you file any charges against him?"

"No, I didn't?"

"Why not? You claim that he had brutally abused you. Didn't you wish to see him punished for that?"

"I didn't think it would do any good. I was a homeless man. Who would listen to me?"

"In all those drunk and homeless years, were you ever beaten by any other police officer?"

"Sure, lots of times."

"And were you resentful of these beatings?"

"Well, of course. Who wouldn't be?"

"Yes, precisely. Who wouldn't be resentful of a thing like that?" Wilkinson paused here as if contemplating the significance of this. "Isn't it possible,

Mr. Foster, that you are taking advantage of the fact that you can now get even with all of these brutal policemen by taking it out on Officer Deaver, a man who was left defenseless by a violent act that was visited upon him in the course of performing his sworn duty?"

"No, that's not the way it is. That's not why I came here today."

"Then why did you come here today? Why did you travel all the way from Spokane to testify in a trial that really has nothing to do with you?"

"Because Jesus told me to forgive my trespassers. I came to tell Officer Deaver that I forgive him."

"Are you sure it was Jesus who convinced you to testify? I think maybe it was someone else. Tell me something Mr. Foster. Who was your defense attorney in your trial after you were arrested by Officer Deaver?"

"It was Ms. Lawson."

"Ms. Lawson? This Ms. Lawson? The same Ms. Lawson who is defending Eli March in this trial?"

"Yes. That's correct."

"So, are you trying to tell me that you are here along with Ms. Lawson to fulfill some sort of vendetta against Officer Deaver?"

"OBJECTION!"

"Never mind. I withdraw the question."

27

After Luke Foster's testimony, Judge Walker called for another much needed recess - much needed because as her age advanced her bladder control declined, perhaps one of the primary motivations for her determining it was time to retire. She was finding it to be increasingly problematic to move a trial along when she herself had to run to the bathroom every couple of hours.

When court reconvened it was Eli's turn. Jennifer had carefully timed Eli's testimony so that it would take place late in the afternoon just before Judge Walker adjourned court for the day. This would allow the members of the jury to have time to ponder overnight what they had heard and seen, well before Wilkinson would have a chance to question Eli in front of them. This strategy would also provide her with additional time to coach Eli on what the County Attorney might ask and on how he should respond. On the other hand, it would allow Wilkinson more time to prepare for his cross-examination. In her estimation, however, the pros outweighed the cons.

Eli had altered his appearance considerably for his trial. Clean shaven, and wearing a newly purchased coat and tie, he looked more the part of a handsome young attorney than that of a defendant. When he walked to the stand he could sense all eyes upon him and tried to transmit as much dignity as he could convey.

These last several months, this whole experience, had changed Eli profoundly. He was no longer the shy, unassuming, naive young man he had once been; and the senseless loss of his home, rather than leaving him crushed and defeated, had given him a renewed determination to fight back, a sturdy and potent resolve to meet this struggle head on. Adversity builds character. It had forced him to mature, to find within himself strength, courage, wisdom and hope. And in the company of this transformation came a newborn confidence, a visible self-assurance.

Jennifer began by gently taking him through the basic information: his name, age, schooling, and work history. Although she intended most of these queries as mere filler to eat up time, they were likewise designed to establish Eli as a productive member of the community with a clean record; an undeniably solid citizen. After about fifteen minutes of this socializing, she shifted her tempo, picking up the pace, and transferred her line of questioning to the meat of the matter.

"Eli, how and when did you meet Jolene Sutten?"

"Well, it was last March, and - at the risk of sounding like I'm just repeating what everyone else has said this afternoon - I met her on a Friday night at the Mountain Vista Tavern. She was sitting at the bar by herself, and I went over and introduced myself and bought her a drink."

Jennifer was standing next to Eli and together they tried to make eye contact with members of the jury, each of them hoping that the jurists would perceive Eli as being open and honest, innocent even, as he told what he knew to be the simple truth.

"And on that night did you leave the bar together?"

"Yes. We did. I invited her to come over to my house out on Foothill Road, and she accepted. She followed me out there in her car."

"And when you got to your house, what happened next?"

"Well, she came in and looked around and I asked her if she wanted a drink. She said 'sure' and I told her I had beer and red wine. She asked for wine, so I poured her a glass and got a beer for myself."

"Do you recall what you talked about?"

"Honestly, I don't. I think mostly we talked about other people, you know, like who we both knew…that sort of thing…but nothing important, nothing that sticks in my memory."

"Okay, so you were having drinks, and were engaged in some mindless conversation. What happened after that?"

"Well…she put her drink down, and moved in really close…and she kissed me."

"And what happened next?"

"She took my hand and led me to the bedroom."

"Okay, I think we all get the idea, but just to be perfectly clear on this, I need to ask: did you have sex with Jolene Sutten?"

"Yes, I did."

Jennifer paused for a few moments, letting this one squalid fact sink in, irrefutably demonstrating to the jury that they had nothing to hide.

"After this first evening together, did you see more of Ms. Sutten?"

"Yes, quite a lot, actually. A few days later she called and asked if she could stop by. Sometimes she would just show up, as if she couldn't imagine that she wouldn't be welcome. On Fridays we'd meet at the

Mountain Vista after work, but we always ended up back at my place."

"And how long did this go on?"

"About three weeks."

"Eli, would you describe this arrangement that you had with Ms. Sutten, in any way, to be the beginnings of a relationship?"

"No, not at all. It was purely physical. There was never anything said between us about it being anything more than that."

"There were no declarations of love, no promises of fidelity?"

"No, of course not."

"So in your mind, and, as far as you knew, in the mind of Ms. Sutten, there was a mutual understanding that this arrangement was purely for recreational purposes?"

"Objection," Wilkinson piped in, "calls for speculation on the part of the witness."

Judge Walker sustained the objection, but that didn't matter; Jennifer had made her point.

"Eli, you have just sworn to tell us the truth, the whole truth, and nothing but the truth, have you not?"

"Yes, I have."

"Then tell us, Eli, in your own words, exactly what happened on the night of April seventh."

Eli began his narrative in a very straightforward tone, showing little emotion. He told how he and Jolene had met at the Mountain Vista on that Friday night, and had had some drinks and visited with some friends; he related how he had encountered Marcie, a former girlfriend and Rod, her current boyfriend, and in a friendly manner had introduced them both to Jolene; and he further stated that at this point he saw no indication that Jolene was disturbed, or disquieted in any way.

"After the bar, did you both go to your house?"

"Yes. She followed me in her car, just like the other times."

"And what happened when you got there?"

"When she got out of her car, I could tell something was bothering her. It was weird! It was like in the fifteen or twenty minutes it took to drive out to my place, something had happened that totally changed her mood."

"What did she say?"

"Well, nothing at first. She just walked past me into the house, and she wasn't really looking at me; it was just a vibe, I guess. As soon as we got in the house she turned on me and started yelling at me. She was accusing me of still having a relationship with Marcie, which was ridiculous because when would I have had the time? But she was really worked up, and when I asked her to calm down she only got worse, and it was starting to freak me out. I told her that she was way off base, that Marcie and I were just friends, nothing more, and I reminded her that she and I were not in a relationship anyway, that we were just having sex."

"And how did she react to that."

"Well, that was when she really came unglued. She screamed something about how all men were alike and how much she hated them. My friends had warned me that she was hot-tempered, but it really freaked me out just the same! She was standing in the kitchen next to where I had this wooden block with all these different knives in it, and she reached out and grabbed the handle of one of them and pulled it out and stabbed me in the shoulder with it. Lucky for me, she had grabbed one of the smaller knives, and I backed away just in time, so it didn't go in very far, but it hurt like hell, and bled a lot. Mainly it just scared the cra…I was really frightened!"

As Eli continued his account, his voice rose in pitch, his cool demeanor diminishing, and he became more agitated.

"Go on, Eli. What happened next?"

"I asked why she had done that, and I called her a…"

"What? What did you call her?"

"I called her a crazy bitch!"

"And what was her reaction to that?"

"She screamed at me not to dare call her that! And then she threw the little knife on the floor and drew out a larger one and came at me. I was so scared I didn't know what to do, so I grabbed the phone off the wall and dialed 911. But before anyone answered I had to drop the phone and grab her wrists to keep her from stabbing me. I couldn't believe how strong she was! And the knife was pointed right at my chest! It was all I could do to just hold her off!"

"And how long did this struggle go on?"

"Quite a while! She hooked her leg around mine, and we fell to the floor, but somehow I managed to keep ahold of her wrists. At one point she sort of stopped fighting me, and I let go with my right hand and tried to take the knife away from her, but then all of a sudden she went even more berserk. And all the time she kept calling me a muth… a bad name. I was real scared, and I had no doubt that if I let go she was going to stab me again."

"So what finally ended this altercation?"

Eli glanced across the courtroom to where Scott Deaver sat in his wheelchair.

"I heard a car pull up and its headlights came through the front window. I remember hoping that my 911 call had been traced somehow and that maybe this was a cop showing up. Then there was a loud banging on the door and I shouted for him to come in. I was kind of on top of Jolene trying to hold her down, and my back was to the door. I heard the deputy say 'Okay, buddy, that's enough!' and then he grabbed my ankles and pulled me off of her. At this point I was actually feeling kind of relieved because I thought it was all over, but then he started hitting me right in the kidneys with his flashlight. I realized he had made a mistake and I didn't try to fight him at all. I just curled up and tried to cover myself with my arms, and hoped that he would stop when he saw that I was giving up. But he didn't stop; he just kept hitting me. So I turned over and looked up at him and shouted at him to stop, and told him that it was me that called 911."

"And at that point did he stop hitting you?"

"Yes, he did. But he had this real angry look on his face, and he said 'Oh, no, you're not going to get off that easy!' and then he started to raise his arm to hit me again, so I reached up and grabbed the flashlight to try to stop him. When I did that he stepped back and tried to pull the flashlight free, but he pulled me with it and I got to my feet."

"And then what happened?"

"The flashlight slipped out of his hand and then I was holding it. This all happened really fast, and I was about to tell him that it was over, but before I could say anything he reached for his gun."

"And did you believe that he was about to shoot you?"

"Yes, I guess so. All I remember is that I was real scared, and I knew I had to stop him."

"So what did you do?"

"I didn't really think about it; I just swung the flashlight at him. It hit him pretty hard on the side of his neck and he just crumpled! Right then, Jolene ran out the front door and when she got to her car she turned around and made an obscene gesture and yelled at me that I was really screwed now. Then she drove off."

Jennifer paused in her questioning and paced distractedly until she found herself standing in front of the jury box, her eyes once again locked with those of juror number three.

"Please tell us, Eli, what was going on in your head at this point?"

Eli shifted in his seat and looked across the room to where she stood, and he also made an effort at eye contact with the jury.

"I was more afraid than I'd ever been at any other time in my whole life. The deputy was unconscious on the floor, I was bleeding from where Jolene had stabbed me, and my ribs hurt severely from the beating. I remember thinking that Jolene would probably call 911 from her cell phone as soon as she got to a place where she had reception, and there was no way to know what she would tell them, but I seriously doubted that it would be the truth."

"So what did you do?"

"Well, first I checked on the deputy. I couldn't wake him up, but he was breathing okay, and I thought that he had only been knocked unconscious. Honestly, I had no idea how badly he was hurt! But I could see how this would look to the officers when they showed up, and I didn't think they would believe me when I told them what had happened. I was scared and confused, and I didn't really know what to do. So I decided to take off, and hide up in the mountains until I had a better plan. I guess I was hoping that somehow the truth would come out, that maybe one of them, either Jolene or the deputy, would own up to it, and I would be able to come home."

"Yes, I can see where anyone would be frightened and confused in a situation like that." Jennifer's gaze swept the jury box, and then she turned and walked back to where Eli sat. "Earlier you stated that you have been employed in the past as a hunting and fishing guide, so would it be logical to assume that you are adept at wilderness survival?"

"Well, I've spent most of my life in the mountains. I guess I know my way around as well as anyone else."

"So going up into the mountains was not at all intimidating to you, was it? Would you say that you were going to a place where you felt safe? A place of refuge?"

"Yes, I suppose you could call it that."

"So why did you come back and turn yourself in?"

"Well, about a week later I came out down in the Swan near Condon to get some supplies, and I also bought a newspaper. When I had a chance to read it, I found out how badly Deputy Deaver had been injured, and I felt real bad about it. But I also found out that Jolene had done just as I expected and made up a story that wasn't entirely truthful."

"On that same day that you picked up supplies at the store near Condon, as you were headed back up into the mountains there was something that happened. Would you tell us about that, please?"

"Sure. It was raining down below that day, but the rain had stopped and the sun came out, and there was fresh snow up near the divide. I was hiding in the trees and I saw two snowmobiles enter a clearing. One of them went over the top of a rock outcrop, and the other went below it. The first snowmobiler loosened some snow that fell off the edge of the cornice and started a small avalanche that knocked the other snowmobiler off his machine and left him buried face down in the snow."

"So what did you do?"

"Well, I didn't know how long it would take his partner to find him, so I ran over and dug him out."

"Hardly the actions of a dangerous fugitive. You saved his life."

"Maybe, but I think his partner would have gotten him out in time. He rode up just as I got the guy uncovered, but he recognized me, I guess from the pictures in the paper, or from television maybe."

"So then what did you do?"

"I went back up in the mountains and hid out for a while longer, but my Uncle Dexter came up and found me, and we talked it over, and I kept thinking about the whole situation and how hopeless it was. Finally I decided that I had better come on down and tell my side of things, and hope for the best. Otherwise, I was going to be a hunted fugitive for the rest of my life."

"So you turned yourself in voluntarily?"

"Yes, I did."

"You didn't give yourself up because you were cold and starving from living in the wilderness?"

"No, not at all. I've lived off the land for much longer periods of time than that, and during much harsher weather. No, I turned myself in because I am innocent, and I wanted an opportunity to prove it, and to get on with my life."

28

"Yes, Eli you did very well yesterday, but please don't let yourself get too cocky. Wilkinson is no fool, and he's going to come at you with everything he's got."

Jennifer and Eli were seated in a booth in Nickel Charlie's on Idaho Street having an early breakfast and strategy session before court. Eli was pouring syrup on a stack of oversize pancakes. His performance the day before had been very strong and convincing and he was feeling increasingly optimistic, which was good, but Jennifer felt she needed to caution him against becoming overly confident. Wilkinson's cross-examination could be vicious and brutal, and she wanted to make sure that Eli was fully prepared. Having faced Wilkinson in court many times, she was fully aware of what kind of wily tricks he had up his sleeve that he might be likely to employ in order to shake Eli's testimony and to try to discredit him.

"The County Attorney is going to hit you with a lot of rapid questions designed to confuse you – to trip you up in your story. Don't let him control the pace. Take your time before you answer. Count to ten if you have to. This will not only force him to slow down, but it will also give you time to formulate your answers."

"I know, Jennifer. You've told me this a hundred times already."

Eli spoke around a mouthful of pancake, while Jennifer's omelet remained untouched.

"Yes, I have, and I'll tell you a hundred times more if that's what it takes. It's important that you try to stay in control of yourself. Don't let him get to you."

"Don't worry. I won't."

"Good! Other than that, just tell the truth as you have been doing, and everything should be alright."

Jennifer's words of encouragement were not just for Eli, but for herself as well. There was still the inescapable fact of Scott Deaver sitting in his wheelchair in the courtroom every day, wearing his dress uniform, and looking every bit the part of the victim in this tragedy. If Eli did not fare well under Wilkinson's onslaught, Jennifer had only one more card to play. And it was a wild card.

⁂

Just as Jennifer had predicted, it was an onslaught from the very beginning. Wilkinson did not waste any time trying to soften Eli up, but instead he sprang out of his chair like a boxer coming out of his corner, and commenced throwing quick combinations of verbal punches.

"Do all women throw themselves at you as you claim Ms. Sutten did?"

The very first question was one that neither Eli nor Jennifer had anticipated, and it caught Eli completely - and noticeably - off guard. Before he could articulate a reply, Wilkinson pressed his advantage and blind-sided Eli with another unexpected question.

"What about your former girlfriend? Did you also pick her up in a bar?"

Eli stammered an indecipherable response trying to explain how he had met Marcie at a friend's house, but before he could complete his response Wilkinson threw another inquiry at him.

"It sounds like you spend a lot of time in bars! Is this true?"

Jennifer was about to object, but then she recognized that Eli had finally remembered to count to ten. She saw him sit up a little straighter, and he seemed to be allowing himself no expression whatsoever, trying to convey by his manner that none of this was worthy of an answer.

"Thatta boy," she whispered to herself.

Wilkinson, however, instinctively sensed this alteration in the witness, and backed off for a second, changing his tactic by asking a more straightforward question.

"Mr. March, you stated that Deputy Deaver reached for his gun. Did he actually remove his gun from his holster?"

"No, he didn't. I hit him before…"

"Just answer the question, yes or no, Mr. March!"

"Well…no."

"And did he reach with his left hand or his right?"

"His right."

"Your sure?"

"Yes."

"You were facing him at the time. Maybe he was reaching with the hand that was on your right, which would have been his left hand. It's a common mistake. He couldn't have possibly been reaching for his Taser with his left hand, could he?"

"No, I'm absolutely sure he was reaching for his gun with his right hand!"

“Yes, I’m sure you are!” Wilkinson turned his head meaningfully toward the jury, but whatever point he thought he had made was decidedly vague, to say the least, and did not seem to score any points with the jurors, or anyone else in the room for that matter. Undeterred, he walked to the prosecution table, picked up some papers and turned toward the witness stand.

“I have here a list of items that were found in your house, and among them are several empty boxes of ammunition; one of them held bullets for a .357 magnum, and the rest were .30-.30s. Neither of these guns were found in your house, so would it be reasonable to assume that during the time you were a fugitive hiding in the mountains that you had these firearms with you?”

This was one of the questions that Jennifer *had* anticipated, but hoped would not be asked; but there it was and there was no way around it. After much discussion both she and Eli had acknowledged that the only thing to do would be to answer truthfully; that it would be better in any case not to take a chance at being caught in a lie.

“Yes,” Eli admitted, but then quickly added, “I always carry firearms in the wilderness. For my own safety.”

“I see. But in this case you were a fugitive from the law, and you admit that you were armed, so doesn’t that add up to your having been an *armed* fugitive?”

“I suppose some people would see it that way.”

“Yes, Mr. March! I believe they would! Which leads us to the question – if the authorities had caught up to you, would you have used these weapons against them?”

“OBJECTION!” Jennifer burst in, “Your Honor, this situation did not occur, therefore asking what might have happened calls for speculation on the part of the witness.”

Judge Walker peered over her glasses in palpable scrutiny for a moment, then asked both attorneys to approach the bench.

"Mr. Wilkinson, how do you respond to this?" she asked.

"Your Honor, I wasn't asking what the witness thought might have happened, but was merely trying to determine what his intentions had been at the time."

The judge's brow knitted into deep furrows, producing the fleeting aspect of a wizened elf. "That's a pretty good rebuttal, Mr. Wilkinson, but not good enough. Objection sustained."

Without a glance at each other, both advocates returned to their respective corners. Wilkinson stood next to the prosecution table and continued his questioning from there.

"For the last ten years you have held a State of Montana guiding license for both hunting and fishing. Is this true?"

"Yes, it is."

"So then, guns are tools of your trade, are they not?"

"Yes, I guess you could say that."

"How many guns do you have?"

This was another anticipated question and Eli had a ready answer.

"I have six rifles, three handguns, and three shotguns; all of varying calibers and gauges."

Wilkinson tried to look astonished, "My, that's a lot of 'tools' for any trade!"

Eli saw and opening and stepped into it throwing a quick jab of his own.

"I bet you own a lot more law books than that!"

The comment initiated a small current of light laughter rippling through the courtroom, and even the county attorney allowed himself an amused expression.

"Yes, I suppose I do," he conceded, "Mr. March, you stated that you always carry firearms when you go into the wilderness. Does owning all of this weaponry, and being skilled in its use make you feel safer at these times?"

"I have no fear of the wilderness. I grew up in it. But experience has taught me that it's much better to have firearms with you and not need them, than it is to need them and not have them."

With a disbelieving tone Wilkinson asked, "You have absolutely no fear of the wilderness? With all of its dangers? Grizzly bears, mountain lions, being caught out in sudden storms? None of this frightens you?"

"I have a healthy respect for the wilderness, and I have learned how to avoid most dangers, and how best to deal with them when they are unavoidable."

"I see! You sound like a very brave and resourceful person! So tell me Mr. March: How is it that a man such as yourself, over six feet tall, 200 pounds, unafraid to face all of the many dangers of the wilderness, was frightened out of his wits by 110 pound girl?"

Eli was ready for this one also, and parried it easily.

"Because in the wilderness survival depends on knowledge and experience; recognizing the dangers and knowing how to avoid them. What happened with Jolene was out of the blue. It blindsided me. I didn't see it coming."

"Oh come on now, Mr. March. By your own testimony your friends had supposedly warned you about her. If this is so, how could you have not anticipated it?"

"I guess I didn't take them seriously enough."

"No, I guess you didn't! That is…not if that's what really happened! But that's not what really happened, is it, Mr. March?"

"Yes, it…"

"What really happened is that Jolene Sutten was forced to defend herself when you lost your temper after she questioned you about your philandering. Isn't that so?"

"No, it…"

"And it was Jolene Sutten, in fear for her life, who placed the first call to 911. Wasn't it Mr. March?"

"No, it was the other way around!"

"Well, that's just your word against hers," Wilkinson's manner was cloaked in indignation, "How convenient for you that she's not here to defend herself against your accusations."

Jennifer was on her feet in a furious flash.

"OBJECTION!"

Wilkinson turned his head and actually looked down his nose at her.

"Never mind. I withdraw the question. Statement. Whatever."

The statement may have been stricken from the record, but it was not stricken from the impression the image projected upon the minds of the jurors.

"There's some other things that don't quite make sense, Mr. March," Wilkinson continued, "How is it that you fought with a small woman for over twenty minutes, but you were able to overpower – and cripple for life – a trained policeman in a matter of seconds? And after this violence, why didn't you stay put and wait for the authorities? Or, better yet, why didn't you pick up the phone and dial 911 again yourself? There was a seriously wounded man lying on the floor of your house, in dire need of immediate attention. How could you ignore such a thing? Hasn't it occurred to you that if you had made the call…if you had dialed just three numbers…that you would be no worse off than you are right now? Not to mention that you would look a lot less guilty?

"But instead, you armed yourself and ran away like a guilty person would, placing yourself in danger of being shot by your pursuers! None of this makes any sense, Mr. March! How do you explain all of this?"

"I've asked myself these same questions many times, and the only answer I've come up with is that I panicked. I made a bad choice. I made a lot of bad choices, and I wish I'd done it all differently."

"Yes, Mr. March. I bet you do! No further questions, Your Honor."

"Very well," Judge Walker tapped her gavel, "We will recess for lunch and meet back here at 1:30."

29

Sheriff Mike Montgomery was doing something he had never done before; something that would have shocked his wife, not to mention a lot of other people. He was sitting alone at the bar in the Blue Canyon Grill, drinking a beer at 11:45 in the morning. Although he was in plain clothes, officially, he was on duty, and he was in a very public place. But he didn't really care; in fact, he didn't *really* care about a lot of things anymore.

The bartender had placed a lunch menu in front him that offered a variety of hamburgers and salads, but he pushed it aside. He had lost the once renowned prodigious appetite that his mother had often referred to as extraordinary, and the rest of his extended family had agreed was indeed impressive. He had worn plain clothes every day in court for the simple reason that his uniform - that used to swell at its seams - now fit him like an old sack. In the few weeks since Annie had been gone, he had lost over thirty pounds. A formerly sizeable man, he was now scarcely a shadow of his former self.

Almost anyone who might chance to notice him having his beer in the middle of the day would most likely decline to pass judgment; the whole community knew he was grieving. But grieving was one thing, and what Montgomery was doing was another. Annie would have been ashamed of such desolation - such weakness. Annie had been nothing but strong to the very end, and she would have accepted no less from him. For this reason his depression embarrassed him, and he could talk about it to no one, a denial that left him drifting through his daily routines struggling to seem stalwart, but privately disintegrating.

Each day of the trial he had arrived late, and taken up a position standing just inside the double doors of the courtroom. Most of the trial had held little interest for him. Because it concerned an injured deputy, he felt it was his duty to attend, but during most of the testimonies his mind had been on other matters, and he had often been called away to deal with erstwhile obligations. Conversely, however, the testimony of Eli March had captured his complete attention.

March had handled himself very well, only faltering slightly under Wilkinson's near-bullying blitzkrieg. Montgomery had never cared much for Wilkinson, but, by contrast, he liked Eli very much. In fact, he saw Eli as the kind of Montana-born, self-reliant young man that he hoped his son, Chad, might become. Abetted by his foreknowledge of Deaver's character (or lack of), he was certain that March was telling the truth, and it distressed him that there was practically nothing he could do about it. The Sheriff had done his job; he had more-or-less brought the suspect to justice, if that's what you could call this charade. Beyond that his hands were tied. Once the County Attorney's office had taken over, the investigation had been concentrated on conviction. Truth was not an issue. Justice was of little concern to the prosecution.

Nonetheless, in her indomitable bulldog fashion, Jennifer Lawson had managed to drive home many salient, relevant points and several of those sitting on the jury must have acquired at least some uncertainty as to March's culpability. Although he had often butted heads with her, Montgomery, nonetheless, admired and respected Jennifer's determination and tenacity.

At this point – in Montgomery's mind, at least – it was a draw. If the trial ended now, he could see the jury going either way, and maybe that was the best he could hope for, but it wasn't what he wished. Even if it meant that his department was to be discredited, and his chances at re-election diminished, so be it. It didn't really matter anymore. He wanted to see Eli March set free and Deaver publicly shamed, wheelchair or no wheelchair. For that satisfaction, he would gladly go down as well. He didn't really give a damn anymore. Whether he won the election or not was no longer a concern. Annie was gone and that was all that really mattered.

A single tear emerged from the corner of his eye and skated indifferently down his cheek dripping despondently onto the bar like a drop of blood oozing from a wound that refused to heal.

They say that time flies when your having fun, but the reverse is also true, at least from Eli's perspective. His assessment was that the trial was taking forever; the past three-and-a-half days seemed more like three-and-a-half weeks; months maybe. Especially the first couple of days when this and that witness had incessantly droned on and on about all sorts of things that seemed to have no relevance whatsoever to the matter at hand. The only thing that had presented any significant consequence, had been when they had read Jolene's pack of lies. During this time, he had watched the faces of the jurors closely, but had been unable to read anything there. Subsequently, however, Jennifer had managed to show what a liar Jolene had been - what kind of person she had been – and he thought he had seen at least a few lights go on in the jury box.

He had no strong opinion one way or the other about how Deaver's testimony had been received by the jury. Choosing to believe that they had seen through his pack of lies, he was hopeful that they had likewise been shocked by his angry outburst. Then again, maybe, as Jennifer had suggested, they felt he had every right to be angry.

Nonetheless, it was Eli's own testimony that he was most concerned with. After Jennifer had questioned him, he was feeling pretty cocky, actually thinking he had proven his case and won the jury over. But then that Wilkinson guy had come on so strong, and had hit him with so many loaded questions that he was no longer so sure where he stood.

"It's my last answer that bothers me the most. I admitted to having made bad choices, and I'm not sure how the jury will see that. What I should have said…"

"Don't should all over yourself!" Stephanie admonished him.

"What?"

"I said 'don't *should* all over yourself'! What's done is done. You can't change it. You just have to live with it and hope for the best. For what it's worth, I thought you did just fine, Eli."

It was a warm, sunny Indian summer day, and they were sitting on a bench in a little park next to the courthouse, eating ham and cheese sandwiches that Stephanie had prepared that morning, the ground in front of them carpeted in desiccating yellow and red autumn leaves. It was the third season of this ordeal, this tribulation.

"I did okay, I guess. But what if it just wasn't good enough? I know you love me, Steph, but it might be years we're talking about here. I can't ask you to wait that long. It wouldn't be right."

"We'll cross that bridge when we come to it. *If* we come to it! The trial's not over yet. Jennifer still has another witness."

"I don't know who she could possibly call to the stand that would make any difference now."

Jennifer was sitting at her desk. Her mother had left the office for lunch, knowing full well that it was best to leave her daughter alone at times like these and let her work it out on her own. Jennifer was skipping lunch. Ostensibly, she was preparing for the afternoon session - there were several law books open in front of her, but she wasn't looking at them; mostly she was just sitting and thinking, taking a few notes, and trying to get herself mentally ready for her final witness – a witness she had had long, tiring debates with herself about whether to call at all.

She liked to think of herself as a kind, compassionate person, and she hated the idea that she might be taking advantage of another person's fragility. But Eli was her first concern, and all other complications had to come after that. This was war. She must use whatever armament was within reach to defend her client, regardless of her own ideals.

More than one therapist had suggested that the obvious reason she was so driven was because of what had happened to her father - that she was, in essence, defending her father every time she went to court. Of course there was a certain amount of validity to this, but it was not entirely true. She believed that the reason she fought so doggedly was not *because* of her father, but on *behalf* of her father, and in that way she honored and revered his memory. Whenever she was able to prove the innocence of the unjustly accused, her methods, whatever they may have been, were justified, supportable, and she herself felt vindicated. This time would be no different.

When court reconvened at one-thirty, Judge Walker got right to it.

"Ms. Lawson, do you wish to call another witness?"

Jennifer stood up.

"Yes, Your Honor, the defense calls Sheriff Michael Montgomery to the stand."

Sheriff Montgomery, standing in his customary spot just inside the doors of the courtroom, was surprised to hear his name called, but not near as surprised as County Attorney Fred Wilkinson, who jumped to his feet.

"OBJECTION, Your Honor!"

"On what grounds do you object, Mr. Wilkinson?"

"Your Honor, the defense did not list Sheriff Montgomery as a potential defense witness in discovery."

"Ms. Lawson?" Judge Walker peered over her glasses at Jennifer.

"This is true, Your Honor, but the prosecution *did* list him, and this gives the defense a right to call him."

As Jennifer knew, it was a routine practice of the prosecutor to list anyone connected with the trial as a possible witness just in case he might want to call them to add to, or perhaps dispute, a testimony. This also served to force the defense to spend needless hours vetting witnesses that would never be called. However, the sheriff had not been called, so this was not a recall for purposes of cross-examination. It was one of those gray areas that was left up to the judge's discretion, and, thankfully, Jennifer had been accurate in her assumption that the judge would rule in her favor.

"Objection overruled. The witness will take the stand and be sworn in."

All eyes followed Sheriff Montgomery as he walked down the short aisle and through the oak half-gates to the stand and was sworn in. Jennifer found that she was dismayed at how thin and haggard he looked, and she had to brace herself in order to proceed.

"Just for the record," she began, "you are currently Sheriff of Flathead County, is this correct?"

Sheriff Montgomery was a very experienced witness, and he answered her questions succinctly and with brevity. His tone was straightforward and unemotional.

"Yes, it is."

"And for how long have you held this office?"

"For three-and-a-half years."

"And how long have you been with the sheriff's department altogether?"

"Altogether, seventeen years."

"When did you first meet Deputy Scott Deaver?"

The Sheriff shifted in his chair uneasily before answering.

"About five years ago when he first joined the department."

"And what was your position with the department at that time?"

"I was Undersheriff of Flathead County."

"In the capacity of that position, were you privy to Deputy Deaver's background information?"

Montgomery, sensing where this was leading, faltered only a moment before answering. "Yes. I was."

"Were there any red flags in his background? Anything that you felt you had to keep an eye on?"

Jennifer was fishing, but she was quite certain that a lunker lurked in this pool, and, with only another moment's hesitation, Sheriff Montgomery accepted the bait.

"Yes, there was. Deputy Deaver had transferred from the Kalispell Police Department after some informal warnings."

"And what did these informal warnings concern?"

Of course Jennifer knew the answer to this question having studied Deaver's record thoroughly, but she also knew it would have a more profound effect coming from the Sheriff. Before answering the question, Montgomery looked around the courtroom, ultimately letting his eyes lock with those of Scott Deaver.

"Excessive use of force."

A susurrating murmur filtered through the room. Fred Wilkinson started to rise and voice an objection, but Judge Walker waved him down. Deaver scowled.

"Had any formal charges ever been brought against Scott Deaver?"

"No."

"Why not?"

"I can only speculate as to why not. You would have to ask the Kalispell Police Department about that."

"I see. And did you, as Sheriff ever have any issues of this sort with Deputy Deaver?"

Montgomery faltered; the composure that he had previously exhibited seemed to be evaporating. He could feel the eyes of everyone in the courtroom fixed on him; their collective bated breath was palpable. But the presence he felt most, the force that stressed his spirit and strained his soul, echoed from the grave like a resonating refrain: *Do the right thing!*

"Yes. I did."

An audible exhalation, elusive as a lament, fled like a fugitive throughout the room. The cat was out of the bag. In those three words it was all there for all to see. Jennifer was careful to keep her expression neutral as she smiled inwardly. The only thing she had left to do was to nail down a few details, but from this point on it was all over.

"Did this happen more than once?"

"Yes… It did."

"Sheriff Montgomery, am I hearing you correctly? Are you telling us," she waved her hand to include the judge and jury, "that several times you verbally reprimanded Deputy Scott Deaver for repeated use of excessive force, but that you never brought any type of charges against him? No administrative leave? No investigation?"

"That's right."

"Why not?"

"I'm ashamed to admit it, but it was for political reasons. I'm currently running for re-election, and I didn't want any negative publicity. I thought it might endanger my chances. It was my intention to watch Deputy Deaver closely, and wait until after the election to put him on administrative leave, which would begin the procedure of having him eventually dismissed."

"But you didn't watch him closely enough, did you, Sheriff? And as a result, he nearly killed my client, and got himself disabled in the process, didn't he?"

"I couldn't say for sure because I wasn't there, but, yes, I believe that's what happened…and I regret it very much. But…"

Montgomery vacillated, but Jennifer prompted him to continue.

"Go on, Sheriff."

"My biggest regret is that I allowed myself to be blinded by my own personal needs, and I placed them above the needs of the Department. My wife was very ill at the time, and if I lost the job I also lost the health insurance. I had no idea how I would be able to take care of her. It may seem like a poor excuse, but to me it was the most important thing in my life, taking priority over everything else. I hope that all of you, and the whole community can forgive me."

"I hope so, too," Jennifer responded sympathetically, "No more questions, Your Honor."

Wilkinson did not bother to cross-examine. It was all over and he knew it, and he was fully aware that the jury also knew it. But, even so, no one knew the half of it. No one had even begun to glimpse what lie beneath the deceit. No one could fathom the depths to which genuine evil can descend. Although a portion of the truth would soon be revealed, the remainder would be a long time coming.

As Jennifer announced that the defense rests, Deaver wheeled himself angrily from the courtroom.

Wilkinson's closing arguments were brief and predictable. He quickly re-examined the evidence, reiterated a few testimonies, and he went over Deaver's record of public service and his subsequent disability. He almost, but not quite, managed to make it seem as if Deaver had left the courtroom in disgust, rather than disgrace. When he asked the jury to deliver a guilty verdict, it was obvious that he was simply going through the motions. There was no conviction in his voice.

Jennifer's summation was more an indictment of the community than a defense of her client. She spoke for twenty minutes about the way Eli had been hounded by the media, lost his job, treated with contempt almost everywhere he went, and had his house burned to the ground by vindictive vigilantes.

"At the heart of American jurisprudence is the concept that a person is innocent until proven guilty, but Eli March was never given that consideration. He was prejudged by many, and pre-sentenced by a spiteful and malicious few. He was unjustly accused and has been forced to suffer the consequences of the legal system in a small town where rumors are all too often accepted as truth by an otherwise well-meaning citizenry. There is no way to right this wrong. What's done is done. If Eli March had a home left to go home to, I would ask you to please send him there. Nonetheless, he deserves to be set free."

In less than an hour, just enough time for a bathroom break, and perhaps something to drink, the jury returned with not-guilty verdicts on both counts.

30

A few minutes before midnight, a black 2008 F-250 diesel with only its fog lights illuminated, cruised slowly up Woodland Drive and eased to the curb less than a block from Jennifer Lawson's house. The driver turned off the engine and sat for a long time in the darkness behind the pickup's smoked glass windows, his shadowy presence imperceptible to passing cars or any pedestrians who might chance to stroll by at this late hour.

Most of the lights in Jennifer's house were still on, and she was in the solarium fussing with her plants, a glass of red wine cradled in her left hand. After court had adjourned, they had all gone to Scotty's Bar to celebrate over burgers and beer, and had stayed late. Angela was spending the night with Cricket and Nikki; and Bob, Eli, Stephanie, and Doreen were all still at Scotty's. Dexter had been conspicuously absent, and had still not shown up an hour ago when Jennifer had finally succumbed to the rigors of the trial, and had excused herself from the festivities and driven herself home. It had been a long day – a long week – and this was one of her best ways to unwind, alone with the intimacy of her florae, the tart, but mellow taste of merlot sharp on her tongue.

She was glad this trial was over. Even though the outcome had been favorable, she had struggled, nonetheless, with her own personal demons; not the least of which was that she had been obligated to extract a painful public admission from Sheriff Montgomery, a man she truly respected. Rationalizing that it was essential, that it was vital to her case, did not ease the pain she felt at its necessity, and she hoped with all her heart that it would not cause him any further embarrassment, and, especially, that it would not result in the loss of the election. On the other hand, he had seemed to practically welcome her interrogation, almost as if it offered him an opportunity to unburden himself. As he stepped down after his testimony he had actually smiled.

Eli was free. Although he had suffered and lost so much, she was confidant that he would someday realize how much he had gained, as well. Perhaps he did already. Over these past months Jennifer had witnessed Eli's transformation into a man in full, a man to be honored and respected. A man who had earned the love of a very brave, and loyal young woman. She was extremely proud to have represented and guided him, and she was exceedingly pleased that she had been able to help him get his life back on track. This gave her an immense sense of satisfaction. This was the payback. This was why she did what she did.

It was rare that she experienced this level of gratification; it bordered on contentment, which was a sensation that was all but foreign to her. But it didn't have to be! Maybe Eli wasn't the only one who had been transformed; maybe she had undergone a makeover of her own. Maybe this trial had wrought a change in her, as well.

This made her consider all the wrongs she had perpetrated, all the things she wished she could do different, and she knew exactly where to begin. She felt badly about the way she had treated Bob. He was really a wonderful man, kind and patient; and she really did love him. Maybe it was time to try again. Maybe this time it would stick.

Nearly a half-hour had passed before the driver's door of the black pickup opened and a man dressed in dark sweats stepped out. He walked around behind his pickup topper, shielding himself from view through any of the windows in Jennifer's house. Like an injured animal, he slunk across the neighbor's yard to a clump of shrubbery at the corner adjacent to Jennifer's property.

From past experience he knew that most of the residents of Kalispell did not bother to lock their doors until they went to bed, some not at all. There was so little of that type of crime. People felt safe. Without hesitation he proceeded in a shuffling gait to the front door of her house and placed his hand upon the knob.

The wine and the solarium were not doing their job. Instead of relaxing, Jennifer still felt keyed up – but in a good way. Habitually after a difficult trial, no matter if she won or lost, she would feel herself slip into a mild depression, a minor funk, but one that often lasted for days. Forcing herself to proceed with routine, she would drift through the hours feeling tired and listless, and she would fall into her bed at night, dreamless, and wake with the impression that she had just laid down; but not this time.

This time was different. She didn't feel tired at all; in fact, she felt energetic and vital to an extent that was nearly euphoric. She felt that she understood and comprehended herself with an enhanced clarity that had been absent for most of her existence. For once in her life she knew what she wanted, and she didn't want to wait another second; and right then she decided to call Bob on his cell phone and ask him to come over. She turned around and started toward the dining room table to get her phone, and then suddenly she gasped and stopped dead in her tracks, dropping her wine glass, which shattered on the slate floor. Scott Deaver was standing – *Standing?* – in her living room pointing a large handgun at her heart, which was thumping wildly in her chest.

Although she was aware that she was in mortal peril, her disbelief impelled her to ask an unthinkingly stupid question whose answer was obvious, "You can walk?"

"Had you fooled, didn't I?" Deaver seemed proud of himself. "Had them all fooled! No one ever even guessed that I was faking it!"

As the initial shock began to wear off, Jennifer experienced an adrenalin-induced queasiness. She struggled hard to regain the kind of clarity she had experienced only moments before. She was going to need it if she was going to survive.

Like most cowardly bullies, Deaver liked to brag. She knew that she had to keep him talking, and that the best way to accomplish that would be to appear impressed by his ingenuity, his cunning. It was equally critical that she show no fear. A predator will quickly attack a fleeing prey, but will be hesitant with an animal that stands up to him.

Jennifer stalwartly resisted the tremor that tried to force its way into her voice. "Well, you certainly managed to deceive me! But what makes you think you're going to get away with this?"

"It's simple! Who would ever suspect a cripple?" Deaver sneered at her. "Besides, your boy wonder is the one who's gonna to get nailed for this!"

"What makes you think that?"

Deaver gestured with his head toward the gun in his hand. Jennifer now saw that he was wearing surgical gloves, and the truth suddenly dawned on her.

"That's Eli's gun!"

"Yes it is," Deaver agreed with a sinister smile, "And what's better yet, it's registered in his name. I can get rid of you, and he'll get the needle for it."

Deaver was delusional. What motive could Eli possibly have for killing her? Just because he owned the weapon, didn't mean that he pulled the trigger.

The realization that Deaver had had Eli's gun all along confronted her with another, gruesome deduction.

"You killed Jolene Sutten." It was not a question.

"What a nice little package! How much luckier can a guy get, than to have her stepfather, who happened to be on parole from prison for abusing her, just lurking around at the scene of the crime! How perfect!"

"But, why? Why did you kill her? Her story backed you up!"

"I couldn't take any chances. I was all set up to get disability pay for the rest of my life. I was going to go to Mexico where no one would know me and have my checks sent down there. I'd be living like a king! But if she changed her testimony I wasn't just going to lose my disability pay, I might've lost everything! *I* might have gone to jail! I couldn't risk it."

"And then you burned down Eli's house." This was not a question either.

"That wasn't my plan, but it just turned out that way. Originally, I was going to make it look like a murder/suicide. He kills her, and then goes home and blows his brains out. But that didn't work out. Linnell arrested him before I could get to him. And then when they let him go, I found out that he had a solid alibi.

"But then I got to thinking that there still were plenty of reasons for him to want to kill himself. It would make sense for him to commit suicide. But when

I snuck up on his house that night that fucking dog started growling through the door, and I knew I'd have to shoot the dog first, and that might alert March and give him a chance to get away....or he might even get me first. I had already seen how fast he can move. It was too chancy. And that was when I saw that can of charcoal lighter on the shelf next to the barbeque grill. Problem solved." Deaver sneered malevolently, "But what a lucky son-of-a-bitch! How the fuck did he survive that?"

None of this made sense. Deaver wasn't merely delusional; he was downright insane. Jennifer had only thought she knew what kind of person Scott Deaver was, but she had not even begun to comprehend the depths of his depravity. She had never in her life witnessed such degeneracy, such unadulterated evil.

"So, what do you hope to gain by killing me? What's that going to do for you?"

Deaver smirked at her again.

"You know, the other killings were necessary, but I think I'm going to enjoy this one."

Killings?

"Besides," he went on, "it'll be like whacking two birds with one stone. March hurt me bad. The son-of-a-bitch broke my fucking neck! Up until about three months ago I didn't think I *would* be able to walk. And I'll probably never be able to walk like I did before, let alone run. That fucking asshole needs to pay for that. Will pay for that! And you...! Huh! Ya know, you were the reason I had to leave the Kalispell Police Department in the first place! And, as if that wasn't enough, now you've gone and made me look like a fool right in front of everyone! You fucked up everything! And I ain't about to let a bitch like you get away with that kind of shit! You have no idea how long I've looked forward to this!"

He started to raise the gun, but then suddenly he went rigid as if he'd been stung by a giant hornet, and he crumpled to the floor writhing in convulsions, discharging the weapon as he fell. The impact of the bullet knocked Jennifer off her feet and she landed hard on the slate surface of the solarium.

Sheriff Montgomery stepped into the room, the Taser still in his hand, and when he saw Jennifer, her blood pooling out around her, he knew he had to act fast. There was barely enough time to pocket the gun and quickly frisk Deaver to make sure he had no other weapons. Because he had no handcuffs on him, he could not secure Deaver, and, regardless, he had no time to do so. Dropping to his knees he grabbed a throw pillow off the couch, and pressed it into the wound in Jennifer's abdomen, simultaneously opening his cell phone and calling dispatch with the speed dial. Montgomery spoke urgently, giving the dispatcher the address, and requesting an ambulance and a patrol car. While he was thus occupied, Deaver regained his senses somewhat, and scuttled out the door. Montgomery reported this to dispatch, but otherwise let him go; he couldn't be bothered right now.

Jennifer was struggling against the pain and mumbling incoherently, and then abruptly all of the fight drained out of her, and her body went limp in his arms. Her eyelids began to flutter, and her eyes rolled back in their sockets.

"Hold on, Jennifer! Hold on, Goddammit!"

And he began to administer CPR.

Epilogue
Six Months Later

People began to arrive early on Saturday morning. The sun was just now cresting the shadowy mountains that rose otherworldly, framing the eastern horizon like an apparition behind Eli and Stephanie, with only a few delicate white clouds billowing in the cobalt sky. The air was suffused with the piquant aromas of the forest. It was a cool dawn in late April, but the forecast called for temperatures in the high sixties by mid-morning.

Ray and Bennie were the first to drive up, Bennie hanging out the window of his truck shouting, "Hey, Eli! Let's kick some ass!" Random ran to greet them barking wildly. Bennie's dad, Gary, pulling the Greenwald Construction job trailer, was right behind them, followed closely by all the others who had come to offer their assistance.

"How cool is this?" Stephanie remarked, "Do you remember that movie *Witness*, with Harrison Ford. You know the one where he's hiding out from the bad guys with some Amish people? There's this scene where they have this barn raising, and all the neighbors for miles around come to help, and they build this whole barn in like one day! Remember that? That's what this reminds me of!"

Eli felt truly humbled. He had never expected this many people to show up.

"But where's Bob?" Eli questioned. "He's the one who put this whole thing together. He shoulda been here by now."

"Don't worry," Stephanie assured him, "He'll show up."

The plan was to get the new house for Eli and Stephanie dried-in in one weekend. Over the past couple of weeks, the old burned-out remains of the cabin had been removed, and a new foundation had been poured. The new house would be a little larger, with two bedrooms – Eli and Stephanie would be needing that second bedroom in about six months. Eli hoped to be able to finish the house on his own before then.

Several volunteers pulled campers into Nate Newman's field next door, planning to stay the night so that they could work late and get an early start in the morning. Everyone brought food to share.

Jon Krack drove up in a black pickup towing a flatbed trailer loaded with several large rough-sawn timbers that Old Montana Building Company had left over from a few of their projects. He had generously given them to Eli and Stephanie for a wedding present. In his dusty wake came an out-and-out battalion of carpenters and other tradesmen.

"I'm just blown away!" Eli exclaimed, "I mean it's one thing for people to donate lumber and stuff, but it's quite another when they all show up to help! Look! Here comes Delroy, the plumber! That guy doesn't even like me!"

"You know, Eli, we've lived here all our lives, and I think that sometimes we take for granted what a wonderful place this is. People here like to help each other out, especially when they're given a chance to make something that is very wrong into something that is very right. It's just one of the reasons it's called 'The Last Best Place'!"

Stephanie smiled at Eli, but then saw a shadow pass across his face.

"Eli? What's wrong?"

"Nothing…I just wish Jennifer could be here to see this."

Stephanie touched his arm in sympathy.

"I know, Eli. But if she can't be here in body, you know she's here in spirit."

⁂

The floor was on by mid-morning, and they were already laying out the exterior walls, amid the racket of hammers, nail guns, and Skil saws. Whenever someone stopped to get a drink or take a break, someone else took his place. Eli had the plans spread on a piece of plywood that that been laid over a couple of sawhorses, and was going over a detail with Gary and Bennie, when a young man with long blond hair that he did not recognize approached them with a smile on his face and his right hand extended to shake. As Eli shook his hand he noticed that his face was deeply tanned, which was unusual at this time of year, but there were white circles around his eyes as if he spent a lot of time outdoors wearing goggles.

"Hi, Eli, I'm Troy Davies." Seeing the confusion in Eli's face he remarked, "You don't remember me. Do you?"

"No, I'm sorry," Eli responded, "I don't."

"Well you should," Davies smiled, "I owe you my life!"

Eli's confusion deepened.

"I guess I don't know what you're talking about."

Davies laughed at Eli's bewilderment.

"No, I guess you don't! Maybe if I plant myself upside-down in a snow bank, you'll be able to recognize me. I'm the guy you dug out after the avalanche."

"Oh!" Eli shook his hand again, "Sorry! I never knew your name!"

"And I've never had a chance to thank you," Davies admitted, "But I heard about this thing…and I'm not a carpenter, or anything…but I, uh, just wanted to come and help out anyway I can. I mean, I wouldn't even be here if it wasn't for you!"

"Well, sure, Troy. Thanks for coming! But I don't know about saving your life. Truthfully, I think your friend would have gotten you out in time. But I'm glad you're here. And I'm sure we can find something for you to do."

Dexter and Sheriff Montgomery were standing next to a large yellow Igloo water cooler capped with a red lid that had been set up under one of Eli's apple trees – the same tree that Eli had leaned against last summer as he had watched his cabin burn to the ground. Montgomery had won the election last November by a huge margin. As it turned out no one had liked his opponent, Sergeant Ruben Broussard, very much, but, even more so, everyone had seemed impressed by Montgomery's honesty, and his willingness to confess his mistakes. Being re-elected had gone a long way toward helping Montgomery get over the loss of his wife. He had regained some of the weight he had lost and had discovered that he could smile again, and even find things to laugh about.

"I have to admit," Montgomery said, "That was actually pretty funny, what you did!"

"What are you talking about?" Dexter responded.

"Letting the air out of Deaver's tires. In a sick sort of way, it was hilarious!" Montgomery chuckled,

"Can you just imagine how it must have looked to the patrolmen when they picked him up on Willow Glen Drive flapping down the road on four flats?"

Montgomery made a jerky circular motion with his hand in imitation of a flat tire. Dexter smiled and laughed with him.

"If you hadn't called me that night after the trial, I would've never figured it out on my own," Montgomery continued, "But how did you know? What made you suspicious in the first place?"

"It was just a nagging feeling I had had all along, like there was something I couldn't quite make out that was lurking in the shadows. So I did a little *private* investigating, and I found out something that spiked my curiosity. Dr. Santay had written in Deaver's charts that the injuries to his spinal cord were minor. He should have been able to walk. Everyone who knew the facts, including Dr. Santay - and even you, Sheriff - seemed to be ready to chalk it up as being psychosomatic. But I was just a little skeptical, I guess. So, after the trial I staked out his house. When I saw him back out of the garage in that black pickup, well, that's when I called you from my cell phone."

"And it's a good thing that you did! I'm glad you didn't try to apprehend him yourself."

"That was never an issue. I am no longer skilled in the arts of combat, nor do I wish to be. I am a man of peace."

Montgomery nodded respectfully a few times, but then his expression rearranged itself inquisitively, "But how did you happen to see Deaver's charts in the first place?"

"I can't say."

"What do you mean: you can't say?"

Dexter smiled secretively.

"Just be glad I figured it out, and that Deaver's in jail."

Montgomery seemed to accept this.

"That he is! And he'll most likely spend the rest of his life there."

⁂

At noon everyone took a break for lunch. Several folding tables and chairs had been set up, and Stephanie and Eli's mom, along with Doreen Morningstar and numerous other women busied themselves with laying out food and filling drink glasses. Eli was sitting next to Bennie, eating a chicken salad sandwich when he saw Bob's pickup finally turn off of Foothill road and drive up to the jobsite. When he saw who else was in the vehicle, a big smile spread across his face, and he put his sandwich down and stood up, walking toward them, Random at his heels wagging his tail merrily.

Bob was helping her down out of the cab, and holding an aluminum walker until she had steadied herself.

"What are you doing here?" Eli asked, "You told me you weren't yet well enough to get out!"

Jennifer was obviously in some pain, but she managed to smile at him.

"I wouldn't have missed this for anything. Besides, I have my little helpers." She rattled a bottle of pills at him.

"Are you still having to take pain killers?" Eli sounded concerned.

"Now, don't you start in on me, too! I'll be off them soon enough," she assured him, "Help me find a place to sit down. I've got to get off my feet."

Bob had opened up a comfortable looking camp chair and was setting it in the shade under the apple tree near the yellow water cooler. As Eli helped to lower her into the chair - she seemed to weigh practically nothing - he noticed that a band of sweat beaded her brow, and that her overall complexion was pallid and chalky. It was the first time since the shooting that he had seen her out of bed, and he was shocked at how gaunt she appeared.

Concerned, he inquired, "Are you sure this is a good idea? You coming out like this? I thought the doctor had told you at least six more weeks!"

She reached fondly for Eli's hand. Her fingers felt skeletal, birdlike.

"It's been a long journey," she pronounced, "from death's bed to here. But I assure you I'm only going to keep getting better. Hopefully, I'll be able to work again before too long. There's still something we need to do."

"What's that?"

"I intend to file a civil action on your behalf against the state for the misconduct of Scott Deaver, and compensation for the costs that you incurred. I'd also like to file a wrongful arrest suit, but I doubt it would succeed. They wouldn't have much trouble proving probable cause. Nonetheless, this has cost you and your family a lot of money, and I believe you should be reimbursed."

Eli smiled at her.

"You really look after me, don't you, Jennifer? This isn't just another attorney/client relationship, is it?"

Jennifer smiled back wanly.

"You're very special, Eli."

From amidst the construction clamor someone called out to Eli, and he excused himself, and joined the crew that was already plumbing and lining walls with long 2X4 braces. Delroy was right behind them drilling holes to run pipes through, and Bob was emptying bags of powdery mortar into his gas-powered mixer. The din was deafening.

Dexter brought Jennifer a tall glass of lemonade. Unfolding his own chair, he sat down next to her, and held her hand companionably, waiting patiently for a lull in the noise before he spoke.

"I got a license, you know!" He spoke the words with that inscrutable Native-American inflection that he seemed to be able to summon at will.

"A license? What are you talking about? What kind of license?"

"I'm official! I got a private investigator's license. So now you won't have to worry about hiring me!"

"Oh, right, Dex!" she guffawed, "No one has to worry about you, do they?"

He replied with an unreadable smile, which she returned in kind.

"Honestly, though," she continued, "I doubt I could have won without you!"

"Don't short-change yourself, Jen. You did an awesome job."

"No, Dex," she gave his hand a feeble squeeze, "*We* did an awesome job."

Dexter bobbed his head a few times in contemplation.

"Yup," he simply stated, "*We* sure did!"

"I guess we make a pretty good team! Don't we, Dex?"

Made in the USA
Charleston, SC
23 April 2014